"We obviously
at the same tin

"Please don't say
Promise me," Lea

"Okay…but on one condition." His gunmetal-gray eyes snagged hers.

"What's that?"

"That you'll help me pick out a wife." He held up his own package of letters with a crooked grin.

"Why do you need *my* help?"

"You're a great judge of character, and you know me better than anyone else. Do we have ourselves an agreement or not?"

"Agreed." Leah smiled up at Jake and the dimples on each side of her pink lips winked. How he would love to— Jake stopped his mind from taking him down that well-worn path to nowhere. Soon Leah would be another man's wife.

"Well, let's get this over with," Leah said, her smile looking forced now.

"Have to put it that way?"

"No, no. I just meant…"

Jake placed his fingertips on Leah's soft lips. "It's okay—I know what you meant."

Debra Ullrick
and
Noelle Marchand

Groom Wanted
&
A Texas-Made Match

LOVE INSPIRED
INSPIRATIONAL ROMANCE

LOVE INSPIRED®

INSPIRATIONAL ROMANCE

ISBN-13: 978-1-335-44873-6

Groom Wanted & A Texas-Made Match

Recycling programs for this product may not exist in your area.

For questions and comments about the quality of this book, please contact us at CustomerService@Harlequin.com.

Love Inspired
22 Adelaide St. West, 40th Floor
Toronto, Ontario M5H 4E3, Canada
www.Harlequin.com

Printed in U.S.A.

CONTENTS

Debra Ullrick is an award-winning author who is happily married to her husband of over thirty-five years. For more than twenty-five years, she and her husband and their only daughter lived and worked on cattle ranches in the Colorado mountains. The last ranch Debra lived on was also where a famous movie star and her screenwriter husband chose to purchase property. She now lives in the flatlands, where she's dealing with cultural whiplash. Debra loves animals, classic cars, mud-bog racing and monster trucks.

Debra loves hearing from her readers. You can contact her through her website, debraullrick.com.

Books by Debra Ullrick

Love Inspired Historical

The Unexpected Bride
The Unlikely Wife
Groom Wanted
The Unintended Groom

Visit the Author Profile page
at Harlequin.com for more titles.

GROOM WANTED

Debra Ullrick

A man's heart deviseth his way,
but the Lord directeth his steps.
—*Proverbs* 16:9

To my daughter, Sharmane Wikberg.

Remember, kiddo, when you brought home those Christian romance books from the library eons ago, and how you had to beg me to read them? Look what happened when I finally did. Who would have ever thought it, huh? Thank you, Sharmy. And thanks for being such a loving daughter. God sure blessed me when He gave me you. I love you, girl.

((MEGA HUGS))

Chapter One

Paradise Haven
Idaho Territory, 1886

Nine men had replied to her "Groom Wanted" ad.

Leah Bowen couldn't believe she'd received so many that quickly. Her heart skipped as she fingered the envelopes that might very well hold her future and her only avenue of escape from the nightmares that plagued her.

"You, too, huh?"

"Twinkling stars above!" Leah gasped and whirled toward the sound of Jake Lure's deep voice. Her nose came within an inch of jamming into the napped wool shirt covering her friend's massive chest. Pleasant scents of springtime and sunshine floated from him.

Near the front door of Paradise Haven's post office Jake stood, looking over her shoulder at the posts in her hand. Most people were intimidated by his massive size, but she wasn't. Underneath that outdoorsy, muscular exterior was a gentle giant.

"What—what do you mean, 'you, too'?" Leah glanced at the top envelope with the very noticeable masculine script and tucked them into her reticule. She tossed the end of her purple knit scarf over her shoulder and gathered the edges of the collar of her wool coat closer together.

Jake held up a packet of letters. "Got these in the mail today."

"Oh? What are they?" she asked with all the innocence she could muster.

"Same thing as that stack you just put in your purse."

"What? You mean letters?"

"Those envelopes you have aren't just any ole letters." One of Jake's eyebrows rose. "They're answers to *your* advertisement."

Advertisement? She swallowed hard. Did he know she'd placed an ad for a husband? "What are you talking about?" Leah hated playacting, but she had no choice. She refused to offer Jake any information concerning her personal ad. Just because he had mentioned how he wanted to place an advertisement for a wife during one of the many times she and Abby had visited him over the past eleven months didn't mean she had to confide in him that she, too, had wanted to do that very same thing. So how did he know? Or was he only speculating?

Jake cupped her elbow.

Her gaze flew to the spot where his large calloused hand rested, then back onto his face. "What are you doing?"

"Taking you someplace where we can talk without being overheard." Even through a whisper, his voice sounded deep.

Their footsteps echoed on the plank-covered boardwalk as he led her away from prying eyes to a more secluded place to protect her reputation, no doubt, for which she was extremely grateful though she still tried to look annoyed. Truth was she didn't want people getting the wrong idea about the two of them. They were friends and nothing more.

They'd become good friends after he'd slipped on some shale at the top of a hill on his place almost a year ago. He'd tumbled down and hit his head, leaving him with a bleeding gash on his forehead and rendering him unconscious. If Leah's brother Michael and his wife, Selina, hadn't found Jake that day, he may have died. Selina's kindness in doctoring him and making sure he had food and his needs were met changed Jake. He realized how wrong he had been for judging her for her lack of social graces and regretted his heckling. After that, he changed, and he had become the person to everyone else that he had always been to her.

Through it all, Leah had always believed that Jake was a nice man, a good man, even when he was heckling people. Years before, she'd learned that most people who teased others were either jealous or insecure or did it to protect themselves. Leah wasn't sure just why Jake had. But her friend Dottie Aimsley had once told her that she'd heard the reason Jake acted like that was because when he was growing up he himself had been ridiculed because he had a fear of crowds. Although Leah didn't know all the particulars of his phobia, hearing that had secured her compassion toward him, and the two had quickly become the best of friends.

And he was a handsome friend at that.

A man who could charm any woman. Except her, that was. Leah had her sights set on a different type of man. A man exactly like her late father—before he had become a rancher. The mere thought of him brought the pain surging into her chest. She couldn't let it reside there, though. She had to evict it as she had so many times before or it would escalate until it became so bad she could barely breathe.

She sighed and blew out a long breath. It really was a shame Jake wasn't a city man. City men didn't encounter anywhere near the hazards farmers and ranchers did. She knew that for a fact because, even though it had been fifteen years since her family had moved from New York to the Idaho Territory, she still kept in contact with her friends back East and all of their fathers were still alive.

Marrying a farmer or a rancher who risked his life every day working with unpredictable animals and dangerous farm tools and equipment wasn't for her.

And Jake was one of them. Her father had been one of them, too. Getting away from city life and owning a ranch had been her father's dream. It was that dream that had gotten him killed.

Her heart felt the pain of his loss as if it had just happened yesterday instead of years ago. Her hand balled into a fist and pressed against the center of her chest as she tried to make the memories stop. But they came with even greater force. In desperation, her mind grasped backward through time to the father who had doted on her.

Had loved her.

Had made her feel special.

Secure.

Protected.

And fearless, even.

Oh, sure, after his death her older brothers—Haydon, Jesse and Michael—had tried to take his place. Tried to make her feel secure. But no one could take the place of a father. Especially in a little girl's heart. No one.

And no one could stop the nightmares that visited her on a regular basis since his death.

She'd learn to suppress the nightmares because she had to be strong for her little sister, Abby, and her mother, whose grief at that time had ripped at Leah's soul. Oh, if only she hadn't heard her father gasping for air as his lungs filled with blood or had seen his broken body crushed underneath that huge tree. But she had.

Leah slammed her eyelids shut to blot out the gruesome memory that chased her like a haunting ghost. In one shaky breath she willed her father's healthy face to come into focus, but only a shadowed image filled her mind. Time had faded his features until she could no longer see them clearly. And that scared her.

It was all Paradise Haven's fault. She despised and blamed the Idaho Territory for the loss of the one person she had loved most in the world. Moving back to New York would help the nightmares stop. Of that she was convinced because there were no phantoms there. Only fond memories.

Memories of better, happier times.

Memories of her father walking and talking and holding her until whatever was bothering her at that time disappeared. Father had made everything okay. Only he couldn't make this okay. Nothing would bring him back to life. This place had killed him.

New York was where she longed to be.

Getting there couldn't happen fast enough for her. Why she had waited this long she didn't know. But the sooner she moved, the better off she would be. And maybe, just maybe when she finally got there, those dreaded nightmares would end.

"Leah?"

She blinked and yanked her attention upward and onto Jake. "What?"

"You okay?" His dark blond brows met in the middle.

"I'm fine." Or she soon would be when she moved away from here.

The look on his face said he didn't believe her. "You gonna answer my question?"

"I just did. I said I was fine."

"No. Not that question. Still waiting for an answer to—" he pointed to the stack of posts in her reticule "—if those letters are what I think they are."

"I don't know. What do you think they are?"

He gave a quick glance around. No one milled about anywhere close to them. "Answers to your advertisement."

She studied his eyes, gazing at her from under his brown cowboy hat. His irises were a light silver-gray with a dark gray circle surrounding them, reminding her of a tabby cat she once had. A knowing look filled them. There was no denying it any longer.

"How did you know?"

"Put two-and-two together."

"What do you mean?" Panic and fear settled into her spirit, knowing that if anyone in her family discovered what she was doing and why, they would put a stop to it right away. It didn't matter that Haydon and Michael had gotten wonderful wives that way. There was no way they would let their sister traipse off to New York by herself to meet a complete stranger, even if she was twenty-four years old.

Jake's gaze slipped to the boards at their feet. "Truth is, Leah, I saw your advertisement when I looked through the papers for the one I'd placed. We obviously posted ads for a spouse at the same time."

Oh, no. He did know. Fear dug its claws into her chest.

"You don't look too good. You okay?"

She nodded, then changing her mind, she slowly shook her head. "No." She gazed up at him, imploring her eyes to show how much this affected her. "Please don't tell my family."

"You mean they don't know?"

"No. I didn't tell them. Please don't say anything to them, Jake. Promise me you won't." Desperation pricked her skin.

He ran his fingers down the place that once had a thick, dark blond mustache but now only held stubble and kept repeating the action. "On one condition." His gunmetal-gray eyes snagged onto hers.

"What's that?" Worry nipped at the heels of her mind as she waited for his response.

"That you'll help me pick out a wife." He held his own package of letters up, and his lips tilted into that normally lazy, crooked grin of his. The one that really was quite endearing.

"Are you serious?"

"Yep. Sure am."

"Why do you need me to help you do that?"

"'Cause. I don't trust myself. When it comes to women, I haven't had the best of luck."

Heat rushed to her cheeks. Turning down Jake's marriage-of-convenience proposal a couple months back had nothing to do with his luck with women but with her wanting to flee this place. "What makes you think I'll do any better?"

"You're a great judge of character, and you know me

better than anyone else. Not only that— Women seem to have a sense about these things. Men don't. So. Do we have ourselves an agreement or not?" He held his hand out for her to shake.

She stared at it, debating what to do, until she realized she didn't have any other choice. Having peace in her life depended on her moving. With a short nod, she clasped his hand, and gave it a quick shake before releasing it. "Agreed."

Jake shook Leah's hand and plastered a smile on his face. He wasn't kidding when he said he needed help picking out a wife. His past record had proven that. At eighteen he'd asked Gabby Marcel to marry him, but she'd said no, saying she wanted to marry Jeffrey Smith. He didn't even know she liked the man. Jake thought Gabby was in love with him, but she'd just used him to get close to his friend. Backfired on her big time. Jeffrey wanted nothing to do with her and neither had Jake after that.

Then a few months back Leah had turned him down, too, saying she had her reasons and that it had nothing to do with him, but her.

Too bad she hadn't accepted his proposal. He didn't blame her for rejecting him, though. Nothing had been mentioned about love. Only about how it would be nice since they were friends and all. A friendship he treasured and didn't want to lose. Jake's hope at the time had been that if they did marry one day his heart would love Leah the way a man loves a woman, but right now he only felt friendship toward her. So, it was probably best she'd turned him down.

Besides, she was way out of his league, anyway. Going from a large home to a small three-room house would be hard for anyone used to living in the luxury she was accustomed to. Plus, staying where she was, Leah never had to want for anything. If she married him, she would. Oh, he could support her by keeping food on the table and clothes on her back, but there wouldn't be much left for anything extra. And the woman deserved every good thing life had to offer. None of that mattered now, anyway. Leah had made it clear that nothing would stop her from moving back to New York. Why she wanted to go there, he had no idea.

Personally, he hated the city and would go crazy if he ever went to one again.

Literally.

His childhood had seen to that. In 1864 fire blazed throughout Atlantic City. The crowd had gone berserk trying to flee to safety and in the process he had gotten separated from his mother. The crowd trampled him, leaving him for dead at six years old. Ever since then, he had a fear of crowds. He could be around a small group of people, but he couldn't handle being closed in a building or surrounded by people—he felt trapped. For twenty-two of his twenty-eight years he'd tried to overcome his fear. Had even made a trip back to Atlantic City. Big mistake that was. While walking down the crowded streets, suddenly everyone seemed as if they were right on top of him again, just like when he was six.

He'd felt trapped.

Closed in, even.

His heart had pounded hard and fast, his breathing came in short gasps, his arms felt heavy, his palms coated with moisture, and his head swam until his vision clouded.

The need to flee had pressed in on him.

Only when he had escaped to an open field had his heart stopped racing and his breathing returned to normal.

Even now, whenever he found himself crowded in, even by the smallest mob of people, fear stampeded over him. His only recourse was to get alone until his heart and breathing returned to normal and the fear lifted. When people asked him what was wrong, he'd make up an excuse because a long time ago, he'd learned not to tell anyone or ask for help. The few times he had he'd been made fun of and he hated how small that made him feel. For a man his size, it was hard to make him feel small, but ridicule did. The worst part of this whole thing was his phobia punctured the dream of him ever moving to New York to be with Leah.

"You do know, Jake, that I will have to bring Abby with me again. Propriety and all that, you know." Leah's voice snatched his mind back from the dark caves of the past. "That means she'll know what you're doing, too."

"Already figured as much. Wouldn't have it any other way. Wouldn't do anything to ruin your reputation, even if that means having Abby know what I'm up to." He gave a quick nod. "So be it. Besides, I enjoy your sister. Who wouldn't? She's a pistol."

"She sure is. A very discreet pistol, though, I assure you." Leah smiled and the dimples on each side of her pink lips winked.

"Well, let's get this over with."

"Have to put it that way?"

Leah waved her hand, "No, no. I didn't mean it like that. I just meant…"

He placed his fingertips on her soft lips. "It's okay, Leah. You don't have to explain. I know what you

meant. Was just teasing you." When he realized where his fingers were, he quickly removed them.

"When do you want to start?" She fiddled with the strings of her reticule.

"Now, if that works for you."

Leah's gaze brushed his. She tilted her head in that cute way of hers, then stared at him as if she were considering his offer.

"Hmm." She settled her fingertip against her lips. "I am finished in town, and Mother isn't expecting me until later. So now will work just fine. I'll run and go get Abby, then follow you to your place."

"No."

"What do you mean, 'no'?" Leah tilted her head even farther and a blond lock slipped across her eye.

He reached to brush it away, then snatched his hand back to his side. Doing that seemed intimate somehow. A line friends didn't cross. "Think about it, Leah. How would that look, us riding off together?"

Leah tapped her forehead. "How could I have been so dim-witted? Of course, you're right. Thank you, Jake."

He glanced out to the dirt street that ran right through town. "Tell you what. I'll head on out now. You and Abby leave ten or fifteen minutes after me?"

"What time is it now?"

He pulled his pocket watch out of his vest pocket and flipped it open. "One forty-five."

"I'm supposed to meet Abby at her friend Phoebe's house around two. So that will work perfectly." There were those dimples again.

"Great. See you at my place in about half an hour then?"

This smile went all the way up to her eyes. Eyes the color of a spring day dotted with clouds.

"We'll be there."

Unable to think of anything else to say, Jake clasped the brim of his hat, gave a quick nod and headed toward the blacksmith shop to pick up his horse.

"Phoebe!" Leah gaped at Abby's friend, who was a little more than a year older than Abby's seventeen. "Your wedding dress is absolutely gorgeous. You look so beautiful in it. Like Cinderella at the ball."

Phoebe's lips curled upward and her face turned as red as her hair. Her big green eyes were shielded when her eyelids lowered. How the sweet girl ever managed to snag Markus Donahue, the banker's son, when she was so shy was beyond Leah, but she was glad Phoebe had. If anyone deserved a nice man like Markus, it was Phoebe.

"Tomorrow's the big day. Are you excited?" Leah curled a stray strand of hair around her ear.

Phoebe dipped her head down and nodded. Two seconds later her head popped upward and alarm marched across her face. "You two are still coming, aren't you?"

Leah walked over to Phoebe and grabbed her hands. "Of course we'll be there. Nothing would stop us from coming."

"But you know how unpredictable the weather is here in May. What if it rains or snows and you can't get into town because the roads are too muddy?"

Horrified was the only way Leah could describe Phoebe's face.

"Then we'll ride the horses into town. They'll be able to make it even if the buggy can't."

Phoebe's head jerked with short, nervous nods. "Oh. Okay."

Leah clasped Phoebe's hands again. "We'll be there, Phoebe. I promise. Now." She released her hands. "Come on, Abbynormal." Leah used the nickname she often called her sister. The one that best suited Abby's personality. Abby was anything but normal, but Leah loved her sister for it and envied her at the same time. How wonderful it would be to be so carefree. "We need to get going."

Abby stopped talking with Phoebe and faced her. "Why?"

"Because…" She gave Abby that look. The one that let her know she was going to Jake's again. Something the two of them had done ever since his accident many months back when he'd fallen and hit his head. Back then, the idea of him alone and needing help had eaten at Leah until she couldn't bear it. She was so glad Abby had agreed to go with her to help him until he had healed. During that time Leah and Jake had become great friends.

Make that the three of them. Abby enjoyed going to Jake's farm as much as Leah did and thought it was great fun playing the role of her older sister's chaperone. Leah was glad she found it fun, but it was necessary more than anything. If she didn't drag her sister along, Leah could never have gone to a single man's house alone. It would be improper and, most importantly, her reputation would be ruined.

Being seen with Jake too much in public would give people the wrong idea about the two of them. Like a wildfire out of control, all of Paradise Haven would spread rumors that they were courting. She'd seen it happen to several other couples who eventually wed or

ended the whole thing in a ruinous scandal—neither of
which she wanted with Jake. Besides, it wasn't like that
between her and Jake. To be sure, they enjoyed each
other's company, but neither of them had feelings that
went beyond friendship.

Leah loved having a male friend as special and caring as Jake. She looked forward to their visits. Despite
the fact they wanted different things out of life, he was
the one person she felt she could talk to about anything.

Well, almost anything.

He didn't know the real reasons why she had turned
down his proposal and why she wanted to move. No
one knew about the nightmares except for her former
friend Marie. Former for two reasons—one, Marie had
moved away, and two, Leah hadn't associated with her
since the day she'd confided in Marie about the nightmares and how she blamed this place for killing her
father. Marie had laughed and said she was just being
silly and that she needed to get over it. Oh sure, as if
it were that easy.

"Ohhh." Abby nodded, then turned to her friend.
"I'd better scoot along now, Phoebe. Sister dear has
places to go and things to see. But fear not, I shall see
you on the morrow. You have my word." Abby, the
dramatic one in the family, grabbed her cloak, swung
it around her shoulders with the grace of a queen and,
with her arm outstretched holding her cloak, glided
toward the door.

"Thank you so much for helping me make my dress
and for putting the finishing touches on it." Phoebe
scurried after Abby and hugged her.

Abby pulled back and waved off her friend. "You
are quite welcome, my dear." Abby's British accent
imitation needed help. She sounded nothing like the

Manvilles, their British neighbors back in New York City, or even like Rainee, their sister-in-law, who mixed British with Southern quite nicely. "And now, I must make haste and take my leave." Abby swung the door open and, with a flourish, headed outside.

Leah shrugged toward Phoebe's direction. "What can I say? You can't help but love her." With that, she followed Abby out the door and onto the wagon. They turned and waved goodbye to Phoebe before she disappeared into her house.

"So, we're heading to Jake's again." Abby waggled her eyebrows.

"We sure are."

"Well, then, sister dear, what are we waiting for?" Abby faced forward. "Make haste. Make haste, my dear."

Leah shook her head. She should have never let Abby read the well-worn copy of *Pride and Prejudice* that Rainee had given Leah years ago. Ever since then, Abby imitated the British often. She hoped Abby never found the copy of *Sense and Sensibility* that she kept hidden in the bottom lining of her trunk. She shuddered just thinking about how Abby would act after reading that one.

Leah wondered if Abby would follow in her footsteps.

The real Mr. Darcy in *Pride and Prejudice,* not the one Elizabeth Bennet thought he was before she had gotten to know him better, reminded Leah of her father. Mr. Darcy had rescued Elizabeth's family when Lydia's infidelity would have shamed them. He was a man with integrity, a big heart, a protector, just like her father. From the moment that realization had struck Leah, her love and respect for Mr. Darcy had her pray-

ing that someday she would find her very own Mr.
Darcy—a man who represented everything her father
had stood for.

"C'mon, Leah. What are you waiting for?"

"Pushy."

"Me, pushy? You were the one who was in such an
all-fired big hurry to go." Abby nudged Leah's shoulder.

"True. True. I hate it when you're right." Leah tit-
tered and with a quick slap of the lines on her horse's
rump the buggy pitched forward. "Oh, you won't believe this, Abbs, but Jake knows about my advertisement."

Abby whipped her head so fast in Leah's direction that one of her curls whacked her sister across the
face. "How'd he find out?" Abby's eyes gleamed as
she searched Leah's. Her sister loved a good story and
loved to tell them, too, but she wouldn't tell this one.
She'd been sworn to secrecy.

"He started getting newspapers from all over, including back East where I placed mine. When he
searched the papers to see his ad, he saw mine and put
two-and-two together."

"Oh. What are you going to do if he tells Michael?"

"He won't."

"How do you know he won't? Jake and Michael are
good friends. If Michael finds out, you know he'll tell
the rest of the family. And Haydon and Mother will put
a stop to your plans."

"They won't find out because Jake and I made an
agreement and shook hands on the bargain."

"Oh, yeah? What kind of agreement?"

"Well—" she shifted toward Abby "—he won't tell
anyone if I help him find a wife. You know, help him
decide which of the letters he should respond to."

"Ohhh. This could be fun." Her sister's eyebrows danced.

Fun? Leah hadn't thought about it being fun. But it just might very well be. She gave a quick flick of the leather lines to get her horse to pick up her pace. "Don't tell anyone, Abbs. This whole thing will be our little secret, okay? Promise?"

"I haven't said anything to anyone before, have I?" Her sister looked slighted.

"No, you haven't. And I know you wouldn't, either. But with this concerning Jake, too, I just thought I would remind you, that's all. Okay?"

"Okay."

They rode in silence for a time. The only sounds were the horse's hooves clunking on the hard road and a flock of geese honking above them.

"It's too bad you have your heart set on moving to New York. Otherwise, Jake would make a great husband for you," Abby said out of nowhere.

Leah glanced over at her sister. "Jake is a friend and nothing more. But if I wasn't so dead set in pursuing my dreams, who knows, I might have considered Jake." Turning down his proposal hadn't been easy because she enjoyed his company immensely. Good thing she wasn't in love with Jake. Saying no would have been extremely hard, but necessary.

"You would?" Abby clasped her hands together and her eyes sparkled.

"I said if, Abbs, if."

"But Jake is sooo handsome," Abby said dreamily with her clasped hands pressed against her heart.

"If you think he's sooo handsome, then why don't you marry him?"

Abby yanked her hands away from her chest and her

wide eyes stared at Leah. "Me? He's way too old for me. But if he wasn't, I sure would try for him."

"Why?" Leah found she really wanted to know.

"What do you mean, 'why'? Just look at him. He's dreamy and so handsome."

Handsome, yes. But dreamy? She never thought about Jake as being dreamy. "Jake is handsome. I'll give him that. But looks aren't everything, and he is not my type."

"I know, I know." Abby rolled her eyes. "Your type of man is one who wears waistcoats, ties and fancy suits and lives in a big city."

Only because that was how her father used to dress. Another pleasant memory she held on to.

Abby laid her hand on Leah's. Gone was the humor from her face. Serious now replaced it. "What if you find someone, Lee-Lee, and once you get out there, it isn't anything like what you dreamed it would be? Then what?"

Good question. Just what would she do? What if she got out there and the nightmares didn't stop? No. She couldn't think that way. She had to hold on to that hope. She just had to. "That won't happen, Abbs, because before I go anywhere, if a man intrigues me, I'll request a picture of him and ask a lot of questions. If I like his answers, then I'll go out and meet him in person first."

"You know Mother won't let you go alone."

"She won't know."

"You mean you're not going to tell her?" That same horrified look she saw on Phoebe earlier now shrouded her sister's face.

"No. And neither are you."

"I don't like this, Leah. Not one little bit."

Neither did she. But her heart was set on moving

out East and nothing would stop her. Not her mother, her brothers or Jake. Jake? What did he have to do with any of this?

Chapter Two

Jake rode into the yard of his farm faster than ever before, unsaddled his horse and turned Dun loose in the corral. He ran to his house and stepped inside. One glance told him it was as bad as he had feared. Boots and jackets were sprawled on the bench and floor, dishes covered the table and newspapers surrounded his living room chair.

Every time Leah had come to his house, their visits had been planned and he always had a chance to spruce up the place first. This time that wasn't the case because he hadn't expected to see her today, much less invite her over. "Better hustle, Jake." He snatched up his jackets and hung them on the hooks, then lined his work boots neatly underneath the bench.

Dishes rattled and clanged as he gathered the breakfast mess, tossed the dishes into the sink and covered them with a towel. After washing the table down, he flocked the pile of newspapers together and laid them in a neat pile on the coffee table he'd made.

Next he plucked his clean undergarments, shirts, pants and socks down from the clothesline he'd rigged near the cookstove, tossed them onto his unmade bed and closed the bedroom door behind him.

Banjo's barking reached his ears. He peered out his living room window and saw Leah's carriage coming down the lane.

He darted toward the wash basin and checked his reflection in the shaving mirror. His thick blond hair, part of his Norwegian heritage, stuck out everywhere. He snatched up his comb and smoothed the strands down, then headed out the door and met Leah and Abby right as they pulled in front of his house.

"Hush, Banjo." His mottled-colored Australian shepherd tilted her head both directions, then darted onto the porch. Banjo laid down on the top step, placed her head between her legs, leaving her front paws dangling over the step, and let out a slow, pitiful whine.

Jake looked back at the ladies sitting in the buckboard phaeton with the parasol top, another reminder of the differences in their financial statuses in life. This phaeton was only one of the expensive carriages the Bowen family owned.

"Hi, Jake!" Abby waved.

"Howdy-do, ladies." He nodded, then offered Leah a hand.

"Thank you." She smiled up at him when she reached the ground.

He returned her smile, then helped Abby down.

"Thanks, Jake." Abby looked around the yard. "Where's Meanie?"

"In the barn. Had to put her in a stall."

Leah tilted her head. "How come?"

"Kept running off. Down to Mabel's barn. Eating all her grain. Caused all kinds of ruckus. Ornery old goat anyway."

"Jake!" Leah gasped and her eyes widened. "That isn't nice. Once you get to know Mabel, you'll discover she's really a very sweet lady with a soft heart."

Abby giggled and darted up the steps, flopping down next to Banjo.

Jake couldn't help but laugh. "Wasn't talking about Mabel. Was talking about my pet goat, Meanie."

Leah's cheeks turned a nice shade of dark pink, the same color as the dress she had on, and her perfectly formed lips formed an *O*.

"Shall we get started?" He motioned toward his house. They walked side by side up the wide steps, past Abby and onto the porch. Jake opened the door and moved out of the way.

"You coming, Abby?"

Abby turned sideways. "Do you mind if I stay out here? It's too nice to go inside. Besides, Banjo's better company. Isn't that right, girl?" Abby rubbed his dog behind her ears.

"Hey." Leah planted her hands on her slim waist.

Abby glanced back and winked. "Just kidding, Lee-Lee. But I would like to stay out here on the porch, if you don't mind. Even though the air's a little nippy, the sun sure feels good."

Leah looked up at him as if to question if it was okay or not.

Jake shrugged, seeing no reason why she couldn't. "I don't mind if you don't."

"I don't mind. That's fine, Abbs."

"Would you like something to drink, Abby?"

"No. I had a cup of hot cocoa at Phoebe's house right before we left, so I'm fine. But you two go ahead if you'd like," she said, keeping her back to them as she continued to pet Banjo.

"You change your mind, just holler," Jake said before he and Leah stepped inside his house.

"Where do you want to sit?" Leah asked him.

"The table. That way we can spread the letters out and be in plain view of Abby."

"Sounds good to me."

Jake took Leah's wrap and hung it on a peg near the door before Leah headed toward his kitchen table.

The slab table with pine legs and the kitchen chairs made out of lodgepole pine with slab seats looked shabby next to Leah's fancy kitchen furniture. Never once had she turned her nose down at them, though. She even made a comment one time about what a great job he'd done making them, how nice his handiwork was and how beautiful she thought they were. It meant a lot coming from her.

"Want something to drink?"

"No, thanks."

A quick nod, then he hurried around Leah and held out one of the chairs and waited for her to be seated before he sat in the chair on her right. He removed the stack of envelopes from his inside vest pocket and laid them on the table in front of him.

Leah scooted her chair closer to his, and her skirt brushed against his legs when she did. Lilacs and crisp spring air swirled around her. "Well, which one would you like to read first?"

He glanced down at the pile and thumbed through them until he came across one from Tennessee. "This one."

"Any particular reason why you chose that one first?" Curiosity fluttered through her eyes.

"Yep."

"Care to share?" She looked hopeful.

He debated whether or not to tell her. She might think he was strange if he did. Clasping his hands in front of him on top of the table, he drew in a deep breath and said, "Know this sounds odd, but ever since Michael brought Selina here, I've been hoping to find someone like her."

She shook her head and grinned. "You sound like Michael."

"Come again?" he asked, not understanding her meaning.

"Well." She dropped her hands onto her lap. "Ever since Rainee arrived, Michael wanted someone just like *her*."

"He did?" That was news to him. Shocking news at that.

"Yes."

"Don't get it. Selina's nothing like Rainee."

"I know. Everything in her letters indicated she was like her, but her friend had written the letters for her and lied so Selina would find a good husband. It was a deceptive thing for her to do, but I'm so glad she did. Selina is a remarkable person. And I'm so thrilled to have her for a sister."

Everything Leah just mentioned made him rethink what he was about to do. What if he, too, got a woman who lied to him and wasn't what she said she was? Or even worse, what if he found someone who interested him and she turned him down because *he* wasn't what *she* expected? After all, he'd been turned down twice before. Could he handle another rejection?

Leah studied Jake's face. It went from fear to confusion to sadness.

"Maybe I shouldn't do this. Maybe I should just

give up this whole crazy idea." Jake plowed his hands through his bulky blond hair and sat back from the letters, staring at them.

"Why?" Leah couldn't imagine what had caused him to change his mind so suddenly.

"Well, what if the woman who writes me is nothing like she portrays herself to be?"

Oh, that's why. Leah let out a relieved sigh. "Jake, because Michael was needed on the ranch, he married Selina without going out to meet her. You don't have to do that."

"I can't afford to leave, either." Again his fingers forked through his hair. Only this time they went all the way down the back of his head until they reached his thick, muscular neck where they lingered.

"You don't have to. You can have her come here."

His hand dropped to the table. He frowned. "Why didn't Michael do that?"

"Because Selina's father wouldn't let her leave until she was married. Michael had prayed about it and had peace so he married her sight unseen."

Jake scooted back his chair, scraping it against the rough wood floor, and rose. Leah's eyes trailed up his tall, broad frame, wondering what he was doing.

He went to the sink, which she noticed was stacked with what she presumed to be dirty dishes, though a large towel covered them. Nervousness permeated his every movement. "I know I already asked you this once, but would you like something to drink now?"

"Yes. Thank you. A glass of water would be great." Her mouth felt dry as trail dust. She watched as he held the glass under the spout and raised and lowered the water pump handle in the sink. His broad shoulders and arm muscles bulged as he filled the glass. Only a few drips of water landed onto the dish towel. She hoped to find someone as tall as Jake. He had to be at least six-foot-four or -five. And at five-foot-eight-and-a-half, she was either the same height as most of the men she knew or taller. The thought of being taller than the man she married bothered her.

Jake turned and walked back toward her. What a fine male specimen he was. He would make some woman a good husband. Of that she was certain.

He set a glass of water in front of her and one in front of himself before lowering his bulky frame onto the chair. Worry creased his forehead. This time she thought she knew why.

Wanting to put his mind at ease, she laid her hand on top of his arm, and his hard muscle jumped under her fingertips. She removed her hand and rested it on the table in front of her. "Listen, Jake. Before you get too involved with someone, you could always make it clear you want to meet them in person and spend time getting to know them before either of you make any real commitment. And…" She sat back in her chair. "I don't know what your financial situation is, but you could inform her that you would send her a round-trip ticket in case things don't work out."

His shoulders relaxed and the creases in his forehead disappeared. "That's a good idea. Think someone would do that?"

"Of course they would. It's done all the time. I know I'm going to. There is no way I'm going to marry someone without meeting him and without spending time with him and his family first."

"You scared, Leah?"

Was she? "A little. But the sooner I get away from here, the happier I'll be."

"You sure about that? Won't you miss your family?"

"Yes and yes. To be perfectly honest, the idea of staying here bothers me more than the idea of missing my family or the fear of the unknown does. I actually find that part rather thrilling."

"What do you find thrilling?"

"The fear of the unknown."

He narrowed his eyes and searched hers. "Why do you dislike it here so much?"

She shrugged, wishing she could confide in him about the nightmares and just why she hated this place as much as she did. But she didn't want him to think she was being silly like Marie had, so she used her standard reply. "I miss New York City and the lifestyle I used to have back then. Plus, I want some excitement in my life. As crazy as this may sound, I crave adventure." That part was true. She could use some adventure in her life.

"The Idaho Territory doesn't provide you with enough adventure?" A hint of humor warbled his voice.

"No. It's so boring here. Nothing exciting ever happens."

"You don't call the war with Nez Perce Indians exciting?" His blue eyes sparkled with mischief.

"There was nothing exciting about that war. Frightening was more like it." She shifted in her seat. "But I don't want to talk about that. Let's take a look at those letters. Would you like to read them first, or do you want me to?"

"If you don't mind, I'd rather you read them." Jake opened the envelope from Tennessee and gave the letter to Leah.

Leah could hardly decipher the sloppy penmanship.

"Hello, my name is Betsy. I'm a single mother of four young children."

"Whoa." Jake's hand flew up. "Forget that one. Not ready to be a father yet. Especially to a herd of kids." He frowned. "How old is she, anyway? Does she say?"

Leah scanned the letter. "She's thirty-nine."

His eyes widened. "Thirty-nine? That's eleven years older than me. No, thank you." He tugged the letter from her hands and ripped it into several pieces before setting the shredded pile far from him.

Leah took the liberty of going through his stack of posts. She couldn't believe how many women were looking for husbands. "How about this one? The post-mark is from Mississippi."

He shrugged, then nodded.

"Dear Mr. Lure. Me name is Samantha O'Sullivan. I be twenty-seven years old, six feet tall and one hundred and twenty pounds. Me hair is fiery red and me eyes are brown. Me pa said I must be gettin' married soon afore I become an ole maid. I dinna want to wed, but me pa said if I dinna and dinna write to you that he would toss me backside outta the house."

Leah looked over at Jake and put on her most serious face. "I think she sounds just like what you're looking for. You should write her back right away."

"You—you do?" The shock on his face pulled a guf-faw out of Leah.

"No, no. Don't look so worried. I'm just teasing you, Jake."

Relief flooded over his face and his taut lips relaxed. "Whew. Had me worried there for a moment."

Leah sat up straight and in her best Irish imitation she said, "Blimey, Mister Jake. Ye must pick me. Aye, ye must, even tho' I dinna wanna marry. And even tho' me be gone in da head for even tellin' ye such a thang in da first place, won't ye please consider sendin' fer me anyway and spare me from becomin' an ole maid?"

She laughed and so did Jake, but his laughter had a nervous flutter to it.

Seconds later, Jake shredded that letter, too. "Next."

Leah continued reading the responses he'd received. Each one was worst than the first, but Jake didn't shred any more of them— He just stacked them in a pile. She opened the last one and a photograph slipped out. Leah picked it up and her mouth fell open.

"What you got there?" Jake asked.

Leah slid her attention from the photo and onto him. "She sent you a picture."

"Who did?"

Leah handed the picture to him and looked at the signature at the bottom of the letter. "Evie Scott. She's very lovely, isn't she?"

"Yep, she's pretty." He said it with very little enthusiasm.

Was the man blind or something? The woman was striking, and yet Jake seemed unfazed by her beauty.

He laid the photo on the kitchen table. "Don't care what a person looks like. I care about the type of person they are in here." He pointed to his heart. "What's her letter say?"

Leah drew in a breath and read the letter. "Dear Mr. Lure. My name is Evie Scott. As you see, I have enclosed a photograph of myself. I am twenty-two years old, five-feet-seven inches tall. Ever since the War Between the States, men have been scarce out here in Alabama. It is my desire to marry and to raise a family. I am willing to travel out West and marry straightaway, or if you so desire, we can spend time getting to know one another first before a commitment is made by either one of us. Of course, I will expect proper accommodations for a lady of my standing and—"

"Whoa. Stop right there," Jake interrupted.

Leah looked at Jake. "What's the matter?"

"Heard enough. She's not someone I'd consider marrying."

Leah tilted her head and frowned. "Why? She sounds lovely."

"Obviously, she's a woman of rank. I want a wife I can feel equal to. Not someone who comes from money."

She came from money, so why had he asked her to marry him? Wait a minute. Did he think she had turned him down because he didn't have money? That bothered her. A lot. She didn't care about that. But she didn't want to ask and embarrass him, either. So she'd let it go. For now, anyway. "Okay." Leah placed the photo in the letter and put it back into the envelope. "What now?"

"Nothing." He shrugged. "I'm in no hurry to get married. I'll wait to see if anyone else answers my ad."

"Oh, okay." She nodded.

Neither spoke.

"Leah." Abby chose that moment to appear at the door. Leah looked over at her sister. "We'd better get on home or Mother's going to wonder where we are. She may even send out a posse or the cavalry looking for us," Abby said with her usual dramatic flair.

"What time is it?"

Jake pulled out his pocket watch and told her the time.

"Sweet twinkling stars above. Abby's right." Leah scooted her chair out. "I've got to go. Mother will be worried."

Abby darted down the steps. Banjo followed her, leaping and hopping at her heels.

"Meant to ask you, where'd that expression come from, anyway?" Jake asked, following her out. "You're the only one I ever heard say it."

"Say what?"

"'Sweet twinkling stars above.'"

"Oh, that." Her face lit up. At the edge of the porch she gazed up at the sky. "When my father was alive, many warm summer nights we'd grab blankets and go lay outside. Father used to tuck me under the crook of his arm and we'd stare up at the stars. Father used to say that back in New York you couldn't see them as clearly as you could here. He even made up a song about sweet twinkling stars above and used to sing it to us."

"How's it go?"

Leah turned her attention onto him, then to where Abby was, near the phaeton playing with Banjo.

"Sweet twinkling stars above; there to remind us of our Heavenly Father's love. Each one placed by the Savior with care; as a sweet reminder that He will always be there. Oh, sweet twinkling stars above. When my children gaze upon you remind them, too, of my love. Each twinkle is a kiss from me; a hug, a prayer, a sweet memory. Oh, sweet twinkling stars above." Leah stopped singing in the softest, sweetest voice he'd ever heard. One filled with reverence and joy. And yet, her face now only showed sadness. "Okay. Now you know. And I need to get going," she blurted as if her tongue were on fire, and down the steps she bolted.

Jake caught up to her and they walked side by side until she reached her carriage. She stopped and faced him. All of a sudden, something barreled into her backside and sent her flying forward. Her face smacked into a firm wall. Her arms flung out, clutching onto something solid. Something warm. Something very muscular.

Jake stared at the top of Leah's head plastered against his chest. Her hands clung to his upper arms as he caught and held her there. He froze in place and the air around him suddenly disappeared. Having her this close to him, her hands touching him and her head so near his heart, caused his pulse to buck and kick like an untamed horse. That had never happened to him before. Course, she'd never touched him that closely before, either. Still. What was going on?

"Um, Jake, could you help me up, please?"

Jake blinked. "Oh. Yeah. Sorry." As soon as she was steady on her feet, he released her.

"What just hit me, anyway?" Leah ran her hands over her skirt.

"Meanie's what hit you," Abby said from behind Leah.

Abby had Jake's pet goat by the collar, yanking it away from her sister.

"Meanie! How'd you get out?" Jake grabbed the goat's collar and tugged her close to his leg. The animal stretched her head toward Leah and started gnawing on her skirt.

Jake yanked the cloth from the nanny's mouth and tapped her on the tip of the nose. "Stop that, you ornery old goat." Meanie latched onto Jake's fingers and shook her head fast and hard.

Banjo barked and bit Meanie in the backside. The goat chomped down harder on Jake's fingers. Jake struggled to pull them away while simultaneously holding the goat and knowing he looked like a blooming idiot. "Down, Banjo!"

The dog immediately dropped onto his belly.

Jake tugged, trying to free his now-throbbing fingers. One more yank and they were free. Shaking his hand, he glanced over at Leah. "Gonna hang that brother of yours. Should have never let Michael talk me into taking this goat off his hands."

Leah covered her mouth with her hand and her eyes crinkled into a smile.

"Go ahead and laugh. We both know you want to."

Her laughter pealed across the farmyard. It only took a second before he and Abby joined her.

With a hard jerk on his arm, Meanie broke free and took off in the direction of Mabel's house. Banjo ran after her, nipping her heels and dodging the goat's quick kicks.

"Oh, no! Not again." Jake darted after them, hollering over his shoulder, "See you ladies tomorrow. Got a dog to stop and a goat to catch."

Their laughter followed him.

It took a quarter mile, but he finally caught up with Meanie and the dog, corralled them both and headed back to the house. He fully expected Leah and Abby to be gone, but they weren't. Keeping a tight hold on Meanie, he walked up to Leah's rig, panting from the exertion. "Something wrong?" he asked between gasps of breath. He struggled to keep the nanny from breaking free again.

"You said you would see us tomorrow, but I can't come by tomorrow."

"Won't be here even if you did."

"Huh?" Leah tilted her head in that charming way of hers.

"Guess Michael didn't tell you, then."

"Tell me what?"

"Starting tomorrow, I'll be working for him." He jerked on the goat's collar to keep her under control.

Leah's eyes widened. "Y-you are?" She glanced around his spread and then turned her attention back onto him. "But who's going to take care of your place?"

"Only gonna work part-time, until Smokey gets back from taking care of his folks' affairs and Michael feels comfortable leaving Selina home with the twins. Can you believe it? Michael. A father? To twins?"

"It's hard to picture Michael a father. But I'm so happy for my brother and Selina. It's hilarious watching him with those babies. Every little whimper and he rushes to their cradles. Selina has to almost wrestle him to the ground to keep him from picking them up all the time. He's paranoid to leave them and Selina alone.

"Mother, Abby and I promised him we'd help, but with Lottie Lynn and Joseph Michael only a few days old, he doesn't want to leave them or Selina. And if he does, it's only for a minute or two. I can understand that." She looked at Jake and her smile lit up her whole face. "I'm glad you'll be at the ranch, though. It'll be fun having you around."

Jake's insides grinned at her announcement. Maybe being a hired hand on the Bowen ranch just might be a fun thing after all.

Chapter Three

Leah removed her coat and scarf, hung them up on a wooden coat tree near the front door of her house and looked around. Dinner was on the stove waiting to be heated, everything was sparkling clean and the laundry was finished. With Abby still outside and her mother only who knew where, the house was so quiet that the only sound she heard was the grandfather clock ticking. Knowing she was alone and that she wouldn't have to wait until later to read her letters, her spirit skipped with excitement. She darted toward the stairs.

"Where are you off to in such a hurry?" Mother's voice stopped her.

Masking her disappointment for the delay in reading her posts, she put her reticule on the step and turned toward her mother. "Hi, Mother. Sorry, I didn't see you."

"Of course you didn't. I was in my room until I heard the front door. Did you have a nice time in town today?"

"I had a wonderful time." Soon Mother would know just how wonderful of a day Leah really did have. Right now, however, she had to keep that information tucked inside those hidden, secret compartments in her mind. When the time was right, she would tell Mother of her plans.

Arm in arm they went to the living room and sat down. Mother crossed her legs in Leah's direction. "Were you and Abby able to help Phoebe get everything finished for her wedding?"

"Yes, we did. Oh, Mother, Phoebe's gown is so pretty, and she looked so beautiful in it. Markus will absolutely love it."

"I'm sure he will. I wish you could find a nice man like Markus. Anyone caught your eye yet?" Eagerness and hope brightened her mother's beautiful face.

"No. Sorry, Mother. Not yet." *But hopefully someone will very soon.* She thought of the letters sitting on the stairs, waiting for her and calling out to her to come read them.

Mother patted her hand. "You will. God has someone special for you. I'm sure of it. When the time is right, He'll bring the right man into your life. Unless He already has and you don't know it yet."

She tilted her head and frowned. That same strand of hair that always seemed to escape its pins fell across her cheek. She reached up and curled it around her ear. "What do you mean? Do you have someone in mind?"

Mother leaned forward. "Let's just say I've been praying." She reached for Leah's hands and held them in her own, hands that were starting to show a few age spots and wrinkles. "Sweetheart, sometimes God places something right before our eyes but we don't see it because we're too busy looking somewhere else or for something else. Something that may or may not be God's will for us."

Did her mother know about her plans? No, she couldn't because only Abby, Jake and Selina knew, and none of them would have said anything to her. Of that she was certain. The need to know what her mother meant hovered inside her until she could no longer stand it. "What do you mean, Mother?"

"I'm just saying that there are a lot of young men here who would make a wonderful husband."

That was true. But the problem was they lived here, not in New York.

"What about Jake? You two seem to get along really well. You even entered the sack race at last year's harvest party with him. He's a nice man who loves the Lord. He'd make a wonderful husband."

Her eyes snapped to her mother's. "Mother, Jake is a nice man, but he's not the one for me."

"How do you know that?"

"I just know. Well, Mother—" Leah rose "—I'm sorry to end this conversation, but I have some things I need to do."

The look on her mother's face said Leah wasn't fooling her, but she nodded and smiled. "I need to get busy, too. Just think about what I said, okay?"

"I will." They hugged, then Leah headed up to her room. She removed the letters from her reticule and locked them in her nightstand before heading back downstairs and out the door where she planned on having a long talk with the Lord. After the conversation with her mother, she needed one.

Two hours later, after the dinner dishes were finished and the kitchen cleaned, Leah excused herself and went up to her room, shutting the door behind her. With one right turn of the passkey she locked the door, then tossed the key in her armoire drawer and quickly readied herself for bed. Against the headboard she propped up her pillows and settled herself on top of her lavender quilt. With a quick turn of the brass skeleton key, she unlocked her nightstand drawer, removed the letters, a pencil, and her Mr. Darcy diary and opened it up to the next blank page.

Dear Mr. Darcy, she penciled in as she had been doing ever since Rainee had given her the journal. Somehow Leah had felt silly just writing to her journal, but this way she felt like she was writing to a real, live person somewhere—someone who understood what she was going through. Someone who didn't make fun of her. She thought about calling it her Dear Daddy diary, but that hurt too much, so she named it the next best thing after her father, Mr. Darcy.

> *Today, I was pleasantly surprised to see that I had received many letters to my advertisement. I can't wait to read them, and I want you here when I do. My greatest hope is that I will find you in one of them.*
>
> *For years I've dreamed of finding someone as wonderful as my father. You're the closest thing to that. But you already know that, don't you? I've shared it with you enough times.*
>
> *I so desperately need to move. To escape the nightmares. I can't take them much longer. They're getting even worse and are coming more often. I just have got to find the peace I had before tragedy took Daddy away from me.*

She grimaced.

Before the Idaho Territory took him from me.

Fresh anger roiled inside her.

*I hate this place, Mr. Darcy! My father would
still be alive if we hadn't ever moved here. I miss
him terribly.*

She brushed away a tear, let out a long sigh and
forced her shaking hand to continue.

*I want to go back to New York. That's why I
placed an ad in the* New York Times. *I'm going
to stop writing now so I can read my letters, but
I'll be back to let you know how they are. See
you in awhile.*
Love,
Leah

She set her diary off to the side and picked up the
first letter postmarked from New York. Her heart raced
as she tore open the envelope. Was this it? Was this
the man who would make everything good again? She
couldn't wait to see.

Dear Madam,
*I am answering your advertisement because I am
in need of a wife. It is my father's wish that I marry
a woman who is willing to bear me many sons
so as to continue the Hamlen name and lineage.*

Leah felt heat rush into her cheeks. The man was
rather forward with his mention of bearing children.
Such an intimate detail for him to openly share. Most
inappropriate. But then again, if that was his design
in marrying, then she could understand why he would
bring it up. Still, the very idea that he did made her
uncomfortable.

With uneasiness squirming through her, she continued to read.

> *The women here refuse to submit to my authority, and I will not have that. I will say straightaway that I am a strict believer in the Bible and where it says that the man is the head over the woman and she is to submit to her husband. If you do not have a problem with being submissive to me and calling me Lord, then please contact me. If not, do not bother responding.*
> *Signed,*
> *Mr. Gregory Joseph Hamlen III*

Leah laughed. No wonder the man was still single. What woman in her right mind would ever marry such a man as he?

She imitated Jake and tore the letter and envelope into pieces. After she did, she wished she hadn't and instead kept it to read to Jake. "If he thought some of his letters were bad, well, this one topped any of his," she whispered into the empty room.

Leah scanned through the pile of letters. One with precise penmanship snagged her attention. She looked at the return envelope and her heart skipped a beat. *Sweet twinkling stars above!* She clutched the envelope to her chest and looked upward. "Lord, is this a sign from You?"

Pulling her attention back onto the letter, she read the name on the return label again.

Fitzwilliam D. Barrington.

Fitzwilliam was Mr. Darcy's first name. She wondered what the *D* stood for. Darcy? No. Surely not. That would be too weird, even for her. Brushing all those thoughts and the strand of hair that had fallen against her cheek aside, she flipped the envelope over and carefully ran her finger over the red waxed seal with the fancy script *B* insignia.

Dear Miss Bowen,
As I have just moved to the United States of America from England, I have not had the pleasure to make many acquaintances as of yet. The women I have met do not share your good opinion to travel and to explore the world. I must confess, your exuberant advertisement has quite intrigued me, and I must meet you. If it is agreeable with you, perhaps I could come on Tuesday next or within a fortnight to meet you. We could spend time getting acquainted to see if there could be a future for us together. If this is agreeable, then please send a post to me straightaway.
I hope to hear from you soon.
Sincerely,
Fitzwilliam D. Barrington

Relief drizzled over her. Mr. Barrington was willing to come here. She wouldn't have to risk breaking her mother's heart by traipsing off to New York by herself. She tossed everything from her lap onto the floor and rushed over to her writing desk.

Retrieving her best stationery, she dipped her pen in the ink well and penned her reply, making sure to use the swooping letters that looked so beautiful. Everything about this reply had to be perfect. After all, Fitzwilliam would make his decision about her and their future from it. Tomorrow she would take it to the post office. Bubbles of excitement popped through her. In her heart of hearts she felt she had at last found her very own Mr. Darcy who would come and whisk her away.

Jake saddled his horse and made his way to the Bowens' house. No one would be expecting him for at least another hour, but he couldn't sleep so he'd decided to head to their place early in hopes of seeing Leah. The morning nip brushed across him on a light breeze. He pulled the lapels of his wool coat tighter together, hoping the morning sun would soon penetrate the chilly air.

As he rounded the bend of pine trees nestled against the mountain leading to the Bowen ranch, his anticipation of seeing Leah caused his heart to beat erratically as he rode into their ranch yard. Leah had a way of making him feel special. He loved spending time with her.

He glanced toward the barn. There she was, sitting on a bench outside the barn door, petting Kitty, the family's pet pig. Jake reined his horse in that direction. Leah raised her head and leaped up. Grabbing the ends of her light pink wrap together, she scurried toward him, her lavender dress swinging like a bell around her feet as she did. Her warm welcome made his heart smile.

"I was hoping I would catch you this morning. You won't believe what I have to tell you." She was practically bouncing on her feet.

"Morning to you, too." He grinned.

There were those dimples again. Her eyes sparkled and her face shone brighter than the morning sun glistening off the dewdrops. Something had put that glow on her face. How he wished it was him, but he knew better.

"What won't I believe?" He dismounted and stood

in front of her. Kitty nudged her nose into the palm of his hand.

"Kitty, leave Jake alone."

"She's all right."

"She's a pest." Leah leaned over and tapped the pig on the nose. "Aren't you, girl?"

Kitty sniffed the air with her round snout. Jake patted her shoulder and gave a quick scratch behind her ears. Content with the attention, Kitty waddled slowly in the direction of the field blooming with purple camas flowers, no doubt to have her fill of camas bulbs. "That pig's quite a character."

"She sure is." Leah laughed, then turned her attention from the retreating pig back onto him. "Come and sit down. I can't wait to tell you my good news." She grabbed his hand and pulled him along.

There was a lilt to her walk. The air around her rolled with joy. She let his hand go and he followed her to the same hewed-out bench she'd been sitting on when he'd arrived. After he tied his horse to a nearby hitching post, he sat down with her, careful to keep the appropriate amount of distance between them.

"Okay, bright eyes. What's your good news?"

Her smile bracketed by those dimples was contagious, and he found his own lips curling upward.

"I think I found my husband."

He wasn't expecting that, and it took him a minute to gather his wits about him. "Oh, yeah?" He knew he should be happy for her. That it would happen someday. But the thought of losing his best friend made his gut twist into a painful knot.

"Yes. He moved from England to New York City and he wants to come here to meet me. I'm sending my consent today. I'm so happy. He sounds like just the type of man I've been looking for." She went on and on oblivious to the pain her declaration was causing him. Pain he couldn't articulate.

"Morning, Jake." Michael's voice drifted toward him from yards away. "I wasn't expecting you here so early."

Jake snapped himself together and stood. "Morning, Michael."

Leah hopped up beside him. "What are you doing here?" she asked. "I thought you didn't want to leave Selina alone."

"I don't. But she's finally asleep now."

"What do you mean, 'finally'?" Leah tilted her head.

"The babies kept her up most of the night."

Jake anchored his arms across his chest. Concern for a woman he'd come to greatly respect pressed through him. "How's Selina doing?"

"Other than being exhausted, she's doing well. Having twins is a lot of hard work. But Joseph and Lottie Lynn are sure worth it." His eyes sparkled, then a wide yawn stretched his lips. It was then that Jake noticed the bags under Michael's eyes.

"So, what are you doing here?" Leah inquired again.

"I wanted to show Jake what to do."

"Can't Haydon or Jess do that?"

"They could, but…"

"You know both Haydon and Jess are going to hang you for not trusting them to show Jake what to do," Leah interrupted her brother.

Michael frowned. "It's not that I don't trust them. I wanted to be here to welcome Jake. To show him around and…"

They continued to talk about Jake as if he weren't standing right there between them.

"Fine, fine. If you insist on being the one to show him what to do, I'll run over and sit with Selina and the twins until you get back. I know that will help put your mind at ease and help you to relax a bit."

"It sure will. Thank you, Leah. But don't wake her or the babies. And don't knock. Just open the door quietly and let yourself in."

"Yes, yes, Michael." Leah dragged out the words and rolled her eyes at her brother. "You worry too much. You really need to learn to lighten up."

"Just wait until you have children. Then it will be my turn to tell *you* to lighten up."

She shook her head and glanced over at Jake. "See you later, Jake."

He gave a quick nod and watched her as she headed toward Michael's house.

"You like her, don't you?"

Jake yanked his attention to Michael. "Sure I like her. She's been a great friend to me."

"She's more than a friend. I can see it in your eyes."

Jake shook his head and waved Michael off. "The only thing you see in my eyes is respect."

"If you say so, buddy." The smirk on Michael's face bugged Jake. Couldn't a guy have a female friend without everyone making a big deal about it?

Best change the subject before Michael put together any more pieces that didn't fit. "So, what do you want me to do?"

"Changing the subject, huh?"

"Michael." Jake sent Michael a warning glare. "I'm here to help, not discuss my *friendship* with Leah. You want my help or not? Besides, thought you didn't like leaving Selina alone."

Worry crowded into Michael's face immediately

followed by determination. He glanced at his pocket watch. "Oh, man. I've got to hurry. I've been gone ten minutes already."

"Ten minutes? That long, huh? We'd better hurry, then."

"Okay, wise guy. Just wait until you become a father. Then you'll understand. Come on." He motioned for them to go inside the barn.

Jake hoped someday he would know exactly how Michael felt. Once again, he wished Leah hadn't turned his marriage offer down. He knew she'd make a good wife and mother, and he admired her and respected her more than any other woman he knew.

Thoughts of Leah answering some strange man's ad and inviting him there trailed through Jake's mind. Would he be able to handle seeing his best friend hanging out with another man?

A man who could possibly become Leah's husband and take her away from him?

God, give me the grace to let my friend go and to make it through this time. Make it a large dose. 'Cause I'm sure gonna need every ounce You can spare.

Chapter Four

Steps creaked under Leah's feet. She cringed, hoping the noise wouldn't wake Selina. Michael would give her a good scolding if she did. Of that she was certain. Quietly she opened the door and stepped inside. Her eyes popped open. She'd never seen Selina's house this messy before. Never.

Dishes were scattered all over the table and piled in the sink. If Selina saw them, she would be so upset, and Leah couldn't have that. After she peeked into Selina's bedroom to make sure everything was all right, she closed the door. Leah grabbed an apron from off the hook, rolled up her sleeves and, as quietly as she could, she washed the dishes and tidied up the house.

Squeaking hinges caught her attention. She turned to find Michael stepping inside the house.

"Is she still asleep? Are the twins okay?"

She barely heard his questions his voice was so low.

"Yes. They're fine." She, too, kept her voice down.

"Good." He nodded. "Leah, would you mind doing me a favor?" He looked away and then back at her. "Oh. Thanks for doing the dishes and picking up the place. I really appreciate it. I hadn't gotten to that yet."

"You're welcome, Michael. That's what sisters are for." She smiled. "Now, what did you want?"

"We have a cow that's down and needs doctoring. Everyone else is busy and Jake will need my help. Would you mind staying here with Selina a bit longer? I don't want to leave her alone." He ran his hand over his face. "Man, I wish I didn't have to help. I hate leaving Selina. But Jake can't do it alone and no one else is around."

Leah laid her hand on his arm. "I can stay with her. She and the twins will be just fine."

Worry crowded his face. It was happening a lot these days.

"Michael." She turned and gave him a push toward the door. "Go. They'll be fine. Selina's a strong woman."

"She is, isn't she?" Pride puffed out his chest.

"Yes. Now go. I'll wait until you get back."

"If you need anything—"

"Michael, she'll be fine." This time, Leah pushed him out the door.

"I'll be back in about an hour."

"I'll be here."

She watched Michael leave, then shut the door.

With Selina and the babies still sound asleep, Leah searched her brother's cellar and pantry and made a pot of stew and some biscuits.

Nearly an hour later, Leah heard a baby cry. She headed over to the bedroom, slowly opened the door and peered inside. Lottie Lynn's little arms were moving in short, choppy movements. A wail came from Joseph's bed and his arms and legs imitated his sister's. Leah scurried inside, not knowing which one to reach for first.

"They sure have mighty good lungs," Selina said with a voice filled with sleep.

She started to rise, but Leah shot up her hand. "You stay there. I'll bring them to you."

"I ain't helpless. I can get them."

"I know you're not. But Michael would have my hide if he knew I let you get out of that bed."

Selina rolled her sleepy eyes. "Such fussin' that man does over me. I can do it."

"Please, Selina. You stay there. Let me do this for you," Leah said over the wails of the twins. She picked up Lottie Lynn, who stopped crying instantly. Leah hugged the baby girl to her chest. Someday she hoped to have a houseful of her own children. Her thoughts went to the letter still in her pocket, the one destined to be mailed today. Maybe that someday wasn't too far off.

She changed the baby's diaper and handed her to Selina who was now sitting propped against the pillows, looking more tired than Leah had ever seen her. No wonder Michael seemed so worried. She made a mental note to tell her mother that despite Michael's protest, they needed to come and help Selina…and Michael.

"Thank ya kindly, Leah."

"You're welcome."

Joey's loud wail pierced the air. Leah scuttled over to his crib and, securing his head, lifted him out. Muddy diaper odor stung Leah's nose with its potency. Ewwww. She wrinkled her nose and blinked her eyes.

"Sweet twinkling stars above. You need changing, little man," she cooed to him as she walked over to the changing table Michael had made. She laid him on the wooden slab with the feather-filled flannel quilt on top and changed her nephew's diaper. His crying stopped. She picked him up, kissed his cheek and turned toward Selina. A light blanket covered Lottie Lynn's head while she nursed.

"Do you want me to leave and you can holler when you're finished?"

"No. It don't bother me none. Unless you're uncomfortable."

She shook her head, sat down in the rocking chair next to the bed and rocked Joey.

Leah knew it was time to make the announcement. She let out a long breath to settle the butterflies flitting about in her stomach. "Well, I finally did it."

Busy with the baby, Selina hardly looked up. "Did what?"

"I placed an advertisement for a husband. And I've already received several answers."

Selina's eyes went wide as they jerked up, and her brows puckered. "Does your family know?"

"No."

"They ain't gonna like it. You goin' off to who knows where."

Leah found that weird coming from Selina, who had traveled across the country to be with Michael.

"I know what you're a-thinkin'. I did it. And I personally see nothin' wrong with it. But your family is mighty protective of you."

"I know they are. But…" She handed Joey to Selina and took the newly fed Lottie Lynn from her mother. With a cloth draped over her shoulder Leah patted her niece on the back until a loud burp echoed in the room. Selina and Leah giggled.

Selina settled Joey and then turned her attention back to Leah. "But what?"

"But, I don't think they'll have a problem with it

once I tell him that Fitzwilliam will be coming here, and I won't be traveling alone."

"Fitzwilliam? Ain't that an interestin' name. Never heard it before."

"I love his name. And—" she shifted Lottie Lynn and cradled her closer "—I really believe God is in this."

"Why's that?"

"Well, ever since reading *Pride and Prejudice* I've prayed for a man like Mr. Darcy. In the book, Mr. Darcy's first name is Fitzwilliam."

"Oh. I see." She waved her head back and forth, confusion flooding her face. "No, I don't see. What's that gotta do with anythin'?"

"It's simple, really. I've been praying for a man like Mr. Darcy. Then I get a letter from a man with Mr. Darcy's first name. And he lives in New York City." Oops. She shouldn't have said that. Leah didn't want Selina asking her why that was important, so she rushed on before she could. "You see, these are all signs."

"Signs?"

"Yes. From God."

"Leah, it ain't none-a my business—"

"What isn't any of your business, sweetheart?" Michael interrupted Selina as he stepped into the room.

Leah's gaze flew to Selina. With her eyes only, she begged Selina not to tell him.

Her brother strode into the room and kissed Selina, then took Lottie Lynn from Leah. "So, how are my favorite people in the whole world doing?" Michael sat on the bed next to Selina.

"Oh, I didn't know you thought of me as one of your favorite people. I'm honored, and I'm doing great," Leah teased her brother.

"Very funny. Ha-ha. I wasn't asking you."

"Really? Could have fooled me," she teased him again.

Michael turned to his family.

Whew. Thank You, Lord. Michael's forgotten all about his question. Leah stood. "It looks like you don't need me anymore, so I'll be on my way. There's stew on the stove and biscuits in the warmer."

Michael glanced over at her. "Thank you, Leah. I appreciate your help." He turned back to Selina.

"Thank ya kindly, Leah." Selina peered around him. Then, as if she weren't even there, her brother and his wife started talking. They were so adorable to watch. Leah silently prayed for a marriage like theirs, like the marriages of all her siblings and her parents. Out of the house she bounded with a spring in her step. Time to ready her horse and head into town to mail the letter that might very well give her the future she desired.

Jake finished mucking the stalls. Rivulets of sweat streamed from underneath his cowboy hat. From his back pocket, he pulled out a handkerchief that had definitely seen better days.

"You need a new one of those." Leah stepped in front of him, and what a beautiful sight she was.

He looked at the holes in his kerchief. "Sure do."

"I'll make you some."

"You don't need to do that."

"I know I don't need to, silly. I want to."

It was hard for Jake to accept charity—always had been. He hated feeling less than in front of anyone. Feeling that way in front of Leah was even worse. "Only if I pay for them."

Leah planted her hands on her slender hips. "No. You will not pay me for them."

"Won't take them then." He crossed his arms over his chest and stood his ground.

Her eyes trailed the length of him. For some odd reason, he hoped she liked what she saw. "You think that stance is going to stop me? Well, it won't. Besides, you have a birthday coming up and you can't refuse a birthday gift from a friend. It would be rude."

She got him there. He picked up the shovel again and changed the subject. "How are Selina and the twins doing?"

"Great. They're so cute. You should see them."

"I'll give Selina a few more days to recuperate before I do. Besides, don't think Michael's gonna let anyone near her for a few days."

They laughed.

"He sure is protective of them, isn't he?" Leah said through a giggle.

"I would be, too."

"I bet you would. You'll make a fine father someday." As she realized what she'd said, her face turned a deep shade of red. She spun and headed toward the tack room.

Jake followed her. "What you doing?"

"I'm going to get Lambie ready so I can head into town to mail my letter." She kept her back to him and reached for a halter.

His heart felt as if it had been thrown from a bucking bronc, but he reached for the tack just the same. "Here. Let me do that."

She turned to him and her smile was filled with gratitude. "I can get her. But thanks anyway."

Jake gently tugged the halter from her grasp. "How

about you let me help—or no handkerchiefs?" He grinned down at her.

She tilted her head and gazed up at him with those big blue eyes. "Okay. You win. But—" she held out her hand "—only if you promise me you will accept my gift."

Jake glanced down at her hand. "Deal." He accepted her handshake. Her hand felt small in his larger one. Soft, too, except for the few calluses he felt.

"Um, Jake." Leah glanced down at her hand. "You can let go now."

His attention drifted to her face and then to where their hands were still joined. "Oh, right." He dropped her hand as if it were on fire and felt heat rush up his neck and into his face. He couldn't believe it. He was blushing. Blushing. Like a woman.

Embarrassed, he spun on the heel of his boot and strode to her horse's stall. "How you doing, girl?" he asked, slipping the lead rope around Lambie's neck and then the halter on her head. Jake led the mare from her stall over to where Leah stood by the phaeton.

While they worked together to hitch up her horse Jake asked, "Lambie's a weird name for a horse, ain't it?"

"Yes. Abby named her."

"Did she name Kitty, too?" He referred to the pet pig with the huge personality.

"Yes. When she was younger she wanted to name all the animals. My brothers didn't have the heart to refuse her. They're sorry for it now." She laughed.

"Why's that?"

"Well, we have a horse named Lambie and one named Raven. Kitty the pig." She ticked each one off her fingers as she mentioned them. "Miss Piggy, the cat." She paused. "Oh and there was Taxt, one of our bulls."

"She named a bull Taxt?"

Leah laughed again. "Everyone asks that. And the answer is yes, she did."

"Poor bull."

Leah's giggle at his comment pulled a chuckle out of him. Ever since they'd become friends, he'd found himself laughing more and more. It felt good. Real good in fact.

"There. All finished."

"Thank you, Jake, for helping me."

"Welcome. Anytime."

She grabbed the lines under the horse's chin and tugged on them. Jake hurried ahead and opened the double doors.

Outside the sun had knocked the midmorning chill out of the air.

Leah looked up at the sky and all around. "It's sure a lovely day today."

Jake shifted his focus from her sleek, graceful neck and placed it upward, glad his hat shielded the bright sun from reaching his eyes. "Sure is."

"Well…" Her eyes collided with his. "I'd better go now. Mother wants me to pick up a few things for her, and I need to mail my letter." Her face brightened at that, and his outlook dimmed.

Pushing his own stupid feelings aside, he offered her a hand into the buggy, even though he really didn't want to aid her reason for going. "Mind picking up my mail while you're there?"

"No. I'd be happy to." She sat down and faced him.

"Leah." He gathered the lines but didn't hand them to her. "You sure you wanna do this?"

"Do what? Go to town? I have to. Mother needs—"

"No," he interrupted her, unable to keep the frustration from his voice. "Answer that man's ad."

"Of course I'm sure. Otherwise I wouldn't be doing it."

"How can you be so certain?"

Her eyes brushed over his face as if she were contemplating her answer. She looked away and then her attention settled on him. "For years I prayed for a man like my father and Mr. Darcy."

"Mr. Darcy? Who's that?"

Her eyelids lowered to her lap.

Jake watched as she nervously tugged on her fingertips. In a bold move, he reached for her hands and held on to them. "Leah, look at me."

Slowly, she raised her head toward him. "We're friends. You can tell me who Mr. Darcy is." Jake wondered if Mr. Darcy was the man who had just bought the livery stable. He couldn't remember the man's name, only that it started with a *D*.

"Promise you won't laugh?"

"Promise." He hiked his foot up, set it on the phaeton step and rested his forearm on his leg, waiting for her answer.

"Mr. Darcy is the hero in *Pride and Prejudice*."

"What's that?"

"A novel."

Jake forced his eyes not to bounce wide open. A novel? She wanted a man like some imaginable character out of a book? Whoa! He hadn't seen that one coming. Right now, laughing was the furthest thing from his mind.

"I know it sounds silly. But the man reminds me so much of my father."

"So this Mr. Darcy is a rancher?"

She shook her head and her bouncy curls wiggled with the motion. He longed to wrap his finger around one of them, just to see if they were as soft as they looked. "No. He's not a rancher. He reminds me of my father—before we moved here, that is." She clamped her lips together tightly.

Jake thought he saw a shimmer in her eyes but wasn't sure because she looked away. He placed his foot back onto the ground, not sure what to say or do.

Seconds ticked by. With a slow turn of her head, she dropped her attention onto him. "I'd better go, Jake. I have lots of errands to run."

That was it. No explanation. He scanned her face. Though she tried to smile, he could see in her eyes that she was upset. He hated to see her leave like this, but he didn't know what to say or do to make it better because he didn't even know what was wrong.

She reached for the lines. Reluctantly, Jake laid them in her hand when what he really wanted to do was snatch them back and ask her what was wrong. But he didn't. She said she needed to go, and he needed to respect that. He stepped back, out of her way. "Be careful."

"I will. Thank you."

"For what?"

"For helping me with my horse and for not laughing at me."

"Nothing to laugh at." His grin was meant to reassure her.

She nodded and flicked the lines. Jake watched the buggy pull out of the yard. Curious about what type of person this Mr. Darcy fellow was, he decided that he needed to purchase a copy of that book. What was it called? Oh, yes. *Pride and Prejudice*. The title alone made him nervous. He'd never been much of a reader in school, but this was important. He could only imagine what was stuck in between the pages and who this Mr. Darcy fellow was. The sooner he found out, the better.

Chapter Five

Leah couldn't believe she'd almost slipped. Telling Jake about wanting a man like her dad was bad enough, but she'd almost started to tell him why. Good thing she'd caught herself.

Two hours later, after running all of her errands, she headed for home. Seven letters had come for her and sixteen for Jake. She looked at the large bundle of Jake's posts, and without warning or understanding, jealousy snipped at her. Why, she didn't know. She wanted her friend to be happy. And if one of the women in those letters would make that happen, she'd be happy, too.

A light breeze swept by her and over the field of blooming camas. The purple flowers waved as the gentle wind drifted over them. Spring was her favorite time of the year. It meant winter was coming to an end and new life, new growth and new births were being ushered in.

From afar, she noticed Jake out in the field tending to the cattle and grinned. He had a way of making her smile. Another click of the lines, and she coaxed Lambie into a fast trot.

Jake spotted her, swung into his saddle and headed

toward her. Her heart picked up as he neared. That happened a lot lately.

"Howdy-do." Jake pulled his horse up alongside her buggy and rode next to her.

"Howdy-do yourself." She pulled her horse to a stop and raised her hand to block out the sun as she gazed up at him.

Jake moved his horse until he blocked the sun from shining in her eyes. "Did you have a pleasant trip?" He thumbed the brim of his hat upward, and she got a clear look at his tabby-gray eyes.

"I sure did." It was even more pleasurable now that her best friend was here. "How'd your day go? Did my brothers work you too hard?"

"Naw. I'm used to hard work. Think they went easy on me today, though." There was that lazy grin she enjoyed.

"Why's that?"

"'Cause. Didn't do much." He leaned over and rested his arm on his saddle horn and gazed down at her. His horse shifted and stomped its leg, trying to get rid of a pesky horsefly. Jake didn't even flinch but remained relaxed.

Leah envied how relaxed he always was, whereas she was always restless and fidgety inside and out. Oh, to have his peace. Someday. Someday soon, she encouraged herself. "What all did you do?"

"Milked the cows. Doctored a few heifers. Cleaned the barn. Checked to make sure the pigs were all okay. That was it. I'm done for the day already."

"Already?"

"Yep."

"Sweet twinkling stars above. They really did go easy on you." She grinned and nearly laughed outright.

He chuckled. "Yep. Told you they did." Jake sat up straight. "Before I forget, did I have any mail?"

"Oh. Um. Yes. You did. Quite a bit, actually." She moved her reticule, grabbed the tied bundle of his mail and handed it to him.

"You weren't kidding." He took the generous bundle from her and turned it around.

"Sixteen, to be exact."

His attention drifted to her. "Sixteen, huh?" A knowing smirk accompanied his question.

Heat rushed to Leah's face. She wished she could blame it on the warm sun, but the sun had been there for hours, and her red face hadn't. She dipped her head and only let her eyes look up at him. "Yes. Sixteen."

There was that chuckle again. "How many you get?"

"Seven." She raised her chin, hoping her face was no longer red.

"You busy now? I mean, after you take your supplies home."

"No. Why?"

"Well, was wondering if you'd help me go through these." He raised the package of letters.

"Sure. You want to go through them now?"

"You mean right here?"

"Yes."

"What about your supplies?"

"They'll be fine. Besides, I got done earlier than I thought. Mother won't be expecting me home for another hour or so. We could…" She looked around and pointed to the trees. "We could go sit on that rock over there in the shade?"

Jake followed her line of view. "Works for me."

He dismounted, gathered both reins under his geld-

ing's neck, and wrapped them around the saddle horn
and let go.

"Won't he leave?" Leah asked, referring to his dun-
colored horse.

"Nope. Dun's trained not to go far when his reins
are tied to the saddle. We do this all the time."

"Our horses are trained to stand still when the reins
are down, but I've never seen anyone do it like that
before."

"Yeah, well, I'm different."

"That's for sure." A smile lit up her face.

It must have been lost on Jake because he whipped
his head in her direction and his tone sounded defen-
sive. "What's that supposed to mean?"

"Oh. I see how that must have sounded, but I meant
that as a compliment. Truly. That's one of the things
I like about you, Jake. You do things differently than
most folks."

"Like what?" His forehead wrinkled as he tied off
the lines on her carriage.

"Well, for one, you keep that silly goat and put up
with her silly antics when no one else would."

"Yep. I do. 'Cause I know if I gave that little escape
artist to someone else they would probably destroy her.
That's why I keep her."

"Exactly. They would have put her down. And so
you put up with all the trouble she causes rather than
risk someone else destroying her." Leah watched as he
shrugged off her compliment. "You're a softy when it
comes to animals, Jake. That's one of the things I admire about you. And another thing you do differently
is… You asked another woman to help you pick out a
wife. I don't know anyone who's ever done that. Do

you?" She danced her eyebrows up at him and sent him a smirch of a smile.

"Got me there." His lazy grin appeared. "Speaking of. We'd best get to it so we can get ready for Phoebe's wedding." Jake slipped the tied bundle of letters from her hand.

Under the clear blue sky the knee-high bunchgrass rustled as they walked through it side by side until they reached a large flat-topped boulder and sat down.

"Okay. What do we have here this time?" Leah pointed to the letters Jake held.

He untied the string and handed her the first one. Leah opened it and scrunched her face.

Jake leaned toward her. His breath brushed the hair near her ear, sending chills rushing up and down her back. Not understanding why that would happen, she turned her head, and her face was inches from his. Her gaze soared to his gray eyes. Eyes that searched hers, questioning hers, as her eyes did his.

A moment passed in which neither moved.

Then Jake pulled back, cleared his throat and looked straight ahead. Leah, realizing she hadn't been breathing, drew in a long, quiet breath, wondering why her insides were suddenly fluttering.

Jake willed his heartbeat to return to normal. The urge to kiss his friend just now was so strong that he'd almost given in to it. Nothing good would have come from it, of that he was certain. And he would do nothing to risk his friendship with her.

No one understood him like she did.

No one accepted him just as he was like she did.

And no one filled his thoughts more than she did.

And therein lay the danger.

She was leaving soon.

It was time for him to find a wife. He looked back at her. "Well. Let's get to it."

Leah tilted her head. "Get to what?" Confusion infused her face.

Did she know he had been about to kiss her? If so, is that what she thought he meant? "The letters. Get to the letters."

"Oh. Yes. Oh, um. Right. The letters." Her attention dropped to the post in her hand. "I think we have to forget this one."

"Why's that?"

"Because." She placed it under his view. "I can't even read it."

He squinted, trying to make out the sloppy cursive. He could make out only a few words. Saloon. Toothless. And ten babies. "Whoa!" He balled the letter up faster than he could say the word *no*.

"What?" Leah glanced at the wad in his hands.

"You don't wanna know."

"Well, now you've got me curious. Tell me?"

Reluctantly, he un-balled the letter and smoothed the wrinkles as best as he could. Heat drifted up the back of his neck as he pointed to each of the three words.

Leah's eyes opened farther and farther with each one he pointed to. "Sweet twinkling stars above." Her hands flew to her flushed cheeks, and her wide eyes darted to his. "Oh my." She shook her head. "Oh my, my, my, my, my."

"'Oh my' is right." He took the letter from her and wadded it up again before he shoved it into his pocket to burn later. Apprehension and fear fisted inside him as he stared at the remaining pile. "Not sure I wanna do this anymore. Bad idea."

"What's a bad idea?" Leah's color had returned to normal and she seemed to have recovered from the shock.

He wished he had. His gut was still being punched around. "Don't think I want you to read anymore."

"Why?"

His own eyebrows pointed upward. "Why? You ask me why after reading that letter?"

Leah's lips quivered and her nostrils danced.

He watched, amused at her trying to hold back her laughter. His own lips now curled and twitched. Soon a belly laugh rolled out of him.

Leah's hand rested on his arm and her sweet laughter joined his.

He didn't know how long they laughed, but it was long enough that Leah had tears rolling from her eyes.

He would offer her his handkerchief, but it was too worn and would be too embarrassing. No need, anyway. She reached inside the pocket of her skirt and pulled a lace hankie out and dabbed at her eyes.

When they both had composed themselves, Leah asked, "What do you want to do with these?"

"Burn 'em!" he blurted.

They burst out laughing again.

"Seriously," Leah said through a twitter. "What do you want to do with them?"

"Told you already. Burn 'em."

She tilted her head. "Surely they can't all be like her."

He hiked a brow.

"Okay, Jake. Tell you what. I'll turn my back to you and read them so you can't see my face. If they're bad, then I'll slip them back into the envelope. If they aren't, I'll read them to you. Sound fair?"

After that last letter, he didn't care what was in any of them. He no longer had any faith in this process. He'd rather remain single the rest of his life than marry a toothless woman who had worked in a saloon and wanted ten babies.

"Well, what do you think?"

"Think I'll just forget the whole thing."

Once again her hand rested on his arm and lingered there.

His attention trailed there and to the heat that now raced up his arm.

"Oh, sorry." She yanked it back and rested her hand on her skirt. "You sure you want to do that, Jake? There might be some lovely ladies in here." She patted the stack.

Debate did a roundup through his brain. He really wanted to get married, but some of the letters he'd received were downright scary. Okay, a few of them were. Still. Did he dare take a chance on one of them?

"Jake." Leah's soft voice reached his ears and he looked at her. "I know you're scared. So am I. But if you don't step out in faith, how will you ever know? Besides, like I said before, you can always have her come here before you make a decision. I mean, it isn't like you have to marry her or anything before meeting her." She shrugged. "What have you got to lose?"

Her words pinned his heart to the hard ground. It was once again obvious that she would never consider him. If she would, she wouldn't have suggested he send for someone else. *Is that what's been holding me back? Hoping Leah would change her mind and marry me?* Truth smacked him upside the head. That was it. Knowing that, he decided he might as well give it a try. "You're right. Don't have anything to lose. Okay. Open the next one." If only she knew how hard those words were for him to say. When what he really wanted to say was, *Are you sure you won't reconsider my proposal and stay here? At least I know what you're like. These other women are downright scary.*

Leah pulled out the next one. One after another she read, and the second to the last one caught his attention.

Dear Mr. Lure,
My name is Raquel Tobias. I am a Christian woman looking for a Christian man to share my life with. I'm twenty-three years old, five foot seven, 130 pounds, with auburn hair and blue eyes. I'm currently residing in Chicago, taking care of my beloved Aunt Sally who encouraged me to not follow in her footsteps wishing she'd married. Therefore, I decided to take a chance by answering your advertisement.

Aunt Sally insists on paying my way there and back in case things do not work between us. It is her way of saying thanks for being a companion to her all this time. Aunt Tillie, her sister, is recently widowed and will be coming to live with her, so my aunt will not be alone if I leave.

So, if you would like to meet me, please reply to this post.
Thank you and God bless you.
Raquel Tobias

Leah shifted her focus from the letter onto him. "What do you think?"

"Well," he stood, pondering Miss Tobias's words. Seconds passed. "Like you said, I need to step out in faith, so I'll answer her." And what a leap of faith it would be. Bigger than any he'd ever taken before.

"Do you want help writing her back?" For some odd reason, the prospect of Jake actually responding to a woman who could potentially become his wife made Leah uneasy. Was the feeling a warning from God that this woman wasn't right for him? She didn't know. She couldn't rightly discern why she felt the way she did. All she knew was something didn't feel right.

"You okay?" Jake asked, shifting his vision down on her.

Leah gazed up at him. Once again, Jake, being the perfect gentleman, blocked the bright sun from shining in her eyes. She shook out the confusing thoughts. He was going to think she'd lost her mind. "Yes. Of course. I'm fine." Only she didn't feel fine. No. In fact, she felt sick. Even so, she forced a smile onto her face. Later on, when she was alone, she'd try to figure out just what was bothering her about this whole situation. After all, from the looks of things, everything seemed to be working out exactly as she had hoped. She realized then she was just being silly about all of it.

"Thanks for the offer, Leah, but I can manage." Jake crossed his arms over his chest and shrugged.

That threw her completely off track, and she turned wide, confused eyes at him. "Manage what?"

"The letter." He nodded at it still in her hand.

"Oh. Yes. That. Silly me." She gathered the letters, handed all of them to Jake and then stood. "How could I have forgotten so soon?"

"'Cause you're a woman."

"Hey." She slapped him on the arm. "What's that supposed to mean?"

"Just teasing you, Leah." He winked at her.

Winked. She couldn't believe her friend just winked at her. Even more befuddling…she couldn't believe how her heart leaped in response to his wink. What was going on with her? Whatever it was, she wasn't sure she liked it. "Yes, well, um. I'd better get home now. I have much to do before Phoebe's wedding. So, I'll see you later, Jake." She brushed past him, scurried to her buggy and climbed aboard.

"What's your hurry?"

"Me? I'm not in a hurry," she answered without meeting his eyes.

Jake hiked a brow and stared at her. "Okay, Leah. Something's wrong. What is it?"

Her hands shook and her insides weren't any better, but she forced herself to not show any of it. "Nothing's wrong. I just have a lot on my mind, that's all. And I really do have much to do before the wedding."

His eyes searched hers, though she wasn't really looking at him. She couldn't. If she did, he would see everything.

He shook his head. "Not buying it, Leah. But neither will I push you into talking about what's bothering you." Hurt and disappointment marched across Jake's face. "You got a right to keep your own counsel, I guess."

Anger with herself for handling it all so badly trounced over her. Gathering her courage, she looked down at him. "Jake, I'm honestly not sure what's bothering me, or I would tell you." She looked him right in the eye, wanting to ask but not sure she should. "Do you ever feel like something's wrong but you don't know what it is?"

"Yep. Lots of times."

"You do? What do you do about it?" It was odd being so blunt about what she was feeling. So often, her own feelings had to be tucked away in deference to duty. She took a short breath and pushed those thoughts away.

"I pray and ask God to show me what it is and what to do about it." Conviction gripped his words. He looked so settled, so solid.

"Pray," she whispered. How simple, yet why hadn't she thought of that? "That's what I'll do. Thank you, Jake."

With his free hand, he handed her the lines. "Leah, you know you can talk to me anytime about anything. That I'm here for you, right?"

"Yes." She knew without a doubt he was. "And I thank you for that. You know that I'm here for you, too, don't you?"

"Yep." Jake nodded and smiled a half grin.

After a few moments of gazing silence, he stepped back, out of the way of her buggy. "Better let you go so you can get whatever it is you need to do done. See ya this evening."

That's right. She would see Jake this evening. Joy sang through her leaping heart. She gave him her sweetest smile. "Yes. I'll see you later. I'm looking forward to it." She meant that more than even she understood and that scared her. She was starting to realize that she needed to be careful because the more time she spent with Jake, the harder it would be for her to say goodbye to him. But say goodbye she must. Her peace of mind and her very sanity depended on it.

Chapter Six

Dressed in her blue-violet dress, Leah stood at the full-length looking glass in her bedroom and studied her image. The sheer, ruffled lace around her neck, sleeves and skirt looked out of place in the Idaho Territory. Yet tonight it wouldn't be. Phoebe was marrying the banker's son, so everyone would be dressing in their best attire.

Leah gave one more glance at herself. Then she turned the key on her jewelry box, removed the tortoiseshell hairpins, placed them into her coiffure hairstyle and stared at them. Father had given them to her for her tenth birthday.

She closed her eyes as memories of that day crashed in on her. Father had been so proud of the combs he himself had picked out. "A special gift for my special girl," he'd said before tucking them into her hair. He'd stood back and admired her. "You look beautiful, Leah. I'm so proud of you, princess." He'd hugged her, and she felt the warmth and security of that moment even to this day.

Melancholy shoved through her as she remembered also that there would never be any more hugs from her father. He was gone and nothing could bring him back. This wretched place had stolen him from her.

Short, huffy breaths whooshed between her clenched teeth. She yanked the combs from her hair and put them back into her jewelry box where she couldn't see them anymore. The reminder of who gave them to her hurt too much.

Without warning, the image of her father gasping for air invaded her thoughts. She slapped her hand over her mouth to stifle the scream the unwelcome intruder regurgitated. Gurgling sounds of her father trying to draw breath flooded her ears. She pressed her hands over them to snuff the ghastly noise from her anguished soul. But neither the image nor the sound stopped.

The urge to scream once again siphoned up her esophagus. She wanted to let it out. To yell at the ugly things attacking her to leave her alone, but she couldn't— Her family would hear her.

She pinched her eyes shut and swallowed hard as if that would somehow make everything better. When that didn't work, she leaned over, placed her hands on her knees and drew in several long breaths, exhaling slowly each time until finally the grisly images and sounds faded, and the jitters ceased. Having won that battle, she straightened and pressed her shoulders back. Ghosts of the past would not ruin her evening. Chin up, she headed downstairs.

"Oh, Lee-Lee. You look beautiful." Abby glanced over her.

"You look pretty gorgeous yourself, Abbs." The yellow cotton frock layered with white lace on the bodice, skirt and neck brought out the yellow highlights in her sister's hair. Abby had done an incredible job on that dress. What an excellent seamstress she turned out to be. Leah was so proud of her baby sister.

"Well, look at my girls." They both turned toward the sound of their mother's voice. "You both look so lovely. Oh." She pressed her finger on her lip. "That won't do. You girls had better go up and change. You'll outshine the bride, and we can't have that now, can we?"

"Oh, Mother." Leah waved her off and beamed under her praise. "You're so sweet. But I'm certain we, as in the three of us, won't 'outshine' the bride. Trust me. Wait until you see her."

"Yes, Mother." Abby cupped her fisted hand under her chin, batted her eyes and sighed dramatically. "It's the most beautiful gown ever, and Phoebe looks absolutely fabulous in it."

"What a silly goose you are, Abbynormal." Leah shook her head at her sister. "You are so dramatic."

"Yeah. But you love me."

"I sure do." She pulled Abby into a hug.

"Okay, ladies. We'd better go or we'll be late." Mother gathered her wrap and picked up the gloves that matched her simple yet elegant blue silk dress. "I hope you girls don't mind, but with Jess and Hannah and Haydon and Rainee having full wagonloads already, I accepted Mr. Barker's offer to come and pick us up."

Leah's excitement plummeted to her button-up shoes.

"We don't mind. Do we, Leah?" Abby beamed.

Leah wished she shared her sister's enthusiasm over her mother's growing friendship with Mr. Barker, but she didn't, and she minded—a lot. The idea of Mother sitting next to someone who wasn't her father bothered Leah enormously. Mother was lonely, that Leah knew, and she hated feeling so selfish. She tried not to think only of herself, but the idea drove through her heart like a railroad spike being plunged into the hard ground.

"Leah." Mother laid a gloved hand on her arm. "You don't mind, do you? If you do, I will have one of the hands get the surrey ready."

Despite how she felt, Leah did what she always did—suppressed her true feelings to spare hurting someone else's. She couldn't bear to hurt her mother like that, even if it was killing her from the inside out. "No. Of course not, Mother. No need to get the surrey. It was kind of Mr. Barker to offer to take us."

The sound of wagon wheels crunching on the gravel and a horse whinnying drew their attention outside.

Wraps and gloves gathered and put on, they headed out the door.

God, please help me to overcome this discontentment and to be happy for Mother. Please.

The ride to the church seemed endless, and Leah sent up many more prayers the whole way there. At the church, Mr. Barker pulled his landau alongside the others. He hopped out and helped her and Abby down, then her mother. Mother looped her arm through his and they strolled toward the church door together. As if they were a couple.

Bile rose up Leah's throat. Everyone was watching. Everyone could see. And they appeared to not even care about that.

Leah wanted to yank her mother's arm from Mr. Barker's, but it was not her place to do so. Her mother had every right to do what she wanted and to be with whomever she wanted. Father had been gone a long time now, and this war raging inside of her was her problem, not her mother's. Still. It hurt. She closed her eyes and fought to keep the tears and frustrations down. The pain, however, was too much to bear.

"It's hard for you to see your mother on the arm of another man, isn't it?" Jake's voice, while low, reached her ears with ease as he stepped up beside her.

She stared up at him, blinking and searching for the answer to her silent question: *How did you know?* She'd told no one.

Without another word, Jake cupped her elbow and led her out of the earshot of others. This time she didn't care what anyone thought. Right now she needed a friend more than ever. And not just any friend. She needed Jake. He had a way of comforting her. Of making her feel better when no one else could or did.

It wasn't until they'd made it around the corner of the building that she looked up into his face. "Whatever do you mean?"

"I saw the hurt on your face just now when you watched your mother walk away with Mr. Barker, Leah. And I have to say, I know exactly how you feel."

"You—you do?" She searched his eyes for the truth.

"Yep."

"How can you possibly know?"

"I know because when my mama decided to get remarried, I had a terrible time with it. Hated seeing her with someone other than Papa. But the truth is, it didn't take long to get over it."

"Why's that?" Leah needed to hear his answer. She needed the selfish feelings she harbored about this over, too. Those same feelings that now had her head lowering in guilt and shame.

"Because I saw how happy Mama was, that's why. And I realized how selfish I'd been by not considering how lonely she was without Papa around." He tilted her chin upward with his forefinger. "It gets easier. Honest. And Mr. Barker's a good man."

Tears blurred her vision and coated her heart. "But he's not Father."

"No. He isn't. And no one can take your father's place. But your father's gone, Leah. You're mother isn't. Life goes on whether we like it or not. You have a big heart. Open it up and let Mr. Barker in. If you can't do it for you, then do it for your mother. She needs you to." He released her chin.

After a brief moment, Leah shifted her attention over to the small flock of people heading into the church. "I know you're right," she said not looking at him. "I need to. For Mother's sake, if nothing else. It's just so hard sometimes. And it hurts so badly. My father was a wonderful man." Her throat constricted. "And he and Mother were so happy." She closed her eyes, fighting back the flood of unshed tears.

Jake gently turned her face toward him and held it just long enough, until her eyes opened and their gazes locked. The compassion in those soft gray eyes of his revealed just how much he really did understand what she was going through. Knowing he understood what it was like to lose a father one dearly loved, she wanted to pour out her heart to him, to tell him about the nightmares she had and how hard it had been for her all these years since her father's death.

The opportunity passed with the ringing of the church bell at that precise moment.

Another time, perhaps. She took a deep breath and let determination fill the place sorrow had been.

"We'd better get inside," Jake said as if he'd read her thoughts. He led her to a small group of people near the door. Once there, he stepped back, waiting until everyone preceded him, including her. To keep the tongues from wagging, she couldn't sit with Jake, so Leah joined her mother and even managed to smile at Mr. Barker, who returned it with a large one of his own.

Mother beamed. Her lips curled with approval, and her eyes twinkled with joy.

Yes, Leah decided. She could do this, and she would. For her mother's sake she would try her hardest to. However, in the very next second, doubt assailed her with the question: If she accepted her mother's relationship with Mr. Barker, was she somehow denigrating the memory of her father?

Jake sat on the small bench nearest the door. Being close to a quick means of escape was the only way he could handle being shut in with such a close group of people.

The pastor began the ceremony. He talked about marriage and how sacred it was and how it shouldn't be entered into lightly.

Jake's focus slid to Leah, sitting directly in front of him. He wished it was he and Leah standing there exchanging their vows. Immediately he scattered that wishful yet ridiculous thought away with a shake of his head.

The words "Do you promise to love her?" echoed off the rafters.

Love. Markus's love for Phoebe was written all over him and the conviction of it was in his strong response, "I will."

Again Jake glanced at Leah. He knew he couldn't make that same promise before God. Sure, he cared deeply for Leah. But love? He didn't think so. He wasn't even sure how a person knew when they were in love.

Jake forced himself to remember it wouldn't be Leah standing up there when the time came, anyway. He wondered about the nameless, faceless person that would stand next to him. What would she be like? And could he ever love her the way Markus loved Phoebe?

A latecomer slipped in through the door, breaking through his thoughts. An old man looked down at Jake and with a quick jerk of his thumb motioned for Jake to move over.

Jake froze.

The world tilted and then began to close in around him. The man now stood between him and his only way of escape. There wasn't room for the man to slip between him and the pew in front of him because of Jake's long legs and the man's portly size. So he chose the only other option left to him. Jake shifted his legs sideways and motioned the large man who was about as round as he was tall to the other side of him.

More wrinkles lined the man's weathered face. His lips pursed and his eyes narrowed. With a quick jerk of his chubby thumb, he signaled for Jake to move. Then he moved his rotund body closer, until he towered over Jake, crowding him in.

Jake fought to keep down the rising panic in his chest. Not because the man scared him, but because he suddenly felt trapped. Every Sunday he came to church there and sat in his spot near the door, knowing he could leave at any time. But that wasn't the case now.

His eyes darted about the room that seemed to be getting smaller and smaller.

His fingers tingled, and his palms dampened.

Chilled sweats crawled up and down his spine.

His heart tapped rapidly against his ribs.

Air.

His lungs needed air.

And now.

Jake sent the man the most intimidating warning glare he could muster to get him to move out of his way. The old man's eyes widened and he stepped back. Relief barreled over Jake that it had worked. Jake stood and fought the urge to bolt from the church. He left the building as fast as he could without causing a scene or disrupting the ceremony. Once outside, he scrambled into the woods behind the church as far and as fast as he could, hoping and praying no one had noticed his leaving.

He stopped in the midst of a cluster of cottonwood trees and rested his back against one of the large trunks, wheezing in the cool air.

His arms ached. Felt heavy even.

Sharp pains pressed into his chest. He flattened his hand against his heart. In rapid successions it thumped, thumped, thumped against his fingers.

Closing his eyes, he groaned as the feeling of impending doom blanketed him. Thinking straight was beyond his ability.

He panted like an overheated mountain lion.

It was all he could manage just to stay standing.

"Jake?"

Leah.

Oh, no.

He yanked himself up from the tree but swayed dangerously with the sudden movement. Jake didn't want her to see him like this, so he turned his back to her and tried harder to right his breathing and regain control over his body. It wasn't working nearly as fast or as well as he would have liked.

A second passed and she came around to the front of him.

He turned, placing his back to her again.

"Jake?" She moved in front of him again.

He started to turn, but her hand clutched his forearm with a strength he didn't know she possessed. "Jake, look at me." She shook him not hard but enough to cause the swimming in his head to stop. "What's wrong? Do you need a doctor?" Concern warbled through her voice.

Jake wanted to comfort her, but he simply couldn't right now. He needed to concentrate on breathing.

"I'm going to run and get Doc Berg."

Jake grasped her wrist. He shook his head and held up his hand. "No. Don't," he said through gasping breaths. "I don't need a doctor."

Fear shrouded her face and darkened her eyes. "Jake, you're scaring me. What's wrong? Why are you clutching your chest? And why are you breathing so strangely?"

"Give me. A minute." He leaned over, placed his hands on his knees and coached himself like he had so many times before when this happened. *Breathe, Jake. Slowly. Relax. Breathe. You're okay. No one's going to trample you out here.*

"Can I do something?"

He shook his head and continued to pull air into his lungs. Moments later, his lungs were finally satisfied, his chest quit hurting and his arms returned to normal. "That's better." He stood, feeling more like himself. "Whew."

"What happened? Why did you leave?"

Before he answered her question, he needed to know something. "Did anyone else see me?"

"No. I don't think so. I just happened to notice you leaving from the corner of my eye. I wondered why, so I followed you. What happened back there, Jake? Why did you leave?" She tilted her head, and worry and confusion streamed through her eyes.

Did he dare tell her? Would she laugh at him? And could he bear the one person whom he admired most in the world thinking less of him?

"Jake." Her face hardened. "Remember when you said that if I ever needed to talk that you were here? Well, that goes both ways. I'm here for you, too. Talk to me."

Hearing those words, he wanted to pour out the whole sordid story, to bear his soul to her. But it was Phoebe's wedding, and Leah was missing it. "You're missing Phoebe's wedding."

"This is more important. *You're* more important, Jake."

His heart warmed at her words. He gave a quick nod and looked for a place for them to sit. An old bench by the church's woodshed would have to do. "Let's go sit over there, and I'll tell you."

Dust layered the bench. Not wanting Leah's fancy dress to get dirty, he removed his handkerchief and brushed it over it. Not clean enough, he removed his Sunday jacket, the only nice one he had, and moved to lay it across the top of the bench.

"Oh, Jake. Don't do that." She snatched it from him. "You'll ruin it." Before he could protest, she handed it to him and sat down on the smudged bench.

Seeing no way to argue, Jake slipped his jacket back on and sat on the wooden slab, leaving at least a foot of space between them, then faced her.

Leah rested her hands in her lap. Curious eyes

roamed over his face, but he felt no pressure from her to rush. He appreciated that.

Drawing in a long breath of courage, he plunged forward. "I used to live in Atlantic City until the fire in 1864 broke out. When it started, everyone ran in different directions, screaming. No one paid attention to anyone else. They were all fleeing for their lives. Mama and I got caught in the middle of the confusion and were separated. Mama said she tried to get to me but couldn't break free from the crowd." The memory crammed in on him, and the air around him dissipated again. The scene played before his eyes as if it were happening all over again, right then and there. Unable to sit still, he stood and began pacing. Sweat broke out on his forehead and hands. His lungs burned as he tried to pull air into them.

"Jake."

When he said nothing, Leah grabbed his hands. "Oh, Jake." She must have seen the anguish he felt written all over his face and her arms came around him in pools of gentleness. She ran her hand over his back in a circular motion, cooing words of comfort. He drew strength from her soothing gesture.

His lungs filled again and the tormenting fear lifted. He backed up, grateful for her, and gazed into her eyes. "Thank you, Leah."

She nodded and let her arms fall back to her side. He wanted to snatch them back and put them around him, but he didn't. Instead, he put some distance between them, and Leah sat back down on the bench. "What happened next?"

"All I saw were legs and boots. I tried to roll into a ball, but people trampled over me anyway. Pert near killed me. If it hadn't been for Mama, I'd probably be dead. Somehow she broke free of the mob and found me. Took the bones in my arm and leg a long time to heal, though."

He heard her sharp intake of breath. "Oh, Jake. How awful."

Seeing her compassion and not repulsion gave him the courage to go on. "The bones healed. My mind didn't." He was ashamed to admit it. "Ever since then, anytime I feel crowded in, my hands sweat and tingle. My chest hurts. My arms feel heavy. It's hard to catch a breath. All I feel is fear. I have to run, get away, or I feel like I might lose my mind."

"I know exactly how you feel."

He opened his mouth to protest that she really couldn't and to ask her what she meant but didn't get to because Abby called her name from somewhere nearby. "Leah!"

"Here!" Leah called back and stood.

"There you are." Abby looked at her sister then over at Jake. "Hi, Jake. Boy, don't you look nice." She whistled.

Heat rushed up the back of his neck. "Thank you. So do you."

"I do, don't I?" She whirled. "It's my new dress. You like it? There's something about a new dress that just makes a gal feel better and prettier. Not that I'm saying I'm pretty or anything. I'm just saying…" Jake listened as she babbled on, smiling and laughing at her antics. The girl was such a character. "And now… I really hate to steal Leah away from you, Jake, but Mother sent me to find her. They're getting ready to head to Markus's father's house for the reception and dinner. Come on, Leah. Mother's waiting."

Leah looked up at Jake. Her silent question if he was okay showed through her concerned expression.

A short nod and a quick jerk of his head toward the direction of the church told her he was. "You two go ahead. I'll be there in a minute."

"You sure?" Leah asked.

"I'm sure."

Leah hated leaving him alone, especially after what she'd witnessed. She thought what she went through with the nightmares was bad, but now they seemed mild compared to Jake's experience. Torn between leaving him and going with Abby—and knowing there was no way she could tell Abby without betraying Jake's trust—she finally conceded. "Okay. See you later."

"Count on it." Jake smiled, and she returned his.

Leah and Abby headed to the white clapboard building where Mother and Mr. Barker were waiting in his carriage. Mr. Barker hopped down and helped her and Abby into the wagon. They headed down Main Street. Dust rolled from the parade of buggies and wagons in front of them.

In minutes they arrived at the estate of the richest man in town. Mr. Barker pulled his landau alongside the rest of the carriages and buggies and helped everyone out.

"Can you believe the size of this place?" Abby asked, linking her arm through Leah's. Then she leaned in so only her sister could hear. "I bet Mr. Darcy's is bigger than this, though."

"Mr. Darcy?" Leah looked at her sister as they headed up the wide staircase of the three-story mansion filled with windows and verandas. Wrought-iron benches, chairs and tables were situated precisely down the long, covered porch. "What made you think of him?"

"Well, last night I was reading *Pride and Prejudice* for the umpteenth time and thought about Mr. Darcy's wealth. Ours is probably nothing compared to his. I'm sure glad we don't have to live stuffy lives like that and that we can marry for love and not the size of someone's pocketbook like they did back then in England. Wouldn't that be awful?" Abby chattered on with her usual dramatic embellishment, using her arms to help aid with what she was saying. "I can't imagine having to consider my future husband's financial status or his connections or his station in life before even thinking about marrying him. Who cares about those things? Not me. But even worse than that would be having to be someone I'm not. Having to act all properlike. Ick. Can you imagine how boring that would be?"

"I don't think it sounds boring at all. We weren't bored in New York, and our lives were similar to Mr. Darcy's."

"I guess I was too little to remember. But Mother said Father told her that he wanted us girls to marry for love, not money, not for what the man did for a living or who he knew. And Father would have made sure the man loved us. That's the way it should be, Lee-Lee. Marrying for love. Not all that other stuff."

Abby's words struck a chord in Leah. She was right. Father would not have allowed his girls to marry without knowing they were in love and loved in return. If the man they loved didn't have money, Father would have made sure his daughters had a nice home and plenty of money to live on. He did make sure by seeing to it that she and Abby had sizable dowries. Still, was she settling for less by marrying just to move away from this place? If her father were alive, how would he feel about that?

She gave a silent snort. If he were still alive, she wouldn't even be thinking about marrying a stranger and moving away from those she loved.

Just when she and Abby had walked up the steps to the front door, Leah didn't know. She was so caught up in her thoughts that she hadn't realized the butler was waiting to take her wrap. "Oh. Um. Thank you, sir."

"You're welcome, miss." The slightly balding man held his chin up high. His white, pristine, high-collared shirt, white bow tie, black tailcoat and trousers were as stiff and starchy as he appeared to be. His black shoes sparkled, and when he went to receive her coat, she noticed his white gloves didn't have a speck of dirt on them. He draped their wraps over his arm, stepped back and stood stiff as a wooden plank until they passed. Only one word came to mind. Abby's word—stuffy.

"C'mon, Lee-Lee." Abby grabbed her hand and tugged her forward.

They strolled through the foyer. At the end of the vestibule, two men stood statue-still, one on each side of the doorway, wearing somber expressions on their faces and dressed the same way the butler was, only their ties were black.

Inside the massive main room, Abby told Leah she'd see her later and strode toward Phoebe, who squealed with delight at seeing her friend. Leah suddenly felt alone in the sea of strangers. Women who hadn't attended the wedding ceremony at the church stood talking and fanning themselves. Their bustle gowns were made of fine silk, brocaded tulle, crepe de chine and velvet materials. There were other styles and materials Leah didn't recognize, also. Leah glanced down at her new gown. It was nowhere near as fashionable as these ladies' dresses were. Suddenly she felt like an ugly caterpillar amid a swarm of beautiful butterflies.

She tugged on the collar of her dress. Spotting the open glass doors, she strode in that direction and stepped outside into a beautiful garden with tall, sculptured hedges. Bouquets of various flowers greeted her nostrils, mostly wild pink roses, white and lavender syringa bushes and a hint of the powdery, carroty scent of irises.

Trickling water lulled her toward the center of the garden, where a massive greenish-gray marble statue of a woman with one hand held above her head and the other next to her side holding a bowl stood on a pedestal in the center of what looked to be a large clamshell. Underneath the shell were large carved leaves that ran down the length of the fountain and touched the ground.

Leah's eyes drifted shut as she ran her fingers over the smooth marble, relishing the cool wetness of the slick stone.

"Sure is something, ain't it?"

"Sweet twinkling stars above!" Her hand flew to her neck as a gasp snapped through her. Jake's voice, along with his breath so very near her ear, nearly caused her to go toppling into the statue.

She spun toward him, but Jake stood so close to her that she couldn't, so she turned her neck and glanced up at him.

"'Sure is something' is an understatement. It's breathtaking," she whispered.

"This whole place is…it's…" He moved to her side.

"It's lavish. And so beautiful. Like something out of a fairy tale."

"Fairy tale, huh? Still believe in those, do you?"

"I sure do." She smirked at him. "I think every young woman wants to see her very own Prince Charming ride up on his white horse and swoop up and rescue his fair maiden."

"White horse, huh?" He chuckled.

Leah planted her hands on her hips. "You go ahead and laugh, but you'll see. I'll have my happily-ever-after. Mr. Darcy, I mean, Mr. Barrington, will come and take me away from all of this."

Jake's smile dropped and sadness took its place. "What you doing out here anyway? Why aren't you inside with everyone else?" He changed the subject, and she felt the relief of it. She didn't like him laughing at her dream of a fairy-tale ending.

Leah tilted her head and looked up at him. "Why aren't you?"

"Too crowded in there for me." He shrugged, but she saw how embarrassed he really was about his phobia.

She hated seeing him like that and wanted to make him feel better. She rested her hand on his arm. "It's okay, Jake. If you can't go in there, you can't go in there. It's nothing to be ashamed of. We all have something in our lives that we can't do. Besides, you have a good reason why you can't."

He nodded, but he didn't look convinced. "You never answered why you came out here."

Her hand fell from his arm and her gaze fell with it. "Well, if you must know, I came out here to think."

"About what?"

She'd gone that far, what sense did it make to stop now? "About Mr. Barrington."

"What about him?"

"I just wondered if this is the type of lifestyle he lives."

"How do you feel about that?"

Good question. How *did* she feel about that? Moments ago she felt underdressed and out of place. Did she still? A little. But she would overcome her insecurity. She'd learn to dress as fine as all the ladies in New York if need be. After all, she had before, when she was younger and living in New York. She could do it again. Of that she was certain. "I love the idea."

"You do?"

"Yes. Seeing all those beautiful gowns reminds me of when I was a young girl." She gazed out into nothingness as memories of her childhood wove through her mind. "I remember attending many elegant balls and wearing dresses as fine as, if not finer than, those ladies in there." And feeling every bit the princess, but she kept that thought to herself, especially after he'd laughed at her earlier.

"I can hardly wait to meet Mr. Barrington, to be whisked away to a life full of style and beauty. What girl wouldn't?" She couldn't keep the contentment or the happiness that idea brought on from curling her lips upward. Her very own Mr. Darcy would be coming soon. She would finally get away from this place and the nightmares to live the lifestyle she dreamed of living once again. Nothing would stop her from returning to where she had always been meant to be.

Chapter Seven

Three days later, Jake stood next to Leah at the front door of Michael and Selina's house. "Hi, Michael."

"Hey, what are you two up to?"

"Jake wanted to see the babies, so I told him I'd come with him. I haven't seen them for a while," Leah said, bouncing at his side. Yes, he had mentioned it, but he didn't think she'd drag him right over there right away like she had.

"That's right. It's been one whole day." Mischievousness sparkled through Michael's eyes. "And I'm sure this was all *Jake's* idea."

Jake chuckled.

Leah elbowed him in the side. "It's not funny."

He thought it was—in more ways than one.

"Don't just stand there, y'all. Michael, let them in." Selina's voice came from somewhere behind Michael.

Michael moved out of the way and Jake and Leah stepped inside. Jake hung his hat on a long peg near the door, feeling a little sheepish and very much out of place. He'd never been to the house of brand-new parents before, and truth be told, the babies scared him a mite more than he wanted to admit.

His attention went to Selina sitting on the couch, her legs stretched out before her and covered with a blue lightweight blanket. Two wooden cradles sat on either side of the rocking chair near her. "Sure nice to see ya again, Jake. Can I get y'all some coffee or tea or somethin' to eat?" Selina tossed her coverlet aside, but before she could even move her legs, Michael had sprung over to her and stood in the way of her moving.

"Don't you dare move. I'll get it," Michael ordered. The way Michael acted made Jake chuckle again and Leah, too, though she covered her amusement better than he did.

"Why don't you let me get us all something to drink?" Leah said from beside him.

"I can get it, Leah. I do know how to get refreshments." But the look on Michael's face said how much he'd appreciate her help.

"Oh, please. I'm surprised you managed to stay alive until Selina got here the way you cook. You two go sit down. I'll get it." Leah pursed her lips and narrowed her eyes at Michael. That threatening look would have made Jake obey.

Finally Michael shrugged. "Fine. I know better than to argue with you, sis. What would you like to drink, Jake?"

"Coffee, if you have some already made."

"Just made a fresh pot. It's there on the stove, Leah."

"Of course it's on the stove, Michael. Where else would it be, you silly goose?" She walked past him and tapped him on the arm.

"Watch it, or I'll turn you over my knee."

"You'd have to catch me first." She wrinkled her nose up at him.

"Don't tempt me."

Jake loved watching the interaction between the two siblings. He didn't have any family there to interact with. His sister and her husband lived in Oregon and so did his mother and her husband, Jed.

"When y'all get done horsin' around, me and Jake here would like some coffee," Selina piped in with her slow Southern drawl.

"You lucked out, sister dear. Selina just saved your hide from a good tanning."

"Sure I did." Leah glanced at the ceiling and shook her head, then headed to the kitchen stove. With her back to her brother, she asked, "You want coffee, too, Michael?"

"Yes," Michael answered, then turned to Jake. "Shall we?"

They moved to the living room.

Michael sat in the rocking chair situated next to Selina and the babies.

Jake chose a spot on a chair across the way. Curious, he craned his neck, looking into each cradle to see the babies' little sleeping faces. Lottie's was round and Joseph's was square. Joey's hair was blond and Lottie's was brown. "They sure are cute."

Envy roped through him. Someday he hoped to have a wife and family, too. He glanced over at Leah, standing in front of the stove, looking every bit the part of the homemaker. If only she'd said yes to his proposal, she'd be at his place right now, making a home with him. He sighed. No sense wishing for something that would never be. She'd made it very clear she wasn't interested in that kind of relationship with him. She'd also made clear the lifestyle she wanted to live and the type of man she wanted to live it with. *Pride and Prejudice* popped into his mind. She said that Mr. Darcy fellow was the kind of man she wanted. He really had to read the thing to find out what sort of man did interest Leah. Not that it would make any difference. Still, he wanted to know.

"So how'd Phoebe's weddin' turn out the other day?" Selina asked, adjusting the coverlet that had slipped when she'd changed positions. Michael leaped up and immediately helped her with it.

Jake glanced over at Leah, wondering just how he should answer that.

Leah came into the living room carrying a tray with four cups of coffee each sitting on a small plate, spoons, a bowl with sugar and a creamer jar. "Phoebe looked fabulous," Leah responded with her back to Michael and Selina. She offered Jake a half wink of understanding, and his heart jerked when he realized what she was doing. She was protecting him. His admiration for her went up another notch. "Markus was so cute," she continued as she handed each of them a cup and waited while they added what cream and sugar they wanted to their beverage. "Markus couldn't take his eyes off of Phoebe the whole time. Especially when she walked down the aisle."

As she went on telling the details, Jake thought back to the reception and how he'd finally talked Leah into going back inside. It was sweet of her not to want to leave him out there by himself, but he didn't want her to miss out on a fun evening because of him. He'd said goodbye, told her he was going to leave but not until he saw her safely inside. He'd walked her to the double glass doors, and Leah slipped inside with her head held high, walking with the grace of a queen. Stepping back into the shadows, he watched her mingle with those high society ladies, looking every bit as if she belonged there. An ache filled his heart even now, knowing he could never compete with that.

"I sure do wish we coulda gone, but Michael wouldn't hear of it." Mercifully, Selina's voice pulled Jake from the deep, black hole of sadness his heart had started to fall through.

"Selina." Michael drew out her name. "We've been over this a million times already. It's only been a week since the babies were born. You know how fatigued you get. You need your rest."

"Sure, I get tired, but I'm about to shanty up the stair rail. I can't just sit around here doin' nothin' all day."

"You can and you will, sweetheart." Michael's order sounded like a request, too.

Selina hiked one brow. "You'd best be careful orderin' me about like that, Michael, or whenever I get stronger, I'll fix you up a mess a crawdad tails. Or snails."

Jake's attention darted between Selina and Michael. Was she serious? He'd heard about the crawdad tails before but not snails. Had she fed Michael those, too? Jake swallowed hard just thinking about how disgusting that would be. His wife had better never serve him anything like that. Once again, his attention slid over to Leah, sitting in the chair across from him, her attention on Selina.

"Would you really do that, Selina? Feed him snails and crawdads?" Her blue eyes blinked. She looked so cute and shocked.

Jake couldn't help but smile. He'd like to hear the answer to that one, too.

"Yes, ma'am. I would and already have." A look passed between Michael and Selina. They smiled at each other and the tension dropped. His hand slid over hers and caressed it.

"She sure did." He kissed Selina's hand and smiled at her again.

"You're kidding me, right?" Leah's forehead crinkled. She looked back and forth between them, blinking as she did.

"No, we're not kidding. In Kentucky they eat them all the time. The crawdads aren't too bad. I don't know about the snails. Haven't had those. No offense, sweetheart, but I hope I never do, either. And I refuse to get too worked up over it. It's part of who Selina is, and I love her for it."

Jake didn't know if love would ever be enough to make him eat fish bait. Just the thought of that stuff made him squirm.

They visited for about forty minutes and left.

Forest dirt, fern, kinnikinnick bushes and pine trees surrounded them as they walked side by side to the main ranch yard.

"So, what do you have to do now?" Leah asked.

"A few more chores before I head home. You?"

"Since Mother hired Veronique to help around the house, there isn't much to do anymore. We all pitch in and help with the cooking and laundry, so it doesn't take nearly as long as it used to. Sometimes Veronique's sisters, Colette and Zoé, come and help, too. Because of that, I'm able to go to town a lot more now."

"What do you do in town?"

"Visit with friends. Shop. Work on quilts. Stuff like that."

"I see." They reached the barn door.

After a few minutes of neither of them saying anything, Leah looked up at him and said, "Well, I think I'll go visit Rainee for a while. I'll see you later, Jake."

He gave a quick nod, and she headed in the direction of Haydon and Rainee's house.

He got to work filling a bucket with fresh, clean water and gathering everything else he needed to doctor the Palouse horse. Who'd-a thought the horse would have spooked at Kitty? That sweet little pig wouldn't hurt a leaf. Butterfly must not have agreed, though. When Kitty got too close to her, she took off running and ended up scraping her shoulder on a tree branch. Nothing anyone tried had helped Butterfly to get over her fear of pigs. Even getting her around Kitty hadn't worked.

Tethered outside, Butterfly pawed the ground and shifted her spotted rump around. She turned her neck and stared at Jake with those blinking doe eyes, probably wondering what he was up to.

Jake picked up the full bucket of water and a clean rag and headed to the front of the horse. He patted the mare on the neck. "Who names their horse Butterfly, anyway? This is one interesting family. I'll tell you that." His voice drifted into the midmorning void.

With one hand he held on to the lead rope and with the other he dipped the rag into the cool water and blotted the wide scrape across the horse's shoulder to soften the dried blood. On first contact, she shifted. "It's okay, girl." Jake patted her neck again and she stopped moving, so he continued to work at cleaning the wound.

"How's Butterfly doing?" From several yards away, Haydon dismounted his horse and came around to the front of the Palouse.

"Doesn't look too bad. Scraped the hide off is all it looks like."

"That's good. Hate to see her all scarred up."

"Don't think that'll happen. The hair should grow back just fine."

"From the looks of it, I agree." Haydon stepped away from the inspection of the animal. "When you get finished here, what're you going to do?"

"Was going to head home. Why? Need something?"

"Yes, actually, I do. Could I get you to do me a huge favor? Unless you have to get home right away."

"Nope. No rush. Got up earlier this morning and did everything I needed to. Wheat's doing fine. What can I do for you?"

"Can you run into town for me? I'd send one of the other hands, but Jess keeps them so busy, none of them have time to go."

"I can do that. What you need?"

Haydon pulled a list out of his pocket and handed it to him. "You'll need to take the wagon. Just have them put that stuff on my account."

Jake looked at the list and nodded.

"Well, I've got to get back out there." Haydon untied his horse and swung onto the saddle. "Thanks, Jake. I appreciate this. I'll pay you extra for your time."

Jake wanted to argue with him. But when Michael offered him the job, Jake had offered to help without pay, saying that's what friends do. He'd never wanted to take their money, but none of them would hear of it. They refused his help even unless he agreed to let them pay him. Jake had to admit, as much as he hated taking it, the extra money came in handy. Especially because he was looking to marry soon.

Leah knocked on Rainee's door. Children's voices and scuffling noises came from inside. The door flew open. "Auntie." Rosie threw her arms around Leah's waist. She returned her niece's hug and kissed her on top of her head. The girl released her and glanced up at Leah with those fawn-colored eyes that matched her mother's perfectly. Rosie even shared the same fawn-colored hair as Rainee.

"Hi, Auntie." Emily's arms slipped around Leah. Her hug wasn't as exuberant as Rosie's. It was more dignified. Emily might look more like Haydon with her blond hair and blue eyes, but she acted more like the Southern belle portion of her mother.

"Mother's feeding Haydon Junior. Want me to go tell her that you're here?" Emily asked.

Leah glanced toward Rainee's closed bedroom door, debating what to do. "No. I can come back later."

"Ah. Please don't go, Auntie," Rosie begged.

"Yes. Please don't go. Mother bought us a new book and we were reading it. Won't you please join us?"

"You could read to us." Rosie clapped her small fingertips, her eyes wide and expectant.

How could Leah say no to them? She didn't have anything planned, anyway. "Okay."

They each grabbed one of her hands and led her into the living room. Leah admired Rainee's new furniture. The old furniture was so worn out, yet Haydon couldn't convince Rainee to order a new set, so he had. The blue material with small, light gold roses, the button-tufted backs and mahogany-legged sofa and the matching chairs were beautiful. The pattern reminded her of the English tête-à-tête sofa they had back in New York. *New York.* Her heart flipped at the thought.

Rosie tugged on her sleeve. "Aren't you going to sit down?" Emily looked up at her from the couch. There was just enough space between the girls for her to fit.

Knowing she would be leaving soon, she wanted to spend as much time with her nieces as possible. She smiled and sat down between them. "Yes, I am. Now, who's going to read to whom?"

"You first, okay?" Rosie gave her that hopeful look that melted an aunt's heart into submission.

Leah took the book from Emily and read the title. "*Hans Brinker, or, the Silver Skates: A Story of Life in Holland* by Mary Mapes Dodge. I haven't read this before. This will be fun." She settled comfortably into the sofa and both girls tucked into her sides as she read.

"Oh. Hi, Leah. How long have you been here?" Rainee headed toward her and took the seat across from them.

"Not sure. Enough to read—" she looked down at the open book "—twenty-four pages."

"Did the girls offer you something to drink?"

Emily's eyes widened. "Sorry, Mother. We forgot."

"That happens. Would you care for some tea or something, Leah?" Rainee started to rise.

"No. I'm fine. I can't stay too much longer anyway. I need to help Mother and Veronique get lunch ready."

Rainee looked at the girls. "You two run outside and play. I want to visit with your aunt Leah for a bit."

"Ahhh," Rosie whined.

Emily stood and grabbed Rosie's hand. "Come on, Rosie. We'll go play hide-and-seek. You can hide first."

Rainee sent Emily a smile of approval, and the girls headed out the door.

Her sister-in-law shifted her body toward Leah. "So, how are you and Jake doing?"

"Me and Jake?" Leah tilted her head, wondering what she was talking about. Rainee knew she and Jake were only friends.

"You two have been spending more and more time together. I just assumed you were…you know…getting ready to make an announcement."

Leah's mouth widened along with her eyes. Her lips moved but no words came out.

"Oh. I am so sorry, Leah. I… Oh, my. I have really done it now. I have quite jumped to conclusions and embarrassed you."

Leah wondered if other people were thinking the same thing. She hadn't realized she and Jake had spent that much time in public together. And even though she'd gone to his house many times, it was only with Abby, and no one else knew of those visits. Did they? Surely not. "We're just friends, Rainee."

"I see." She didn't look convinced.

"I do enjoy Jake's company. He's a very nice man, but that's as far as it goes. Truly."

Rainee still looked unconvinced but said nothing further.

Leah chewed on her lip, wondering if she should confide in Rainee about her plans. All the years she'd known her, never once had Leah heard Rainee talk about others, unless it was to say something good about them. The decision was made. "Rainee, can I tell you something? If I do, will you promise me you won't tell anyone? Not even Haydon? That it won't go any further than this room, even?"

"Of course, Leah. You have my word it will go no further than you and me."

"Okay." Leah shifted in her seat. "I placed an advertisement in the *New York Times* for a husband." Leah waited for the shock to show on Rainee's face, but it never came. That gave her the courage to plunge forward. "I've already responded to a gentleman's post, and I'm waiting to hear back from him to see when he's coming for sure."

"I see. Where is he from?"

"New York City. Well, he's actually from England and has recently moved to New York. His name is Mr. Fitzwilliam Barrington."

"Fitzwilliam? As in Mr. Fitzwilliam Darcy from *Pride and Prejudice?*"

"Yes." Leah's insides played leapfrog. Excited, she scooted to the end of the couch and poured out the whole story. "So, you see, Jake and I really are just friends."

"Well." Rainee smiled. "I wish you both all the best. I know it works. That is how I ended up with Haydon, as you very well know." Happiness set its glow onto her sister-in-law's face. "I pray you will find a man as wonderful as your brother."

"Who do you hope will find a man as wonderful as me?" Haydon strode over to Rainee and kissed her on the cheek and said hi to Leah.

Leah's insides quivered from anxiety. Had Haydon heard their conversation? *Please, Lord, no.* "Hi, Haydon." She stood. "Well, I need to get home and help Mother. I'll see you two later." She turned and headed for the door.

"Okay. See you later." Haydon held up his hand and gave a quick wave.

"'Bye, Leah. Thank you for stopping by." Rainee stared after her.

Leah nodded and as fast as possible closed the distance between Haydon and the door.

"Who do you hope finds a man as wonderful as me?" she heard Haydon ask.

Leah listened for the answer as she reached for the brass doorknob.

"We were just talking, Haydon. Now, what are you doing home in the middle of the day? And to what do I owe this honor?"

Leah breathed a sigh of relief. She opened the door and closed it behind her. That was a close call. A little too close.

Chapter Eight

The list Haydon gave Jake included dropping a bridle off at the smithy; picking up grain, chicken feed and horse liniment; and getting the Bowens' mail.

Jake was surprised when the postmaster assumed that meant all of the Bowens' mail, including Leah's. On the top of the stack was a letter addressed to Leah from Fitzwilliam Barrington—New York, NY. If memory served him right, he was the man coming to possibly court Leah.

Outside the post office Jake looked around. The urge to yank the letter off the top of the pile and burn it was powerful, but he couldn't. Not and live with himself, anyway. Unable to bear looking at the thing, he tossed the mail under the wagon seat and headed to the Barker Hotel and Restaurant to grab a bite to eat before heading back to the Bowen ranch.

Annabelle Schmidt, one of Mr. Barker's waitresses, walked up to his table. "Hi, Jake." Dreamy eyes gazed down at him. The petite woman had made it clear she wanted to be his wife. He'd been flattered, but he couldn't see himself with her. A farmer needed a woman of strong constitution to survive that lifestyle.

Leah could, but she didn't want to. Annabelle wouldn't survive a day.

Would the women who responded to his advertisement be able to? It was something he needed to make sure of before he sent for any of them. Good thing he hadn't sent that letter off to Miss Raquel Tobias yet. It sounded like she lived in comfort. What if she was a frail, delicate woman? That wouldn't do at all.

Jake hurried through his lunch of roast beef, mashed potatoes with gravy and apple pie. The best thing he could do was to get away from Annabelle, who kept coming by in between customers and flirting with him. Normally he was a slow eater, but this time he devoured his meal within minutes, paid his bill and excused himself. He all but ran from the place and to the wagon, thanking God he was able to get away.

Back at the Bowens' place, he hopped down from the wagon just as Leah stepped off Haydon's porch. She looked his way and gave him an exuberant wave, warming his heart with her sweetness. If only he didn't have to give her the letter that might very well take her away from him. But he did. He motioned for her to join him.

Her smile reached him before she did. "Hi, Jake. Did you need something?"

"Yep. The postmaster gave this to me." He handed her Mr. Barrington's letter.

Without looking at it she tilted her head, then gazed up at him with a frown. "Why would he give you my mail without my consent? Not that I mind or anything, but I'm curious."

"Haydon asked me to get the ranch's mail."

"Oh, I see." Leah's focus shifted to the letter. "Oh my, Jake. It's from Mr. Barrington."

He already knew that, but it wouldn't do any good to tell her that. "Didn't you just write him a few days ago?"

"Yes." She did a quick hop of excitement. "It must be good news for him to have written back so quickly, don't you think?"

Now it was Jake's turn to frown. Barrington wouldn't have gotten her post already. Curious about what it said, he hoped Leah would share it with him. Then, as if she'd read his thoughts, she tore open the letter and read it aloud.

Dear Miss Bowen,

Forgive me my impatience, but I could not wait to see if you would respond to my post. I had to meet the woman who has intrigued me. Therefore, I have taken the liberty of booking tickets on the train forthwith. My sister Elizabeth and I will be arriving at Paradise Haven, if my calculations are correct, within a day or two after you receive this post. Please do not trouble yourself to make accommodations for us as we will book rooms in the nearest hotel.

All I can hope for is that you are not yet attached. If you are, I, of course, will be disappointed, but my sister and I will then use this time to take in the countryside out West.

When we arrive, I will send word where we are staying. If you would like to meet me, then send word back with the carrier. If I have been too presumptuous, then inform the carrier that you do not wish to meet me, and Elizabeth and I will be on our way.

Sincerely,

Fitzwilliam Barrington

Leah studied the envelope. "Sweet twinkling stars above. Judging from the postmark, and if his calculations are correct, he'll be here in three days. The fourth of June." Leah slid her attention from the letter onto Jake. Joy, confusion and uncertainty crawled across her face.

"How do you feel about that?"

She looked around the yard with a blank expression before landing her attention back onto him. "I'm not sure. Of course, I'm excited and scared and apprehensive." All the things he'd seen on her face. "What should I do, Jake?"

"What do you mean, what should you do?"

"I know he said I didn't need to, but should I head into town and make accommodations for him and his sister? Should I invite them to stay here? Would Mother even allow such a thing? I mean, she did with Rainee, but that was different. Haydon had his own house."

Why was she asking him? He didn't know the answers. If he had his way, he'd advise her that as soon the carrier came she should tell him no.

"Oh, no."

"What?"

"I haven't even told Mother anything about him yet."

"You haven't?"

"No. I was waiting to hear back from him, then I was going to tell her. Of course, I've already been preparing for this day and made a couple of new dresses, but I had thought I would surely get into town for some more material to make at least one more dress before..."

New dresses? Jake was struggling to keep up with her. The topic had gone from what should she do to she hadn't told her mother and then on to new dresses.

He glanced at her simple yellow garment. "Why'd

you make new clothes? What's wrong with the ones you have?"

She looked down at her dress as if seeing it for the first time. "What's wrong with it? Everything is wrong with it. I need to go. I have to tell Mother."

He'd never seen Leah this scatterbrained before. "Want me to go with you?"

She tilted her head and frowned.

"For moral support," he clarified. "That's what friends do."

"Oh. Oh." Understanding replaced the frown. "Of course. Moral support. Friends. Yes. Right." She pressed her finger against her lips and her eyes glanced around before landing back on him. "No. No. I better not. As much as I would love for you to, I need to tell her myself. But thanks for the offer just the same."

"You're welcome." He didn't feel all that welcoming, however. Panic gripped him when he realized she really was about to walk out of his life. "Oh, Leah, before I forget. I know you're gonna be busy with everything, but I was wondering something."

"What's that?"

He hated to ask because it was clear her mind was on other things. "Would you have time to go over another stack of letters?"

"Huh? I thought you were going to write Raquel Tobias. Did you change your mind?"

"Praying about that still. Need to ask her a few questions first, too. Meantime, I'll keep reading the posts I get."

"How many more did you get?"

"Eight."

"Eight!" Her eyes widened. "Sweet twinkling stars above. You sure are well liked."

"Nah. Just a lot of desperate women."

Her brows pulled together. "Is that how you see me? Desperate? Because I placed an ad looking for a groom?"

"What? No." He took a step backward, raised his hat and pushed his hand through his hair before placing the hat back on his head. "Didn't mean it that way. Just meant there are a lot of women out there desperate to marry."

Her head dipped sideways again, sending that spiraling curl down her cheek. How he wanted to brush it away, but when the palm of her hand rose, the urge skittered with it.

"Forget I said anything. So. Think you'll have time to come by? If not, it's okay. I know you have things to do."

"I can do it. No, make that I want to do it." She smiled. "This afternoon would work. I know Abby isn't doing anything. We can come to your place, if you want?"

Jake wondered why they didn't just go over them here, but he would do whatever worked for her. "Sounds good. Well, best get this wagon unloaded and get home. See you there."

The only way to describe the smile she flashed his way just now and how it affected him was sweet summer sunshine. "Looking forward to it."

So was he. So was he. And that wasn't good.

Leah ran to the house with more excitement about going over to Jake's than meeting Mr. Barrington. How strange was that? Nerves. It had to be nerves.

"Where are you running off to in such an all-fired hurry?" Abby caught up to her.

Leah stopped and had to catch her breath before she could get anything coherent out. "Boy, am I glad to see you."

"Why?"

"Because I need to see if you can go over to Jake's with me this afternoon." She hooked her arm through her sister's and nudged her forward but away from the house and any listening ears.

"Sure. I love it there. Besides, I don't have anything better to do."

"Thanks. You sure know how to flatter a girl."

"I didn't mean it like that." Abby nudged Leah with her hip, knocking her off balance.

"I know you didn't, but I have to tease you to keep you on your toes. Oh, and if you don't mind, I would really appreciate it if you'd be there with me when I tell Mother."

"Tell Mother what?"

"About my advertisement."

Abby stopped walking and unhooked her arm. "I don't want to be there when you tell her. She's going to be so upset with you."

"Surely you wouldn't abandon me now, would you, Abbs? Come on," she pleaded. "I really need you there for support."

"Why don't you ask Jake?" Abby did a little hop and a skip beside her as if she'd just given her the perfect solution, then she tugged Leah forward, resuming their walk.

Leah waved her off as if that wasn't even important , though her heart leaped with the sweet memory of Jake's thoughtful offer. "He already offered, but after my talk with Rainee, I didn't think it would be wise to have him there."

"What talk with Rainee?"

"Nothing of significance, really. But while I was there she wondered if I would be making an announcement soon about me and Jake."

"No." Her sister's blue eyes widened. "She didn't."

"Yes. She did. All because she said she saw us together so much."

"Well, yes. But I thought everyone knew you two were just friends."

Leah twisted her mouth and shook her head as if the whole idea was ludicrous. "Apparently not. And I know if I walk in with Jake, Mother will wonder, too. She already basically asked me if I would marry him."

"She did?" Again with the wide eyes. "When did all this happen? You never said anything about it."

"It was the other day. Anyway, forget all that. It's really not important. Would you please be there with me when I tell her?"

"I wouldn't miss any of this for the whole wide world." She flung her arm out with a flair. "So, have you heard from any of the gentlemen yet?"

It was then that Leah realized they should have been walking much slower, but it was too late. The boards creaked under their feet as they made their way up the porch steps and into the house.

"I'll tell you more about them later."

"You'd better." Abby's warning look belied her smiling smirk.

"Mother! We're home," Leah hollered.

Mother stepped out from behind the laundry room door. Her dress was soaked, and some of her hairpins had come out. She ran the back of her hand over the sweat beads pooling on her forehead.

"What are you doing?" Leah asked.

"Laundry."

"Why didn't you say you needed help? Where's Veronique? Isn't she here?"

"*Oui.* I mean, yes. Am right here." Veronique peeked around from behind Mother. Strands of brown hair with gold highlights stuck to the moisture on Veronique's oval face. The five-foot-ten, stocky Frenchwoman was hard-working, honest and a great cook. A real blessing to have around.

"Do you need us to help?" Leah waved her pointed finger between her and Abby.

"No. I just got tired of sitting around so I thought I would help Veronique for something to do. What time is it?"

"Eleven forty-five. We thought we'd come in for a bite then Abby and I are going to go for a ride."

"A ride. That sounds like fun." Mother's face brightened.

Leah swallowed down the dread that rose up inside her. Was her mother hinting that she'd like to go? What would Leah do if she did?

"I wish I could go with you girls, but I promised Michael I would stay with Selina for a couple of hours this afternoon. He had some errands to run."

Whew. Leah let out the breath she was holding slowly and quietly so as not to draw attention. "You mean he's actually going to leave her for that long?"

They all chuckled.

"Tell Selina hi and kiss the babies for me," Leah said.

"For me, too," Abby added. "Hey, what's for lunch, Mother? I'm starving."

"You're always hungry," her mother teased. "Veronique made venison stew earlier."

Leah suddenly wondered if Jake had eaten. Maybe he ate in town. He did that sometimes. If so, had he run into Annabelle? The poor woman had a mad crush on Jake. Everyone in town knew it. Annabelle didn't even try to hide her feelings for him. Leah smiled at the thought. Of course, Jake had been gentle with her when he let her know he wasn't interested in marrying someone who was ten years older than he, but that didn't stop her. Poor Jake. The smile in her heart increased. He was such a kind man.

"Did you hear me, Leah?"

Leah snapped her attention onto her mother's. "What? Oh. No. I'm sorry, Mother. I didn't. What did you say?"

"I asked if you would get us some bowls."

"Oh. Um. Sure." She scurried to the cupboard and gathered the bowls. After they were all filled, she set them, glasses of tea, biscuits, butter and pear preserves on the table. She, Mother and Abby sat down, bowed their heads and prayed. Leah added her own silent prayer that her mother wouldn't be too upset and that God would give her the words she needed to say.

Leah buttered her biscuit, smeared a dollop of the homemade pear preserves on it and took a bite. Cinnamon and nutmeg filled her taste buds as she chewed slowly, enjoying the sweet fruit and putting off the inevitable. Knowing she didn't have much time before she headed to Jake's, she put her biscuit down and drew in a long breath. "Mother?"

"Yes?" Mother put a spoon of stew into her mouth.

"I'm not sure how to tell you this, so I'm just going to come right out and say it, okay?"

Mother stopped chewing and looked at her. She nodded.

"A while back I placed an advertisement in the *New York Times*."

Mother swallowed with a gulp and reached for her water. "What kind of advertisement, sweetheart?"

Leah looked over at Abby, who nodded to keep going.

"For a husband."

"What?" The glass clattered to the table and barely stayed upright. Mother closed her eyes and shook her head in a jerky motion. She opened her eyes and stared at Leah. "Did I just hear you say you placed an ad for a husband… in New York?"

"Yes, Mother. That's what I said."

"Why? Why would you do that, Leah? And why wouldn't you ask me first?"

Abby picked up her spoon, suddenly finding interest in her stew. Leah wished she could do the same.

"Because I was afraid you'd say no, that's why, and I have my heart set on moving back to New York."

Her mother set her spoon down and wiped her mouth off with a napkin. "Why, Leah? Why would you do such a thing?" The anguish on her mother's face flooded Leah with guilt.

"Because I miss New York." She couldn't tell her that she hated this place and why. Mother wouldn't understand. No one would. So she dived into the other part of the story. "I knew the only way you and the boys would let me go is if I were married. So, I placed an ad, and I've received an answer."

Abby's spoon hit the table and she stared openly at her sister, soup forgotten.

"You—you have? From whom?" Mother's face paled and she suddenly looked sick.

Even more guilt assaulted Leah. She honestly hadn't

thought her mother would take the news this badly. Yes, she knew she'd be upset but not to where it made her ill.

Bad as she felt, there was nothing she could do about it now, anyway. What was done was done. The man was already on his way. Besides, Leah didn't want to stop him from coming. She might be a tad scared and a bit apprehensive, but she still couldn't wait to meet Mr. Barrington and hopefully marry him. If she had to, she'd deal with consequences of that decision later. She squared her shoulders and lifted her chin. "His name is Fitzwilliam Barrington, Mother. And he's from England."

"England!" Mother gasped. "You're moving to England?" She waved her hand in front of her face, looking even paler.

"Mother? You okay?" Leah pressed her fist into her belly, which was twisting with torment for what she was putting her mother through.

"England?" Abby asked in horror. "You can't move to England, Lee-Lee!"

"Mother? Are you okay?" Leah jumped from the table to assist her mother should she pass out, which was looking like a very real possibility at the moment.

Mother raised her hand to wave her daughter away. "I'm—I'm fine. Just shocked is all."

Leah looked over at Abby, who didn't look much better than her mother but still managed to send Leah a sympathetic shrug.

"Don't worry, Mother. Abby." Leah eyed both of them for a brief moment and resumed her seat, thankful she no longer had to stand on her shaking legs. "I'm not moving to England. Mr. Barrington moved to New York City recently and saw my ad."

"So, you're going to New York to meet him?" Mother's words were spoken as if they were shards of broken glass.

Leah didn't think her mother's complexion could get any paler, but it had. More guilt dumped on her. "No."

The tension in her mother's face softened. "Oh, good. I'm so relieved to hear that." She patted herself above her heart.

"He's coming here with his sister. We're going to get acquainted first to see if we are compatible. Then we'll take it from there."

Mother remained quiet. She pushed her half-filled bowl away from her and rested her folded hands on the table.

Leah didn't know if she was praying or thinking. No longer hungry herself, she pushed her own bowl out of the way and laid her hands over her mother's. "Mother." She waited until her mother looked over at her. "Please don't be upset. I'm sorry I didn't say anything to you. I never meant to hurt you. But I am twenty-four years old. It's time I found a husband. Everything will work out. You'll see. I tell you what, Mother. If you don't approve of him, then I won't marry him. How's that?" Leah couldn't believe she was saying that. But she couldn't stand to see her mother so upset.

"Leah, I know everything will work out only because I have just now given it over to God. But I am hurt that you didn't discuss this with me first."

Leah opened her mouth to respond, but Mother held up her hand. "I understand why you didn't. I just don't understand why you would want to leave me. Leave your family."

She didn't want to leave her mother or her family—just this place. The idea of leaving them hurt, but when she considered the nightmares and the guilt that haunted her, leaving her family was her only option. "Mother, this has nothing to do with you or with the family. It has to do with me. I'm sorry if you feel I'm doing this to you. I never meant it to be that way. I'm doing this for me. It's something I've dreamed of for a long time. Besides, I'll come back often. Mr. Barrington wants to travel, too. I'm sure he won't mind traveling back here. Okay, Mother?"

Mother said nothing— She only stared at her. The minutes ticked by agonizingly slow until Mother finally spoke. "God's will be done." That was all she said. But it was the way she said it—with so much confidence and assurance— that made Leah nervous.

Judging from past experience, when her mother prayed, things happened—and not always the way her children had wanted them to. Mother prayed fervently for Haydon, and he'd done something he said he'd never do again—get married.

Mother prayed for Michael to love Selina, something he said he could never do, and then Michael fell deeply in love with her. Both were wonderful answers to prayer. Still, Leah couldn't help but wonder how or what Mother was praying for her and why she had that knowing smile on her face.

"Oh, before I forget, girls—" Mother dropped a glance onto her and then one to Abby "—I won't be here for dinner this evening. Mr. Barker's invited me to dine with him."

"You sure have been seeing a lot of him, Mother," Abby said with a wide smile.

Her mother returned the smile with dreamy eyes. "Yes. Yes, I have."

"Do you like him?" Although Leah hated the idea

of her mother with another man, she had to know the answer to the question.

"Yes, I do. Very much so. In fact—" her mother picked up her coffee and took a drink before setting it down again "—I'm hoping our relationship will develop into something more very soon."

Why did it suddenly feel like the situation reversed? Leah's head spun with the thought. "You mean marriage?"

"Yes. I mean marriage." Mother's face glowed.

"That's wonderful, Mother!" Abby jumped up and threw her arms around her.

Leah wished she could share her sister's enthusiasm. Seeing her mother on Mr. Barker's arm at Phoebe's wedding had been hard enough, but to actually hear her mother say the *m* word... That she couldn't bear.

Chapter Nine

Jake sat on his front porch listening for the sound of horse's hooves, but only the creaking of the rocker and an occasional bee buzzing by filled the quietness around him. That is, until Meanie started that frustrated bleating she so often did when he locked her in a stall to keep her out of trouble. Trouble. That was all the little critter had been since he'd taken her in. He could do nothing short of letting Meanie loose to fix that situation, but he'd never do that. Truth is, he'd grown kind of fond of the ornery goat.

He glanced at the copy of *Pride and Prejudice* sitting on his lap. Curious about what type of man Leah was interested in, he began to read. It was slow going, but determination prodded him on. The more he read, the more he wanted to slam the book up against the wall, to burn it, to do anything but read about some prideful, arrogant man who only cared about position, power and money.

All the things Jake despised in a man.

How could Leah be attracted to that? He shook his head in disbelief and bewilderment. Knowing Leah like he did, nothing about the kind of man she said she wanted or anything else was adding up or making any sense. Jake sent up a silent prayer for her, then glanced down the road to see if there was any sign of her yet. When there wasn't, he continued reading to see if Mr. Darcy had improved any.

Ten pages later buggy wheels crunched on gravel and Banjo barked. Jake turned his attention to the road. Leah. He glanced at the book in his hand. Not wanting Leah to know he'd purchased *Pride and Prejudice*, he darted into the house and shoved the book under his pillow. Outside and down the steps he dashed, arriving just as Leah pulled her carriage in front of his house.

"Hi, Jake." Abby greeted him with a smile and a happy wave. Before he had a chance to help her down, she jumped down from the buggy, crouched and rubbed her nose on Banjo's.

"Howdy-do, Abby." Jake turned his attention to Leah and offered her his hand. She shifted the reticule onto her wrist and laid her hand on top of his.

"Hi, Jake." Those dimples made an appearance again.

He helped her down and released her hand. "You ready for this?"

"I sure am." She looked pretty, all gussied up in her dress with the curly-tailed teardrop design. Paisley. That's what he'd heard someone call the pattern, though he didn't know much about material or dresses. It didn't matter what it was, she looked beautiful in it. Of course, as far as he was concerned, she'd looked pretty in just about anything. Even an old, worn-out grain sack. Leah was a beautiful woman. A woman any man would be proud to have on his arm.

Before he allowed any more thoughts of her to enter his mind, he reined them in like he would a runaway horse and anchored his gaze onto the porch. *She's here as a friend, Jake. To help you choose a wife.* Forgetting that again might be the death of him.

Side by side they climbed the steps. Leah stopped at the top of them and turned around, her dress swishing at her ankles. "Abbs, do you want to join us?"

"No. If Jake doesn't mind, I'd like to go down to the barn and see Meanie."

"That's fine. Just don't let her out of the corral. She's a tricky one."

"I'll be careful." With those words Abby scurried toward the barn with Banjo prancing at her side.

"Sure sweet of Abby to accompany you here every time."

"It sure is. She says she does it because she likes your company, but I think it's the animals' company she likes most."

"Think you're right." They chuckled.

He gave a yank of his head toward the door. "Wanna go inside or sit here on the porch?"

"Out here would be great. It's too nice a day to be cooped up inside."

"I agree. Let me just grab us something to drink and the letters and I'll be right out." He disappeared into the house and peeked back to make sure Leah couldn't see him before he swiped his sweaty palms down the front of his jeans. What was with him today? Emotions he couldn't decipher were whirling through his brain like a destructive dust bowl.

Jake hurried to get everything he needed. When he stepped outside, Leah was sitting in the chair with her reticule resting in her lap, rocking, staring out into the trees, looking every bit like she belonged there. But she didn't. And never would. Not because he didn't want her to, but because she didn't want to be here. Her rejection still stung. But, no sense dwelling on that now— It was a well-traveled road that went nowhere.

"Here you go." He handed her the letters, set their drinks on the stand between the two rockers and sat down.

Leah took a long drink of her water.

"Must've been thirsty."

"I sure was. It's so dry that on the way over here I think I swallowed a bucket of road dust." She took another drink, then set the glass down.

"Jabber-jawed that much, huh?"

"Hey." She reached over and whacked his arm with the backs of her fingers.

He chuckled at the smile twinkling in her beautiful blue eyes.

"Oh, before I forget, I have something for you." She opened her reticule and pulled out three brand-new handkerchiefs and extended them toward him.

He glanced down at them and then his attention trailed to her face. "It ain't my birthday today."

"So." She shrugged with a grin. Then she grabbed his hand, laid the handkerchiefs in his palm, folded his fingers over them and pushed his hand back.

Jake slowly opened his hand.

The initials J.L. stared up at him. "Um-hm." He cleared his throat to choke back the rising emotion. He'd never had anything so nice before. He ran his fingers over the raised letters and was deeply touched not only by the detail, but also by the amount of time it must have taken her to make these. But how could he accept such a gift? He looked over at her. "I can't accep—"

"You have to take them, Jake." Leah stopped him. "There's no giving them back. It's your initials that are on them, so they belong to you. Besides, I don't know any other J.L.'s to give them to. Sorry, mister," she said, "but you're stuck with them." With a dramatic sigh that would rank right up there with one of Abby's, she sat back and crossed her arms over her chest, looking playfully smug.

Truth was, he really didn't want to give them back. He'd treasure them forever. There was only one problem with them— They were too nice to use.

"All joking aside…" Leah sat forward. "Please accept my gift and use them until they look as worn as your old ones."

His gaze flew to hers. Had she read his mind? "Not sure I can. Don't want to ruin them."

Leah wrinkled her nose. "Huh? But that's what I made them for, for you to use. It would mean a lot to me if you did, Jake. It isn't much, but it's my way of showing you how special you are to me. I've never had a friend as wonderful as you before. Now—" she shook her finger at him "—if you don't use them, I'm not going to help you with your letters. So, are you going to use them or not?"

Mischievousness snaked through Jake. Keeping his eye on her, with a quick snap of his wrist, he unfolded one of them, raised the kerchief to his nose and using his voice only, he pretended to blow into it. He folded it up, not so neatly either, then flashed her a smug smile. "Feel better?"

Leah tossed her head back and laughed. "I sure do," she said when she stopped laughing. "Thank you, Jake."

"No. Thank *you,* Leah." The humor had gone from his voice, replaced with gratitude.

"You're welcome."

They stared at each other for a few seconds, then

Jake broke the connection. "Oh, how'd the talk with your mother go?" He picked up his glass and took a drink before setting it back down, being extra careful not to spill it.

Her dimples disappeared, and lines formed around her eyes.

"That bad, huh? Wanna talk about it?"

She nodded, then looked away, off down the road. "I felt so bad for Mother. I honestly didn't think it would affect her the way it had. I thought she was going to faint." She paused and drew in a deep breath. "I think Mother was mostly hurt that I didn't say anything. But, when I told her he was coming here, she seemed to feel better about it, although she doesn't understand how I could want to leave her or the rest of the family."

He heard the melancholy in her voice and dipped his head to get a better look at her face. "That bother you, Leah? Leaving your family?"

"Yes. But not nearly as much as the idea of staying here bothers me." She turned her attention back on him. "Know what Mother told me and Abby?"

He shook his head.

"That she likes Mr. Barker a lot and is in fact hoping for more than a friendship with him."

"As in marriage?"

"Yes. Seeing her with Mr. Barker has been hard enough. But to actually hear her say she wants to marry him. Well…" Her fingers fiddled with the strings on her reticule. "I know we talked about this the other night… And maybe you were able to handle your mother getting married, but I'm not sure I can. I'm trying. Honest I am. But—but…" She slammed her eyes closed and frustration ripped across her face. "Aaaccck! I can't stand this! I'm so tired of feeling this way. Tired of feeling guilty because of my emotions." She uncrossed her legs.

His heart softened for her pain and the confusion she was feeling. He'd been there once, too, and it wasn't a fun place to be. "It's a normal reaction, Leah. But I promise you, it does get easier."

She shrugged as if she had her doubts, which she probably did. All he could do was pray for her and be a friend for her. As long as he could, anyway.

"I'm just glad I won't be here when and if she does marry Mr. Barker."

Again he was reminded of her leaving, and it was like a gunslinger's bullet to his chest. "Does your mother know how you feel?"

"No, and I would never tell her, either."

"How come? Maybe it would help to talk to her about it."

"No. No, it wouldn't." She shook her head. "Nothing would help me feel better about this. Nothing." She raked in a breath and let it go. "Let's not talk about this anymore. It's just too upsetting. Now." She picked up one of the envelopes, slid her finger under the seal and pulled the paper out. "Let's find you a wife. I'll feel much better about leaving if I know my dearest friend is happily married." The smile she gave him was a forced one because no dimples showed up.

At that moment, Jake silently sent up a prayer that God would give Leah grace and mercy to help her to deal with whatever decision her mother made regarding Mr. Barker. Jake's attention shifted back to Leah when she started to read.

Dear Mr. Lure,
Your ad said, "When you write, tell me about

*yourself." Well, my name is Blossom Pearson.
I'm twenty-five years old, five foot nine and
weigh 145 lbs. My hair is brown and my eyes
are green. You didn't say nothing about a picture, but I thought I'd send you one.*

Leah stopped reading and peered into the envelope.
"Sorry, Jake, I didn't even see this." She handed him a
small picture without looking at it.

Jake's eyes trained in on the woman in the photo.
He had to admit she was a beauty. Stocky, too. Looked
like she could handle just about anything. Something
about the softness in her eyes drew him. He'd like to
hear more about her. "What else she say?"

"That pretty, huh?"

Jake snapped his attention over to Leah. "That
doesn't matter."

"Sure it doesn't. If you say so." She giggled. The
dimples were back.

If she wasn't a female, he'd smack her on the arm
like she had done to him earlier. But she was definitely a woman. With all the right curves in all the right
places. "Just keep reading, woman."

She giggled again. "Okay. Let's see."

*I was born and raised on a farm, so I'm used
to hard work. And I'm strong as an ox. I can
manage a plow, milk cows, garden, do canning,
cook and do just about any kind of farm work that
needs done. I'm real good with animals. Especially horses. Broke a few myself. Well, that ain't
exactly true. I think it was more like they broke
me. Or maybe we broke each other.*

Jake laughed. The woman had a sense of humor. That was good.

> *Well, don't know what else to say except hope to hear from you soon.*
> *God bless you through Christ our Lord.*
> *Blossom*
> *P.S. Yes, Blossom is my real name. If you want to know why, you'll have to send for me to find out.*

Leah folded the letter. "Jake, she sounds perfect for you."

"Think so?" He searched her face for any kind of doubt.

"Yes, I do. I think you should write her right away." A seriousness permeated her voice that hadn't been there before.

"You do?" He had hoped she would at least show some sign of disappointment at the idea of his getting married. After all, once he did, their friendship would have to end. Neither of their spouses would allow them to continue on like they had been. Jake wondered if Leah had ever considered that, and if she had, how did she feel about that?

"Did you want to me to read the rest of these?"

He flipped his mind back to the task of finding a wife. None of the posts he'd gotten so far intrigued him like Blossom's had. One thing was for certain—after hearing her letter, he knew he wouldn't write to Raquel. He wasn't even sure he'd write Blossom back, either. Or any other woman, for that matter. What he really wanted to do was to wait and see what happened between Leah and that Barrington fellow. Call him a fool, but somewhere deep inside of him, he still hoped for a chance for him and Leah to marry.

Not that it would ever happen, but he would hold on to that hope a little while longer. After all, Leah wasn't married yet. In the meantime, he'd concentrate on finding someone else just in case things didn't work out as he hoped they would.

Time and again, Jake had seen men and women marry for convenience, and somehow it had worked out. All he had to do was look at Michael and Haydon, who were both happily married. And although Jake would rather marry Leah, someone he knew and respected, rather than a total stranger, he knew better than anyone else that probably would never happen, so he needed to stop dwelling on it. Brooding on it would only lead to more heartache.

"Well, Jake," Leah said after four more letters that he really hadn't heard, "I've been here over an hour. I'd better go get Abby and be getting home. I need to get things ready for Mr. Barrington's arrival."

He nodded and they stood.

Leah picked up her reticule from the table, and side by side they walked down the steps and headed to the corral.

"Abby, are you ready to go?" Leah called.

Nothing. The barnyard was quiet.

"That's odd. Where could she be?" Leah asked.

"Don't know." Jake hiked a shoulder.

"Abby!" Leah hollered.

"Over here." Abby's voice came from the direction of the woods.

They headed that way. Abby met them halfway. Banjo followed close behind with her mouth wide open and her tongue hanging out the side of her mouth, panting.

"Have you seen Meanie?" Abby asked, puffing.

"Meanie?" Jake crossed his arms over his chest. "That ornery old goat escape again?"

"Yes. I'm really sorry, Jake," Abby said between gasps. "When I stepped out of the pen, I held the gate close to me so she wouldn't get out. But she rammed into my legs and knocked me down and took off running into the woods. I haven't been able to find her anywhere."

"It's okay, Abby. Told you she was tricky. I'll find her."

"We'll help. Then we really do need to go home," Leah said.

Abby went one way, Leah went another and Jake another.

Within minutes he heard Leah hollering, "Give me back my reticule, you ornery brat."

Jake glanced at the sky and rolled his eyes. "Oh, no." He bolted toward the sound of Leah's voice. When he got there, he saw Leah in an all-out tug-of-war with Meanie over her purse. Leah's hair was dancing around her head as curls came scrambling out of their holdings.

"Meanie!" Jake hustled to her.

Leah's attention flew to Jake and in the process she lost her grip on her bag. Meanie took off running with it as Leah landed on her backside in the dust. Jake darted after the goat as Leah scrambled to her feet and followed close behind them.

"Get back here!" he yelled, dodging and ducking through the trees. Suddenly, with no warning at all, his foot caught a tree root, and he tumbled to the ground. Only a half step back, Leah didn't have time to change course and with a thud she landed right on top of him.

Their faces were mere inches from each other.

They were so close their breaths mingled.

Neither moved.

Leah's wide eyes stared into his. She looked so cute, so disheveled and surprised. Even her lips were parted in shock.

The desire to kiss those lips barreled over him.

As if she'd read his mind, she blinked, yanking his senses back to where they belonged.

"You okay?" He shifted her off of him, careful not to hurt her.

"I'm… I'm fine." She brushed the tousled hair from her face and the dirt from her dress. "I look like a mess, but I'm all right."

Jake stood and helped her up. Then he brushed the pine needles out of his hair and off his arms and legs while Leah brushed them off of herself.

Her cheeks were flushed. He wondered if his were, too. For sure they would have been if he had followed through with his desire to kiss her. Thank goodness he hadn't. Not because he didn't want to. Leah's outward and inward beauty, her love for the Lord and her fun, sweet, generous nature would be a temptation for any man. Including him. No, especially for him. But kissing her would have been a huge mistake.

Heat once again rose up Leah's neck and into her cheeks at the certainty that Jake had been about to kiss her. She tried to steer her thoughts a different way as she turned the carriage for home, but they clung to her mind and her heart.

"Why's your face so red?" Abby asked her in the carriage.

She wanted to lie but found she could not. "I'm not

sure, but I think Jake was going to kiss me back there in the forest."

"What? Are you serious?" Abby shrieked.

"Like I said, I'm not sure—but I think so." Leah took her eyes off the horse clomping down the hard-packed road from Jake's place and looked over at his flourishing wheat field.

"Why? What did he do?"

"Well, when I fell on top of him, our—"

"You fell on top of Jake?" Abby interrupted with a gust of surprise in her voice.

"Yes, I—"

"When? How?"

"Abby, if you'd stop interrupting me, I'd tell you." No frustration came through, only a slight reprimand. For a brief moment, Leah's attention went to a pair of gray partridge birds flying above them before her focus returned to Abby.

"Sorry." Her sister didn't look one bit sorry. That was okay— Leah knew she was excited to hear the story. And Leah was glad she could share these things with her sister. Seven years separated them, but they'd grown close over the past year.

"Okay, so, I spotted Meanie near the cottonwood trees on Jake's property. You know the ones I'm talking about, don't you?"

Abby nodded, blinking, waiting expectantly.

Leah held her chuckle inside at seeing her sister like that.

"And?" Abby dragged the word out.

"Well, as soon as I reached for her halter, she snatched my reticule from me. I yelled at her to give it back. I'm surprised you didn't hear me."

"How could I? I was the opposite direction from you. Who cares about that, anyway? Keep going."

"Well, Jake heard me. He came right away. Meanie took off running. Jake ran after her, and I ran after Jake. He tripped on something. I think a tree root, or something, I'm not sure. Anyway, doesn't matter what he tripped on. Whatever it was, he fell and I landed on top of him." The memory burned through her like wind whipping embers into a blaze. "It was so weird. His face was so close, Abbs, and he had this look on his face...."

"Ooooh. How romantic. Then what happened?" Her sparkling blue eyes stared expectantly at Leah.

Leah jerked her head from side to side. "You've been reading too many romance novels. Jake and I, we're not like that."

"But you could be." Was that hope on her sister's face?

"No, Abbs. We can't. I'm leaving, remember? And besides, I don't feel that way about him, and I know he doesn't feel that way about me."

"But he was going to kiss you."

"No." The more she thought about it, the more she talked herself out of it. "I said I thought he was going to kiss me, but I must be wrong. Jake doesn't think about me like that."

"How do you know that?"

"Because." She studied Abby's eyes a moment. "Look. If I tell you something, you have to promise not to say anything to anyone, okay?"

"You always ask me that. Do I ever?" Abby questioned her with not only her words, but also her looks.

"No. No, you don't. And I appreciate it more than

you will ever know." She smiled at Abby. "A few months back, Jake asked me to marry him."

"What?" Abby's brows darted upward. "You're kidding? What did you say?"

"I said no."

"No." Abby's face scrunched. "Why?"

"You know why. Besides, he said it would be a marriage of convenience between two friends."

"Ouch."

"Ouch is right. But that's okay. It wasn't right—he and I. And now, with me leaving, I'm just glad I don't love Jake in that way or it would be too hard to move if I did."

"Do you think he loves you, Lee-Lee?"

Leah frowned. "Why would you ask that? I just told you his proposal was one of convenience, not love."

"Yes, well, you also said you thought he wanted to kiss you. And you two do spend a lot of time together."

"Yes, we do spend a lot of time together because we enjoy each other's company."

Abby's eyes brightened.

"As friends, Abbynormal, as friends. It's nice having a male friend. They're more rational and not so emotional. And Jake is easy to talk to. He says the same thing about me. As for him wanting to kiss me, well, perhaps I imagined it. Because as soon as I looked at his mouth, he couldn't get away from me fast enough. He jumped up and brushed himself off, and I had a hard time keeping up with him on the way to the barn."

Was the thought of kissing her that repulsive to him? The idea of him kissing her wasn't to Leah. How strange was that? She'd never thought about Jake kissing her before. Or what it would be like. Until this very moment. *Sweet twinkling stars above.* Her eyes widened on the thought. Not good. Not good at all. She swallowed hard and clicked on the lines. "Giddyup, Lambie."

Minutes later they rode into the ranch yard. "Uh-oh," Abby said.

Leah's gaze trailed toward the direction Abby was looking. She was so busy thinking about what had happened earlier, she didn't see her brothers standing in front of the barn with their arms crossed. For Michael to leave Selina's side, whatever they were up to could not be good. "'Uh-oh' is right. Mother must have told them about my plans."

Chin up, she guided Lambie toward the front of the barn, but before she could get close, her brothers were next to the phaeton.

Jesse grabbed the lines near her horse's bit and stopped her.

Haydon was the first to get to her. "We need to talk." He offered Leah a hand down, but it didn't feel very helpful.

"Hello to you, too." One glance at Haydon's face said he wasn't amused.

By that time, Jess and Michael had joined him like a wall in front of her.

Abby was at Leah's side in an instant. Two against three was better than one against three at least.

"What's this we hear about you placing an ad in the *New York Times* for a husband?"

Leah darted a glance at Abby, who looked pale as a dandelion seed. "Mother didn't waste any time, did she?"

"Never mind that," Haydon cut in. "I can't believe you did something like that without talking it over with us."

"What?" Leah bobbed her head forward with a tilt

and scrunched her face. "Are you serious? I'm not a child anymore. I'm twenty-four years old and more than capable of making my own decisions."

"You might be twenty-four, but you're still our sister and under our protective care. There's no way I'm letting my little sister marry a complete stranger. I can't believe you did this. That you would go behind our backs like this." Haydon raised his cowboy hat and shoved his fingers through his blond hair. "Why, Leah? Why?" Nothing but concern filled his voice and eyes.

"Haydon—" Michael laid his hand on their oldest brother's shoulder "—we're all upset about this. But, we need to remember, we got wives like this, too."

"I don't care. This is our sister we're talking about here."

"Well, Rainee and Selina were someone's sister, too," Michael said as if he had all the calm in the world.

"Rainee's brother doesn't count," Haydon counteracted with a grunt.

"True, but Selina's does. Her brothers loved her as much as we love Leah."

Leah's heart melted at those words. They really did love and care about her.

Haydon stared at Michael, then looked over at Leah. She saw tender love for her along with confusion. She could tell he was torn, that a battle was going on inside him. Finally, he said, "Leah, would you promise one thing?"

"What's that?" Leah pushed away a strand of hair that had breezed across her eyes.

"If we don't feel right about this guy, would you take our advice and not marry him?" Up until this moment her brother Jess had been silent. "That's all we ask, Lee.

We'll all be praying about this to see what God has to say about it. Fair enough?"

"I *did* pray about it, and I have peace about my decision."

"No offense, Leah, but you women let your emotions rule you," Haydon said, clearly wishing he could put a stop to it and that be that. "Besides, we're on the outside looking in. So would you trust us to pray about this and heed whatever God shows us?"

She glanced up at Haydon. As the oldest this had to be hard on him. He'd been the one to step in, to try to take her father's place when he'd died. This had to be killing him. A ghost she'd rather not deal with floated just behind his eyes. "Okay."

"Wise decision, Lee-Lee," Abby interjected.

"Hey, whose side are you on?"

"Both, of course." Abby wrinkled her nose at her, then smiled.

So much for secrets. She turned her attention to other pressing matters. "Oh, while everyone is here, I want to talk to you guys about something. What do you think of Mother and Mr. Barker's relationship? Did she tell you that she was interested in pursuing a serious relationship with him?"

Haydon was the first to respond. "She did."

"And? What do you think about that?"

"We—" Haydon pointed at Jess and Michael "— think it's great."

Leah crossed her arms, not terribly happy with the answer. "You do? But what about Father?"

"What about him?" Jess asked.

She came uncoiled. "What do you mean 'what about him'? Am I the only one this bothers?"

"Leah." Michael put his arm around her shoulder

and tucked her next to his side, a move that made her all the more angry. He glanced down at her. "Look, I know it's hard for you to think about Mother with anyone but Father. It is for all of us."

"It is?" She brightened, no longer feeling alone in her guilt-ridden thoughts.

"But…"

Her heart sank back into the abyss it dwelled in where her father was concerned.

"Father's gone. And he has been for a long time. We all see how lonely Mother is. We thought her and Mr. Svenson would get together until he decided to go back East. His leaving was hard on her. But now she seems happy again. Mr. Barker is obviously the one who is making her that way. He's a good Christian man who will take good care of her."

Leah looked away, annoyed to be the only one who was upset, and feeling guilty at the same time.

"It'll be okay, sis. You'll see." Jess tried to reassure her, too.

She couldn't even nod. Her heart was torn. She knew Michael was right, but that didn't make it any easier. The only good thing about any of it was that she wouldn't be there to see her mother with another man. It would hurt too much.

Michael gave her a squeeze before releasing her. "Now, we need to talk about what to do with this fellow who's coming. When's he supposed to get here?"

They discussed Fitzwilliam and his arrival. Just thinking about his coming in three days stripped away the melancholy that plagued her moments before. She had so much to prepare—herself most of all.

* * *

Later that evening, Leah sat in her bed and pulled out her diary and quill.

Dear Mr. Darcy,
Today I think Jake wanted to kiss me. A part of me wonders what it would be like. Another part of me is really glad he didn't. That would change everything. I would be uncomfortable around him if he had. In fact, tomorrow I'm wondering if it will be awkward around him after that incident. I hope not, but I still wonder. Anyway, I just wanted to let you know that in three days I'll be meeting Mr. Barrington. I can hardly wait.

Leah continued to write about her day and all that had transpired with her brothers. A wide yawn brought moisture to her eyes. She wiped it away, signed off with a *Good night, Mr. Darcy,* closed the journal and locked it securely inside her nightstand. Another long yawn and she decided it was time to get some sleep. She had a lot to do before Mr. Barrington arrived.

Snuggling underneath her covers, she nestled her head into the downy pillow and prayed that Mr. Barrington would like her.

Her eyes drifted shut.

"Father, where are you?" Leah hollered, running through the forest. Pine needles pricked her bare feet, stinging them, but she ignored the pain they inflicted. She had to find her father.

Deeper into the forest she ran, her shouts now filled with panic.

The sun settled behind the mountain and darkness shrouded everything.

Cedar, pine and cottonwood trees pressed in, encapsulating her and looming over her like the monsters they were.

Right before her eyes, their branches morphed into hands, and their knotholes turned into sinister eyes and mouths.

Evil now glared down at her.

Her heart slammed against her ribs with such force that Leah thought they would surely break.

With slow, menacing movement, the branches descended their arms downward toward her, straining closer and closer.

Leah ducked until she could duck no further. "Father, help me! I need you!" Her screams sucked all the air from around her. Breathing became difficult.

Long, spiky fingers dotted with leaves spread wide to take her into their grasp.

Leah pinched her eyes shut, waiting for the hand to grab her.

Seconds ticked by and nothing.

She slowly opened her eyes.

Her hands flew to the side of her head.

She screamed into the black void, "No! No!"

The monstrous tree had captured not her but her father, burying him underneath its mighty trunk. Only his legs, arms and head stuck out from underneath the massive beast.

Leah stared in horror.

Blood ran from her father's face in rivers.

"Lea—Leah. I—I love you, princess." Each word came out gurgled, slow, in painful gasps. Suddenly, his eyes rolled toward the back of his head and he went limp.

"Nooo! I'm sorry, Father! I'm sorry!" she wailed, her heart splintering from her chest.

Leah bolted upright and her gaze darted about the darkened room. Her heart beat so fast it throbbed in her ears as the images pursued her, even in reality. Blinking them back, she struggled to shake herself completely awake. With a toss, she yanked the covers back and swung her feet onto the cool floor.

The nightmare left her gasping for breath.

Tears slipped down her cheeks.

Those horrific dreams always ended the same— with her saying she was sorry. Sorry for what? She had no idea.

Exhausted, she wanted to lay her head back onto the pillow but couldn't. The gruesome image of her father might haunt her again.

Instead, she lit her kerosene lamp, lifted her Bible from the drawer and opened it to where her ribbon lay. *The Lord is my shepherd; I shall not want. He maketh me to lie down in green pastures: he leadeth me beside the still waters. He restoreth my soul: he leadeth me in the path of righteousness for his name's sake. Yea, thou I walk through the valley of the shadow of death, I will fear no evil: for thou art with me; thy rod and thy staff they comfort me. Thou preparest a table in the presence of mine enemies: thou anointest my head with oil; my cup runneth over. Surely goodness and mercy shall follow me all the days of my life: and I will dwell in the house of the Lord forever.*

Two more times Leah read Psalm Twenty-Three before closing her Bible. She slipped her peach-colored muslin robe over her nightgown and walked over to her bedroom window. She tied back the curtain and lowered herself into the chair in front of her open window, resting her arm on the windowsill. Staring up at the stars, in the quietness of her mind she sang the song her father had made up. *Sweet twinkling stars above; there to remind us of our Heavenly Father's love. Each one placed by the Savior with care; as a sweet reminder that He will always be there.*

Too weak to battle the tears from coming, they streamed down her cheeks, and she ran a hand over them to wipe them dry. *Oh, sweet twinkling stars above. When my children gaze upon you remind them, too, of my love.*

She sniffed back the rest of the tears, but more replaced them.

Each twinkle is a kiss from me; a hug, a prayer, a sweet memory. Oh, sweet twinkling stars above. Sniffing as the tears continued to fall, she sang it over and over until finally a blanket of peace covered her. She could almost feel her father's arms around her. It was the one sweet memory from this place that held any sway over all of the bad. She sighed with the hard-fought contentment.

Insects hissed and clacked their wings.

Coyotes howled somewhere faraway.

Leah listened to them, enjoying the peace and quiet.

How long she sat there, she didn't know. Only when the grandfather clock downstairs chimed five times did she move from the window. With a heavy sigh, Leah went and washed up, got dressed and headed downstairs. She had a lot to do before Mr. Barrington arrived. Two days. It seemed an eternity.

Mr. Barrington. Her heart said the name again.

The man who might very well become her husband. At the word *husband,* Jake's face slipped into the front of her mind, and Leah shook the notion from her brain. As much as she enjoyed Jake, he would not be a part of her future. He couldn't be. She was leaving. And after that nightmare, the sooner she got away from this place, the better.

Chapter Ten

For the first time ever, Jake's insides squirmed like a restless snake at the thought of seeing Leah. He wasn't sure how things would be between them after he'd almost kissed her. Or if she even knew how, for that one brief second, he'd thought about doing just that. He had a feeling she did because her attention had fallen to his mouth. Truth was, he wouldn't mind seeing what it would be like to kiss her. To see if her lips were as warm and soft as they looked. *What are you doing? Stop it, buddy boy. Best get your mind off of her and get your work done. Thinking like that could get you in trouble, that's for sure.*

Jake haltered another cow and sat down with his back to the barn door. Streams of milk pinged into the bucket. A few squirts later, he spurt some of the warm, sweet liquid into his mouth. "Ah. Nothing better than fresh milk." He wiped his mouth and continued milking the Jersey. He had just finished when he heard someone coming into the barn. This early, it either had to be Jess or Haydon.

The familiar scent of roses reached his nose.

Leah.

His insides writhed with a mixture of excitement and uncertainty.

"Good morning, Jake." Leah's greeting and light-hearted step eased the tension inside him.

Whew. Leah was acting as if nothing was out of the normal. "Morning, sunshine." Jake continued milking, keeping his sight trained on Leah as she strolled up to him. To get a better view of her, he thumbed his hat off his forehead and stopped milking. Worry crowded in on him the second he got a good look at her.

Dark, puffy circles sagged underneath her eyes.

"You all right?"

"I'm fine. Why?"

"You look tuckered out." He moved the bucket behind him and stood.

"Oh, that." She smiled, but it was forced and drowsy. "I didn't sleep well last night."

"How come?"

"I had a lot on my mind." Her hands slid into the pockets of her light blue skirt and she fiddled with something inside them.

"Getting ready for that Barrington fellow, huh?"

"Yes. I have a lot to do to get ready for his arrival. But Mother asked if I would take care of the milk this morning because Veronique can't. With Mr. Barrington and his sister coming, Mother wants Veronique to make sure our house is sparkling clean." She looked around and stopped when she spotted the two covered pails he'd just finished. "Have you taken any milk to my brothers' houses yet?"

"Nope. Not yet."

"Would you mind if I go ahead and take those?" She pointed to them.

"Nope. Don't mind at all, but what's your rush?" He suspected he knew, and both reasons ate at him.

"I want to hurry and get done so that Mother, Abby and I can head into town to buy some more material. I want to look my best when I meet Mr. Barrington."

He tipped his hat again and gazed the length of her. "You always look nice, Leah."

"Ah, that is sweet of you to say. Thank you, Jake." Those dimples appeared again when her lips curled. It was a friendly smile and cuter than a six-week-old kitten.

"Just a minute, okay? Don't go anywhere." He released the Jersey into the corral, where she'd stay until he finished milking the rest of them, then he'd shoo them back out into the pasture.

He haltered another one and moved the cow where the other one had been.

Leah stood on the cow's left, staring at the animal with inquisitive eyes. "This is going to sound strange, but I've never milked a cow before. I always wanted to, but my brothers always did it. Would you mind showing me how it's done?"

Jake looked at her clean yet simple dress. "You might get dirty."

"So?" She shrugged. "It doesn't matter if I do. This dress is old. I wear it when I help Mother and Veronique around the house. Besides, I'll change before I head into town so no need to worry about soiling it." She glanced at the cow and then back at him. "What do you say? Would you be willing to show me how it's done?"

Was he? Sure. Why not? Could be fun even. He gave a quick nod, grabbed the brim of his hat and lowered it back into place. "Come around to this side. Make sure you walk out and back far enough that she can't kick you."

She did as she was instructed to. Farther than necessary, even.

"Okay. Sit down." He motioned for her to sit on the stool.

She tucked her skirt under her and sat with her shoulder against the cow's right side.

He placed the bucket underneath the udder, squatted down next to her and rested his weight on the heel of his boot. "Okay. Here's what you do. Reach under here and grab the…um…grab the…uh…" Heat rose up the back of his neck. From the corner of his eye, he peeked at Leah. Her face reminded him of a ripened tomato.

God, help me out here, okay?

He roped some courage to himself and after a deep breath, he said, "Wrap your hand around…um…this right here." Jake demonstrated where she should place her hand. "Keep it close to the…um…" He cleared his throat. "The udder. Then squeeze." A stream of milk landed in the pail. "Okay. Now you do it."

He avoided looking at her face but watched as she did just as he'd told her to. Nothing came out.

She turned toward him with concern. "What did I do wrong?"

"Don't know. Try it again."

She did, and again nothing happened.

"You squeezing hard enough?"

"I don't want to hurt her." She blinked wide eyes at him as if what he'd said was the most absurd thing she'd ever heard.

Jake chuckled. "You won't hurt her. Here. Let me show you how much pressure to apply." He laid his hand on top of hers. Her small hand disappeared under his larger one. Gently, he guided her hand with his and the milk spurted out. A couple of tries later, he removed his hand. Milk continued to splatter into the bucket.

"I did it." The sound in her voice and the look on her face reminded him of a child who'd just learned to catch a ball for the first time.

"You sure did." He watched as she continued to milk the cow and even managed to get most of it into the bucket. "Hey, you're not doing too bad for a girl."

"What's that supposed to mean?" She cocked her head the way she did so often.

"You said your brothers never let you milk a cow. Figured they didn't 'cause you were a girl."

"Don't see what being a *girl* has to do with anything. Lots of *women* milk cows."

He noticed her emphasis on *girl* and *women.* Her way of letting him know she wasn't a girl but a woman. No need for her to point that out to him. That detail definitely hadn't skipped his notice. "Prissy little *women* like yourself don't," he teased.

"Prissy? Me?"

Just then drops of milk hit the top of his cheekbone. She giggled.

"Hey." He jumped up, raised his hat and ran the back of his sleeve over his face.

Another round of drops splattered against his neck. She chuckled again.

"What is wrong with you, *woman?*" He grabbed the ratty handkerchief from the back pocket of his jeans and wiped off his neck.

"Nothing's wrong with me." She sent him a cheeky grin, then dipped her fingertips in the milk bucket again and flicked the liquid toward him. This time it landed near his mouth. After a quick swipe to remove the splatters, before she could hit him again, he dropped to a squat, dipped his hand in the bucket and tossed it at her. The milk landed in her hair.

She squealed, then nailed him again in the ear with a handful before he had a chance to block it.

He scooped another handful, and this time the milk landed on her cheek.

She shrieked and started to shove the stool out of the way, but one of the three legs caught on the dirt floor, and the stool tipped over. Her arms shot out in front of her. He tried to catch them but couldn't. She landed on her rump, then her back, and ended up with her legs draped up and over the stool.

"What's going on in here?" Michael strode in the barn door and right up to them, where he put his hands on his hips to survey the mess.

In one fluid motion, Jake rose and helped Leah up. He faced Michael, expecting to see anger but instead saw a face spiked with humor. Jake knew what Michael was thinking, but he needed to set that right and fast.

Leah wiped her soiled hand on her skirt and brushed the dust and hay particles from her dress. Stems of hay hung in her hair, but he wasn't going to remove them and give Michael any more wrong ideas to speculate over. He quickly used his handkerchief to wipe the milk from his hand.

"Uh. Hi, Michael," she said before Jake got anything out. "I, um, I asked Jake to show me how to milk a cow."

"Oh. Is that what you were doing?" Michael rubbed his chin.

"Yes." Leah slammed her hands on her slender hips. "I've always wanted to learn, but you would never teach me how. So I asked Jake to. And I'm pretty good at it, too." Leah gave her brother a smug look filled with pride.

"Yes, real good." Michael peered into the nearly empty pail and then at the two of them. "Looks like you got more on yourselves than in the bucket."

Her eyes narrowed. "What are you doing here, anyway? Don't you have something better to do? Seems to me you've been leaving Selina a lot more often lately. You sure that's wise?"

Michael shrugged as Jake assessed Leah out of the corner of his eye. He didn't dare do more. "Abby's there. And I don't leave her for long periods. Besides, they were all sound asleep when I left." He frowned at Leah. "What are you doing here so early?" Michael eyed Jake and Leah suspiciously.

"If you must know, Mother asked me to come get the milk." She looked over at Jake. "May I have those two?"

Jake snatched up the two cloth-covered buckets sitting on high shelves off of the dirty floor. "I'll carry these up to the house for you."

"You don't have to do that. I can get them. But thanks anyway." She reached for the buckets, but Jake refused to hand them over to her. They were heavier than they looked.

"I said I would carry them for you." He sent her a look that left no room for argument, then turned his focus onto Michael. "Did you come down here for a reason?"

"Yes." Michael looked at Leah. "Would you excuse us for a minute?"

She glanced at Jake and the pails.

"I'll bring them up to the house in a minute, okay?"

Leah nodded, then picked up the milk pail he and Leah had dipped their hands in. "I'll take this and give it to the pigs." She left the barn with a quick glance over her shoulder.

Jake faced Michael and waited.

"I was wondering if you'd do me a favor."

"What's that?"

"Leah posted an advertisement in the New York paper for a husband." Michael stared at Jake, waiting for his reaction, no doubt.

"I know."

"You do?"

"Yep." And that was all he was going to say about it.

Michael's mouth twisted. "Well, some man answered it and he's coming out here in a couple of days. I… We… That is, Haydon, Jess and I were wondering if you'd take Leah into town to pick him up. Jess and Haydon can't, and I don't want to leave Selina that long. Would you mind? We'd feel a whole lot better if we knew you were with her."

Jake wanted to ask why they'd feel better about him being with her, but he didn't. He would do it to protect her and keep an eye on her—and to meet this dandy who was about to take his place. His place. Listen to him—as if he had a place in Leah's life. "Be happy to."

"Thanks, Jake." Michael laid his hand on Jake's shoulder. "I'll feel a lot better knowing you'll be there."

So would he. So would he.

Leah paced the kitchen floor, wondering where Jake was and what was taking him so long. She couldn't wait to get the milk. The sooner she did, the sooner she could take care of it so they could head to town.

"Leah, would you sit down? You're going to wear a path in the floor. Pacing isn't going to get that milk here any faster." Mother added another uniformly diced potato into the large cooking pot filled with cool water. She wanted to have everything ready for when they got back from town to fix pyttipanna, better known in America as Swedish hash.

Veronique normally did most of the cooking, but with all the extra housecleaning she had to do, Leah and Mother would take care of the cooking and baking for the next couple of days.

The sound of heavy boots climbing up the steps to the kitchen stopped Leah's fretting. She darted toward the door and swung it open.

"Where do you want these?" Jake had a bucket in each hand.

"On the table will be fine."

"Good morning, Katherine." Jake's muscles bulged beneath his shirt when he hoisted the pails onto the table. The man sure had nice muscular arms.

"Good morning to you, too, Jake."

He smiled then looked at Leah. "When you're ready to head into town just let me know and I'll get the buggy ready."

"Thanks, Jake." Leah watched the broad-shouldered man walk out the door and down the steps. Jake was the sweetest, gentlest man she knew. Someday she hoped he would find a nice woman to marry. She tilted her head, wondering why that thought pinched her soul.

"Leah, are you listening?" Mother asked from only inches behind Leah.

Leah whirled and blinked. "Sorry, Mother. I didn't hear you. What did you say?"

"I said, are you going to stand there gawking at Jake all day or get that milk taken care of?"

"I wasn't gawking at Jake," she murmured under her breath after she brushed past her mother. She snatched up the pails of milk and headed to the cream-ery room. The heavy buckets weighed her arms down as she trekked through the pantry and into the room farthest away from the heat of the kitchen. Inside the cool room, she continued to murmur. "Sweet twin-kling stars above. First Michael and now Mother. Can't a woman admire a man without everyone assuming they're a couple? Or that they're in love? Jake and I have fun together. So what?" She thought about their playful encounter. Jake had such a playful side to him and was so much fun. Too bad Michael had to show up and ruin it.

Leah set the buckets down and tugged at her lower lip, pondering over what Michael could possibly want to talk to Jake about that she couldn't hear. Something about that bothered her.

She quickly finished taking care of the milk, set the table and helped her mother finish dicing the ham and onions. Thankfully this time they wouldn't be adding any bacon or eggs to the pyttipanna or it would take them even longer to finish. Leah could hardly stand it now. She couldn't wait to head into town.

"Those babies are so cute," Abby said, bursting through the kitchen door. She flopped down into one of the chairs with her legs sprawled in front of her and her arms draped at her sides. "I can't wait until I be-come a mother."

Leah couldn't picture her baby sister a mother, al-though Abby was growing up fast and becoming a beautiful, outgoing woman. When had that happened?

"That's the last of the chopping." Mother stood. "Shall we put this up and get ready to head into town?"

"Yes." Leah jumped up and loaded her arms with bowls of chopped food. "Abbs, would you go down to the barn and see if Jake is still there? If he is, would you ask him to get the phaeton that seats four people ready, not the buckboard one?"

"Sure." Abby breezed out the door as fast as she'd breezed in.

That night, after a long day of shopping, Leah wrote about the events of the day in her Mr. Darcy diary. She read the new letters she'd received in response to her post. Not one of them intrigued her like Mr. Barrington's had. She slid them in the drawer and readied herself for bed, praying the nightmares wouldn't come. She needed sleep. Tomorrow would be another long day of preparations to meet Mr. Barrington.

Chapter Eleven

The day before had gone by in a blur of activities, including attending church. Today Mr. Barrington would arrive.

Leah studied her reflection in the mirror.

"You look beautiful, Leah." Mother stepped up behind her.

Leah glanced in the looking glass at her mother's reflection. "Thank you, Mother. And thank you for helping me finish this gown. It's beautiful." Leah turned her attention to the soft-pink satin gown.

The gathered, short sleeves and swooped neckline made her cameo necklace stand out against her sleek neck. She and mother had made a sash that hung below her waist and swept around to form a bustle in the back with a row of pink roses holding it together on the sides. Underneath the sash in front were layers and layers of delicate white ruffled lace that ended about a foot from the bottom hem of the dress. Directly underneath the lacy ruffles they'd sewn a four-inch-wide piece of pink lace all the way around the dress and bustle, leaving the last foot of the gown to match the top. Long, white gloves finished the ensemble.

Earlier, Mother had helped her sweep her hair back, leaving Leah's long curls flowing down in the back. She had even woven beaded ribbons through her blond tresses.

"I haven't lost my touch," Mother whispered.

"What do you mean?" Leah peeled her eyes off of her reflection and onto her mother's.

"Back in New York, we used to dress like this all the time. There was always a grand ball somewhere. Or someone was hosting a party. You remember going to them, don't you?"

"Yes." She turned to face her mother. "Do you ever miss it? I mean New York and the balls?"

"Sometimes yes. Most times no."

"What do you miss about it?"

"I miss being able to wear beautiful dresses once in a while. Not the corsets, though." They laughed. "I especially miss feeling feminine and pretty."

"But you are pretty, Mother."

"That's what Charles, I mean, Mr. Barker, says." At the mention of his name, especially his first name, Leah stiffened. "If he and I do marry, I'll be able to wear more gowns again. You know how elite his establishment is. Almost everyone who goes there dresses up," Mother continued, oblivious to Leah's discomfort. She was trying to be happy for her mother, she really was, but she couldn't help but wonder if anyone even cared about her father anymore except for her.

"Well, enough of that. You need to go or you'll be late meeting…" She paused. "What was his name again?"

"Fitzwilliam. Mr. Fitzwilliam Barrington."

"Oh, that's right. Well, run along now. I'll be praying for you."

"I'll need it. My insides are shaking so badly. I just hope I don't faint."

"You won't. Just remember to breathe."

"Who can breathe with one of these things on?" Leah squirmed in the uncomfortable corset that Rainee had loaned her, saying she didn't care if she ever got it back. She'd only worn the thing two or three times before. No wonder Rainee refused to wear them. Corsets really were the most uncomfortable contraptions ever made.

Mother walked her downstairs and out the door. Standing on the porch, she pulled Leah into a hug and then let her go with a smile and an unshed tear.

With the grace of a lady, Leah stepped down the porch stairs. At the grass, she turned and waved at her mother, then she raised the pink parasol that matched her dress and glided toward the barn, feeling prettier than she'd ever felt before.

Her heart skipped when her eyes landed on Jake, standing near the phaeton with the fringed parasol top, dressed in the same suit he had worn to Phoebe's wedding and looking every bit as handsome as he had that evening.

She strolled over to him, and he removed his black cowboy hat, pressed it over his midsection and, with a slight bow, he made a sweeping gesture toward the carriage. "Your chariot awaits, my lady."

She laughed at his antics, then cocked her head and eyed him. "What are you doing here?"

"I'm your driver."

"My driver?"

"Yep. You don't think your brothers were going to let you meet this man without a chaperone, do you?"

"Well, no. We discussed it the other day, so I knew

that someone was going with me. I just didn't know who. I figured it would be one of them."

"Well, Michael asked if I would take you. I told him I'd be happy to."

Truth be known, she was happy he was taking her, too.

"By the way. You look beautiful."

"Thank you." The compliment meant a lot coming from him.

"Shall we?" He stood at the backseat of the carriage and offered her his hand.

"What are you doing?"

"Can't have you sitting up front with the chauffeur, now can we?"

"You're not my chauffeur, Jake. You're my friend." She snapped her parasol shut, brushed past him, stopped at the front seat and perched her gloved hand toward him. "Now, I'll take that offered hand up if you don't mind, kind sir."

His smile of approval caused her heart to flip.

He reached for her gloved hand and steadied her as she rested her foot on the step and climbed aboard. She gathered her skirt inside and placed her parasol next to her.

Jake ran around and climbed in on the other side.

Although she knew it wasn't proper for her to be seated next to him like this, she didn't care. She was proud to be sitting next to him instead of in the back like some spoiled rich girl, treating her friend like a hired servant. As for what the townspeople would think when they saw them riding into town together like this, well, she didn't care about that, either. Nor did she have to worry about it. After all, she was going to pick up her future husband, so that should keep the tongues from wagging about her and Jake.

Maybe it hadn't been a good idea to let Leah sit next to him on the way to town. All the way there, Jake struggled with her intoxicating scent of roses and soap. Not only that, Leah looked even more beautiful than she normally did. However, seeing her dressed like that reminded him once again of how different their lifestyles were and how it was a good thing she had turned down his proposal. The two of them marrying would be like mixing fire and water.

Leah squirmed in the seat for what seemed like the millionth time.

"Pretty nervous, huh?"

She nodded and sighed.

"Try not to get too worked up. You'll make yourself sick."

"I know."

The train depot came into sight at the edge of town.

"Jake, could you stop here a moment?"

"Sure. Whoa." He halted the perfectly matched black and white spotted horses. Lines firmly in hand, he gave her his undivided attention. "What's wrong?"

"I wondered if—" her eyelids lowered, then rose back to look at him "—I wondered if you would pray with me now."

She looked so hopeful there was no way he could refuse her. "Sure." He reached for her hand. They bowed their heads, and when he finished praying, he realized his prayer hadn't only been for her benefit but for his, too. He knew this was going to be hard, but he hadn't realized just how hard until that moment. If Leah and this Barrington fellow got along or, worse, fell in love, then he would lose the best friend he ever had. Pain clawed at his heart. If only she would have said yes to him before. But knowing it was a good thing she had turned down his proposal and living with that decision were two very different battles.

"Thank you." Leah's voice was soft.

Jake nodded, clicked the lines and headed into town. In the distance, the train wheels clacked against the iron track. Within minutes it would be here. Now it was his turn to be nervous. But, for Leah's sake, he wouldn't let it show. He needed to not only be strong for her, but also for himself. His sanity depended on it.

At the front of the depot, Jake helped Leah down. Their boots tapped side by side against the wooden planks as they walked down the plank board platform to meet the train.

The train whistle pierced the air. Smoke billowed from the black stack, and the clanging of the wheels grew louder as it neared.

Leah's hand touched on his arm. A range of emotions battered across her face.

"Relax. Everything will be okay. You'll see." Brave words coming from a man who was as nervous as she was.

They turned their focus to the passengers now disembarking. The conductor helped a lady wearing a green dress every bit as fancy as Leah's from the train. Behind her was a man in a tail suit, holding a cane in one hand and gloves in another and wearing a top hat. A proud peacock showing off his feathers came to mind.

That dandy had to be Mr. Barrington and the lady with him, his sister.

The man stepped beside the woman, stopped and looked around.

Jake decided to take matters into his own hands. "Wait here," he said to Leah.

She nodded.

Jake strode over to the couple. "Excuse me. Are you Mr. Barrington?"

The man turned dark, condescending eyes and surveyed Jake with disdain.

Jake pressed his shoulders back. No man, rich or otherwise, would make him feel bad about himself. He'd suffered that sting enough to last a lifetime. "I asked if you…"

"Yes. I heard you. And yes, I am Mr. Barrington. Who might you be?"

"Jake Lure." Jake offered the man his hand.

All the fellow did was glance at it as if it were poison.

Jake let his hand fall to his side. What he really wanted to do with it was rearrange the haughty man's face.

"Jake." Leah's confused voice sounded from beside him.

He glanced down at her, then shifted his attention to the Barrington fellow. "Leah, this *gentleman* is Mr. Barrington." Gentleman. Ha.

Barrington's face brightened. "Ah. Capital. I see you've received my post."

Capital? What was that supposed to mean?

The rascal removed his hat and bowed. Then he fastened his hand onto Leah's fingers, raised her hand to his lips and kissed it. When he straightened, his eyes raked up and down Leah's body approvingly.

Jake's fists clenched at the audacity of this man. To avoid embarrassing Leah, he restrained himself from ramming his fist in the man's eyes for disrespecting her like that.

"You are every bit as lovely as I had imagined. Quite striking, actually. It is a real pleasure to make your acquaintance, Miss Bowen. I am sure we will get along quite famously."

A smooth talker this one was. Jake was determined to keep his eye on this fellow who portrayed himself to be a gentleman but was nothing more than a shed snakeskin.

Heat rose into Leah's cheeks at Mr. Barrington's compliment. Judging from the admiration on his face, his study of her must have met with his approval. "It's a pleasure to meet you, too, Mr. Barrington." Leah gave him a small curtsy and a smile, relieved that she remembered the social graces from her childhood.

He returned her smile. His teeth, although white, were slightly crooked. His brown eyes, hair and long sideburns reminded her of the chocolate squares she indulged in every now and again.

"Miss Bowen, may I present my sister, Miss Elizabeth Barrington?"

The woman, who looked identical to her brother, curtsied, and so did Leah. "It's a pleasure to meet you, Miss Barrington."

"Please, call me Elizabeth. May I call you Leah?"

"Yes. Yes, you may." The woman's silk, royal-blue bustle gown must have cost a small fortune. As had her matching parasol, reticule, ribbon sash hat and matching slippers.

Those slippers won't last long out here.

"May I call you Leah, as well? I know it is highly improper unless we are courting, but I feel it is just a matter of time before we shall be." Mr. Barrington smiled.

"Of course. Leah's fine."

"Capital. And you may call me Fitzwilliam."

"Thank you, Fitzwilliam." Leah loved listening to his British accent. The man was extremely handsome. And tall, too. Not as tall as Jake, but taller than she at least. "I hope you don't mind, but I've made arrangements at Mr. Barker's hotel. It is the finest hotel in town." Leah had done that the day she, Mother and Abby had gone to town to get the material for the dress she was now wearing.

"That was most considerate of you, Miss Bowen. I mean, Leah." He hooked her arm through his.

Leah looked at their linked arms, then over at Jake. Jake shrugged.

"You, sir. Get our bags." Mr. Barrington's tone boasted with authority aimed at Jake.

Her mouth fell open and her eyes widened. "You mean Jake?" Leah asked.

"Jake? You address your servant by his first name?"

"Servant? Jake is not my servant." Annoyance rolled inside her at that, but she would not let her face show it— She'd let her voice instead. "Jake—" she emphasized his name "—is my friend. A very dear, very close, very special friend." She smiled at Jake.

"I see." Mr. Barrington's eyes narrowed at Jake, and he looked like he'd just tasted sour milk.

"Brother, I'm sure Mr. Lure or Leah might know someone we may hire to take our belongings to the hotel." Elizabeth smiled at Leah and Jake with a hint of an apologetic smile if Leah wasn't mistaken. Elizabeth's eyes lingered on Jake rather than on Leah, a fact that Leah did not miss. She found her own gaze going to him and sticking, too.

"No need, Miss Barrington. I'll see to them," Jake said, swinging a large bag to his hip.

"Jake, you don't need to do that." Leah slipped her arm out of Mr. Barrington's and stepped beside Jake. "I'll see if Mr. Barker will send someone over to get them."

"I don't mind." He shrugged.

"*You* may not, but *I* do." She sent him a look to let him know she really didn't want him carrying them.

He stared at her for a moment, then set the bag down. Leah sent him a smile, letting him know how relieved she was he'd followed her silent request.

Another nod from Jake. She turned toward Fitzwilliam. "If you're ready, we can take you to the hotel now. If you haven't eaten, we can eat lunch there." Leah's attention slid to Elizabeth. "You must be exhausted from your long journey."

"I am."

"If you'd like, you can have a hot bath and rest awhile."

"That would be lovely, Leah. Yes. You are quite right. A hot bath and a soft bed sound most agreeable. Thank you."

"That's very thoughtful of you to consider my sister's needs, Leah. I must admit, I could use a bit of a rest myself. Perhaps after we've done so, we could hire a carriage to take us out to your ranch?"

"Brother," Elizabeth said. "May we do that tomorrow? I am in need of nourishment and a good night's rest."

"Very well, sister. Even though I am quite anxious to spend time with Leah, I can see you need your rest. We shall wait until the morrow then." Fitzwilliam smiled at Leah. "Though it shall be an interminable wait."

What a sweet man to think of his sister's needs, even above his own wants. "Very well, let's go get you two settled in then. Would you like to walk to the hotel or ride?"

"If it's not too far, I would prefer to walk. I have been sitting much too long," Fitzwilliam answered.

"Yes, we have. Taking a turn would do us good." Elizabeth smiled up at Jake.

She sure seemed to do a lot of that.

"Shall we?" Leah glanced at each one. When Leah turned toward the direction of the hotel, Mr. Barrington looped her hand through his arm again and tugged her forward, away from Jake's side. She glanced over her shoulder at Jake and was about to mouth *sorry* when she felt another tug on her arm.

Jake gave her a quick nod to go on ahead.

"Miss Barrington, may I?" At the sound of Jake's voice, Leah turned her head enough to see Jake offer Elizabeth his arm and smile warmly at her.

Something about that didn't sit right in Leah's belly. But she'd think about the why of it later. Right now she wanted to concentrate on Fitzwilliam.

The walk to the hotel was pleasant enough except for the fact that Leah spent more time listening to the conversation behind her than she did to the one she was a participant in.

"Here we are." She stopped at the large three-story hotel.

"Impressive. Quite impressive. Allow me." Mr. Barrington turned the brass knob on the large mahogany door.

Leah smiled at him and stepped far enough inside to

let the others in. She quickly studied the room, trying to see it from the Barringtons' viewpoint.

Crystal chandeliers loaded with fresh candles hung from the high ceiling. Light and airy, white swag curtains covered the three big windows in front and the three big windows on the sides. The white drapery material dotted with dainty pink and blue roses matched the fabric on the mahogany Chippendale chairs and the tablecloths that covered the matching tables.

On the far end of the room were two long, curved staircases, one on either side of a long mahogany registration desk. Next to the bottom of the stairs were entryways into the kitchen, one door for going in, the other for coming out.

"Don't worry, Leah. Even they would have to agree it's a fine establishment," Jake whispered near her ear from behind her.

He knew her so well. She went to respond to him but never got the chance because Mr. Barrington clutched her arm and propelled her forward.

Fitzwilliam was obviously jealous of Jake, and Leah completely understood why he might be. After all, he didn't know how it was between her and Jake. If he did, he would know he had nothing to be jealous about.

"Leah."

Leah stopped and turned to find Mr. Barker heading her way. "Mr. Barker, how nice to see you again." She really did like the man, she just didn't like the idea of he and her mother married. But she was trying. And she would be polite.

"It's nice to see you again, too, Leah."

Leah glanced over at Jake. "You know Jake Lure."

"Yes, I sure do. How are you doing today, Jake?"

They shook hands, and Mr. Barker's smile radiated his respect.

"Fine, sir. And you?"

"Never better." He glanced at Leah. She knew what he was referring to. Her mother and their relationship.

She didn't want to think about that now so she turned to introduce Fitzwilliam to Mr. Barker. Once again, his eyes were narrowed in Jake's direction, but he recovered quickly.

Poor Jake. He didn't deserve Fitzwilliam's disdain.

"Mr. Barrington," Leah said, liking how refined and dignified he looked there.

Fitzwilliam turned his head toward Leah and the frown disappeared, replaced with a smile that didn't quite make it to his eyes.

"I'd like you to meet Mr. Barker. He's the owner of this establishment."

Fitzwilliam's eyes brightened considerably then. "Pleasure to meet you, sir."

Mr. Barker extended his hand, but Fitzwilliam didn't take it. He bowed.

Mr. Barker did a quick glance in Leah's direction, then let his arm fall slowly to his side.

"And may I present my sister, Elizabeth?"

"Nice to meet you, ma'am." Mr. Barker gave a quick nod.

Elizabeth curtsied. "Thank you, sir. It is a pleasure to meet you, as well."

Seconds of awkward silence passed until Leah spoke up. "Mr. Barker, we've come to have a bite to eat before my guests retire to their rooms. I've reserved two rooms here for them."

"I'll take good care of them, Leah." For an older man, Mr. Barker was very handsome. She could see what her mother saw in him, still… *Not now, Leah,* she silently scolded herself. "Follow me and I'll show you to your table." Mr. Barker led them to the best spot in the dining area and seated them.

"I'll send Carina over to take your orders. And now, if you'll excuse me, I have business to attend to. If I can be of service to you for anything, just ask Carina to send for me, okay? It was a pleasure to meet you all." He glanced down at Leah and smiled. "Tell your mother hello for me."

Although her insides cringed, she said, "I will." She watched him walk away.

Jake leaned close to her and whispered, "Remember. It gets easier. I promise." Like a butterfly alighting on a branch, his hand brushed hers under the table and he squeezed it gently. Gratefulness for his solid presence in her life drifted over her heart.

Their gazes locked for a moment. Leah willed her eyes to show him her gratitude. Jake gave a quick nod, shifted back into his chair and removed his hand.

Leah pulled her focus off of Jake and slid it onto Fitzwilliam, who was once again glaring at Jake. She needed to explain the friendship to Fitzwilliam. Not now, though. And not in front of Jake.

"Hi, Leah." Carina stepped up to the table, dressed in a light green gown. "Hi, Jake." Her smiling green eyes lingered on Jake as did her generous, full-lipped smile.

"Carina, this is Mr. Barrington and his sister, Elizabeth."

"It is a pleasure to meet y'all." Their pretty waitress glanced at Elizabeth and stared at Fitzwilliam.

Fitzwilliam sat in his chair like a statue. Leah waited for him to say something to Carina, but he didn't. How odd. First Fitzwilliam didn't shake Jake's or Mr. Barker's hands and now he didn't respond to Leah's introduction to Carina or even acknowledge her presence. Is that how things were done in England? Or was the man just nervous or shy? Leah hoped it was the latter—that at least she could understand. The other, she couldn't and wasn't sure she wanted to try.

"It is a pleasure to meet you, as well." Elizabeth didn't seem to have a problem acknowledging Carina. "Carina is such a lovely name."

"Thank you, ma'am." Carina pressed a finger to her lip. "I don't recognize the accent. Where y'all from?"

"England. But we live in New York now," Elizabeth answered.

"Really? What are y'all doing here?"

"Carina, I'm sorry to interrupt, but my guests could use a drink and something to eat." Leah gave her a small smile. Carina was a sweet girl, but once she got wind of something, the whole town eventually did, too.

"Oh, of course. How thoughtless of me." Carina smiled a half smile. "What would y'all like to drink? We have tea, coffee, water, milk or wine."

"Leah, what would you care to drink?" Fitzwilliam asked with a smile.

"Tea with cream and sugar."

"The lady would like a spot of tea with cream and sugar," Fitzwilliam told the waitress as if she hadn't heard Leah.

"'A spot of tea'? What's that?" Carina's face wrinkled.

"A cup, madam. It means a cup full of tea." There was no condescension in his voice, which pleased Leah.

"Oh." Carina shrugged and looked at him like he was nuttier than a walnut grove.

"I'll have the same, Miss Carina," Elizabeth said when Carina looked at her.

"Jake, what'll you have?"

"Milk."

"Milk? How very odd." Fitzwilliam frowned at Jake, who looked completely unfazed by it.

But she was.

"And you, sir? What would you like?" Carina gazed down at Fitzwilliam with admiration in her eyes. Leah rolled hers at Carina's obviousness.

"Wine. White if you have it."

Wine? The man drank wine? At a few minutes past twelve, even. Was that something the British did? Leah made a mental note to ask Rainee about that. If it wasn't, she didn't want someone who drank, no matter how desperate she was to leave this place.

"What's on the menu today, Carina?" Jake asked as Leah threaded her way through the questions.

"You have your choice of roasted pork with mashed potatoes and gravy and glazed carrots." She ticked the choices off with her fingers. "Beef stew. Chicken and vegetable pie. Or fried trout with fried potatoes and green beans."

They all placed their orders and Carina brought their drinks.

"So, did you have a nice journey?" Leah asked Fitzwilliam, then took a sip of tea.

"Yes, we did. The countryside was quite to our liking."

Leah tried to think of something else to say, but nothing came to mind. She picked up her tea again, hoping Fitzwilliam would say something. Without looking directly at them, Leah noticed that Elizabeth and Jake weren't having any trouble with conversation. She would join in with theirs but it looked like they were engrossed in whatever it was they were talking about. In fact, Jake looked completely enraptured in what Elizabeth was saying. A twinge of jealousy brushed across Leah.

"Leah."

She looked over at Fitzwilliam. "Yes?"

"How far is your ranch from here?"

The conversation picked up then as did the passing of time. Leah found herself completely engrossed as Fitzwilliam regaled her with one interesting story after another, and her excitement about getting to know him grew. Fitzwilliam turned out to be an interesting man whose travels had taken him to exotic lands—many of which she could hardly pronounce. Each sounded more fascinating than the one before. They were all lands she couldn't wait to see.

When lunch was over, Jake made arrangements for their luggage to be sent over. Leah helped them get their room keys and invited them to come to the ranch the following afternoon and stay for dinner. Goodbyes were said, and with that, she and Jake headed down the boardwalk to the buggy.

"So, what did you think of Fitzwilliam?" Leah asked Jake as they walked slowly down Main Street. Fitzwilliam's antagonism toward Jake made the whole ordeal miserable. Elizabeth was nice enough. Easy on the eyes, and Jake enjoyed talking with her, but that Fitzwilliam fellow...

Jake wanted to tell Leah exactly what he thought of Fitzwilliam, but he held his tongue. "Haven't been around him long enough to know just what sort of fellow he is yet."

"But he seems really nice, though, don't you think?"

Jake shrugged. She didn't want to know what he really thought.

Her boots tapped against the boardwalk as they made their way toward the train depot. At the carriage, Jake helped Leah up and then climbed aboard beside her. "What did you think of Elizabeth?" she asked.

Now that he could answer and be honest about. "She's a very nice, interesting lady." An attractive one at that. He turned the horses toward the Bowens' ranch.

"What all did you and her have to talk about?"

"She asked me what I did and where I lived. I told her. She sure surprised me."

"In what way?" Leah asked as they headed onto the dirt street out of town.

"The woman wants to live on a farm. Said she hates city life."

"Has she ever lived on one before?"

"Said she did. She loved being around the animals. Getting her hands dirty. Something she said English ladies never do. Especially one of her social standing. Didn't seem overly impressed with her own social status." Jake could see why, if she had to live a stuffy, boring life like that Mr. Darcy fellow in the book he'd finished reading. He had to admit, though—in *Pride and Prejudice* Mr. Darcy turned out to be a nice guy. Jake hoped that would be the case with Fitzwilliam Barrington. But he had his doubts. He'd seen the ugly, evil glint of jealousy in the man's eyes.

Years before, Jake's uncle Urias killed a man in a fit of jealous rage. Before they'd hanged his uncle, he'd warned Jake of the evil of venomous jealousy. Said no woman was worth killing someone over. If looks alone could kill a man, Jake was certain he'd be dead right now. Thinking about that Fitzwilliam fellow turned his blood to stone. He just hoped that Leah would see it before it was too late.

Father, there's something about that man that doesn't sit right with me. If he's not the man for Leah, would You drive a wedge between them? And please do it before Leah gets hurt.

The ride had been quiet. Each of them was lost in their own thoughts. He dropped Leah off at her house, put the horses and buggy up and glanced at his pocket watch. Time to head to the designated meeting place. Michael, Jesse and Haydon wanted to hear his opinion about the man before meeting him. He'd tell them exactly what his first impression of the man had been. After all, that's what they wanted.

Chapter Twelve

Leah pressed her hand into her midsection, willing it to calm down. In twenty minutes Fitzwilliam and his sister would be arriving for dinner.

Colette and Zoé, Veronique's younger sisters who Mother hired on occasion to help Veronique out with household duties, hustled about in the kitchen.

Veronique charged into the room.

"Is everything ready, Veronique?" Leah asked for the tenth time.

"*Oui*, Leah. All is ready." Sometimes Veronique's French accent was hard to understand. Wearing her best black dress and white apron, both pressed to perfection, Veronique reminded Leah of the maids they'd had back in New York.

Leah may have been young then, but those delightful, fun-filled memories had never left her. Ballrooms filled with the elite of New York society wearing elegant gowns and exquisite jewelry and men dressed in fine suits. Footmen and maids dressed in black-and-white who scurried about waiting on their guests, making sure they had plenty to drink and finger foods to eat.

How Leah longed for those days. She most remembered the days spent with her father. Where he proudly waltzed her around the floor and introduced her to people she'd never met before. Leah could hardly wait to get back to New York and that lifestyle. Fitzwilliam reminded her of those times, just as she had hoped he would. The man was handsome, and his manners were to her liking. Exciting tales of his travels intrigued and excited her. And the way he tended to his sister's needs, well, if that was any indication of what he would be like as a husband, then she had found herself a real gem. And that gem was due to arrive any minute now.

Leah hiked up her skirt and rushed upstairs to check herself in the mirror. The light blue gown wasn't as elegant, nor did it have the lace or ruffles or a bustle like the one she'd worn to meet him had, but, then again, she'd worn her best gown yesterday because she'd wanted to make a good first impression. Hopefully she had.

She wound her finger around the side curls she'd left down in front of her ears and replaced the few pins that had slipped.

The sound of voices downstairs caught her attention. Her family had begun to arrive. In a way she wished they weren't coming, but they wanted to meet Fitzwilliam. Leah couldn't blame them. They were concerned about her and wanted to get to know the stranger their sister might marry. She made her way downstairs, sending up a quick prayer that all would go well.

The house buzzed with people. At the bottom of the staircase, Leah stood undetected for a moment, smiling and watching the family she loved so dearly. Her brothers stood on one end of the vast living room talking while the women congregated to the other end, passing around the babies.

"Some gathering, isn't it?"

Leah turned to find Jake dressed in brown pants and cowboy boots, a tan shirt with brown buttons and a brown vest. His hair was neatly combed, his chin and upper lip were shaved clean, and the air around him bespoke of masculine, woodsy spices. Her heart waltzed knowing her best friend was there. "Hi, Jake. I'm so glad you decided to come."

"Wasn't going to. But couldn't resist that pouty look on your face."

"Hmm." She placed her fingertip on her lips. "From now on, I'll have to remember to pout every time I want something." She cut him a brief smile before turning somber. "Seriously, Jake. I really am so glad you came. I feel a lot better *and* calmer knowing you're here. Thank you."

"Hey, you two, get in here," Haydon ordered with not one ounce of authority.

"We're being summoned." Jake smiled down at her.

They walked side by side into the living room, where Jake headed to the group of men and she to the women. Leah said her hellos, ending with Selina. "I'm so glad you came. Are you doing okay? Do you need to sit?"

"All I done lately is sit even though I'm feelin' finer than frog's hair."

"Yes, but you must not overdo it, sweetheart," Michael said from behind Leah.

Leah glanced at him, then back at Selina.

"He's a bossy one, ain't he?"

"He sure is," Leah agreed, then winked at both of them. She looked around for Lottie and Joey.

Seated on the sofa were Mother, Abby, Rainee and Hannah.

Abby cooed to Joey. Seeing her nephew dressed

in the blue cotton pants and shirt she'd made for him brought a pleased smile to Leah's lips.

Hannah cradled Lottie in the crook of her arms. Lottie looked like a princess in the lacy pink dress Abby had sewn for her.

Mother dangled eleven-month-old Haydon Junior in front of her and rubbed noses with him. His dark blue pants covered his tiny feet and the light blue shirt Mother had sewn fit him to perfection.

Rainee bounced Hannah's eighteen-month-old giggling Rebecca on her knees. With each bounce, the white ruffles on her red dress went up and then down, up and then down.

Contentment hovered on each glowing face. Leah couldn't wait to become a mother.

She felt a slight tug on her skirt and looked down.

Her nine-year-old niece Emily gazed up at her with those same blue eyes as Haydon's. "I think they're here, Auntie."

Seven-year-old Rosie scurried up behind Emily. "I got a peek at them, Auntie. Boy, is she ever pretty. And he's handysome just like my daddy." Rosie's fawn-colored eyes sparkled up at her.

"Handsome," Emily corrected.

"That's what I said." Rosie put her little hands on her hips and jutted out her chin.

It amazed Leah how Rosie was a little miniature Rainee and Emily a miniature Haydon.

"Never mind that now," Emily said. "Auntie, did you hear me? They are here."

"Yes. Yes, I did. Thank you." She tapped Rosie on the tip of her nose. "I'll go greet them now. You girls want to come?"

"Can we?"

"No. You may not," Rainee said.

"Sorry, girls." Leah kissed each one of their cheeks, then floated like a graceful swan to the door.

Jake slipped away from the men, went into the parlor away from the noise of the living room and stood near the open window closest to where Fitzwilliam and Elizabeth disembarked. He stood back far enough to remain undetected and watched and listened.

Jake overheard Fitzwilliam say the house wasn't very large and that they must not have as much money as he had hoped. Was the man after Leah for her money?

"Who cares about that, brother?" Elizabeth's tone came with a rebuke. "I certainly do not. And neither should you. We lack neither fortune nor consequence."

If they had more than enough, then Jake didn't understand why it mattered to the man. Unless Fitzwilliam was like those characters in that novel he'd read. Where money was all that mattered to them. That and position.

The porch steps echoed with footsteps and the front door squeaked. Leah met Fitzwilliam and Elizabeth at the top of the stairs. "Good evening, Fitzwilliam. Elizabeth. Welcome to my home."

"Thank you for inviting us." Elizabeth's kind voice drifted through the window as she gave a small curtsy.

"Good evening, Leah. You look rather lovely." The man peered at Leah and then around her. "Where are your footmen and butler? Why did they not greet us and answer the door?"

"Footmen? Butler?" Leah tilted her head and her curl slipped across her cheek. "We don't have footmen or a butler. Not out here."

"You don't? How very odd."

"I don't think it's odd at all." Jake detected a hint of insecurity and uncertainty drizzling through Leah's words.

How dare that man make her feel inferior. Jake wanted to step outside and put the pompous rogue in his place.

"Brother, you must remember we are not back in England. This is the West. They do things differently out here. And I for one love it."

No need to. Elizabeth just had. Jake wanted to hug the woman for it and for saying something he knew would put Leah at ease. It was hard to believe those two were related. Miss Barrington was nothing like her brother.

"Quite right, sister. Forgive me, Miss Leah. As my dear sister said, I am used to things done a certain way. Please bear with me as I try to adjust to your customs."

"Will Jake be here?" Elizabeth asked, peering over at the house. They had yet to make it to the porch.

It warmed Jake to know she asked about him.

"Jake." His name spoken from Fitzwilliam held only disdain. Jake wondered if Leah noticed it, too. "Sister, dear. Why would the hired help be invited to a formal dinner?"

Hired help? When was the man going to get it through his thick skull that he was a friend of the family and only working for them to help them out?

"As I said before, Mr. Barrington. Jake is *not* the hired help." Leah sounded miffed, and Jake wanted to hug her for it. It must be an evening for hugs, Jake thought, grinning to himself. "He has been kind enough to help my brothers out when they desperately needed him. He has put his own affairs aside to do so. Jake has his own farm to run. And a nice one at that." Jake heard the pride in Leah's voice. Her words meant a lot to him. They warmed his insides clear down to his toes. "Most importantly, Jake is not only my dear friend, but he's also a close friend of the whole family." She turned to Elizabeth. "To answer your question, Elizabeth. Yes, Jake is here."

"How delightful. I cannot understand why you haven't captured him for yourself. He's such an agreeable, handsome man."

"Sister!" Fitzwilliam boomed the word.

Jake chuckled quietly and found himself flattered by Elizabeth's comment about him. There was a lot more to her than he had first guessed.

"Well, 'tis but true, brother."

"I am quite delighted Leah hasn't. For then I would not have the pleasure of making this lovely woman's acquaintance."

"Thank you, Fitzwilliam." Jake heard the pleasure and blush in Leah's voice.

The man was sure slippery. Knew just how to charm a woman. Surely Leah saw right through it, though. Didn't she?

"Shall we go inside?" Leah asked.

Fitzwilliam offered his arms to both women and disappeared toward the front door.

Jake moved away from the curtain and slipped back into the living room.

Michael stepped up to him. "I appreciate you keeping an eye on them for me."

How did Michael know what Jake had been doing? Jake opened his mouth to say he didn't do it for them but for himself, but Leah chose that moment to enter the living room on the arm of the snake.

"Excuse me." Leah's voice rang out loud and clear.

She gazed up at Fitzwilliam, whose eyes widened for a brief moment, but he quickly masked his shock. The highfalutin snob probably didn't approve of Leah raising her voice.

Jake eyed Fitzwilliam up and down. The other men present all wore nice suit jackets, pressed trousers and cowboy boots. Not Fitzwilliam. How out of place the man looked in his starched white shirt with a silk neck cloth, gray waistcoat with his gold watch fob chain showing, his black tail suit, gray top hat and gray shining shoes. Like a peacock in a goat show.

Jake's eyes landed on Fitzwilliam's. Disapproval sneered through those brown eyes of his, but once again the man quickly covered up his disapproval before Leah saw it.

Leah introduced him and Elizabeth to everyone in the room.

Rainee and her daughters curtsied and the men offered Fitzwilliam their hands, but he refused them and instead bowed. Jake watched each interaction. Leah's brothers didn't look overly impressed.

After his brush with royalty, Michael walked over to Jake and leaned close. "A little on the pompous side, don't you think?" Michael spoke in a tone meant for his ears only.

Jake nearly bit his lip off to keep from laughing. "Among other things."

"He sure doesn't like you, does he?"

"You noticed that, too, huh?"

"I'd say it's probably a badge of honor myself."

They chuckled, and Michael left to stand at Selina's side.

Minutes later, Leah's mother announced, "Dinner is ready. Shall we all head into the dining room?"

The men dispersed and gathered their wives and children.

Rainee's red-headed maid, Esther, and Ruth, the petite brunette who worked for Hannah on occasion, came to gather the babies.

"If you need anything or have any trouble, I want you to come get me immediately. And if Joey and Lottie start fussing—"

"Michael," Selina interrupted her husband. "These women will take good care of the children. Rainee wouldn't-a hired them iffen she didn't trust 'em. Lottie and Joey will be just fine. So come on. Let's go sit down and eat and enjoy ourselves. It won't be long before they'll be needin' their mama to feed them again."

Jake watched uncertainty waltz across Michael's face.

"Michael, your babies are in good hands. I promise," Rainee interjected.

"We all know how hard it is leaving them with someone for the first time." Jesse hit his younger brother's shoulder. "But they'll be fine. I promise."

"They'll be right there in the next room, Michael. You can check on them whenever you want." Haydon added his two bits, too.

"I'll go check on them for you, Uncle Michael." Thomas, Jess's oldest son, pressed his shoulders back and stood up tall. Tall for an eleven-year-old anyway.

"We will, too," Rosie and Emily both said.

"Me, too," Jess's other son, William, tossed in. It was obvious the six-year-old didn't want to be left out.

Jake smiled, taking it all in. This loving family supported one another and cared for one another. Watching them made him wish he had brothers and a family like this one. Homesickness for his own family drizzled through him. He wondered what they were doing now.

"Okay. Okay." Michael handed Joey to the maid, but his attention stayed riveted on the babies until they disappeared into the next room.

Leah hooked her hand through Mr. Barrington's. "Shall we?"

His feet remained in place. "Pardon me, Leah, but it is highly improper for us to go in before our host."

"Huh? Oh." She waved him off. "We don't care about stuff like that out here. Out here, guests go first."

His forehead wrinkled. "Highly improper. Most disagreeable to be sure."

Jake scanned the Bowens' faces, hoping the man hadn't offended them, but no one seemed to have heard him but Leah, Elizabeth and himself.

"Brother." Elizabeth laid her hand on his arm. "Please, do not make a scene," his sister whispered, her cheeks a dark shade of red.

Jake stared at Fitzwilliam with one brow hiked and sent the man a warning glare that he'd better fall in line.

Fitzwilliam sent a disapproving look back at him, one that turned into a challenging, smug look, then he looked at his sister. "You're right, Elizabeth dear. Thank you for pointing out my own faux pas."

Faux pas? What in the world was a *faux pas?*

Fitzwilliam turned his attention to Leah. "My apologies to you, Leah. My sister is correct. Again, I must beg you to bear with me. I am quite used to things done differently, but this is your home and we are your guests. Please accept my sincere apology."

Leah's smile showed her relief and her pleasure. "Of course I accept your apology. Now, let's head into dinner." She glanced at Jake. "You coming?"

"Wouldn't miss it." Jake sent his lazy grin her way, the one she enjoyed. Then it was his turn to send Fitzwilliam a smug look. Narrowed eyes stared back at him until Leah turned toward him. Immediately Fitzwilliam's glare changed to a smile. That man was phonier than a fifteen-cent piece.

"May I?" Elizabeth offered her hand to him.

Jake smiled down at the woman who was inches shorter than he. "You may." He looped her hand through his arm and followed Leah into the dining room, thinking how interesting this evening was going to be.

Leah glanced at Elizabeth's hand draped over Jake's arm and his hand patting it in a friendly gesture. Her gaze slid to Elizabeth's face. Miss Barrington stared up at Jake with stars in her eyes. Leah wished she could see Jake's eyes, but from where she stood, they were hidden from her view.

A throat cleared. Leah's gaze slid to Michael, who nodded for her to head into the dining room. Oh. She stepped inside and thanked God that her mother knew how to entertain the wealthy and elite society. From what she'd seen so far, Fitzwilliam was both. That both excited and intimidated her.

She raised her chin and proudly led Fitzwilliam into their formal dining room. Surely he couldn't find fault with anything in here. Two years before, her brothers had added on to Mother's house a large parlor, a library, an office and a formal dining room. For Christmas that year they had all gotten together and surprised Mother with a solid oak Queen Anne dining set, including chairs, table, china hutch and serving table, along with a blue, gray and maroon Victorian rug that gave a nice ambience to the room. Last year they'd bought her two silver candelabras and a crystal chandelier laden with fresh candles, which went great with Mother's bone Limoges china with delicate purple and blue roses and gold trim.

Little by little they were restoring what Mother had left behind to move here. And little by little the place was starting to look like their home back in New York. Except this home wasn't as large, and Leah had to admit, it was much homier.

Mother strolled to her place at the head of the table, and Haydon pulled out her chair. After all the women were seated, the men took their places.

Haydon sat at the other end of the table, opposite his mother. Rainee sat on his right, then Emily, Rosie, Jess, Hannah and two of their children, Thomas and William.

Michael sat on Haydon's left, then Selina, Fitzwilliam, Leah, Jake, Elizabeth and Abby.

"Let's pray."

Leah closed her eyes and bowed her head. She felt Fitzwilliam shift next to her. She slatted one eye and peered at him. His gaze traveled around the room and landed on her. He slammed his eyes shut and quickly bowed his head.

Leah smiled. He'd been caught. She couldn't blame him for being curious. She would be, too. For a brief moment, her attention touched on Elizabeth. Unobserved, Leah watched Elizabeth as the woman stared moon-eyed at Jake until Haydon finished the prayer and everyone said amen. Uneasiness stroked Leah's soul. Later on she'd ask herself why that bothered her.

Veronique and Zoé came in and served the first course.

Fitzwilliam picked up his spoon, tipped it away from

him and took a sip. "This is quite delicious. What it
is it?"

"It's ärtsoppa." At his frown, she explained. "Pea
soup."

"I see." He took another sip and so did she.

Leah reached for a slice of kavring—dark rye
bread—dunked it into her soup and took a bite. She
turned to ask Fitzwilliam if he'd like some but didn't
because he looked aghast. "Something wrong?" she
whispered.

He leaned toward her and spoke quietly. "Is this another American custom? Eating with your fingers?"
His gentle tone belied the shock plastered on his face.

"Yes. Is something wrong with that?" Rather than
take offense, Leah reminded herself that Fitzwilliam
had asked her to bear with him.

"Brother, would you please pass me that delicious-
looking bread?" Elizabeth made direct eye contact with
Fitzwilliam, and his face unpuckered instantly.

"No. No. Not at all." He smiled, and she smiled back
at him, relieved that everything was okay.

He picked up the plate and handed it to Leah. She
passed it to Jake, and he handed it to Elizabeth. Their
hands lingered longer than necessary. Leah frowned,
then shook herself mentally, driving the image from
her mind.

During the whole time they ate their meal of mashed
potatoes, Swedish meatballs, cream sauce, carrots with
parsley sauce, kavring bread with lingonberry jam and
apple pie with sweet whipped cream on it, her brothers
bombarded Fitzwilliam with a million questions. Mr.
Barrington answered each one graciously. He also po-
litely pointed out what he considered to be a faux pas
in dining: using the wrong fork.

Eating with her fingers.

Not using a knife to gather her food onto her fork.

Talking when her mouth wasn't empty and so on.

She paid close attention, knowing she would need to learn those things if they were to marry. After all, she wouldn't want to embarrass him or herself.

By the time the meal ended, however, Leah was torn. She enjoyed Fitzwilliam and found him extremely handsome and loved his accent, and she was grateful he showed her the correct way to do things, but being around him and talking to him wasn't anything like being around or talking to Jake. With Jake she could just be herself. She didn't have to worry about what fork to use or anything else. Now she was worried about everything.

Leah looked over at Jake. He and Elizabeth were engrossed in a conversation. Elizabeth's eyes lit up and she held on to Jake's every word. Was it her imagination, or was Jake leaning closer to Elizabeth than necessary? Leah stared. Feelings she'd never experienced before stirred inside her. Feelings she didn't understand.

Thankful her brothers occupied Fitzwilliam, Leah continued watching Jake interact with Elizabeth. Then, as if he sensed her watching him, his ear turned her way, and then his head, until those gunmetal-gray eyes that reminded her of a beautiful gray tabby cat locked onto hers. He offered her that lazy grin of his, and her heart tripped.

Jake turned to Elizabeth, "Excuse me a moment, Elizabeth." He shifted his focus back onto Leah. "Everything okay?"

"Sure." She nodded. "How about you?"

"Yep. Having a great time."

Was he having a great time because of Elizabeth? If so, why did that bother her?

"I'm here with you and your family, Leah. How could I not have a great time?" That lazy grin of his showed up again.

The heaviness lifted from her heart. Jake always had a way of making her feel better.

Jake sat on the porch swing, rocking his heels back and forth. Leah's brothers and their families had gone home hours before, and Fitzwilliam and his sister had finally left, too. The man didn't want to until Jake had assured Fitzwilliam he, too, was leaving as soon as he finished up a few evening chores for the Bowens. Truth be known, he'd had every intention of doing that very thing until Leah had invited him to stay for some Swedish bird nest cookies and milk.

Leah stood at the door holding a tray. Jake jumped up and opened the door for her. She set the tray on the table next to the porch swing and sat down. The swing creaked when he lowered his tall frame next to her.

She handed him a saucer of cookies and a glass of milk and grabbed the same for herself. He took a guzzle of milk and a bite of a cookie, which had strawberry jam in the thumbprint center hole and walnuts surrounding it. "So, how do you think dinner went?" he asked, brushing the crumbs off his lips and trousers.

Her hand froze midair. She placed the cookie back onto her plate and looked at him. "It was okay. I know one thing, though."

"What's that?"

"I can see why Rainee despised all those rules. There's so many of them. Who cares what fork you use or if you eat with your fingers? Fingers were here before forks, anyway. Even though I know I need to learn all those things..." She shrugged and left her sentence hanging.

"What are you talking about?" Jake continued to eat his cookies and drink his milk.

"Well, during dinner Fitzwilliam pointed out things I was doing wrong."

"Doing wrong? Like what?"

"Oh, that I ate with my fingers, that I used the wrong fork, that spouses never sat next to each other at the table. That children were to be seen and not heard and never should have been allowed to sit with the adults at the dinner table. I know he's only trying to help."

Jake didn't agree, but he'd keep that thought tucked inside. Leah needed to decide for herself if that Barrington fellow was the man for her.

"He also thought it was strange that we had a French maid who served Swedish food."

Jake frowned. "What's wrong with that?"

"I don't know. I didn't ask. To tell you the truth, I didn't care why." She giggled.

"What's so funny?"

"I was thinking about the look on his face when Haydon told him we raised pigs. He couldn't believe anyone would want to be around those 'smelly, filthy animals.'" Leah imitated his British accent. "Then Rainee chimed in about how before she'd come here she was scared to death of them and now she loved them. I thought he was going to choke on his food, he gasped so hard."

Jake laughed over that one. "All joking aside, what do you think of Fitzwilliam? You think he might be the one?" He slowly raised the last bite of his cookie to his mouth and popped it in. Leah did the same. Waiting for her answer was pure torture.

"I'm not sure," she finally said several swallows later. Her answer did nothing to alleviate his fear of losing her forever.

Chapter Thirteen

Leah stretched in bed and glanced at the clock. 7:45. Last evening had been a long night. Jake hadn't left until after eleven. She yawned and wondered if he was as tired today as she was, especially because he had to get there even earlier than normal so he could finish his chores in order to go on their ride this morning. Before he'd left, Leah had invited Jake to go along with her and Fitzwilliam and his sister on a horseback ride around the ranch, and Jake had readily agreed. Had his readiness been because of Elizabeth? After all, he didn't seem to care for Fitzwilliam. He hadn't said as much, but she saw it in his eyes when he looked at the man.

She herself still wasn't sure how she felt about Fitzwilliam. He made her laugh, but not as much as Jake did, of course. Then again, he wasn't Jake, and she needed to remember that and give Fitzwilliam a chance. After all, she'd only known him all of two days.

She glanced at the clock again and sighed. 7:52. If she was going to get ready by the time they got here, she'd better get going.

Leah bathed in a tub of rose water. After drying off, she slid into a brown, split riding skirt and a tan blouse before lacing up her brown brogan boots. Today, she didn't have to worry so much about her appearance as she had the first two times she'd been around Fitzwilliam. And she knew Jake didn't care what she wore.

Down the stairs she skipped. She didn't know if her excitement stemmed from the idea of seeing Jake or because she was about to spend more time getting to know Fitzwilliam. Either way, happiness brightened her heart like the sunshine that now filled the clear blue skies outside.

"Morning, Mother," she chirped. Leah kissed her mother's soft cheek and grabbed a biscuit, two slices of bacon, and a cup of coffee and sat down at the table. "Thank you for letting me sleep." She folded the two slices of bacon between the biscuit and took a bite.

"You're welcome. I knew you didn't get to bed until late. Did you and Jake have a nice visit?"

She and Jake? Why didn't she ask about her and Fitzwilliam? "Jake and I always have fun. So—" she leaned forward with her elbows on the table "—what did you think of Fitzwilliam?"

Mother set her coffee down and looked at her. "He seems nice. Rather formal, though. It seemed like all he did was correct you. You sure you want to marry someone like that, Leah? Are you ready for a lifestyle filled with necessitates?"

The sunshine in her spirit dropped a notch. No. She wasn't sure. All she knew was that she'd craved it all her life. It would take some getting used to again, of that she was certain. Who better to help her and mentor her than the well-traveled, handsome Mr. Barrington? "Yes. I think I am."

Mother pursed her lips and nodded. "I hope so. And I hope you know what you're doing."

"I do, Mother." She scooted her chair out.

"Aren't you going to finish eating?"

"No. I'm not hungry. I'm too excited to eat." She looked around the tidy kitchen. "Where did Veronique put the lunch I asked her to pack?"

"In the pantry."

"Where is Veronique, anyway?"

"I sent her home. She needed a rest after last night."

"She sure did. Veronique and her sisters did an amazing job. They are such hardworking people. And so sweet. I really like them."

"Me, too."

"Well, I'd better run, Mother. I'm meeting Jake down at the barn at nine."

"Jake?"

"Yes, Jake. I invited him to go with us."

"I see."

Leah didn't like the look on her mother's face. "It's not like that, Mother. I invited him to come along to keep Elizabeth company."

Mother just smiled. A smile with a slight smirk to it, one Leah wasn't sure she liked. "Well, run along and have fun, dear. I'll see you later. Oh, I almost forgot. I'm dining with Charles, I mean, Mr. Barker, this evening."

Leah forced a smile. Just hearing those words made her cringe. This was so hard. She wanted her mother to be happy. She truly did. But the struggle was too much for her. She looked forward to getting to know Fitzwilliam better in hopes that he would want to marry her and take her away from this place and all its troubles as soon as possible.

"Okay." She gave her mother a quick kiss again, grabbed the food and a wrap, then flew out the door and down to the barn. "Jake." She swung the door open. Disappointment met her instead of Jake. Where was he?

She checked all the outbuildings and couldn't find him. Worry pounced on her. Surely he made it home safely last night, hadn't he? Leah saw Jess near the woodshed and hurried over to him. "Have you seen Jake?"

Jess leaned on the ax handle resting on a tree stump they used to split wood. "Good morning to you, too."

She tsked and rolled her eyes. "Morning, Jess. Now, have you seen Jake?"

Jess laughed. "Yes. He's standing right behind you."

Leah whirled. Behind her stood Jake with his arms crossed and a smile on his face. His horse grazed in a clearing in the trees.

"When did you get here?"

"Been here and back home already."

"You have?" She took in his freshly clean appearance.

"Yep."

"What time did you get here this morning?"

"Five."

"I told him he didn't have to come in at all today, but he wouldn't hear of it," Jess interrupted. "Guess he can't stay away from this place. Can't imagine why." Jess shot her a cocky grin, then looked at Jake with an approving nod.

Jake didn't seem at all fazed by Jess's comment. Perhaps he didn't get her brother's meaning. She sure did. Heat flooded her cheeks. She couldn't believe her brother would imply something like that. When was everyone going to get it through their brains she and Jake were just friends?

"Me, neither." Jake winked at her.

Jake winked at her! And right in front of her brother. What was he thinking? Her whole neck and face warmed this time. To cover her embarrassment, she turned and strode to the barn, calling over her shoulder, "You coming?"

"Yep." His chuckle followed her and continued when he caught up with her. "Why are your cheeks so red?"

She stopped and planted her hands on her hips. "Jake Lure, don't you ever do that again." Her eyes narrowed in a way she hoped looked menacing and angry.

He looked at her with all the innocence of a newborn lamb. "Do what?"

"You know very well what you did."

He raised his palms upward. "What?"

"I can't believe you winked at me. And in front of my brother, no less. What is wrong with you? You'll give him the wrong idea about us."

"He already has the wrong idea. Or…maybe not." Jake walked away, leaving her standing there with her mouth open and her eyebrows buried under her bangs.

Jake couldn't believe what he'd just said. He had to leave before he saw her reaction. He grabbed three halters and headed to the corral. Just as he reached the corral gate, Leah caught up to him. "Which horses do you want for Elizabeth and that fellow?" he asked.

"That fellow has a name. *Fitzwilliam.* And don't think you can say something like that to me and just walk off, either. What did you mean 'or maybe not'?"

He gazed down at her, chastened. "Was just teasing, Leah. You should know me by now."

"I do. But I thought you quit all that heckling stuff long ago."

"I did. That wasn't heckling. That was teasing.

There's a difference." He didn't dare tell her he'd really meant it. The truth was he'd started to develop feelings for her. Real ones that went beyond friendship. And that scared the liver out of him. Especially since she was leaving. *Get a grip, Jake. Act normal, and she'll take a hint to drop it.* "Okay. What horse you want for Fitzwilliam?"

She looked on the verge of giving him another tongue-lashing, but at the last second she sighed and the anger dropped. "Thank you for helping me get them. How about Moose for Fitzwilliam and Magpie for Elizabeth? I'm not sure how much riding either of them have done, but Moose and Magpie are the gentlest ones we have. I'll have to get out the sidesaddle for Elizabeth, though. Oh, no— It hasn't been used for so long. I hope it's clean. I didn't even think to check."

"It's clean. I rubbed all the saddles and tack down the other day."

"Oh. Okay. Thank you, Jake. I don't know what I'd do without you."

If only she meant that literally. With an inward sigh, Jake gathered two of the horses while Leah haltered Ginger, a horse named after Abby had outgrown naming the Bowens' animals.

Inside the barn, hay dust floated in the air. Horse, grain and cleaned leather smells intertwined with Leah's rose scent.

Jake went to work readying the animals. "You excited about today? Or nervous?"

Leah tugged on the cinch and glanced at him. "Both. I'm just glad you'll be there."

"Me, too." But not for the same reason she was, he was certain. He wanted to spend more time with Leah and keep an eye on that phony dandy. If only Leah had noticed all the times Fitzwilliam had shown disdain over the way she and her family did things. The man not only hid it well, but also masked it before Leah caught him. She thought he was trying to help. *Lord, open her eyes to the truth.*

"Did you enjoy your time with Elizabeth?" Leah grabbed the saddle strings and tied the food sack onto her saddle, then gathered the reins.

"Yep. Sure did. She's lots of fun. Interesting and easy to talk to. And she isn't concerned like her brother is if something ain't done properly."

"She isn't, is she? From what little I've seen, she's the complete opposite of Fitzwilliam."

That's for sure.

They finished readying the rest of the horses in silence. When the task was complete, they led them outside, looped the reins around the hitching post in front of the barn and sat on the bench together, waiting for the Barringtons to arrive.

Minutes passed and still no sign of them. "What time is it, anyway?"

Jake pulled his pocket watch out from inside his vest and clicked it open. "Eight forty-five."

"They should be here any minute now."

"Yep."

Another moment slipped into the sunshine.

"Jake, do you miss your family?" She didn't look at him when she asked it. Her attention was riveted on her lap.

"Yep. A bunch."

"How come you left them to move out here?"

"My farm here belonged to my real Papa's parents. When my grandparents died, they left it to me. Mama

wanted me to sell it. Couldn't do it. I wanted to keep
Papa's legacy going. So, I moved out here."

"Was your family upset that you did?"

"Not upset so much as sad. I was, too, for a while,
but it was the right thing for me."

Leah sat there in the sunshine, head down, her gaze
going nowhere other than her lap. "I wonder if my family will be sad when I move, too."

He knew he would be. His heart said so. "Sure they
will. Will you miss them?" *Will you miss me?* That
question remained locked inside his heart.

"Sweet twinkling stars above! Are you kidding? Of
course I will. I'll miss them more than a hot fire in the
dead of winter."

"Then why are you leaving?"

Hooves pounding on the hard ground and rattling
tack entered the silence that followed. Jake forced his
attention from Leah onto the ranch yard. Annoyance
slid through him at the sight. *Oh, joy.*

"Oh. They're here." Leah pushed herself off the
bench and scurried toward the buggy.

"Whoa," the driver said from up front, covering Leah's boots with dust when the horses stopped.

"Hey, George. Nice to see you again." Jake smiled at
the sixty-five-year-old man who helped Bartholomew,
the town smithy. Jake reached up and shook hands with
the man.

"Nice ta see you, too, Jake. How's that farm of yours
doin'? You sure do have a nice spread." Envy filled
George's eyes.

From the corner of his eyes, Jake noticed Fitzwilliam heeding George's words. "Doing good. Wheat's
growing like weeds."

"Glad to hear it. If ya ever want to sell that place,

you just let me know. I'd love to have it. Me and half the people in Paradise Haven, that is." He cackled.

Jake knew George could never afford it, but it made him feel good the man thought so much of his place. "Not selling, George. I'm here to stay."

"Kinda figured that."

Elizabeth stood in the buggy. Jake hurried to her side and raised his hand to help her down. "Morning, Elizabeth." The woman made a pretty picture dressed in a light blue riding jacket, dark blue skirt and dark blue riding hat. Still, Leah in her plain brown-and-tan riding outfit made an even more splendid picture. Leah could wear a rag and outshine any woman around.

"Good morning, Jake. 'Tis a pleasure to see you again." Every time Elizabeth looked at him, admiration and a look he could only describe as dreamlike softened her large brown eyes.

"What's he doing here?"

Jake glanced over at Fitzwilliam, who was once again scowling at him. He was starting to see a pattern here. This time Jake was flattered by it. It meant Fitzwilliam thought he was a threat to his and Leah's relationship. But he wasn't going to let the man think his look bothered him. So, just for the sake of doing it, Jake sent him an intimidating glare and was pleased to see the momentary shock on Fitzwilliam's face.

"I invited him." Leah tilted her chin like a proud filly. That look said Fitzwilliam had better not say another word about it.

Fitzwilliam must have gotten the hint because he said nothing more but shot Jake a look that could have melted steel. Then, like dew evaporating from the flowers, Fitzwilliam plastered on a phony smile and angled it toward Leah. "Capital idea. I'm sure Elizabeth will enjoy having him about." He sent a smug look of his own back to Jake.

Jake closed his eyes. The two of them were acting like two roosters fighting over the same prized hen. Someone had to lose, and unfortunately it would probably be Jake.

"How are you this morning, Fitzwilliam?" Leah didn't have to look up as far to see Fitzwilliam's face as she did Jake's. She loved Jake's massive height.

"Very well, thank you. And you?"

"Great." Leah looked up at the pale blue sky that smothered her face with warm kisses. "It sure is a beautiful day for a ride."

"Yes. Yes it is. Shall we get to it, then? I'm quite anxious to see how large this ranch of yours is."

What an odd thing for him to say. Why did he care how big her family's ranch was?

"Driver." Fitzwilliam turned to the man still seated on the buckboard. "You may take your leave now. But be back by here by half past six. Do not be late."

George nodded, reined the horses around, gave a quick swat on their rumps and mumbled that his name was George and something else Leah couldn't hear plainly about people who thought they were better than other folks.

"Well, let's get going. We have a long ride ahead of us." Leah looped her arm through his and started toward the horses. "You two coming?" She looked over her shoulder at Jake and Elizabeth.

"Right behind you," Jake answered as he gathered Elizabeth's hand, tucked it through his arm and sent Elizabeth a lazy smile. The same one he gave Leah.

Again jealousy snaked through her. She needed to get a grip on it, and soon.

Mere feet from their horses, Fitzwilliam stopped and glanced around.

"What's wrong?" Leah followed his trail of vision.

"Where's the horse I shall be riding?"

Huh? Did the man need glasses? Right in front of him stood four horses tied to the hitching post. "Uh. Your horse, Moose, is right here." She patted the gelding's white-spotted rump.

"Moose?" One of Fitzwilliam's eyebrows rose and the corners of his mouth fell.

"Yes, Moose." At his look of confusion she went on to explain. "When my sister Abby was younger, she begged my brother Haydon to let her name the animals on the ranch. He couldn't resist her sweet, angelic face so he agreed. I'm afraid you will discover we have many animals with very strange names."

"Ah. I see."

Leah could tell by the low pucker of his mouth that he didn't, but that was okay. Everyone in her family now found the bizarre names humorous. They were just part of what made her family her family.

Fitzwilliam walked up to Moose's side and eyed the saddle. "I've never ridden a saddle like this before."

Leah's countenance fell with her shoulders. Not another faux pas. How long would it take her to learn his ways? And did she really want to? A question to definitely ask herself later.

"But—" he held up one finger "—I shall find it a challenge. And I am quite fond of a good challenge." His gaze slithered from the horse to Jake.

Leah wondered what that was all about. "Oh good. I'm so glad. What kind of saddle do you normally use?"

"One without this thing." Fitzwilliam rested his hand on the saddlehorn.

"It's called a horn," Jake said as he passed them and untied Elizabeth's horse. "This is your horse, Elizabeth. May I?"

Leah watched as Jake placed his large hands around Elizabeth's petite waist. His muscles bulged as he hoisted her effortlessly onto the saddle.

"Thank you, Jake." Did the woman have something in her eyes? She sure blinked them often enough.

Jake smiled at Elizabeth then mounted his horse. His gaze landed on Leah as she stood on the ground among the horses. Their eyes locked. Leah smiled, and so did Jake.

"I do not see another horse with a sidesaddle. Where is your horse?" Fitzwilliam's breath brushed against Leah's ear. She wanted to swish it away and tell him not to talk so close to her ear.

"Oh. This one's mine." She untethered her horse, gathered the reins near the bit and pushed backward on them. "Back, Lambie. Back." Her horse did as she asked it to.

Fitzwilliam followed Leah around the horse, examining as he went. "Where's your sidesaddle?"

"I don't use one. I tried it once and hated the thing." She slipped one rein under Lambie's neck and tossed it over the horse's mane. The other she held in her hand while she placed her boot in the stirrup and swung up and into the saddle, then gathered the other rein.

She glanced down at Fitzwilliam. His expression went from a gaping mouth and bulging eyes to narrowed eyes and a wrinkled nose. Now, what had she done wrong this time? Her sigh was barely contained.

"What's wrong *now?*" She hadn't meant for the frustration to fly out of her mouth, but it had anyway.

"Brother." At the sound of Elizabeth's voice, his features softened.

"Just another American custom to get used to is all." With a shake of his head, he mounted his horse.

Leah heard him mumble about how the saddle was the most uncomfortable thing he'd ever sat on.

She wanted to laugh at the awkward picture he made up there, but instead she rode up next to him and said, "I thought you loved adventure."

Jake's chuckle nearly sent her over the edge of her own laughter, but she caught it just in time.

Fitzwilliam snapped his neck in Jake's direction. "I do." He narrowed his eyes at Jake and then turned a forced smile on her. "Make haste, my dear. And let us go."

To hide her frustration at Fitzwilliam's open display of abhorrence toward Jake, Leah nudged the heels of her brogans into her horse's side, leaving the others to trail behind her.

It was going to be a long day.

As they headed out of the ranch yard, Jake pulled alongside her and Elizabeth next to him. Fitzwilliam rode on the other side.

They rode through the sparse fir trees past several blooming bushes.

"Those are quite lovely. What are they?"

"Syringa bushes," Jake answered Elizabeth.

"They smell divine. And those? What are they, please?"

Leah followed Elizabeth's pointed finger.

"Kinnikinnick shrubs," Leah answered this time.

Leah breathed deeply the strong citrus scent of the

ground-hugging kinnikinnick shrubs with their leathery leaves and pink blossoms mingled with the sweet scent of the syringa bushes.

"I must say, it's quite handsome up here." Fitzwilliam's compliment warmed Leah.

Branches resting on top of the green forest floor crunched under the horses' hooves. Over the lush green rolling hills they rode. Fields of red poppies waved in the breeze that was ever-present.

They headed toward the forest at the base of the mountain. The spiked flowers of Indian paintbrushes dotted the grassy hilltops and field edges with their bright orange and yellow.

Leah explained to Fitzwilliam what they were and about the rich volcanic ash soil and how it came to be there. Fitzwilliam appeared to be interested, but he was more intrigued with where their property line ended.

"Fitzwilliam, what's it like in England?" Leah asked.

"It depends on what part of England one is at. Some places are quite similar to here, very lush and green. Some are not. One obvious difference is that there are no castles or brick mansions in America. Not that I've noticed in my travels, at least."

"You told me about some of your travels, but where all have you traveled to?"

"As I said when we were dining, I have journeyed the world. I've been to France, Ireland, Italy, Germany, Switzerland, Greece…" Fitzwilliam went on and on about where all he'd been, telling her nothing exciting about any of the places, even though she'd asked him questions. Instead, he talked about his many accolades, and all he'd accomplished and his great wealth.

Sorry she had asked him now, Leah kept riding, waiting and hoping the man would stop talking. She knew he was trying to impress her, but for some reason his voice was starting to grate on her nerves. Strange, Jake's voice didn't have that effect on her. She loved listening to him and could for hours and hours without wishing he'd be quiet. Even though Jake was a man of few words, he was a great conversationalist, and not chatty like Fitzwilliam. Maybe Mr. Barrington was just nervous. Tillie, a widowed woman at church, chattered like a magpie when she got nervous. At least she hoped that was the case with Fitzwilliam.

Long, grueling minutes later, Fitzwilliam finally stopped prattling and pulled a long drink from his canteen. Leah took the opportunity to focus on Jake. Leather rasped as she shifted in her saddle to talk to him, but he and Elizabeth were laughing and talking. Leah envied Elizabeth. Jake always had something interesting to say.

Hours later, they stopped and dismounted at a clear spring that ran year-round on the top of the ancient cedar grove mountain.

Jake walked up behind her. "So, how was the ride up here?"

Leah leaned back to make sure Fitzwilliam wasn't close enough to hear her. She blew out a long breath when she saw him and his sister at the base of one of the cedar trees that was at least ten feet in diameter. They gazed up at it, completely engrossed and talking animatedly about it.

Leah turned her attention back onto Jake. "The man never stopped talking. Some of what he had to say was interesting, but most of it was about himself. What do I do?"

"I'll pay more attention and try to help you out, okay?"

"You'd do that for me?"

"Yep. That's what friends are for."

"Oh, Jake, you must make haste and come see this." Elizabeth hooked her arm through Jake's and led him to the base of one of the mammoth cedar trees.

Jake glanced back over his shoulder. Even though he was being led away, Leah knew he would be there for her when she needed him to be. That's just the way it was between the two of them.

Fitzwilliam strode up to her and laced her hand through his arm. "You are quite a handsome woman, Leah. I'm blessed you have chosen to respond to my post. I think we shall get along quite famously. Oh, and as my dear sister so kindly pointed out to me, I must apologize for talking so much. A case of nerves, I fear. I will try to contain myself from here on in."

"Well, if you get to talking too much, I'll let you know, okay?"

He took a step back with shock, then chuckled. "Yes. Fair enough, madam."

"I'm hungry. How about you?"

"Yes. I am quite famished."

"Jake. Elizabeth," Leah hollered and tugged herself away from Fitzwilliam's grasp. "Time to eat." She headed to her saddle and untied the food sack. Jake grabbed the blanket he'd brought and spread it out in a clearing near the spring.

Making sure Leah and Elizabeth were seated, the men sat down. Fitzwilliam sat so close their legs touched. Uncomfortable with the intimacy of that, Leah grabbed the food out of the sack and, as indiscreetly as possible, positioned her body closer to Jake, without touching him.

Leah placed roasted pork sandwiches, cheese slices and the Swedish rye crackers she'd made onto four napkins. She pulled a butter knife from the bag and set it on the blanket, then reached inside the sack and pulled out the small jar of lingonberry jam. Grasping the preserve jar lid, Leah twisted the lid hard but it wouldn't budge.

"Allow me." Fitzwilliam took the jar from her. He strained to open it but again it wouldn't open, so he discreetly set it down on the blanket.

Jake picked it up, and opened it with one try.

Leah smiled at him. Pride oozed from her.

"Aren't you glad we loosened it for you, my man?" Fitzwilliam said.

Leah curved her face toward Jake. Making sure no one could see her, she rolled her eyes.

Jake's eyes twinkled in acknowledgment. "Couldn't of done it without you, Fitzwilliam," he said, and Leah hid her grin.

With all the food out and settled, Leah gazed at them. "Shall we pray?" Fitzwilliam frowned, then nodded. "Jake, would you do us the honors?"

"I can." Fitzwilliam chimed in.

"Oh. Uh. How about next time since I've already asked Jake? After all, it would be rude, would it not, to tell him I've changed my mind?" she asked as if Jake wasn't right there to hear. Which he was, and she knew he'd get exactly what she was doing.

"Oh. Yes. How rude of me. Go ahead, Jake," Fitzwilliam said it as if it were his idea.

"Thank you, Fitzwilliam." A knowing look passed between Leah and Jake.

One thing was for sure—Jake could pray. His prayers were short, sweet and filled with gratitude. The man loved Jesus. Did Fitzwilliam? She had never thought to ask him about his faith. That should have been her first question. She'd been so desperate to leave she hadn't even thought about that. Shame swept over her heart. Everyone started to eat, so Leah made a mental note to ask him later.

Four gray-and-white camp robber birds swooped down from the trees, begging for food. Leah, Jake and Elizabeth tossed morsels of the crackers to the birds, but Fitzwilliam sat watching, his face scrunched. Where was the man who said he loved adventure?

All through their meal, Fitzwilliam talked nonstop. Jake tried to interrupt him several times and had even managed to get a few words in. No longer able to bear his prattling, Leah blurted, "Are you nervous again?"

Fitzwilliam stopped and looked at her, eyes blinking.

Jake chuckled.

Fitzwilliam shot a glaring look Jake's way.

"I'm sorry," Leah said. "I must be getting tired. Forgive my bluntness." Truth was, she was neither sorry nor tired. She was just ready to get this day behind her.

Jake had enjoyed every minute of their outing, mostly because Leah was getting a glimpse of the pompous Mr. Magpie. At the rate the man was going, with any luck at all Leah would send him packing before sundown. Even then, it wouldn't be soon enough for Jake.

"Hate to break up the party, but if we're going to get you home in time for George to pick you up, we'd best head on back now."

"Oh, yes," Leah chimed in. "I forgot about that. Thank you, Jake." Her gratitude sparkled through her eyes. Eyes he'd come to read very well.

Jake stood and offered her a hand.

Fitzwilliam was on his feet faster than it took to pull the trigger on a gun and snatched Leah's hand before it ever reached Jake's. Jake wanted to yank his hand off of Leah's, but he had to remember that he wasn't the one courting her. He was there to be a chaperone. A chaperone with a motive.

They rode into the yard and tethered their horses to the hitching post.

George was already there.

"I'll take care of the horses, Leah."

"Thank you." For Jake's ears only, she said, "When you get done, come up to the house, okay?"

He gave her a short nod.

Elizabeth strolled toward him, looking as fresh as when she'd first arrived. "Thank you, Jake. I don't remember when I've had a more lovely time."

"Didn't do anything."

"Yes. Yes, you did. You allowed me to be myself. I didn't have to perform." She looped her arm through his and led him away from everyone. "If my brother heard me say this, he would have a fit of apoplexy, but I cannot bear being around the people in our society any longer. Every move you make is watched and recorded. Everything is judged by who your family is and how much money they make.

"And of course you must marry someone of good breeding and of good fortune. I care not one whit about those things." She glanced around, and peace settled in the depths of her eyes. "I love it here. It's so peaceful. There's no one you have to impress. Well—" she giggled "—unless you consider my brother. But him, I can manage." She smiled.

Jake nodded, wondering why she was telling him all of this.

"Elizabeth, come. We must away," Fitzwilliam said from across the other side of the buggy.

"'Must away'? What does that mean?" Jake asked Elizabeth.

"We must take our leave now."

"Oh. Evening, George. See you made it back with plenty of time to spare." He glanced at Fitzwilliam, who once again glared at him. If Fitzwilliam knew how much Jake enjoyed annoying him, the man wouldn't glower at Jake so much. The old heckler in Jake wanted to rise up, but he worked hard at keeping that part of him controlled and refused to stoop to the slimy snake's low level.

Like the gentleman he'd been raised to be, Jake helped Elizabeth into the buggy. She pulled her skirt in and gazed at him. "My brother is inviting Leah to come to the hotel for a spot of tea tomorrow afternoon. Please say you will come as well?"

"I'll come," he agreed. Anything to keep his eye on Leah and to keep that man from bamboozling her.

Seeing Elizabeth's eyes brighten, Jake hoped she wasn't getting the wrong idea about the two of them. There was no "them."

"Thank you. I am in need of a good friend right now."

Friend? The word yanked his smile down. Why did women only want to be his friend? What was wrong with him that they couldn't get past a friendship? Not that he was interested in anything more than friendship with Elizabeth, but she didn't know that.

"Capital. I shall see you on the morrow then. I am indeed looking forward to it."

Jake looked over at Fitzwilliam. The man beamed, but Leah didn't. Jake knew her well enough to see that she wasn't at all pleased. He hid his grin. With any luck at all, Fitzwilliam would soon be history.

Leah stood next to Jake and watched the buggy pull out of the yard. When it was safely out of earshot, she let out a long breath. "Am I ever glad that's over."

Jake chuckled.

"What? Aren't you?" Leah asked.

"Yep. Sure am."

Leah's relieved laughter surrounded him.

"Hey, I have an idea. You want to stay for supper? Don't know what we're having yet, and it'll be just me and Abby this evening, but I would love it if you would join us."

Jake wouldn't miss it. It was more time spent with Leah. Something he needed to take advantage of while he still had the chance. "Sounds good."

"Great." Her face brightened all the way. That brought a smile to Jake's heart and melted his insides like wax in the hot sun.

"I'll take care of the horses and see you inside."

"Okay. See you in a few minutes." She took a few steps and stopped. "Hurry up, okay?"

"Yep." He sure would.

Chapter Fourteen

"Abby, I'm home." Leah dashed into the house. "Abbers," she hollered as she went about checking the house for her sister only to find she was nowhere around. Knowing she would be home soon, Leah donned her apron and scrounged around for something to fix. Inside the warmer was a tin plate with a browned pie crust. She pulled it out and took a whiff. Swedish meat pie. One of her favorites. She shoved it back in the warmer and set the table with three place settings.

Heavy footsteps sounded on the porch.

Jake.

Her heart skipped a few beats. Leah ran to meet him at the door.

"Look what I found down at the barn."

Abby peeked around him and flashed a cheeky grin her way.

Leah shook her head. "You, Abbynormal, are a nut."

"I know." Her sister brushed past Jake. "Sorry I wasn't here to help with supper. I just got back from Phoebe's."

Jake stepped inside.

"How is Phoebe? And how does she like married life?"

"She loves it." Abby sighed. "I can't wait until I marry."

"You? You won't be eighteen for three more months."

"So? I still can't wait."

Leah sighed. "If I didn't want to leave here so badly, I wouldn't bother getting married."

"I don't understand you, Lee-Lee. Why do you want to move to the city when you have everything you need here? Including love." Abby yanked her head toward Jake.

"Abigail!" Leah gasped. Heat rushed up her neck and into her face. She swung her attention to Jake, standing near the table and wearing his lazy grin. He seemed nonplussed by Abby's comment. Leah spun around. "Er, um. I need to get dinner." She scurried to the stove.

Leah had no idea how to react to Abby's implication that Jake loved her. Oh sure, she knew he loved her as a friend, but the man wasn't *in* love with her. He couldn't be. She wouldn't let him. She was leaving. And love would get in the way of her plans to escape the nightmares that were almost a nightly occurrence now and to flee the place that took her father's life. She had to stay focused on her mission—to marry someone from New York. Mr. Barrington, to be precise.

Leah brought the pie to the table and set it down. "What would you like to drink, Jake? Milk? Tea? Coffee?"

"Milk sounds good. I can get it."

"No. No. You are a guest. Sit down and I'll get it." Leah returned with a pitcher of milk and some cheese.

Jake rose from the table, pulled out her chair and waited until she was seated before he sat down again.

While Abby was busy slicing the pie into five pieces, Leah filled their glasses with milk and set the pitcher on the table, then reached for Jake's plate.

"Two pieces, Abbs."

"Hungry, are we?"

"No. This is Jake's plate."

"I know that." Abby scooped out two large pieces.

With everyone's plates filled, Leah looked over at Jake. "Would you mind praying, Jake?"

"Nope. Not at all."

They bowed their heads.

"Father, thank You for this food. For the hands that prepared it. For great friends. And for Leah."

Leah frowned. Wasn't she a great friend?

"Bless this food. Amen."

"Amen." Abby picked up her fork and dived into the ground meat pie. "I'm so hungry I could eat a whole pig," she said around the food in her mouth, but Leah barely heard her. She was still wondering about Jake's prayer.

Jake took three bites and a drink of milk. "This is good. Did you make it?"

"Huh?" Leah glanced at Jake.

"I asked if you made this."

"No. Mother or Veronique did."

"Don't you cook?"

"She sure does. She's a great cook, too," Abby answered for her sister.

"That right?"

"Yes. She does all kind of things really well. She can cook, clean, sew, crochet, knit. Just about anything a person would need to make a good wife."

"Abby!" Leah nearly came out of her chair. "What

is wrong with you this evening? You're making our guest uncomfortable."

Abby looked over at Jake. "He doesn't look uncomfortable to me. And he isn't a guest. He's family. Or hopefully he will be very soon."

"That's enough!" Leah shot her sister a you'd-better-stop-it-now glare before turning to face Jake. "I'm sorry, Jake. You'll have to excuse my sister. I don't know what's come over her."

"Doesn't bother me." His shoulder hiked. He cut off a chunk of his pie and put it in his mouth as if nothing had been said.

Leah didn't know what to think or say. Nothing he said or did tonight made any sense.

"So, how did your day go with Fitzwilliam?" Without waiting for Leah's answer, Abby asked, "You aren't serious about that man, are you, Lee-Lee?" Abby wrinkled her nose in disgust before taking a bite of cheese.

"I'm not serious about anyone, Abbs. I'm just trying to get to know Fitzwilliam to see if we can make a marriage work. That's all."

"Whatever you say, Lee-Lee." Abby turned to Jake. "What do you think of Elizabeth, Jake? She doesn't seem anything like her brother. She's nice."

"Fitzwilliam is nice," Leah jumped in quickly, but her voice didn't sound too convincing even to her own ears.

"I was asking Jake, Leah."

"She's nice enough. Must admit. She isn't anything like I thought she'd be."

"What do you mean?" Leah tilted her head in Jake's direction.

"She hates the city. Wants to be a farmer's wife. To cook and clean and raise animals."

"Probably yours, no doubt," Abby mumbled, but Leah heard her nonetheless and was certain Jake had, too.

"Does she know how hard farm life can be?" Leah picked up her glass and took a drink of her milk.

"Don't know. She didn't say. Only said she loved it out here and preferred it over her lifestyle."

Leah pondered Jake's words. Surely she must attend balls and dinner parties all the time. The woman got to travel all over the world to exotic places meeting people from all sorts of cultures. Something Leah only dreamed about doing. How could Elizabeth prefer this lifestyle to her perfect one?

"There's more to life than parties and balls, Lee-Lee." Abby's voice popped Leah's thoughts.

"I know that, Abbs." She allowed her hot annoyance to drift through her voice. "But you've never been to them. You don't know how fun they are. Or how special it was to have Father whirl you around the dance floor." Leah closed her eyes. Her heart ached afresh at the memory of her father dancing with her.

The backs of her eyes stung.

Unable to keep the tears from coming, she scraped her chair back and bolted out of the house. Dodging willow bushes, syringa shrubs, cottonwood trees and pines, she fled deep into the forest. She came upon a felled log amid a batch of ferns, where she plopped down, placed her face in her hands and sobbed.

Minutes later, the log moved, and without looking, she knew it was Jake.

Jake sat on the log and slipped his arm around Leah. "Come here."

Tear-soaked eyes gazed up at him. Seeing her like

this, so sad and so shaken, broke his heart. He wished he could take her pain onto himself. Gently, he pressed her head into his chest. "It's okay."

"It hurts so badly. I miss him so much."

"I know. I still miss my papa, too."

"You—you do?" She pulled back, her eyes questioning him.

"Yep."

"But you said…"

"Know what I said about the papa I have now, and I meant it. It did get easier seeing my mama with him, but I never said I didn't miss my flesh-and-blood papa."

"What do you miss about him?" Tears shimmered on her lashes.

Jake brushed them away with his thumb and wiped them on his pant leg. "Everything."

"Everything?"

"Yep. When he first died, I thought the pain would never end. Felt about as alone and lost as a wayward sheep." He tucked his finger under her chin. "Leah, we all need someone who understands how we feel. Someone that'll listen to us. You know I'm here for you, right? That I understand what you're going through."

Leah's chest heaved in choppy breaths and the floodwaters came gushing out again.

He pushed himself off the log and pulled her into his arms. His heart wept with her.

"It hurts so badly." She'd already said that.

"I know."

"I miss him." She'd already said that, too. But it was okay. All of it.

"I know. Believe me, I know."

Moments later her tears let up again and, with a sigh, she backed out of the circle of his arms. They now felt empty without her. Alone even. He wanted to pull her back to him, but didn't. "Tell me. What are some of the things you miss about your father?"

"Father always made me laugh. I miss that. I miss our talks. I miss how he used to tuck me into bed every night and pray with me. He made me feel so special. Treasured, even. Like a real princess. That's what he used to call me, you know."

"That's important to you? Feeling like a princess?"

"Yes."

"Why?"

Her shrug was a lazy, off-handed one. "Mostly because it reminds me of my father. It makes me feel like he's still here with me. And I need that. Especially when—" Suddenly she sat straight up and shook her head. "Oh. Um. Listen. I'd better get back to the house. Abby's probably worried sick about me." She scurried ahead of him through the trees, her feet and skirt whooshing and crackling as she did.

"Leah, wait!" It took ten steps before Jake caught up to her and stopped her, turning her toward him. "What were you going to say, Leah?"

"I don't want to talk about it anymore, okay? It hurts too badly." That was the third time she'd said that.

The loss of a parent was something one didn't get over easily, but Leah should have healed far more than this by now. It had been a long time. Many, many years. Something was wrong with this whole situation. Jake really wanted to know what was tormenting her. To press the issue. But her pleading, bloodshot eyes kept him from probing further. He frowned, keeping his questions inside with a hard fist of control. "Can I pray with you?"

Leah nodded. "I'd like that."

Jake gathered her hands in his and bowed his head. "Father, You know how much Leah misses her father. Comfort her as only You can. Wrap Your arms around her. Let her know that while she may no longer have her earthly father here with her, that, You, her Heavenly Father, will always be with her, that You never leave her nor forsake her. Help her to find comfort in those words for they're Your words. And Father, this thing that is hurting Leah so deeply, touch that area and heal it as only You can. Surround her with Your love and Your grace. In Jesus's name. Amen." Jake raised his head and his gaze touched Leah's.

"Thank you, Jake." She sniffed, never removing her eyes from his. Instead they searched his, probing deeper and deeper. For what, he didn't know, but he allowed her to keep prying until she found whatever it was she was searching for. Her blue eyes went from hurt to grateful then to... To what? He didn't know. He only knew they held a soft warmth he'd never seen before.

Something in that moment changed in her. He wanted to ask what it was, but deep in his gut, he knew now was not the time. Now was the time for him to be still and let her have her way. Her hands remained buried in his, and he didn't release them because something was going on between them. Something spiritual. As if their souls were connecting on a deeper level.

"Leah!" The desperation in Abby's voice caused them both to blink.

Leah slipped her hands out of his, but her eyes kept meeting his until Abby arrived. "We're over here!"

In his heart, he knew the connection that had begun hadn't been severed, just put on hold.

"Finally. Where'd you go? I was so worried about

you, Lee-Lee." Abby threw her arms around Leah. "Are you okay?"

"Yes, Abbs. Everything is fine." Her gaze touched on his again and the connection was back. When the time was right, he'd find out just what had happened.

Abby looked at him, then at Leah. "Good. Now that I know you're okay, I'm going back to the house and finish eating." She glanced between them again and scuttled away.

Bless her heart.

One more glance into each other's eyes, and they headed back to the house in silence, but it wasn't uncomfortable. Their minds were intertwined with thoughts and words that had yet to be spoken.

Dear Mr. Darcy
Something happened in the forest today. My feelings for Jake have changed. I'm not sure just how, but during the whole time we were talking, when he prayed for me, and even afterward, something happened between us. I feel somehow closer to him. Which scares me. I don't want to care about Jake in that way. It will ruin everything. All my plans. I have to go now. I need to pray about this. I will talk to you later, Mr. Darcy.

Leah shut her diary and locked it in her nightstand. She lay down with her hand above her head and closed her eyes, letting her heart say the prayer she didn't have the words to utter.

When she woke up the next morning, she rushed through her toiletries and hurried into the kitchen.

"Morning, Mother." Leah kissed her cheek. "Morning, Abbs."

"Good morning," they both replied.

"What's for breakfast? I'm starving."

"Äggröra and bacon."

"Scrambled eggs sound good." Leah fixed her plate, grabbed a cup of coffee and sat down at the table.

Leah dived into her food. Not having eaten much last night, she was famished this morning.

"Leah, I hope you don't mind, but there's been a change of plans today."

"What do you mean, Mother?"

"Well, Charles and I ran into the Barringtons at the hotel last night, and we invited them to sit with us. Mr. Barrington seems like a nice man. A bit too talkative for me, but he's very informative and highly intelligent. And he is an extremely savvy businessman. Anyway, Charles invited them to a gathering he's having at his home this evening."

Leah noticed Mother didn't bother to correct calling Mr. Barker by his first name this time. That meant she really was serious. Leah sent up a quick prayer about moving away from there faster and for the strength she needed to be tolerant for her mother's sake. "Oh? What kind of gathering?"

"Well, it's more than a gathering, really. A friend of Charles is passing through Paradise Haven and is staying at Charles's hotel. Mr. Martonella and his company have agreed to perform for Charles. Charles thought your friends might enjoy it, so he invited them along with several other prominent business acquaintances. Mr. Barrington said you had plans to meet for tea." Mother reached into her apron pocket and pulled out a post, then handed it to Leah. "So he asked me to give this to you."

Leah took the envelope and gazed at the waxed seal with the embossed letter *B*. She slid her thumb under the red circle and opened the letter.

My dearest Leah,
I hope you do not mind, but there has been a change in plans. Rather than tea this afternoon, Mr. Barker has been kind enough to invite us to his home this evening to attend an opera. I have taken the liberty of accepting his invitation on your behalf. Also, Elizabeth has requested that you ask your friend Mr. Lure to join us. If this is not agreeable to either one of you, please send a post straightaway to let us know.
With fond regards,
Fitzwilliam Barrington

Leah folded the letter. She'd never been to an opera before. What did one even wear to such a thing? She'd already worn the two new bustle gowns she'd made, and there was no time to make a third.

"Well, what do you think, dear?"

Leah looked over at her mother. "I'm not sure. I'll talk to Jake and see what he thinks."

"Why do you care what Jake thinks?" Abby joined in the conversation, although her question was pointed.

"Because, Abbs. He was invited, too."

"So? What's that got to do with you? Elizabeth invited him."

Leah sighed. "I just meant I need to ask him if he wants to go. If not, then I need to send word to Elizabeth."

"Oh." Abby tossed the last bite of her toast with apple butter on it into her mouth. "If you say so." A twinkle sparked through her eyes.

The comments Abby had made the night before about Leah and Jake flittered through her mind again. Abby was up to something where she and Jake were concerned.

Well, Leah wasn't going to take the bait dangled in front of her. "Mother, I'll go see if Jake wants to accept Elizabeth's invitation. I'll be right back."

"Finish your breakfast first. Then go." Mother pointed to her loaded plate.

Paying no attention to her manners, Leah downed her food in record time and placed her dishes in the sink.

"Tell Jake hi for me. And give him a kiss for me, too. Or better yet, make it from you." Abby winked at her.

Leah sent Abby a warning look, glanced at her mother with a what-can-I-say shrug and made a dash for the door. When she stepped onto the porch, she heard her mother ask Abby, "What was that all about?"

Despite her wanting to know what Abby's response was, Leah didn't wait to hear it. She shuddered just thinking about what it would be.

Down at the barn, Leah searched for Jake, but he wasn't there. She checked the corrals, the chicken coop and the hog barn, but she couldn't find him at any of those places, either. She glanced over at Michael's house, wondering if he went there. Leah rushed over and knocked lightly on the door.

Michael stepped into view holding one of the twins. "Morning, Leah. Come on in."

"Good morning, Michael." She stepped inside and froze. By the fireplace stood Jake, holding the other twin. The baby looked tiny against Jake's giant form. What an image he made. One that made her heart flip.

Jake looked over at her and smiled. "Morning."

"Oh. Um. Good morning to you, too." The words fumbled from her mouth. Embarrassed by her stammering, Leah looked around for her sister-in-law. "Where's Selina?"

"Taking a nice, hot bath."

"Oh." Why had she come again? Her brain was no longer filling her in on such important details.

Michael raised his eyebrows with concern. "Did you need something?"

"What? Oh. Yes. I was looking for Jake, actually."

"Well, looks like you found him."

Leah took the baby from Michael. "How's Auntie's Joey doing?" she cooed and played with his chin until he smiled. She tore her attention from the baby. "When you get a minute, Jake, I need to talk to you."

"We can talk now. I was just getting ready to leave."

"You can't leave yet," Michael blurted.

"Why not?" she asked.

"Because. Who's going to help me with the twins? I can't take care of them myself." Her brother looked absolutely horrified.

Leah cleared her throat to stifle her laugh. "You don't need any help, Michael. Every time I've been over here, you've done just fine with them."

"Yes, but Selina wasn't in the tub then. And you, Mother or Abby was here. I've never been alone with them before."

"Well, it's time you start." She handed Joey back to him. "They won't bite. I promise. Come on, Jake."

Jake looked at her then at Michael, who looked as lost as a puppy in the woods.

"Come on, sis. Don't leave me like this. Please."

She couldn't stand seeing the look of desperation on Michael's face or indecision on Jake's, so she quit toying with them. "Okay. Fine. You win. What I have to ask Jake can wait."

She walked over to Jake. "May I?" She motioned toward Lottie. In a heartbeat, Jake handed her to Leah as if she were a hot coal.

Leah chuckled. Men. They wanted children but couldn't handle them for more than five minutes.

Minutes ticked by. Leah changed both the baby's diapers, put them in a pail inside the laundry room and went back into the living room. When her bustling was finished, Selina was already out and in the rocker with a baby in each arm. Her face glowed. "Mornin'."

"Good morning to you, too. How are you feeling today?"

"Happier than a squirrel with a sack full of hickory nuts."

Leah laughed. Her sister-in-law came up with the funniest sayings.

"Well, I'd better run along." Jake moved to the door. "Still have a couple of things to do before heading home to get ready for this afternoon."

Leah's attention went from Selina to Jake.

"Whatcha doin' this afternoon?" Selina set the rocking chair in motion.

"Going to some tea party." Jake rolled his eyes and shook his head.

"You? Going to a tea party? This I've got to see." Michael chortled.

"Can't picture you at no tea party neither, Jake."

"Yeah, well, somehow I got roped into one."

"Well, you don't have to go," Leah interjected with just a touch of annoyance.

"There's where you're wrong." He lowered his gaze at her, and it held no levity. "I do."

"Why? Nobody's making you go. If you don't want to, don't."

"I have my reasons for going." He took a quick glance at Michael and then back at her.

Leah frowned. What was that all about? "Well, the plans have changed, anyway."

"Oh, yeah?"

"Don't look so relieved, Jake. If you didn't like the idea of a tea party, you're not going to like this one, either."

Chapter Fifteen

Dread pitted into Jake. He couldn't imagine anything worse than a tea party with a pious, arrogant man who was out to steal his best friend. "You can tell me on the way to the barn."

They said their goodbyes and headed out the door and through the pine trees. *Yak yak yak yak*—the fast sound of a magpie greeted them along with an earthy scent of foliage and forest floor.

"So what's this change of plans?" Jake glanced down at her as he kept walking.

A twig snapped under Leah's foot. Her ankle twisted, and she lost her balance. Jake's hand shot out and steadied her. "You okay?"

"Fine. Thanks."

He gave a quick nod and a short frown.

"At breakfast this morning, Mother gave me a note from Fitzwilliam." Hopefully the note said he was leaving town. A man could wish, anyway.

"Mr. Barker's friend is in town with his opera company. They're going to perform for a group of Mr. Barker's friends and business acquaintances this evening. They invited the Barringtons and us to come."

"Us?" Jake throat constricted. A group of people? In a crowded room? His heart raced and his palms started to sweat just thinking about it.

"Jake?" Leah's hand rested on his arm. "You okay?"

He stopped and tried to force a smile on his face, to act like everything was fine, but it wasn't. He struggled to breathe.

"Take a deep breath, Jake." Her eyes locked on his, and he searched them for more direction.

"Come on, Jake. Take in a deep breath. You can do it," she coaxed.

He continued to follow her instructions until his breathing returned to normal. Because of Leah, this time it hadn't taken long.

"Thank you, Leah."

"You're welcome. I'm just glad you told me what happens to you. If you hadn't, I wouldn't have known what was wrong or how to help you."

He nodded, grateful that he had shared his embarrassing problem with her. This was the first time the panic attack lasted only a minute or so. They resumed walking toward the ranch yard.

"I'll send word that you won't be going."

This time he grasped her arm and stopped her. "Didn't say I wasn't going."

"But how can you?"

"Is it indoors or outdoors?"

"Um. I don't know. Mother might. Let's go ask her."

"No. You ask her. I'll be down at the barn. Have to finish mucking stalls. Then I'll be done."

"I don't understand why my brothers give you such dirty jobs. Why don't they have the hired hands do it?"

"They didn't give them to me. I offered."

"Why would you do that?"

"Why not? I'm a farmer, remember? Not some high-falutin man who thinks he's too good to scoop manure. It's what I do. It's how I make my living."

"I didn't mean to offend you, Jake. I know you're not like Mr. Barrington."

"How'd you know I was talking about him?"

"Because I've noticed you don't like him."

"That obvious, huh?"

"Yes, it is. And it's okay. You don't have to like him. I'm not sure I do, either."

"Does this mean you're not gonna marry him?" Hope pounced on him.

"I didn't say that."

"I'm confused."

Leah stopped and turned those beautiful sky-blue eyes up at him. "I'm not marrying for love. I'm marrying so I can leave."

"You'd really marry someone you didn't like? Or love?"

"Why's that so strange to you? It happens all the time. Besides, you asked me to marry you, and you don't love me."

"True. But you and I are good friends. We get along great."

"It still would have been a marriage of convenience."

"Well, yes. So, what's that got to do with what we're talking about?"

"I'm just saying that not everyone is lucky enough to find love. Some people have to marry for convenience's sake."

"True again. But you ought to at least like the person you're thinking about marrying. If you're not sure you even like the fellow, why would you consider marrying him, even out of convenience?"

"Because staying here bothers me more than marrying a man like Fitzwilliam does."

"You really hate this place that much that you would marry a man you didn't like just to leave here?"

"I didn't say I didn't like him. I said I'm not sure how I feel about him. Besides, there's more to it than that, Jake."

"Like what?"

"Like… I don't want to talk about this or Fitzwilliam anymore. Let's get back to what we were originally talking about."

He let out a frustrated breath. "You always do that."

"Do what?"

"Leave or change the subject when it gets too much for you."

"No, I don't."

"Yes, you do."

"Well, even if I do, so what?"

"Look, Leah. I don't want to argue with you, okay? I need to get busy. So if you would go ask your mother, I would appreciate it." He turned on his heel. "I'll see you later."

"Now who's walking away?" Her question bounced off his back.

He didn't answer but kept on walking. Jake couldn't believe she was willing to marry someone just to get away from there.

At the barn, he slid the double doors open and stepped inside. Soiled straw scent lingered in the air. He snatched a hay fork off the nail, picked up the wheelbarrow handles and headed to the first stall. While he cleaned, he thought about Leah and her comment about mucking. That comment only served to remind him that she was out of his league. He had thought maybe they would have a chance, especially after last night, but now he knew there would never be a chance for him. But that wouldn't stop him from doing whatever it took to keep her from marrying Fitzwilliam. His gut had warned him time and again about the man.

Jake tossed the last of the soiled straw into the wheelbarrow, grabbed the handles and wheeled it out of the stall.

"There you are."

He set the wheelbarrow down and faced Leah.

"Mother said Mr. Barker invited about forty people. He's going to have it at his house in the ballroom. I asked if she'd seen the room before and she said she had. I asked about how big it was, if it had doors. She said it was huge and that there were several double glass doors. She wanted to know why I asked, but I didn't tell her."

"Thanks. I appreciate that."

"Do you think you'll be all right in there?"

"Should be fine long as I sit next to the double doors." Jake hated he even had to think this way. That he couldn't defeat this demon that plagued him whenever he was stuck in large crowds.

"Okay, then. I'll make sure you do."

"Look, Leah. I don't want you saying anything to anyone. It's embarrassing enough that you know."

"I won't tell anyone. I'll figure out some way to work it out. Trust me, okay?"

He set his jaw. "Thought you didn't want me to go."

Leah tilted her head. A lone, curly strand slid across her cheek.

Without thinking, he reached for it and tucked it behind her ear. His fingers trailed along her jawbone as he retracted his hand.

Questions lingered across her face and eyes. Questions he had no answers to. Like why he'd allowed his hand to follow the soft contour of her jaw. Why he enjoyed the feel of her soft skin. Or why he had the urge to take her in his arms and taste her sweet lips. *What are you doing? Those kinds of thoughts can only lead to heartbreak.*

He let his hand fall to his side. "Sorry." It was all he could manage before he clutched the handles on the wheelbarrow and headed out the barn and into the dumping area.

"Jake." Leah stood behind him as he raised the wheelbarrow handles and let the soiled straw fall into the pit. "What made you think I didn't want you to go?"

Relieved she hadn't mentioned the incident in the barn, he set the wheelbarrow down and faced her. "Earlier you said I didn't have to go. That nobody was making me. I figured that meant you didn't want me to."

"Sweet twinkling stars above, Jake. That's not it." She shook her head and the soft curls he'd touched moments ago kissed her cheeks, something he wished he could do. This time, however, he roped in his urges before he did something foolish again. "You sounded like someone was making you go. I didn't want you to think you had to for my sake. I know you said you'd help me, but you really don't have to do this if you don't want to."

"Do you want me to go?" His eyes touched on hers.

She lowered her lashes. "Yes. I really don't want to go if you're not there."

"Why, Leah?"

She looked up at him. "What do you mean, 'why'?"

"Why is it so important for you to have me there? To help you? Is that your only reason?"

"I don't know what you're asking me, Jake." Wide innocent eyes frowned at him.

"Never mind." He had hoped for something more. What, he wasn't sure, but something that said he mattered. That their friendship mattered. Anything.

Who was he kidding?

He wanted to hear she couldn't live without him. But that wasn't going to happen. At least not the way he wanted it to. He shoved his hands through his thick hair.

Why did he keep torturing himself with something that was never going to be?

Even if he was in love with her, he didn't think that would be enough to sway her to stay. Good thing his heart wasn't fully engaged. His feelings for her were growing, but he wasn't in love with her. Or was he? He didn't know. He only knew this whole thing about her leaving battered his heart with bruises he thought would never heal. "I'll go."

Leah blinked. "What?"

"I'll go, Leah. I'll be there to help you. But this is the last time."

"What do you mean 'this is the last time'?"

"I mean, you'll probably be getting married soon. It's best I back out of the picture after this. You don't need me hanging around while some man is trying to court you."

"Court me? Fitzwilliam and I haven't even talked about that."

"Isn't that why he's here? To court you? To see if there can be a future between you two?"

"Well, um, yes. But nothing's been said yet."

"Just the same. After today, I won't be going with you anymore."

"What about Elizabeth?"

"What about her?"

"She needs an escort." He could tell by the look on her face that she was grasping at anything to keep him with her.

"This whole thing was your idea, Leah. Not mine."

"Yes, but you like her, don't you?"

"She's nice enough. What's that got to do with anything?"

"Jake." Leah laid her hand on his arm. "Please. Please don't leave me alone with him. I need you there."

"Why?"

"Because I feel protected when you're there."

"Do you need protecting?"

She shrugged. "I don't know why it's important to me. But it is. Please. Please say you'll go with me."

Her pleading eyes stared up at him. How could he refuse his best friend?

Friend.

He was growing to hate that word.

Leah glanced at the clock. Time to head downstairs. She took one last look in the full-length mirror. Today, she didn't take as much care with her attire. She put on a modest blue silk dress that hung around her shoulders. Her hair was rolled at the sides and gathered into a spun bun at the back of her head. No combs or flowers adorned it. Her joy at going this evening had diminished with her talk with Jake.

When he'd told her that she was on her own after this evening, a million needles pricked her heart. She didn't want to think about what the pain in her heart and soul meant. She had an idea, but admitting it, she would never allow.

"Lord, have mercy on me" was all she could manage before descending the stairs.

"You look nice, Lee-Lee."

"Thanks, Abbs. So do you." Her voice was monotone.

"What's wrong?"

"Nothing."

"Leah, something's wrong. I can tell."

"You girls ready to go?" Mother stepped into the room.

"Yes, Mother." Leah forced herself to respond in a normal tone. She didn't want any more questions.

They grabbed their wraps and headed to the landau carriage Mr. Barker had sent. The driver opened the doors and helped them inside. Leah kept to herself and her gray thoughts. Even Abby gave up trying to talk with her, and Leah couldn't blame her sister. Her heart just wasn't in this.

The landau rolled to a stop in front of Mr. Barker's pristine white, three-story mansion with four white pillars in front. Bay windows sparkled on the right and left sides of the house. White and lavender blooming syringa bushes filled the air with their sweetness. Manicured shrubs formed a barrier wall to the backyard. Wild pink roses climbed the outside walls. Their scent mingled with the syringa bushes.

Even though Mr. Barker's house was enormous, it was only half the size of the mansion she'd been born in back in New York, and she wondered for a second what Fitzwilliam would think of it.

The driver helped them out and a footman escorted them into the house.

Inside, they were led to a large oval room with light brown and tan floors so shiny they looked like glass sparkling in the sunlight. Gold and white chandeliers dangled from the ceiling. Ceiling to floor, reddish-brown brocade curtains with gold scarf swags and tassels hung over the three evenly spaced windows at the end of the room. Fine gold and glass sconces centered each one.

At the front of the room a Bösendorfer grand piano stood on the right. Rows of white Chippendale chairs with padded seats covered in the same material as the curtains were centered in the room, leaving plenty of space on each side, down the middle, and even more space behind. Large white pillars like the ones outside Mr. Barker's house surrounded two sizable glass French doors on each side of the chairs.

Leah's chest expanded with relief, knowing Jake would be fine in this room. It certainly was large enough not to feel closed in. Even better, the doors were open and there were several ways of escape.

She glanced around to see if Jake had arrived yet, but she didn't see him. She did spot Mr. Barker, however, amid a group of elegant men and women. The men wore an array of gray, blue and black frock coats with matching trousers, white starched shirts and bow ties. The women wore silk and tulle dresses, satin and lace, faille and lace, and even crepe de chine and velvet, and all were bustle gowns with bows and flowers made from satin ribbons. Exquisite diamonds, rubies and sapphires inlaid in gold adorned their necks and gloved wrists.

Her heart skipped a happy beat. This was the beautiful sort of people she would be associating with once she moved to New York.

"I'll see you two later." Abby let go of her and headed over to Phoebe.

Mother pulled Leah's arm through hers. "Let's go say hello, shall we?"

Leah didn't have a chance to refuse her mother's request because she tugged her along, and the two of them glided toward the group.

When they arrived at the small party of guests, Mr. Barker's attention drifted to Mother's and stopped. His eyes brightened and a huge smile split across his face. "Hello, my dear." He looped Mother's gloved hand through the crook of his arm. "Gentlemen, may I present to you my special lady friend, Katherine Bowen."

They all greeted her with cordial smiles.

"And this lovely young woman is her daughter Leah." Mr. Barker gently pulled Leah into the fold.

Men she'd never seen before greeted her warmly, staring at her approvingly even, but the women only nodded and raked their eyes up and down the length of her.

Seeing their looks of disapproval, heat rushed into her cheeks. At that moment, she wanted to crawl under the floor and pull it over her.

She glanced at her mother to see if she noticed, but Mother only had eyes for Mr. Barker.

Whispers behind gloved hands about her attire reached her ears. How could they be so cruel?

If only she'd taken more time with her appearance and worn her bustle gown and the jewels Father had given her. Elaborate jewels that had belonged to Father's mother. If she had, they would not be looking down their noses at her.

"Miss Bowen." Fitzwilliam's icy tone from beside her caused her gaze to jump to him. No smile or any warmth of feeling ingrained his features. And he'd

called her *Miss Bowen* instead of *Leah*. That couldn't be
good. What gross faux pas had she committed this time?

His gaze discreetly ran down the length of her and
a scowl marred his face. Without even excusing them
from the crowd, he cupped her elbow and led her away
from the small gathering of people near the French
doors.

"Leah, my dear, this is a formal affair with men and
women of great prominence. Why did you not dress
appropriately for it? How could you embarrass me this
way?"

Her heart sank. She had a lot to learn. The only problem was, would she ever? "I'm sorry, Mr. Barrington. I
didn't know it was going to be this elaborate or I would
have taken more care in dressing."

"Did you not know that this was to be an operetta?"

"Well, um, yes. But…" She shrugged.

"But what?"

"Well, I, um… I've never been to one before."

His line of vision trailed to Abby, then to her mother.

"Your mother and your sister are appropriately
dressed." One brow hiked.

He didn't believe her.

He was right not to. She'd been so hurt by what had
transpired between her and Jake that she didn't care.
Nothing mattered if Jake wasn't in her life. She loved
him.

Leah froze, and the blood drained from her face.
It was as she feared. *Dear God, no. I can't love Jake.*

Jake's handsome face, lazy smile and soft tabby-gray
eyes invaded her mind. As did thoughts about how he
accepted her just the way she was, how he didn't even
try to change her, how he made her laugh, made her

feel special. Her knees went weak at the thought and very nearly pitched her to the floor.

"Evening, Leah." Leah stiffened at the sound of Jake's voice.

Drawing in a deep breath, she turned to face him and forced a smile onto her face, forced herself to act as if everything were normal. "Evening, Jake."

Jake's smile slipped, replaced by a concerned frown.

She hadn't fooled him at all. He knew her well. Well enough to know something wasn't right. His eyes never left her face. Seeing him through different eyes, she tried not to notice how handsome he really was inside and out.

Or how his broad shoulders, powerfully built arms and wide chest filled out the light blue shirt he wore under a dark blue vest.

Or how strong his muscular legs looked in the new dark blue pants that covered them.

Leah yanked her attention off of him. Those were things an unmarried woman should not be noticing.

She peeked a glance at Fitzwilliam.

His arms were behind his back and he stared at her with brown eyes of steel.

Her heart didn't care, but her mind did. He was still her way of escape from this place and the nightmares. She couldn't risk his disapproval. But what about Jake? What about her newly discovered love for him? Confusion infused itself into her heart and soul. Desperately she tried to think of a way to stay, to rid herself of the nightmares, of her strong hatred for the place that had ripped her father from her. Every coping strategy she'd tried since his death had failed. Nothing had worked. No. She had no choice. She had to go.

"Leah, can we talk?" Jake said.

"Excuse me, sir." Fitzwilliam pulled himself up straighter, and his tone practically dripped with ice. "But Leah is with me. There are some people I want her to meet. So if you will excuse us."

Before Leah had a chance to protest, she found herself all but being dragged toward the same small group of people who'd made her uncomfortable earlier.

Leah glanced over her shoulder. Jake started to follow her, but Elizabeth stepped in front of him. He peered around Miss Barrington. That was all Leah noticed because Fitzwilliam's yank on her arm forced her to look forward or stumble.

They reached the small group, who were engaged in a deep conversation of some sort. Mother and Mr. Barker were no longer standing among them. They were talking to another small group of people on the other side of the room.

Fitzwilliam forgot all about introducing her and joined in with the men's conversation. In the midst of the small crowd, Leah suddenly felt alone.

One of the women looked at Leah. "Mr. Barrington says your family came from New York City and that your father was a prominent businessman there. What do you think about the wholesale corruption? Do you think William Tweed should have been appointed commissioner of public works?"

Leah had no clue what the middle-aged woman with brown hair, green eyes and a long pointed nose was talking about. "I, um. We moved out here years ago, so I'm afraid I don't know what that is."

"You don't?" The woman ran her disgust-filled eyes up and down Leah's face. "That man purchases things for a pittance and sells it at an outrageous amount, and the Tammany society supports him. Why, that political machine runs all of New York City."

Tammany society? Running New York City. She didn't remember Father ever talking about anything like that.

"My husband thinks it's wonderful."

"He does?" asked a woman with shock on her face. "It's pretty corrupt if you ask me."

"What do you think, Leah? Do you think it's right to do that?"

Leah couldn't believe these women were talking politics. It was something she knew nothing about. Nor did she care to. "Oh. I, um…" She didn't know how to answer that. If she told them the way she really felt, which was, no, she didn't think it was right, then the lady whose husband thought it was a great idea would sneer at her. And if she said yes, it would go against what she believed—that the thing sounded like nothing but greediness to her—then the others women would scoff at her.

"Well, surely even way out here you've heard about the high assessment land value in Manhattan over the past twenty-seven years?" Another beautiful woman with dark black hair and striking blue eyes close to Leah's age joined in the conversation.

"No, I haven't." Heat filled Leah's cheeks at the disapproving looks that woman sent her way. Suddenly, the woman no longer seemed beautiful to Leah. In fact, she and the rest of the ladies who were sending her their scowls appeared ugly to her. Amazing how a person could look lovely on the outside until you got to know them on the inside. The ugliness in them caused even their pretty outsides to appear ugly.

"Does your family invest in stocks?"

How was she supposed to know if they did? Her brothers didn't discuss finances with her. They believed women shouldn't have to carry that burden—that it was a man's burden alone to bear. Her father had felt the same way. She hiked a shoulder in response to her question.

"What do you think about *Le nozze di Figaro?*" the same woman asked.

"I don't know what that is." Leah's eyes dropped in shame.

"Don't you know we've come tonight to hear selections from it?" Ugly shrouded this beautiful woman even more so now.

Knowing she would feel even stupider, she said, "Selections?"

"Yes, selections. I saw the entire opera at la Monnaie when we went to Brussels last year."

"La Monnaie?" *Floor, open up now. Please.*

The lady's laughter held only degradation. "Why, of course, la Monnaie. Surely you have heard of la Monnaie."

"No, ma'am. I have not."

"Where have you been, Miss Bowen? Living with the pigs?" asked another woman who had gray hair pulled back in a bun so tight her eyes were almost slanted. They would have been, too, if she wasn't narrowing them so severely at Leah.

Leah sank further into herself, trying to come up with a suitable response. What would this lady think if she knew she really did live with pigs? She felt like a fly caught in a spider's web with an eight-legged beast heading directly toward her with one mission—to devour her.

That's what these women were doing—devouring

her spirit. She needed to escape them. But she had no idea how to do that without being as rude as they were.

"Excuse me, ladies." Jake stepped next to Leah and looped her arm through his. "But I feel you have had the pleasure of my friend's company long enough. As much as I'm sure it will sadden you all to see her leave, I'm going to have to steal her away."

The women nodded. Their faces lit up with smiles. Jake's massive tall frame and extremely good looks would impress any woman. Even this group of snobby women. Several stared at Jake with dreamy eyes as if he were a prince of some kind. In a way he was. He was Leah's Prince Charming, rescuing her from the dragon ladies. Leah had never loved him so much as she did at that very moment.

They pressed their gloved hands against their lips, dipped their heads and blinked their eyes like schoolgirls with a crush. Not a single one of them could form a coherent sentence. They sounded like blathering idiots.

How did they like feeling the way they'd made her feel?

Leah raised her chin. "If you will excuse me, ladies."

Their heads bobbed jerkily as if someone were shaking them hard by the shoulders.

Jake led her away to a corner on the opposite side of the room.

Finally, Leah could breathe—well, kind of, with the infernal corset hemming her in and the tears of humiliation shimmering just behind her eyelashes.

They lowered themselves onto a white Chippendale bench seat. "How did you know I needed rescuing?"

He shrugged. "Just knew."

"Thank you, Jake." She sent him a shy smile. She'd never felt shy around Jake before.

"Told you I'd be here for you."

"Yes, you did. You're always there for me." Leah had to force her true feelings not to show when she fixed her eyes on him. She didn't want Jake to know she was in love with him.

Her gaze traveled around the room, and she leaned as close to him as possible without causing speculation about them, and for his ears only she said, "Are you doing okay in here?"

Jake skimmed the room. "Not too bad. There are several doors and it's not crowded. So far, so good. Should be fine."

"Oh, good. I'm so glad. When I came in here and saw all the space and doors, I had a feeling you would be." She smiled at him.

"You look really nice. I like the dress. It brings out the blue in your eyes."

A tear pooled in each eye.

"Did I say something wrong?" Concern drifted across his face.

"No. No." She held up her hand. "On the contrary."

"What are the tears for, then?" He brushed each one with his thumb from her cheek as they slid down.

She wanted to clutch his hand, press it into her heart and hold it there forever. But it wasn't hers to do with as she pleased. Her heart and soul heaved a heavy sigh before she answered him. "Since I arrived here, you're the first person to say something nice to me."

"What do you mean? People here been mean to you?" Jake's forehead furrowed.

She gave a long blink and nodded. "Those ladies that were so nice to you, well, they weren't to me. You should have seen the disgust on their faces when they eyed me up and down. Made me feel lower than dirt. Then they started talking politics. Things I knew nothing about nor care to, and some opera house in some place I've never even heard of before. I've never felt so stupid in my entire life. I wanted the floor to open and swallow me up."

The muscle in his jaw jumped. Leah could tell he was working to compose himself. "I wouldn't worry about what they think. You outshine every last one of them both in beauty and attire."

"Oh, you're just saying that to be nice. But thanks." She gave him a half smile.

"No. I'm not. I meant every word." Seriousness dotted each syllable he spoke.

Leah studied his beautiful gray eyes for the truth. She didn't see any falseness in them. Her heart warmed. She pressed her shoulders back, feeling taller and better than she had since she'd walked through the doors of this place. And she owed her renewed confidence in herself to Jake, who never once made her feel the way those ladies just had. Ever. In fact, she'd always seen the two of them as equals. "Thank you, Jake. I really needed to hear something nice. You look pretty fabulous yourself." Boy, did he ever.

Jake appreciated Leah's compliment. Her opinion was the only one there that mattered.

Leah played with her fingertips, rubbing and tugging at them. It crushed him to hear how cruel those ladies had been to her. He wanted to storm over there and give every one of them a good tongue-lashing. But he would not cause a scene and risk embarrassing Leah or Mrs. Bowen.

A quick glance at his outfit, and he couldn't understand why they'd been so nice to him. He was the most underdressed man in the place. He'd taken money out of his winter supply fund to buy a new pair of pants but the rest of his attire was his Sunday church clothes. If people didn't like the way he was dressed, well, that was their problem. He wasn't out to impress anyone. He was who he was and if no one liked it, then they didn't have to associate with him.

"Where's Elizabeth?"

"Don't know. I told her I needed to talk to you." He scanned the room but didn't see her.

"Does she correct your faux pas?" She tugged at her bottom lip and her head tilted at a slight angle.

"My what?"

"Faux pas. You know, social blunders?" She hiked a shoulder.

"Nope. Not once."

"You're fortunate." She glanced at him then down at her lap. "Fitzwilliam took me aside and rebuked me. He told me he couldn't believe I hadn't dressed properly this evening."

The muscle in Jake's jaw jumped as he bore down on his teeth.

"How was I supposed to know how to dress for an opera? I've never been to one before. Not even back in New York. They were always held late in the evenings and we were in our bedrooms by then." She turned her face away from him.

"Leah." He tugged on her chin until she faced him. "Any man who cares about outward appearances instead of what's on the inside where it really counts isn't worth caring about. It's like all those people in *Pride and Prejudice*. All they cared about was outward appearances and how much wealth and power a person had. That ain't right."

"You've read *Pride and Prejudice?*"

Jake clamped his jaw shut. He couldn't believe he'd mentioned that book. No avoiding her question. "Yep."

"When?"

"Finished it the other night."

"What made you read it?"

"You."

"Me?"

"Yep."

"How come?"

Jake ran his hand across the back of his neck. "If you must know, it's because you kept talking about how you wanted a man like Mr. Darcy. I was curious what kind of man he was. Have to admit, I'm surprised you want someone like him. Even though he did turn out to be a nice fellow in the end."

"I keep hoping that's what will happen with Mr. Barrington. He's only trying to help me correct my social faux pas. I'm certain once I learn those things he'll be different, too."

"Leah." Jake locked his gaze on hers. Using his sternest tone he said, "Fitzwilliam isn't some hero in a fictional romance novel."

"I know that."

"Do you? Mr. Darcy isn't a real person, Leah. Life isn't like a storybook, either. Fitzwilliam may or may not change. This may be the way he really is. You need to ask yourself if you're willing to take that chance."

She said nothing in reply. Only stared at him.

He'd frustrated her. But what kind of friend would he be if he didn't speak the truth to her? He had something else he needed to talk to her about, too. But now was not the time or the place.

"Oh, Jake. There you are." Elizabeth glided toward them, her dress swaying side to side like a ringing bell.

Jake rose. He turned to Leah and quickly said, "I have something important I need to tell you. Later, okay?"

Leah nodded.

Elizabeth curtsied at Leah and her smile appeared genuine. "Good evening, Leah. You look lovely this evening."

Jake sent Leah a see-I-told-you-so look.

"Thank you, Elizabeth. You do, too."

It was sweet of Elizabeth to compliment Leah. She would make someone a great wife. Not him, but someone. Elizabeth, too, was out of his league. Plus, Jake couldn't imagine having Fitzwilliam for a brother-in-law. He felt sorry for Elizabeth having a brother like him. And he would feel even sorrier for Leah if she ended up marrying the guy.

The thought of Leah marrying that phony fellow was terrifying. Jake couldn't let that happen. If nothing else, he had to at least talk her into finding someone else. He loved her too much to watch her marry a man like that. He started when he realized the thought that had just gone through his head. He loved her. More than that, he was *in* love with her.

"Time to be seated, everyone." Mr. Barker spoke loudly from the front of the room, stopping Jake's musings.

Fitzwilliam walked up and claimed Leah's arm, and Elizabeth claimed his. Not wanting to lead her on, yet refusing to be rude, he allowed her to, and the four of them made their way to the chairs.

Jake sat in the chair directly across from the open doors and only feet away. Elizabeth sat next to him, then Fitzwilliam and then Leah.

Shortly after everyone was seated, a rotund man started singing. The man had a nice enough voice, but Jake couldn't understand a word he said. For the next hour, two other men and three other ladies joined him. The songs got longer and harder to endure. When the singing finally ended, to avoid getting trapped in the crowd, Jake got up immediately and went to stand next to the open doors. Elizabeth, Leah and Fitzwilliam joined him.

"Wasn't that a fine display of talent?" Fitzwilliam asked Leah.

"He sang beautifully, but I couldn't understand a word he said."

"You didn't? How very odd." Pomposity oozed from the man.

What did Leah see in this jerk?

"Nothing odd about it. I didn't understand a word, either," Jake said with no apology whatsoever.

"That doesn't surprise me—a country bumpkin such as yourself."

"Hey, don't talk about Jake that way," Leah blasted Fitzwilliam and disengaged her arm from his.

"Brother, please." Elizabeth bowed her head in embarrassment. "It was in Italian, after all."

Fitzwilliam turned his attention to his sister. The man was a pill, but he sure loved his sister. You could see it in his eyes.

"Very true, sister." He turned back to them. "My apologies to you both. I don't know where my manners are lately." He gazed down at Leah. "I fear jealousy is causing me to act in a manner most unbecoming."

"Jealousy?" She tilted her head.

"Yes. I must admit, I'm quite jealous of the relationship you have with Mr. Lure here. However, I'm sure I have no need to be alarmed on that account. For very soon, if I have my way, you and I shall be heading back to New York." His smile was fake at best. "In fact, what better time than the present to make my feelings on the matter known? Leah, my darling, please say you will be my wife."

Like a sucker punch to his middle, the wind whooshed out of Jake's lungs. *Marry?* His attention flew to Leah. Surely she wouldn't say yes. *No, Leah. Say no.*

She stared at the man with wide, blinking eyes and an open mouth.

Fitzwilliam fingered her mouth shut, shifted to the other foot, glanced around and then smiled. "Of course, you do not have to answer me straightaway, my dear. I shall give you this evening to consider my proposal. On the morrow you can give me your answer. I shall come by early in the morning if that is agreeable with you."

"Um. Oh. Um. Ye-yes. Th-that will be—be just fine."

A dagger ripped at Jake's heart, shredding it to pieces.

The day had come.

Leah would be leaving.

No! No! He refused to let that happen. He'd rather move to the city than live without her. How he would survive it he didn't know, but if that's what it took… His heart raced, and his palms turned damp just thinking about it. He swallowed hard, hoping the panic would go away.

Somehow.

Somehow he'd figure it out.

He had to.

Before she gave Fitzwilliam her answer, he had to talk to Leah, to see how she felt about him, about them. In the next breath, he hoped and prayed she wouldn't reject him this time. For this time, with his heart on the table, her rejection would surely kill him.

Leah watched as Fitzwilliam gave Jake a smug grin, then he excused himself and headed to the group of prominent men he'd been visiting with most of the evening.

She shook her head, unable to get over how Fitzwilliam had asked her to marry him in front of everyone. More importantly, in front of Jake.

Jake.

She couldn't wait to find out what it was he wanted to talk to her about. But wait she must.

"It sure is warm in here."

Leah turned her attention to Elizabeth. Miss Barrington splayed her fan and waved it in front of her face. "Jake, would you be a dear and get me something to drink, please?"

He turned his attention to Leah. "Would you like something to drink, Leah?"

"Please."

He nodded, and Leah's gaze followed him as he headed toward the refreshment table.

"Isn't he the most agreeable man ever?"

Leah yanked her attention toward Elizabeth. "Isn't who the most agreeable man?"

"Jake." Elizabeth hooked arms with her. She glanced around the room and then she leaned closer to Leah.

"He's been so attentive to me. So much so that I think he's in love with me."

Shocked to the very core of her being by Elizabeth's statement, Leah wondered if what she said was true. Was Jake in love with Elizabeth? Leah's thoughts trailed back to how attentive he had been to the woman.

How he held Elizabeth longer than necessary whenever he helped her down.

How he saw to her comforts.

How the two of them laughed and joked.

How he'd gazed at her and had given her his undivided attention.

How willing he was to go every time Leah had invited him along. It had all been for Elizabeth, not for her.

Is that what he wanted to talk to her about? To tell her that he had fallen in love with Elizabeth and that he wanted to marry the woman?

What had she done? She'd driven the man she loved into another woman's arms.

Her mind scrambled to find a solution, but there was not one. If only God would have shown her a way to deal with the loss of her father. But He hadn't. And now she was about to lose the only man she'd ever loved. It was a no-win situation. If she married Fitzwilliam, Jake would be her brother-in-law. If she stayed, the nightmares and the loss of her father would continue to torment her. Earlier, she'd already made up her mind not to marry Fitzwilliam, and now that decision was cemented. There was no way she would marry Fitzwilliam and have to watch Elizabeth and Jake together all the time.

Jake married to another. That idea ate at her heart like a deadly cancer.

Lord, show me a way to make this work. I can't lose him. I can't. I know You have an answer. I'm asking You to reveal it to me. And soon. Before it's too late.

"Here you go, ladies." Jake's voice pulled her out of the heart-wrenching pit her thoughts had taken her to.

He handed them each a glass.

Elizabeth threaded her arms through his. Jake looked down at her. Never taking her eyes off of Jake, Elizabeth took a small sip. "Thank you, Jake. That was very sweet of you."

"My pleasure."

"Yes. Thank you, Jake." Leah forced a smile onto her lips. Even that was hard when her heart was breaking.

"Jake." His attention went back to Elizabeth. "I was wondering if you removed your advertisement yet. You said you were no longer in need of it."

Remove his ad? He hadn't told Leah he was going to do that.

"Yep. No need for it anymore." He looked at Leah, then back at Elizabeth.

He no longer needed it?

Elizabeth smiled at Leah and gave her a look that said, *See what I mean? He is in love with me. He's even stopped his ad as proof.*

Realization pummeled Leah's soul. Jake had said he needed to talk to her. Is that what he was going to tell her? That he'd removed his ad and that he no longer needed it because he was going to marry Elizabeth? Or that he'd finally decided to respond to one of the other women who'd answered his advertisement? Either way, it was too late for her and Jake. Or was it? Surely there had to be a way to work this whole thing out. She couldn't lose Jake. She just couldn't.

Chapter Sixteen

Leah skipped through the ranch yard and up into the trees singing, "Father. Father. Where are you?" She repeated it over and over as her eyes searched for him. Farther and farther into the forest she went. The foliage thickened as did the trees. Sweet syringa scents swirled around her. She stopped, raised her nose in the air and drew in deeply, then frowned as something awful went up her nose. She looked around, trying to figure out where the stench was coming from.

She watched as a tree fell in slow motion and landed with a crunch.

Leah walked over to the fallen tree and stepped on top of it. Her focus drifted to her feet.

Her eyes widened.

A man was trapped underneath the tree. She couldn't see his face.

With one hop, she leaped off the massive trunk.

"Don't be scared, princess."

"Father?" Leah swung one direction and then another, searching frantically for her father.

"I love you, princess."

"Where you are, Father? I can't find you."

"I'm right here."

"Where?"

"Here."

A single beam of light pierced through the darkness.

Leah shook her head. "No. No. I'm sorry, Father. I'm so sorry."

Leah's eyes bolted open, blinking, searching, trying to get her bearings through the morning twilight. When she realized she was in her bedroom and that the whole thing had been yet another nightmare, tears soaked her face as the fresh pain of losing her father assaulted her all over again.

Dear Lord, will these nightmares ever end? I can't take even one more of them. Please, won't You make them stop? She'd prayed the same prayer a million times over the years. Even though the nightmares hadn't ceased, she refused to stop praying. God was her only hope. And now she needed Him to deliver her even more than ever. Her future depended on it.

At first, she truly believed Fitzwilliam was God's answer for her and that once they were married and moved to New York the nightmares would end and she would be free from the place that had robbed her of her precious father. That might very well be true, but it wouldn't solve the problem of being in love with Jake or having him for a brother-in-law.

Jake? A brother-in-law? She tossed her coverlet off, stormed over to the washbasin and splashed cool water on her burning face.

Despite Fitzwilliam's certain disapproval, which she no longer cared about, when Leah completed her toiletries she dressed in a simple lavender dress—the one she always wore when church was held at their home.

Downstairs, she headed into the kitchen. Veronique had the day off, so Leah put a pot of coffee on the stove, cooked up a batch of Swedish pancakes and fried thick slices of ham. She'd just set them in the warmer when she heard the padding of slippers on the floor.

"Good morning, Leah." Mother entered the kitchen wearing her nightgown and robe. "I'm surprised to see you up and dressed so early this morning. I figured as late as it was when we got home last night, you'd sleep in this morning."

"Couldn't sleep. I thought I'd make breakfast so I could help get things set up for church today." Leah went to the window and pulled back the curtain. "At least it's another nice day today." The sky was covered with its usual large fluffy clouds sprinkled throughout the blue vastness. She let the curtain fall and headed to the stove. "You ready to eat?"

"No. Not yet. A cup of coffee sounds nice."

"I'll get it. You stay seated, Mother."

Mother nodded, placed her elbow on the table, rested her chin in her hand and sighed. "Why don't you sit down and have a cup with me?"

Leah nodded, poured them each a cup of the hot brew and sat down.

"Did you enjoy the opera?" Mother cupped her hands around the beverage.

Leah considered lying but realized she didn't have the energy to fake being happy. "Not really. I didn't understand a word they said. Some of the women's voices were so high they hurt my ears." Those high, shrill voices came from the very ladies who had snubbed her. "Did you enjoy it?" Leah blew into her coffee.

"It was all right. Not something I'd like to hear very often."

"Really?"

"Yes, really. It wasn't my type of music at all."

"Why'd you go then?"

"Because Charles asked me to."

"Does he host those kind of parties often?"

"No. He only did it because the man was his friend. Truth is, Charles doesn't care for them at all, and he couldn't understand a word they were saying, either."

That shocked Leah. Fitzwilliam had made her feel like there was something wrong with her and as if she were the only one who didn't understand. Well, she and Jake, that was.

"How are you and Fitzwilliam getting along? Do you think he's the one?"

"He asked me to marry him."

Mother set her cup on the table and leaned forward. "What did you say?" Was that concern on her face?

"I didn't. He said I could think on it and tell him today."

"Have you decided whether or not you're going to accept his proposal?"

"Whose proposal?" Abby stepped in the kitchen with her hair all rumpled, tying the string on her robe. She flopped into a kitchen chair. "Jake's?"

"Jake's?" Mother sat up straighter, eager eyes blinking in Abby's direction. "Why would you think Jake would propose to Leah?"

Abby straightened, and her gaze flew to Leah's and locked there, screaming, *I'm sorry*.

Leah sent her a brief warning glare to make an excuse and drop it.

Abby shrugged. "Just wishful thinking, I guess. I really like Jake, and if Lee-Lee married him, then she wouldn't leave."

"I understand that one," Mother said under her breath, but Leah heard her nonetheless.

If they only knew how that could never be. She sighed. Tired from all the tug and pull on her heart, Leah rose and gathered the food out of the warmer. Both Abby and Mother wanted her to marry Jake. She wouldn't mind it herself now. Except she was probably too late. As much as she wanted it to be so, marrying Jake wouldn't solve her nightmare problem, or seeing Mother with a man other than her father, or her hatred for the place that killed her father, or her desire to go back to where times were better.

Torn between her love for Jake and her desire to leave, Leah struggled to find a solution that would give her all of her heart's desires. Was that even possible? She wasn't sure. One thing she was sure of— She had to risk talking to Jake and telling him everything. If it wasn't too late, perhaps they could come up with a solution together. After all, he'd helped her so many times in the past.

Breakfast flew by with Abby regaling in her dramatic flair about the evening at Mr. Barker's and how fabulous it was. Leah wished she could say the same, but the whole thing had been torture. When they finished breakfast, each went to their bedrooms to get ready for church.

Leah loved when church was held out on the ranch. So did the rest of the town. Though they had an almost-new church building in town, everyone still wanted to gather at the Bowens' ranch at least once a month during the summer season, and Pastor James had readily agreed.

An hour and half later, the parishioners' wagons started rolling in, and Fitzwilliam and Elizabeth were among them. She didn't know what to tell the man because she hadn't had a chance to talk to Jake yet.

Fitzwilliam stepped down from the buggy and offered his sister a helping hand.

Leah drew in a deep breath and headed toward them, knowing she could not be rude.

"Good morning, my dear." Fitzwilliam kissed her hand. "You look—" His brown eyes took in her attire. He leaned close to her. "Is that what you're wearing to church?" Fitzwilliam straightened and looked around with a smile as phony as a three-headed animal.

Enough was enough. Leah refused to let him belittle her or criticize her anymore. She raised her chin. "Yes. This is what I'm wearing."

His countenance immediately changed to one of disapproval. "We'll discuss this later, my dear." Haughtiness tinged his voice.

"There's nothing to discuss."

"Brother, please." Elizabeth put her hand on his arm.

Leah turned to Elizabeth, whose big brown eyes were pleading with her brother once again.

"Good morning, Elizabeth." The warmth in Leah's voice was no act, even though the woman was a threat to her happiness.

"Good morning, Leah. I fear I must apologize for my brother."

Someone needed to. He sure didn't offer an apology for himself. "How are you this morning?" Leah asked. She really wanted to know. Elizabeth was a sweet lady.

"Very well, thank you." She looked around. "Is Jake coming?"

Guilt pricked Leah's conscious at the thought of hurting someone as sweet as Elizabeth. But then again, what if she and Elizabeth were wrong and Jake didn't

love Elizabeth? Then what? The only way to find out
was to talk to him. If Jake was indeed in love with
Elizabeth and planned on marrying her, then as much
as it would kill her, Leah would forget her plans about
talking to him about everything. She would take that as
God's answer to her prayer about the whole situation.

"Yes. He should be here pretty soon. Would you two
like to go ahead and be seated?" She pointed to the side
of the house where the chairs were set up in the shade.

"We're sitting outside?" Fitzwilliam's eyes widened
in horror.

Leah wanted to yell, "Brother, please," but she
didn't. "Yes. We are." She let out a long sigh, hoping
he'd get the hint.

He emitted a disapproving breath. "Well, one time
shan't matter, I suppose. But things will be different
once we're married."

Leah mashed her teeth together. Now was not the
time to say what was on her mind. Not before church.
But the time was coming and it was coming quickly.
Not quick enough, though.

"Shall we all be seated?" Pastor James said from
the wooden podium.

Everyone flocked to their seats.

Leah sat in the last bench, purposely saving the end
spot for Jake.

Jake. Where was he?

Jake had spent the past hour chasing down his goat.
Meanie had escaped once again. He still hadn't found
her, but he didn't want to be late for church, so he finally abandoned the search for his runaway goat, hoping and praying she hadn't gone to Mabel's again.

With a tuck to his horse's side, he galloped to the

Bowens' and arrived just as everyone had gotten seated. Voices rose in worship to the Lord. He tied his horse to one of the hitching posts near the barn, pulled his Bible out of his saddlebag and strode to the side of the house.

Spotting an empty place on the end, and knowing Leah had saved it for him, brought a smile to his face. He slipped in beside her.

She looked up and her dimples made their appearance. Her smile was different. Warm. Inviting, even. Yet shy at the same time.

Leah turned her face toward the front and continued singing in a low, sweet tone. Jake wished she'd sing louder. She had a beautiful voice. One that kissed the soul of a man.

Minutes later, the worship ended, and Pastor James said, "Please be seated, folks." Everyone did. "If you have your Bibles, please open them to Matthew 6:33."

Pages rustled as Jake and several other folks searched for the scripture.

Pastor James glanced down at the makeshift podium. "Seek ye first the kingdom of God, and his righteousness; and all these things shall be added unto you." He raised his head and leaned his arm on the podium. "Is He first in your life and are you second? Or are you first and He's second?"

Pastor walked around to the front of the podium. "Let me tell you, folks. When we put God first in every area of life and read the Word daily and pray over every situation and decision, our lives will be blessed. I challenge you today to ask yourselves if there is something you're holding on to—an area in your life where you haven't put Him first. Perhaps it's money. Or your time. Or a relationship."

Jake glanced at Leah. Had he put God first in that area?

Pastor James continued, but Jake didn't hear what he was saying. He was busy repenting for putting himself first and God second. As hard as it was, Jake prayed for God's will and not his concerning Leah. He would accept God's answer because he no longer wanted to be first in his life. From now on, he was second.

Leah leaned close to him and whispered, "So, did you really cancel the ad?"

Huh? Why was she asking him about that now? He nodded.

"Why?"

"'Cause my heart just wasn't in it anymore."

"How come?"

Tell her the truth. That still small voice spoke to Jake's spirit.

"'Cause I've fallen in love with someone." Now was not the time to tell her with whom. He'd tell her later.

"Please stand, folks," Pastor James said.

Church ended with a song, then everyone scattered to their wagons. Men handed baskets of food down to their womenfolk. Jake jumped in and helped move the tables and benches.

Fitzwilliam stood at the edge of the crowd, watching, the only man not helping.

Jake shook his head, then turned and hoisted another bench.

"I say, stop that. Get away from me."

Jake swung around with the bench still in his hands.

Meanie had the tail of Barrington's suit in her mouth, and she was yanking him to and fro as he fought to disengage her.

For once, Jake could just kiss that old goat. That wasn't very charitable, but he couldn't help enjoying the scene just a little.

Fitzwilliam managed to swat the goat on the nose, which seemed to have the intended reaction of her letting go. "Stupid animal." Fitzwilliam tsked as he examined his attire.

Meanie backed up and dropped her head.

Uh-oh.

Meanie lunged toward the man and rammed her head into Fitzwilliam's backside, sending him flying forward. He landed on his hands and knees, and his top hat bounced on the hard ground, rolling a few feet in front of him.

"Why you!" He jumped up just as the goat headed for him again.

Kitty stood in the background with her ears flapping and her nose jerking high in the air as if she were cheering Meanie on, as if saying "Hit him, hit him again."

The scene was hilarious. Jake wanted to laugh. But as much as he enjoyed seeing the man get what he deserved, Jake needed to stop his goat before she decided to do it again.

He set the bench down and strode toward Meanie, who was in hot pursuit of the gray trousers.

"Someone do something!" Fitzwilliam screamed like a little girl.

As Jake headed across the yard, his goat stopped and backed up.

Oh, no. Not again. "Meanie!" Jake picked up his pace, but he arrived too late.

Meanie rammed her head into Barrington again. This time he landed sprawled out on the ground.

Several men headed his way to help.

Meanie's focus darted to them, but only for a brief second. Mouth barred open, she chomped her teeth into Fitzwilliam's hat and shook it vehemently.

Jake caught her by the collar and tugged on the hat. "Bad goat. Bad Meanie. Give it back."

Meanie shook her head hard. Jake tugged even harder. So did the goat. But she wouldn't let go.

Rriipp.

Uh-oh. Jake glanced over at Fitzwilliam to see if he'd heard the noise.

Haydon, Michael and Jesse stood above Fitzwilliam, offering him a hand up.

"I can do it." He brushed them away, huffing as he stood.

They stepped back, holding up their hands in surrender.

A look of understanding passed between Jake and the three of them. Right then, Jake knew there was no way Leah would be marrying this man. Not if the four of them had anything to say about it, anyway.

In control of the now-shredded hat, Jake walked over and handed what was left of it to him. "Sorry about your hat."

Fitzwilliam snatched it from Jake's hands. Holding on to the brim, he mashed it onto his head. The whole brim tore off and the ring landed around his neck like a collar. Barrington closed his eyes, and his chest expanded. He brushed himself off, pressed his shoulders back and stormed away, mumbling something about being nothing but a bunch of hooligans.

Jake turned his attention back to Leah's brothers. He fought not to laugh, but when he saw Haydon with his head dipped, his hand over his face and nose and his peering eyes upward; Jess biting his quivering lip and looking everywhere but at him; and Michael with his flared nose, pursed mouth and chin twitching, Jake couldn't help it. Laughter rolled out of him, and the other three men joined him.

"Can you believe that guy?" Jesse shook his head, still chortling a bit.

"You'd think he'd at least try to impress us. But the man doesn't even try," Michael added.

"I don't much care for that pompous jerk. I can't figure out what Leah sees in him. Whatever it is…" Haydon rubbed his chin. "I know one thing. I'm not letting that man marry our sister."

"I agree. There has to be a way to stop her. But how?" Jess asked.

"I have an idea." The brothers turned their attention to Jake.

"Let's hear it."

Making sure no one could hear him, Jake shared his plan with them. "Do I have your permission?"

Haydon placed his large hand on Jake's shoulder and gave it a firm squeeze. "You sure do. Doesn't he, boys?"

The other two nodded their assent.

"Now, we'd better get back over there or they're going to eat without us."

Prayers were said over the food, so everyone fixed their plates. Jake, Elizabeth, Leah and Fitzwilliam sat at one of the smaller tables. Selina and Michael wheeled the prams over to their table.

"Mind iffen we join y'all?" Selina asked.

"No. We'd love to have you." Leah motioned for them to sit.

Jake noticed the scowl on Fitzwilliam's face when he had to move over to allow Selina and Michael to sit on the end of the bench across from each other.

What a jerk the man was.

"How you feeling, Selina?" Jake asked.

"Gettin' stronger than a bull every day."

"And ornerier, too." Michael jerked back in pain. "Ouch! Stop that." If his grin was an indicator, Michael didn't look one bit affronted by whatever just happened.

"Woulda never kicked ya iffen you'd behaved yourself." Selina wrinkled her nose at Michael and blew him a kiss.

"I say. Must you bicker at the table? You're acting like children and it is quite vexing."

Everyone's gaze slid to Fitzwilliam. Didn't he know they were teasing each other? It was all in fun. What an overstuffed shirt the man was.

"They aren't bickering, Mr. Barrington. They're having fun. You should try it sometime." The last five words were added under Leah's breath, but Jake heard them. He was certain a few others had, too, if their dipped heads and grins were any indication.

"Oh, don't go gettin' your trousers in a twist. We weren't bickerin', as you call it. Like Leah said, we was just teasin' each other." Selina eyed Fitzwilliam with disgust.

Fitzwilliam sneered at Selina. "You, madam, are—"

"Brother!" Elizabeth glared at Fitzwilliam.

He clamped his mouth shut. "My apologies to each of you. I can only blame my actions on that wretched goat for that beast has ruined my favorite hat."

Whom and what did he blame his actions on before Meanie?

The rest of the meal went fairly well. Everyone but Leah, who appeared down, talked in between taking bites of Selina's excellent Southern fried chicken, the fried trout, Swedish meatballs, potatoes sprinkled with parsley and melted butter, roast beef sandwiches and even a few foods from Jake's Norwegian ancestry such as lefse flatbread and potet klub—potato dumplings covered with butter. Jake wanted to try all the other dishes, but there were too many and his belly was full.

When everyone finished, Leah helped clean up the food, but the usual bounce in her step was missing. Jake couldn't wait to finish putting everything up and get Leah alone, hopefully before she talked to Fitzwilliam about his proposal.

Jake did double-time carrying the tables to the barn. With the last one in the storeroom, he closed the door and turned, nearly bumping into Elizabeth.

"Oh, sorry. Didn't see you there."

"My apologies. I never meant to startle you."

"No problem."

"Jake, may we talk?" Elizabeth fidgeted with the tips of her gloved fingers.

"Sure. We can go outside and—"

"No. May we talk in here, undisturbed, please?"

Her eyes looked down and then back up at him. The ends of her gloves were now twisted into points. He really didn't want to talk to her now, but he hated seeing any woman distressed. "Is something wrong?"

"No. Nothing is wrong. What I'm about to ask is extremely difficult for me."

"Oh, I see." He brushed the dust off a wooden storage container. "Won't you be seated?" He hoped this wouldn't take long. He couldn't wait to talk to Leah.

They sat down.

"What's on your mind?"

She chewed on her lip. Her chest expanded, then she looked him in the eye. "As I told you before, I lived in an isolated part of the country for years and adored it. I love country living. Especially here. Being a debutante is not for me. As you have daily witnessed, my brother cannot tolerate a lot of things. I, however, could care less about those things."

Where was she going with this?

A woman's shadow appeared on the ground outside the barn door. If he wasn't mistaken, it was Leah's.

"While what I'm about to say is highly improper, I cannot help myself."

His attention swayed back to Elizabeth, but using his peripheral vision, he kept watch on the shadow.

Elizabeth's eyelids lowered to her lap and she continued to massacre the tips of her gloves. "I no longer wish to live that kind of lifestyle. In fact, I detest it. What I'm trying to say is…" Her brown eyes met his. "I wish to remain here. With you. Would you consider marrying me?"

The shadow disappeared. Jake knew for sure it was Leah now. "Excuse me, Elizabeth. But I need to go." He pushed himself off the bench, but Elizabeth grabbed his arm.

"What about my proposal, Jake?" Hope filled her big brown eyes.

"I'm sorry, Elizabeth. You're a very nice lady, but I'm in love with someone else."

"Leah?"

"Yes. Leah."

Elizabeth nodded. "I already knew that. But, I was hoping—" She stood and her voice softened. "Leah's a blessed lady. Go after her, Jake."

Jake kissed Elizabeth's gloved hand, gave her one last look and darted out of the barn and into the trees.

Leah was right where he thought she'd be. The same place she always went when something troubled her. Her forehead rested against her arms that were pressed into the trunk of a cottonwood tree, hiding her face completely but not her sobs. Her body jerked with heart-wrenching cries. Jake's heart bled for her.

In an instant he was next to her, turning her around, pulling her into his arms and pressing her head close to his chest. "Leah, what's wrong?"

"Oh, Jake. I—I…" Sobs tore from her.

"Hey. Hey, what's the matter?" Panic brushed across his soul and settled there. Not wanting to let her out of the circle of his arms, he shifted her enough and leaned his head back until he could see her face. "Leah, please. Talk to me."

"I—I—I don't know how to—to tell you—" she said between gasps. "To tell you—"

"Leah, you know you can tell me anything, right? So whatever it is, just say it. It's all right."

She nodded and then waved her head back and forth. "No, I can't." She hiccupped. "Not now. Not this."

He set her away from him and tilted her chin up, and his gaze captured hers. "Listen to me. There's nothing you can't tell me. Now tell me what's bothering you."

She closed her eyes, then slowly opened them. "Elizabeth told me she thought you were in love with her. Then earlier today you said you'd stopped the advertisement because you had fallen in love with someone. I'm sorry, Jake. I know you're probably going to marry Elizabeth or one of the women who responded to your ad, and I have no right to tell you this, but I'm in love with you. You don't have to change your plans or anything, but—"

Jake pressed his fingertips over her lips and smiled. "I love you, too, Leah."

"What?" She blinked. "What did you say?" Her saturated eyes searched his.

"I said I love you, too."

"But—but what about Elizabeth?"

"I'm not in love with her. I'm in love with you."

She closed her eyes and opened them again. "Oh, Jake. I love you so much it hurts. But I don't know what to do. You see, I—"

"I do." Jake interrupted her. He placed one knee on the forest floor, ignoring the dampness soaking into his pant leg. "Leah, the first time I asked you to marry me was out of convenience. Now I'm asking because I love you. Will you marry me?" He looked up at her, waiting, hoping she wouldn't reject him again.

For one blessed moment he thought everything would be right again. But then her gaze fell from his.

"I—I want to, Jake, but I'm not sure I can."

Was she turning him down again? He stood and scraped his hand over the back of his neck. "I don't understand. You just told me you loved me. That you were *in love* with me. Is the reason you're not sure because I'm poor? Because you're determined to move to New York? Is it Fitzwilliam? What is it, Leah? Talk to me."

"Jake, this has nothing to do with Fitzwilliam. And it has nothing to do with you or you being poor. I don't care about money. You should know that."

No, he didn't. "You said you wanted to go back to New York to live the lifestyle you had before. So how can you say you don't care about the money?" Frustration mounted in him. He lowered himself beside her and studied her face.

"It's not about the money. Never has been. It's the memories. Honestly, Jake. I just don't see any way for us to make this work."

"You're not making any sense. What are you talking about?"

She chewed on her lip and looked around. Then she

whooshed out a long breath of air. "I haven't told anyone what I'm about to tell you, so please don't interrupt me or anything or I'll lose my nerve." She didn't look at him or even in his direction. Instead, she spoke to the floor of the forest. "Ever since my father died, I've had horrible recurring nightmares where I'm searching frantically for my father. I'm in the forest surrounded by trees that come to life. Their limbs look like arms with long fingers that spread out and reach for me." She ducked her head down as if they were trying to get her now.

Jake wanted to comfort her but didn't know if he should. She had asked him not to interrupt. In his gut, he had a feeling if he did that he would be doing that very thing, so he didn't.

"I can feel evil all around me." Her body shuddered. Her eyes glassed over, not just with tears, but with the images of the dream.

His full attention locked on her, he struggled to keep his arms at his side.

"I beg them to leave me alone, but they don't. I scream for my father. I hear his voice, but it's gurgled as if he's choking. Then, I look down and see him. Blood is running out of his nose and mouth." Tears flowed through each painstaking word she spoke. "Just like they did the day he died."

He didn't know she'd seen her father buried under that tree the day he'd died. Ache for her drove further into his soul.

"The nightmares always end the same—with me saying I'm sorry." Her tear-drenched eyes finally met his. "I don't know what to do, Jake. I hate it here. This place stole my father from me." She laid her hand across his cheek. Her eyes overflowed with love and sadness.

"I love you with all my heart, and it will kill me to leave you, but I don't see any way out of this mess except to go back to New York to where memories of my father are pleasant and peaceful, not horrifying. I can see now there is no other answer."

Yes, there was, and he would find it.

Leah's heart hurt more than it ever had before. She pressed her hand into her chest, willing the torturous pain to go away, yet knowing it never would. In leaving, she would be trading one heartbreak for another.

Jake pulled her hands into his. She latched on to them. To him. Needing the connection. Needing his strength. His love spread deep into her soul and wrapped its warmth around her heart. How desperately she needed the strength and love he offered her at this moment. She searched his face, memorizing every line, every crease, every detail.

"Leah."

Her eyes snapped up to his.

"I'm sorry for what you've been through. Wish I could take all your pain onto myself. Make it all go away. But, I can't. I won't ask you to stay here."

A huge chunk of her heart tore off, leaving a wide chasm. She pressed her hand tighter into her chest, willing with everything inside for the pain to leave. Yet how could it? The man she loved was lost to her forever. She doubled over, and the floods descended. Not only was she crying for the loss of her father, but also for the loss of the dearest, most cherished best friend she'd ever had.

Jake's arms encircled her like a protective shield as he pulled her tight against him. "Don't cry. If you'll still have me, I'll do whatever it takes to keep you.

Whatever you need me to do, including moving to New York, if need be."

She yanked her head back and stared into his handsome face. The face she loved so dearly. "You—you would do that?" Her heart leaped with hope. "Move to New York with me?"

"I'd do anything for you." He swallowed, and a tremble emanated from him. Dampness moistened her back where his hands rested, and the veins in his arms throbbed faster. He pushed himself off the log.

Realization pummeled her brain. Jake was having a panic attack just thinking about going to New York.

Hope slipped from her heart. What had she been thinking? How selfish of her to even consider such a thing. She'd witnessed those attacks and how hard they were on him. He could never move to the city. Nor would she ask him to. She loved him too much to let him do that.

Her eyes trailed upward.

Jake stood in front of a large tree with his arms crossed. Behind that tree was an even larger, partially uprooted tree with a thick trunk leaning toward it and Jake.

Sunlight streaked through the trees, silhouetting him.

Quick as lightning bolts, flashes of memory struck into her brain.

Swatches of the day pieced together, spiking terror deep into every part of her being.

Her breath strangled to where not even a gasp could be gotten.

Leah leaped up and barreled into Jake, forcing his body as far away from the two trees as she could. He landed on his side on the cushioned forest floor with a thud. She ended up next to him.

"What'd you do that for?"

Panic gripped her so violently that sanity scattered. "I'm sorry. I'm sorry. I just… I couldn't let it kill you, too."

"Let what kill me?" Jake pushed himself off the ground, shaking the pine needles from his arms. Perplexed, he reached down and helped her up, then brushed the fern leaves and stems off the rest of him.

Looking up at the towering monsters above her, her body trembled so violently she thought her knees would buckle and her heart would stop beating. "That—that tree. I couldn't let it kill you."

Jake stared at her as if she'd lost her mind. Maybe she had. She didn't know. All she knew was something had snapped inside her. Something ugly. Something more frightening than anything she'd ever known before.

"You okay?" Concern covered every inch of his face.

"Yes." She nodded. "No." She shook her head so hard hairpins flew in all directions. "Oh, Jake," she cried as sharp talons shredded her heart and pierced her soul. She knuckled her hand into her chest, but nothing could ease this pain. "It's all my fault."

"What's all your fault?" He tried to pull her into his arms, but she stepped back, holding her arms in front of her like a shield. She didn't deserve his comfort— or anyone else's—for what she'd done.

"I now understand why my nightmares end with me telling Father I'm sorry." She stared at the ground, seeing nothing but her own guilt. Tears saturated her eyes.

"Leah, you're not making any sense again."

She tore her focus from the ground and dragged it over to his. Concern filled those soft eyes she so loved.

She couldn't hold his gaze, though—shame and guilt wouldn't let her. In fact, it was all she could do to choke out the next words. "When I saw you standing in front of those trees, it—it all came back to me. Every bit of it." She shuddered and pointed to the trees she had just shoved Jake away from. "See how that tree's almost uprooted?"

"Yeah?" He frowned. "What about it?"

"See how that other one is leaning toward it?" She pulled her hankie out and wiped her eyes then her nose.

"Yes. There's a lot of trees around here like that. What's that got to do with anything?"

"The day my father died…" She put her hand on the tree next to her to steady herself as reality peeled away leaving only the shadow of memories. "I remember the wind blowing really hard and the rain pelting down equally as hard. I was worried about my father being out in the woods in the storm, so I went to try and find him. By the time I spotted him, it had started lightning, too. It was cracking all around us. I hollered at him. He turned and looked at me and waved. Lightning struck the uprooted tree next to him. The tree toppled over—right on top of him. Don't you see?" Even though it hurt for him to know the ugly truth about her, she willed him to understand. "My father died because of me, Jake. It's all my fault." Uncontrollable sobs rent Leah's body. Her legs buckled, but her body never met the ground. Arms strong, yet gentle caught her.

Jake pulled her close, supporting her weight with his strength. "No, Leah, you didn't kill him. The tree did. It was an accident."

Unable to trust her legs to hold her up on their own

strength, she clung to him, leaned her head back and gazed up at him. "No, it wasn't an accident. It's all my fault. If I had never gone looking for him, had never hollered at him, then he would have never stopped to wave at me, and he would be alive today."

Jake shook his head as he stared into her eyes. "Leah, no— You can't blame yourself. Did you know lightning was going to hit that tree at that exact moment?"

"No. But—"

Jake placed his fingertips over her lips. "There are no buts, Leah. There was no way you could have known lightning was going to strike right then and there. If you did, would you have hollered for him?"

"No." She shook her head.

"Well…" His sentence hung in the air for a moment. "Let me ask you this… If Haydon or Michael or Jess or Abby had gone out looking for him and the same thing happened to them, would you blame them for killing your father?"

"No. No. Never." Her response came out as fast as the lightning that had struck that tree.

Jake hiked one brow her way.

Her mind started to see the logic of what he was saying, was trying to grasp it even.

She would have never blamed her brothers or sister or anyone else if the exact same thing had happened. So why was she blaming herself?

The guilt fell away. Tears drizzled from her eyes, only this time they were tears of relief. "Oh, Jake. You're right. All these years I've carried this guilt inside me." She pressed her fisted hand into her chest where the constant pain had resided. "I never knew why until today. I never understood the nightmares, or why I had them when no one else seemed to. Oh, Jake. Thank you." she whispered into his heart beating against her ear. A heart that now belonged to her. "I love you, Jake."

"I love you, too." His whisper held a caress, one she held on to for more moments than it was there.

Then as if another lightning bolt of truth had struck her, she yanked back. "Sweet twinkling stars above."

"What?"

"Mother was right. I've been so blind and foolish."

"Now what are you talking about?" His brows puckered.

"You." Her eyes danced back and forth and the love she had for Jake reflected from hers into his. "Mother said that sometimes God places something right before our eyes but we don't see it because we're too busy looking somewhere else or for something else. I've always wanted a man like my father. A man who could make me feel protected. Secure. Loved. Who would comfort me and make me feel special. Jake, you're that man."

His lazy grin belied the glow on his face.

"I love you, Jake. But I can't ask you to move to New York with me. I can't do that to you."

His smile ended and his face dulled.

"So I'm going to stay here. I want to be with you."

In less than a heartbeat, he crushed her to him in the gentlest way. "My sweet, lovable princess. I love you."

"Hey, you called me princess." Her lips curled upward until she was certain they would take over her face.

"Yep. Sure did. You said being a princess was important to you. You'll always be my princess." Jake's mouth covered hers. His kiss went directly to her heart and soul, melting it with its passion, its warmth and its love. Long moments later, he raised his head and gazed tenderly at her. "I love you, Leah."

"I love you, too."

"So, does this mean you're gonna marry me?"

"Yep." Leah used his own word to answer him.

"Let's get one thing perfectly clear first."

"What's that?"

"This won't be a marriage of convenience, but of love."

"Good. I wouldn't have it any other way." She winked at him.

Jake kissed her again soundly. "Now, let's go tell your family the good news."

Leah quickly brushed her clothes and put her hair to rights. "What about Fitzwilliam and Elizabeth?"

"I have a feeling they won't be there."

"How come?"

"Because Elizabeth figured out that I'm in love with you."

"She did?"

"Yep. But if they are there, we'll share our news later."

"What about my brothers? I don't know how they'll feel about this."

"I do."

"You do?"

"Yep. Already talked to them about us and asked their permission to marry you."

"You did? Ah," she said. "That's so sweet. What did they say?" She tilted her head and a curl fell against her cheek.

"They thought it was about time I came to my senses and realized I was in love with you. They wished me luck and said they'd be praying for me. And for you to say yes." Jake settled the strand of hair behind her ear and ran his finger slowly over her cheek, across her lips and under her chin. He tilted her head up, his soft lips only a breath away.

"Kiss me again, Jake."

His eyelids drifted shut. His lips touched hers, softly, then playfully, then possessively. Her heart sighed and melted into his. The man sure knew how to kiss. She couldn't wait to become his wife.

Their lips eventually parted but with great reluctance.

Jake cupped her hand in his and they threaded their way through the wild ferns and trees.

When the noise of the festivities reached them, Leah stopped and strained to see if Fitzwilliam was anywhere around the ranch yard. She really wasn't looking forward to that confrontation. There was no sign of either him or Elizabeth or the carriage they'd rode in on. "They're gone," she told Jake with a huge sigh of relief.

"Good." Jake stopped her. "Leah, before we get married I want to ask your mother's permission."

"I think that would be nice. Thank you."

"One more thing. What if your mother marries Mr. Barker? Will your living here and witnessing it bother you?"

"I'm not sure. But one thing I am sure of… You'll be there for me if it does."

"Yep." Jake pulled her hand to his lips and kissed it. Love, warm and sweet, went from his lips straight into her heart. "One last thing— You sure you won't mind living in a small, three-room house?" Worry flitted across his face.

"Nope. I don't care about that. I care about you."

"But you said you wanted to go to balls and all that stuff."

"I thought I did. Truth is, after being around all those people at Phoebe's wedding, then at Mr. Barker's the other night, and then Fitzwilliam, I couldn't care less if I ever see another gown or attend another snooty gathering ever again. I no more belong with those people than a pig belongs in a mansion."

"A pig in a mansion, huh?" He grinned and so did she.

Her attention jumped from his to across the yard. "Oh, look. There's Mother. Let's go talk to her." She grabbed his hand and dragged him behind her. For someone who was so against the arrangement an hour ago, she sure had come around quickly. "Mother, can Jake and I speak with you for a moment?"

"Of course."

"I'll talk to you later, Mother." Michael glanced at Jake.

Jake nodded once.

Michael smiled and gave a quick nod of his own, then he turned and strolled over to Selina. Her brother leaned down and said something to his wife. Selina looked over at them, smiling from ear to ear.

Leah's heart warmed knowing they loved Jake and that they approved of her choice of husband. Well, God's choice, really. After hearing the pastor's message about putting God first and ourselves second, during that very service, she'd done just that and look what it had gotten her. The man of her dreams.

"Mrs. Bowen." Jake cleared his throat. "I would like to ask permission to marry your daughter."

"Oh, well, Abby's too young to marry. She's only seventeen." Twinkles glittered her mother's eyes.

"No. I meant…" Jake tugged at his shirt collar.

"Mother. Stop. She's teasing you, Jake."

"Yes, I am. Of course you have my permission to marry Leah. And God's, too."

"What do you mean 'God's, too'?"

"Well, ever since you and Jake ran the sack race, I had a feeling about you two and started praying way back then. And every time I did, it was as if I could sense God's approval."

"Thank you, Mother." Leah threw her arms around her. "Your prayers have been answered. And mine, too. Because of that, we have a wedding to plan."

"The sooner, the better." Jake winked, and getting his full meaning, Leah blushed.

The next morning, Leah bolted upright in bed. She pinched her eyes shut and a deep guttural groan leaked out of her. Her newfound love and revelation hadn't stopped the nightmares. "Why, God?" When no answer came, she hurried through her toiletries and flew toward the barn, hoping Jake was there alone, as was his norm in the morning twilight.

Leah stepped inside the dim interior of the barn. The instant she spotted Jake, she rushed over to him and threw her arms around his waist. Sobs tore from her.

"Hey, what's wrong?" Jake cupped her head snugly into his chest.

"I—I h-had anoth-another nightmare."

"Oh, honey." He pressed her head closer to his chest, his arm tightening around her.

She stayed that way for a moment before leaning her head back and gazing into his eyes. "I don't understand, Jake. Why did this happen? I thought because I'd finally understood why I had them that they would be gone. Or that love would make everything better. What do I do, Jake? I can't take the pain that each one brings. Do I have to leave you and everyone I love and go back to New York for this to be finally over?"

"Leah, love doesn't make bad go away. But it helps us to get through it. I don't know why you had another nightmare. Can't tell you what nobody can know. I can tell you that moving back to New York won't likely solve your problem, either."

"What makes you say that?" She tilted her head sideways.

Jake tucked a strand of hair behind her ear. "I live hundreds of miles from Atlantic City."

What did that have to do with her situation?

"Moving states away didn't solve my problem."

Leah frowned. "Huh? I don't understand."

"Leah, honey. My best memories are on my farm. My worst are in Atlantic City. Changing residences didn't solve what's happening on the inside—only God can do that."

"How? I've been praying about this for years."

"Don't know, princess. Only God knows what it will take. What I do know is 'Two are better than one, because they have a good reward for their labor. For if they fall, the one will lift up his fellow, but woe to him that is alone when he falleth, for he hath not another to help him up.'"

"Ecclesiastes four, nine and ten," she whispered.

"I can't fix everything, princess. Can't even stop the nightmares. Wish I could, but I can't." The same finger that had replaced her curl now rested under her chin. "I can, however, promise to be here with you no matter what. To lift you up. To comfort you, and to protect you through those times."

Leah shifted out of his arms and put her back to him, struggling with what to do. She thought about Jake and how even though he lived miles away from where his problems had started—lived where memories of his family were sweet—panic attacks still plagued him. If Jake could survive what he had to endure, well, so could she. Only now neither of them would have to endure it alone.

Leah turned, and Jake was right there. Just where he said he'd be. Her eyes collided with his. She cupped his face. "My sweet Jake. I love you with all my heart. I promise to do the same and be there for you, too."

Jake drew her into the circle of his strong arms. "I love you, too. Together we can do this."

Their lips sealed the promise between them.

Epilogue

Twenty-one days had passed since Jake had proposed for the second time. During that time he'd courted Leah properly, bringing her gifts and taking her on picnics and evening strolls.

Those three weeks seemed like forever. Today they were finally getting married. Underneath the hot late-afternoon sun, Leah slowly made her way down the aisle, smiling at her friends and family sitting in the rows of benches lined in the yard of her family's ranch. Each step she took, her ivory silk taffeta bustle gown with layers of lace and an asymmetrical skirt with pale pink lace and bows brushed the top of her white button-up boots. It had taken her and Abby hours to sew on the delicate row of pink flowers draped diagonally across the boned corset bodice and neckline. Today she felt like a real princess.

Leah gazed at Jake, who looked more handsome than she'd ever seen him look before—something she thought would never be possible as he was already the most handsome man she'd ever seen.

Their eyes connected and held. Jake reached out his hand and she willingly laid hers in his.

"You ready?" Pastor James asked.

"Yep. Sure am," Jake answered in a rush.

The crowd laughed. When the laughter died, there in front of God and man, Leah said her vows and then Jake said his. He vowed to love, honor, cherish, protect and comfort her. All the things he had spent his life doing already. The very same things that reminded her of her beloved father.

"You may now kiss your bride, Jake."

"Yep. Think I will."

Everyone laughed again.

Jake tilted her chin and kissed her softly, lightly and yet not nearly long enough. When he raised his head, she tilted her head and sent him a questioning look.

He tucked her hair behind her ear. "Later, princess. Later."

She blushed.

After everyone had eaten and the gifts were opened, they said their goodbyes and headed to her buggy—their buggy—decorated with streamers of bowed ribbons and strings of rusty tin cans.

Her mother, brothers, sisters-in-law, sister, nieces and nephews gathered around them. Leah hugged and thanked each one, then Jake helped her into the carriage filled with her belongings.

She tucked herself under her husband's arm and snuggled into his chest on the way to his home. Their home. She sighed.

"What's that for?"

"I can't believe that you're mine. And that your beautiful home is mine now, too." She gazed up at her husband.

Jake pressed his shoulders back and pride marched

across his face. "Can't believe it, either. That you're mine, too."

"Yep." Leah laughed, then captured his lips in a long, breath-robbing kiss.

When the kiss ended, Jake breathlessly said, "Giddyup" and clicked the lines.

At her new home, they unloaded her belongings and while Jake went and put the horse and buggy up, Leah went to their bedroom, where her trunk rested at the end of the bed. She opened it and grabbed her diary.

Dear Mr. Darcy,
You won't be hearing from me anymore. Sorry to disappoint you by saying this, but I found someone even better than you—my very own prince who is everything I always wanted and more. A prince who is my beloved father's equal. So, Mr. Darcy, this is goodbye. Thank you for listening to me all this time.
Love,
Leah

Leah closed the book and clutched it against her chest.

"What you got there?" Jake came up behind her and slipped his arms around her.

Leah turned in his arms with one arm behind her back. She felt behind her and placed the book in her trunk and covered it with an item of clothing. "Nothing of consequence. Not anymore, anyway." With those words, she slipped her arms around her husband's neck and kissed him until her knees threatened to no longer hold her.

The next morning Leah woke up, wrapped in her

husband's embrace. During the night, instead of a nightmare, she had dreamed about her prince of a husband. Hopefully it was the first of many good dreams. But even if it wasn't, she knew Jake's love would see her through the bad times, and that she had finally found the groom she had always wanted.

* * * * *

Noelle Marchand is a native Houstonian living out her childhood dream of being a writer. She graduated summa cum laude from Houston Baptist University in 2012, earning a bachelor's degree in mass communications and speech communications. She loves exploring new books and new cities. When she's not scribbling out her latest manuscript, you may find her pursuing one of her other passions—music, dance, history and classic movies.

Books by Noelle Marchand

Love Inspired Historical

Bachelor List Matches

The Texan's Inherited Family
The Texan's Courtship Lessons
The Texan's Engagement Agreement

Unlawfully Wedded Bride
The Runaway Bride
A Texas-Made Match

Visit the Author Profile page
at Harlequin.com for more titles.

A TEXAS-MADE MATCH

Noelle Marchand

Brothers and sisters, I do not consider myself yet to have taken hold of it. But one thing I do: Forgetting what is behind and straining toward what is ahead, I press on toward the goal to win the prize for which God has called me heavenward in Christ Jesus.
—*Philippians 3:13–14*

Dedicated with love to my father and brother.

Special thanks to Elizabeth Mazer for allowing me
to share all three of the O'Brien's stories!
Also, thanks to Karen Ball of Steve Laube Agency
for all her hard work.

Chapter One

Peppin, Texas
September 1888

Ellie O'Brien was not the type of girl to chase after men.

That might have to change.

After all, today was her twenty-first birthday. While that hadn't stopped her from revisiting her mischievous youth by climbing to her favorite place in the whole world—the top of the waterfall that pooled into her family's creek—it was pushing marriageable age. This wouldn't have been a problem in most Western towns, where the scarcity of women allowed them to take their time picking husbands. The town of Peppin didn't have that problem, though. Women were plentiful, and the competition between them, while friendly, was still fierce. Ellie had never attempted to jump into the fray before. Now, though it might be too late, she wanted to at least try.

But first, one more moment of being a child.

Her fingers teased the hairpins from her hair with a familiarity born of desperation, then tossed them to the dry ground below like the nuisances they were. She shook out her curly golden tresses, reveling in her newfound freedom as the wind made her hair bounce in disarray. Warm mud oozed between her bare toes as she stepped closer to the precipice. The water rushed past her feet, urging her to join its free fall away from the side of the waterfall and into the creek seven feet below. If she took that final step forward, there would be no going back.

Literally and figuratively. She bit her bottom lip as she peered over through the treetops at the rolling green hills that stretched beyond their property. Perhaps it was too romantic to hope that courtship would be as exhilarating as a sheer fall or as refreshing as the cool shock of cold water that followed—but a gal could hope.

It wasn't as if she were only interested in the romance part of getting a husband. Oh, no. Ellie also wanted the adventure that would come with it. After all, her sister Kate had quite the adventure when she fell in love with Nathan Rutledge. Their courtship commenced with a shoot-out, continued with Kate's abduction and was clinched with an arson fire. And then there was Lorelei, Ellie's sister-in-law of nearly one year. She found love through a run-in with a con artist, a secret engagement and a bank robbery.

Ellie blew out a frustrated sigh then whispered to a God she knew was listening. "It isn't as if I want to be abducted or almost killed or anything. I just know what a girl needs to do to get a little excitement around here—find love."

And it worked both ways. There was nothing like a little excitement and danger to make people look at each other in new ways, see things about each other that they hadn't noticed before. In that respect, she could use all the help she could get, living in a town where every eligible man saw her as a little sister.

She couldn't exactly blame them. She'd been a consummate tomboy growing up. She didn't regret one moment she'd spent climbing trees, riding horses, swimming in the creek—they'd all held far more appeal than giggling and flirting with boys like the girls too afraid of mussing their dresses to have any fun. At some point those giggling, flirting girls had started getting beaus who turned into suitors and then into husbands. But not Ellie. Even though she'd abandoned her hoydenish ways years ago, she hadn't been able to shake the label of "tomboy" the town had given her or change the way the young men saw her—yet.

She was ready for the most important adventures of her life, like love, marriage, motherhood. She just needed someone to share them with. And if it took a little danger or excitement to make that happen…well, she was up for it.

"I'm ready to do my part, Lord. Is a little help too much to ask?"

She didn't wait for an answer. She knew only God could join two hearts together—but that didn't mean He couldn't have help. When it came to her siblings, Ellie had helped Him along as much as possible. There was a reason she'd been dubbed the best matchmaker in Peppin. She was the best in town at spotting a match and pulling it off.

But who would help the matchmaker find a match?

No one. That's who. She was going to have to do it on her own, and she was starting today. First things first: she had to figure out a way to climb down from the waterfall without messing up her day dress. *Being adventurous was easier when I wore bloomers.*

There was a simpler way to get down. She peered over the waterfall's tabletop once more, knowing that if she didn't have plans for the afternoon she would have taken that route. Suddenly, Kate's voice shot through the air with startling volume. "Ellie, *don't!*"

She jerked toward the sound, knocking herself off balance and sending her arms churning like a tilted windmill. She fell into the creek with a loud splash. The cool water enveloped her and swept her skirts up around her ears before Ellie pushed off the muddy bottom. She surfaced and searched for her cinnamon-haired sister. Kate's sensible blue dress stood out against the riot of red, orange and yellow wildflowers that painted the banks of the creek.

Ellie swam toward the shore. "I wasn't going to jump. You startled me!"

"Oh, no!" Kate placed one hand over her mouth and another on her hip as she shook her head. "I'm so sorry. What were you doing up there in the first place?"

Ellie shivered in the slight breeze as she stepped onto dry grass. "Reliving my youth."

"You'd better not—after all you put me through." Kate grabbed the picnic blanket from the ground to wrap it around Ellie's shoulders.

"I don't know what you're talking about. I was perfect." She lifted her nose, ignoring a laugh from her sister as she gathered the blanket closer. "What are you doing here so early, anyway? I thought you said I had two hours to myself."

"It's been longer than two hours. We are supposed to meet Ms. Lettie and Lorelei at the café for your birthday lunch in thirty minutes."

"I'm sorry. I must have lost track of time."

"That's all right. So did I." Kate grabbed the picnic basket from the ground and began to lead the way to the farmhouse. "It can't be helped now. You'll have to change clothes and redo your hair."

Ellie paused. "I hadn't thought of that. Do you think it would make a difference?"

Kate tossed a confused look over her shoulder. "Of course it would. You can't go into town drenched."

She laughed. "I forgot you can't read my mind. I meant do you think it would make a difference with men if I changed my hair or clothes?"

"What men? Why should it make a difference? Why would you want to…?" Kate shook her head. "What *are* you talking about?"

"I'm twenty-one. Isn't it time I tried to catch a husband?" It was a little difficult to force the words out through her chattering teeth. "Do you think I even could?"

Kate rubbed her back to try to warm her. "You're more likely to catch a cold if you don't get changed. As for a husband, there's no need to rush. Why? Are you interested in someone?"

"No."

They caught sight of the two-story farmhouse and Kate ushered her toward it. "Then don't worry about it. Go change and try to be quick."

Ellie nodded then hurried into the house and up the stairs to her room. She quickly changed into dry clothes. A distant peal of laughter drew her attention to the large window facing the barn. She grabbed a hand towel from the vanity and dried her hair as she watched her brother-in-law tease her sister about something. Her nieces and nephew danced around their legs in anticipation of the promised ride that would keep them occupied while Kate and Ellie went into town. The couple stole a quick kiss before the whole family walked toward the barn.

The smile that slipped across Ellie's lips preempted a wistful sigh. She combed her fingers through her hair. *It must make a girl feel awfully special to be loved. If a man loved me the way Nathan loves Kate and Sean loves Lorelei, well, it might make up for certain other things.*

On the heels of that thought rode a familiar yet vague feeling of guilt. She pushed it away stubbornly. Today was for celebrating the future, not belaboring distant memories of the past that probably meant nothing. A glimpse of Kate walking toward the house served as a welcome reminder of the need to hurry and sent her rushing to make up for the time she'd spent lollygagging.

Thirty minutes later, Ellie glanced at the three women who'd taken time out of their busy day to help her celebrate her birthday. Kate sat across from her. Their dearly departed mother's best friend, Mrs. Lettie Williams, sat to her right. Lorelei, her sister-in-law, sat on her left. They were all beautiful. They were all strong. They were all married. And Ellie? Well, she wasn't sure she could lay a legitimate claim to any of those things.

Either I'm being obsessive or I'm detecting a theme. She narrowed her eyes as Maddie settled their drinks on the table. "Maddie, would you happen to have a pencil and piece of paper I could use?"

"Certainly." Maddie pulled the pencil from behind her ear and tore a sheet of paper from the small tablet she carried in her pocket.

"Thanks." Ellie tilted her head, then wrote down on one side of the paper a list of the local bachelors who attended church. Then she started going down the list and writing in initials of certain young women in town alongside a few of the men's names.

Lettie's curious voice broke through her thoughts. "Ellie, what *are* you doing?"

Her hand paused in its feverish pace. She glanced up to find all three women watching her. Her gaze dropped to the paper in her hands before she offered them an innocent smile. "I'm finding myself a husband."

Kate nearly choked on the sip of water she'd taken. Lorelei stared at her, mouth agape. Lettie started chuckling and couldn't seem to stop. "The world would be a dull place without you, Ellie."

Ellie grinned. "Wouldn't it?"

Lettie leaned forward. "How exactly is that piece of paper going to help you find a husband?"

Ellie shrugged. "By process of elimination. I'll match the eligible young men with the women they are interested in and go from there."

"Oh, Ellie." Lorelei laughed then leaned across the table for a better view. "Let me help."

Kate had always tried to put a damper on Ellie's escapades. Nathan was content to sit on the sidelines and enjoy whatever scene she'd caused. As a child, her brother, Sean, had always been in the thick of things with her, but eventually he became too sensible to be involved in any excitement she might cause. Then he'd married Lorelei. Ellie's world had not been the same since. She finally had a partner in crime.

Lorelei scooted her chair closer. Ellie glanced up at Kate's exasperated sigh. She didn't buy that for a moment. Kate's eyes were filled with just as much laughter as Lettie's. Ellie picked up the pencil and got back to work. Kate covered her grin by taking another sip of water. "Ellie does seem to have a sixth sense when it comes to detecting romance."

Ellie glanced at Lettie. The woman was responsible for Ellie's "sixth sense" and didn't even know it. Lettie told her at a young age that it didn't always matter so much what a person said as what a person didn't say. For that reason, Ellie had spent her life picking up on the little clues no one else noticed. Like the way Maddie's tone of voice changed when she asked for Jeff Bridger's order, and the way his nervous fingers straightened his collar while he gave it.

She added Maddie's initials to Jeff's name before handing it to Lorelei. "Now, tell me who is left without initials by his name. I'm going to ask you to mark off the men I could not possibly see myself with. Hopefully, we'll find a winner."

"Christian Johansen."

Ellie shook her head. The young man had been her good friend for years, but she couldn't imagine him as anything more.

"Rhett Granger." Lorelei glanced up. "He's handsome."

"I thought I marked him off. He's taken."

Lorelei leaned toward her. "Taken by whom?"

"Never mind that." She leaned back to give the women a knowing glance. "Just mark my words."

"Donovan Turner."

Ellie froze. Her gaze shot to Lorelei's mirth-filled eyes and she frowned. "Lorelei O'Brien, that man was not allowed on my list. He gives me the willies. Who's left?"

Lorelei exchanged a glance with Kate. "No one."

"What? How is that possible?"

Kate leaned over to look at the list. "Everyone else has initials. Some have question marks by them, though. What do those mean?"

Ellie frowned. "It means I'm sure of what the man thinks, or the woman, but not both. I suppose those are still possibilities—until I find out for sure if they're really taken. But there's really no one else without initials?"

Kate shook her head. "You paired off every decent man on the list."

Ellie sat in stunned silence. "I'm going to be a spinster."

"Don't say that." Lorelei sounded horrified.

She buried her face in her hands. "Why not? It's true."

"What's true, Ellie?" Maddie sidled up to the table with their plates.

Ellie spread her fingers to peer up at Maddie. "I'm going to die a decrepit old maid."

Maddie laughed. "Don't be silly."

Ellie straightened abruptly and nearly managed to bump her head on the plate Maddie was setting in front of her. She met the woman's dark brown eyes adamantly. "It isn't silly. It isn't silly at all. I went through every bachelor in town and I'm pretty sure that none of them work."

"You did what?" The woman backed away as if afraid to find out the answer.

"I think you should try again," Lettie said as Kate handed her the list. "Something as serious as this should not be taken lightly or composed hastily. Give yourself time to think about it."

"Ms. Lettie is right," Kate said, though Ellie had

a feeling her sister was just trying to make her feel better about not finding a match. "Maybe you made a mistake."

"You left someone off."

Ellie frowned at Lettie. "I did? I thought I listed every decent, God-fearing man in town."

"That's why." The woman nodded as if the mysteries of the world had been explained to her, while eyeing her thoughtfully. "I don't know why I never thought of it before."

"Thought of what?" Lorelei asked as everyone seemed to lean forward in anticipation.

Lettie exchanged a meaningful look with Kate. At first, Kate's brow furrowed, then slowly the illuminating light of intuition seemed to fill her eyes. "You mean…?"

Lettie nodded.

Kate's eyes widened, then she stared at Ellie before sitting back in her chair. "Hmm."

Ellie exchanged a confused glance with Lorelei. "Who is it?"

A slow smile lifted Kate's lips. "This could be good. This could be very good."

It was always good to get letters from home. Lawson glanced at Nathan Rutledge's letter then turned to the one from the woman he called Mother. Reaching his room in the boarding house, he tugged off his dirty boots, threw his Stetson on his desk and fell back onto his bed, allowing himself to give in to exhaustion for just a moment before opening his mail.

It had been a long, hard year filled with dangerous work and too many secrets. As a Texas Ranger, he'd rounded up more than his fair share of outlaws, and he tried to find some satisfaction in that. But this near-vagabond existence was too much like the life he'd left behind when he'd stumbled into Peppin, Texas, abandoned and alone with nowhere to go until the O'Brien family took him in. A few months later, when he was fourteen, Doc and Lettie Williams adopted him. They'd been the parents he'd always dreamed of. His life in Peppin had been so good that he'd nearly forgotten about the past. Here…he seemed to run across it every day in the smell of liquor, the haunted eyes of the saloon girls, the solitude and the need to be on constant alert.

His commanding officer in the Rangers constantly told him not to lose the chip on his shoulder. "That's what makes you stand out from the other Rangers. That's what makes you tough. That's what enables you to get your man. Never lose that chip."

Lawson wasn't stupid enough to believe him. God was the one enabling him to catch those criminals. As for the chip on his shoulder—well, he reckoned he'd picked it up sometime between being abandoned and wandering into Peppin. Unfortunately, it didn't keep the harshness of this life from wearing away at him, day by day.

Time for a distraction. He tore open the letter from his parents first. It was a thick one so it ought to be good. He lifted the letter above his head just high enough for it to catch the sunlight shining through the window behind him. The room was so silent that he decided to read it out loud: "'Dear Lawson, You really should come home.'"

He sat up in concern and pulled the letter closer. "'Now, don't get all excited. Everyone here is fine. Your pa and I just miss you like crazy. We haven't seen you in more than a year. You haven't come home for any of the holidays. I know you work hard and what you do is important. This isn't to make you feel guilty. This is just to tell you that we love you and we want to see you. Surely you can apply for a leave of absence. Just a few weeks of your company—that's all I ask. Now, I've said my piece so I won't mention it again.'"

She kept her promise and went on to talk about some of the things Lawson had mentioned in his last letter, but he kept going back to that first paragraph. She was right. He hadn't been home since he'd left a few weeks after his almost wedding to Lorelei.

Pretty Lorelei Wilkins had been his sweetheart for years. Asking her to marry him had seemed like the next logical step. He had cared for her, had been determined to be a good husband to her—but before that could happen, she'd run out on their wedding, leaving him literally at the altar. When he'd chased after her, she'd told him the truth: that she didn't think she loved him in the right way to be his wife…and that she didn't think he loved her the right way, either.

She was right. He'd been so hungry to have a family of his own, to make a life for himself that was completely different from the childhood he left behind, that he'd rushed into a wedding that came more from his head than his heart. He'd realized that she deserved more and maybe he did, too, so he did the honorable thing. He let her go. Then he did what his pride demanded, and left. He wasn't there to see her marry Sean O'Brien, Lawson's best friend and the man Lorelei had always secretly loved, though he was happy for her—happy for both of them—that they'd found the love they deserved.

He knew that calling off the wedding had been the right decision, but it had still hurt. The wedding was supposed to prove that he'd overcome his past, that he was starting a new life and a new family. Instead, it seemed to prove the opposite and reminded him of all the rejection he'd experienced before. In truth, it was no wonder she'd walked away so easily. The people who mattered most often did.

He read the letter from Sean's brother-in-law, Nathan Rutledge, then let it fall to his chest as he stared at the ceiling. There must be some conspiracy to make him come home. Nathan wrote that his horse ranch had been doing so well that he'd decided to expand. He was offering Lawson the job of foreman just in case he'd grown tired of being a Ranger.

"Lord, is this from You?"

It was possible that God was bringing his time as a Ranger to a close. If so, Lawson planned to listen. God had been getting Lawson out of danger since he'd been a scraggly ten-year-old fending for himself on the streets, even if he hadn't known Whom to thank for it right away. God had helped him find a fresh start once. Maybe it was time for another new beginning.

Lawson Williams still had something to prove—that he was nothing like the parents who'd given him life then done their best to ruin it. He'd keep proving it to himself over and over again until he could finally believe it. He'd thought being a lawman would provide the opportunity to do that but perhaps the best way to prove it was by going home.

Ellie was trying her best to ignore the young man who'd been trailing after her for the past ten minutes. It wasn't working. She turned and planted her hands on her hips as she eyed the dashing young blacksmith.

"Rhett, if you insist on following me then you might as well make yourself useful."

She pointed to the signs for the booths resting on the church stairs. The Founder's Day activities had already started but the signs needed extra time to dry. Rhett really must have been desperate because he picked them up and began helping her hand them out to the booth workers. "Ellie, I'm sure I'm on your list. You've got to tell me. Jeff Bridger says you told him about Maddie and they are already engaged."

She smiled as she handed Mrs. Redding the sign for her lemonade stand then moved on. "I know they're engaged. I invited you to the party I'm having for them at the ranch. Don't tell me you forgot about it already."

"I didn't forget and you aren't going to distract me." His muscles bulged as he shifted the remaining signs to his shoulder, which somehow made his pleading look seem all the more pitiful. "I've just *got* to know who you think my match is."

She rolled her eyes. It had been two weeks since the fateful day she'd created the "Bachelor List." The whole thing had turned into a disaster. Everyone in town knew about it. She'd had plenty of available men seeking her out after word got around. Unfortunately, they weren't looking for her. They'd just wanted to know whose initials were next to their names on the list.

She could understand them wanting an answer. She'd wanted one, too, but Lettie and Kate never told her who the mystery suitor for her was. Try as she might to extricate the information from them, she'd gained little more for her efforts than a headache.

She sighed. "Well, Rhett, who do you want it to be?"

She followed his gaze as it trailed to where Amy Bradley stood with her sisters. He watched Amy for a full minute before Ellie shook her head and smiled. "Yep, that's what I thought."

His gaze jumped back to hers, and then he grinned. "Thank you."

"I didn't say anything."

He nodded then set off toward Amy. She grabbed his massive arm and dug her heels into the ground to stop him. "Oh, no you don't. You're going to help me deliver all these signs because you're *so* grateful. Isn't that right?"

"Yeah, that's right. I shouldn't get ahead of myself." He patted her hand in brotherly affection and began trailing her again but remained decidedly distracted. He seemed to grow less confident as they continued and when she finally set him free, he went in the opposite direction from where his thoughts had been taking him.

Now, what's wrong with him? She pulled the new list from her pocket and crossed out the question mark beside Amy's initials by his name. He was the only one besides Deputy Jeff Bridger who she'd officially paired a girl with so far. There were plenty of others still with question marks—for now.

She felt someone's eyes on her and turned to find Donovan Turner watching her from near the gazebo. She tucked the list out of sight before barely managing to hide her grimace behind a polite smile and a nod. The man pulled the piece of hay from his mouth and tossed it to the ground before pacing toward her. Now, there was one man who made no effort to hide his opinion of her, which was definitely *not* brotherly. He always seemed to pop up at the most inopportune times—like when she was alone. If he caught her, he'd spend the next thirty minutes bending her ear about that pig farm of his. *If* he caught her; but she wasn't going to let him.

She slipped into a group of people, dashed behind a booth and surfaced behind a tree. She thought she'd lost him, but to make sure, she scanned the crowd as she continued walking backward. She spotted the man scratching his head, glancing about. She was about to turn around when she backed right into someone. She gasped. "Oh, I'm so sorry!"

She tried to step away from the man but strong arms slipped around her waist and pulled her against a solid chest. She froze, then caught her breath as a warm, masculine voice filled her ear. "Hey there, beautiful."

Her eyes narrowed. Slowly, she glanced over her shoulder to look at him. The way his lips curved made her cheeks warm but she forgot all about that when her gaze tangled with those unforgettable hazel eyes. Her breath caught in her throat then her lips blossomed into a smile. "Lawson Williams, as I live and breathe!"

He loosened his arms enough for her to turn around and throw herself back into them. He hugged her back just as tightly as she hugged him. She pushed away to look at his face. "I almost didn't recognize you."

He grinned that slow, steady grin of his that set every female heart in a fifty-mile radius beating wildly. He stepped back to survey her. "Look who's talking. You sure have changed in the last few months."

She laughed. "Last few months? Are you crazy? It's been a year and no less! Of course I've changed. Did you get my letters?"

"I did."

"You only wrote back twice."

"I'm sorry." He shrugged. "I was on assignment most of the time so it wasn't easy to keep up with mail."

She lifted her chin. "Well, how is a person to know whether you fell off your saddle and broke your head or got laid up sick for a week if you don't write?"

He dipped his head to send her a suspicious look. "Were you worrying about me, Ellie?"

"Not me. Just…certain other people."

"I see." His eyes continued to tease her.

She pushed away from his arms, only belatedly remembering the reason she'd run into him in the first place. She glanced over her shoulder to look for Donovan Turner. He'd stopped to speak to someone and they pointed in the direction she'd dashed. She winced. It would only be a matter of time before he found her. Lawson's voice drew her attention.

"I just got into town. I came here first since I figured everyone would be at the celebration. I wanted to surprise my parents, but I wasn't counting on not being able to find them in this crowd." He scanned the flurry of activity around the churchyard. "Have you seen them recently?"

"No." She glanced over her shoulder and saw that Donovan had gotten closer but still hadn't spotted her. She tugged Lawson's arm in the opposite direction. "Let's try this way and hurry up. I'm on the run."

"From the law?"

"No, silly, a man."

His gaze sharply honed in on hers. "What did you do—hit him with a mud pie?"

"No. I'm twenty-one, not twelve."

He snorted. She jostled him lightly with her shoulder and he jostled her right back then caught her around the waist to keep her from stumbling. She rolled her eyes. *Well, that was mature.* Sometimes with Lawson, she couldn't help reverting back to the mischievous ten-year-old she'd been when he'd come into her life.

Lawson glanced around at the crowded churchyard. "This event has gotten larger since I left."

"More people have started coming from outside of Peppin to celebrate with us. Not much else has changed." Satisfied they'd completely lost Donovan, she turned her attention to finding Lawson's parents—or her family since they were probably close together. "Oh, actually, Sean started a new tradition last year when he got up on the podium and proposed to Lorelei in front of everyone. We've all been wondering who'll continue it."

"Naturally, it should be you."

She stopped to stare at him. *"Me?"*

"Well, sure." He tipped his hat up to stare right back at her. "You should try to keep it in the family. Besides, you have men chasing you all the time. That isn't good. You need to pick one and settle down."

"I do *not* have men chasing me. There is *one* man and I don't want him. Everyone else thinks I'm their little sister."

His hazel eyes sparkled with laughter as he stepped a bit closer and lowered his voice. "I bet all those men are just waiting for you to pick one of them so they can declare their feelings."

She tilted her head. "Don't you have that backward?"

"They just need a little encouragement." At her scoff, he narrowed his eyes. "Oh, come on. Show me a little of that charm."

"No."

"I know you have it in you."

"I do not."

"Sure, you do."

She narrowed her eyes at him. He gave her an encouraging little nod then took a step back as though giving her room to work. Her hand went to her hip. A quick glance around told her no one was watching. She stepped close to him and placed a hand on his chest before throwing her head back to stare at him. She batted her eyelashes as fast as she could. "Lawson, honey, it's been you all this time. Tell me how you really feel."

"Well, there's something I've been meaning to ask you for a long time, Ellie O'Brien." His gaze traveled solemnly over her features. Without warning, he sank to one knee and stared up at her. "Will you marry me?"

Chapter Two

Ellie stared at Lawson, speechless. Her brain seemed to stop working. She had to repeat his words in her mind to make sure she'd understood them correctly. Finally, she gasped and punched him in the shoulder. "Get up before someone sees you!"

Her punch knocked him off balance and he put a hand on the ground to stabilize himself. He was laughing too hard to stand. She shook her head even as her lips curved. "You think you're so funny. I can't believe you did that!"

He staggered to his feet but continued laughing. "You should have seen your face."

"I hope it looked as appalled as I felt." She glanced around noting a few curious stares, including a few she recognized. "Don't you know this town is match happy right now? You can't pull a stunt like that. It's dangerous. What if someone thought you were serious?"

That ought to put some real fear into him. Not that it was all that likely since everyone in town knew his taste in women tended to run toward beautiful, sophisticated women like Lorelei. Ellie was more likely to catch a fish than an eligible bachelor like Lawson. He didn't seem concerned as he tried to hide a grin. "Isn't that the pot calling the kettle black? I thought you were Peppin's matchmaking queen."

She pierced him with a glare. "I refuse to discuss it. In fact, I think I'd better walk away from you now."

"Aw, don't leave." He easily kept time with her faster steps. "You promised to help me find my parents. Besides, it was funny. That's why you're trying so hard not to smile."

She rolled her eyes. Of course Lawson would know she was trying not to smile. He'd practically grown up with her and Sean so he had her pegged. That didn't mean she had to like it. "Oh, all right. I'll help you find your parents."

He'd almost forgotten how easy it was to read Ellie's face. Her every thought was written right there for him to see…and what a beautiful face it was. Had he ever taken the time to appreciate the way her full lips were almost always lifted into a smile? Had he ever noticed the faint freckles that danced across her pert nose? Or the way her large green eyes sparkled as if she was laughing at some private joke?

No, he hadn't and he sure as shooting shouldn't be doing it now. Ellie was and always had been his surrogate little sister. Nothing more and nothing less would do. That's the way it would stay. He wasn't about to jeopardize his close relationship with her or the O'Briens by changing things now. No matter how appealing her willowy figure appeared in that green dress. He shook away his odd thoughts to search the crowd for some glimpse of his family.

Ellie stopped and waved a sweeping hand toward the left. He followed her gesture to find his ma standing nearby. He cleared away the emotion in his throat, prompting Ellie to send him a knowing look. As they neared, Lettie turned away to signal to someone. He followed her signal to see Doc wave back. Neither of them had seen him yet.

"Ms. Lettie," Ellie's soft voice called.

The woman turned toward the sound. Her gaze rested on Ellie for an instant before it traveled to him. Lettie's eyes filled with tears even as a smile wreathed her face. He pulled her into a hug. "Hello, Ma."

"You came."

"Of course I did. I always do what you tell me, don't I?" He stepped away and looked down to see her smile.

"You always were a good boy."

Ellie snorted. "Let's not get carried away."

He shot her a glare over his mother's shoulder then glanced past her to see Doc standing quietly to the side with a grin on his face. Lawson stepped forward and met the man with a hearty handshake. "Hello, Pa."

"It's good to have you home, Son."

He stepped back and tried not to feel uncomfortable as everyone just stared at him like he might up and vanish on them. Ellie seemed to recover first. "I guess I'd better round up the rest of the O'Briens and Rutledges."

He sent her a grateful grin. "Thanks. I'd like to see them."

"Then turn around and look," a familiar voice called from behind him.

He turned to find Sean standing behind him, a wide grin on his face. Lawson reached out to one of the few men he'd let close enough to hug. They pounded each other on the back then quickly stepped apart.

Lawson couldn't stop smiling. "How are you, Sean?"

"Fine, just fine." Sean shook his hand for good measure. "It sure is good to see you in Peppin again."

"It's just good to see you period. Where's Lorelei? I heard you managed to get her down the aisle." Lorelei stepped up beside Sean and offered him a hopeful smile, looking just as beautiful as always. She looked so happy—just further proof of how right she'd been to stop her marriage to him just before saying "I do." Everything had turned out for the best, so there didn't need to be any awkwardness between them now. This was home. This was the only family he had and now she was a part of it.

He didn't question his instincts. He just pulled her into a quick brotherly hug then stepped away from her. "It looks like married life agrees with you."

She smiled and slipped her hand into Sean's. "It certainly does."

Nathan and Kate Rutledge appeared with their children. There was more hugging and more talking. Finally, they all settled into a rather familiar group with Kate and Nathan talking to his parents and him with Sean, Ellie and Lorelei. He glanced around at the festive celebration surrounding them and smiled in relief. Just like that he knew he was back where he belonged and everything else seemed to fade into the past.

Ellie glanced over her shoulder to give Lawson a parting smile as the caller had everyone switch partners. Sean spun her around as they danced across the grass together in time with the music. Her gaze traveled back to where it had rested many times since the dance started. Once again, Maddie and Jeff nearly ran into another couple because they couldn't keep their eyes off each other. Ellie frowned.

Sean followed her gaze then glanced down at her. "I would have thought you'd be proud."

"Proud of what? Proud that the tale of my desperate attempt to find a husband has been bandied across town like the joke of the century? Proud that not one of the men who approached me afterward wanted anything more than a point in the right direction? What am I supposed to be proud of, Sean? Tell me, because I'd sure like to know why everyone is patting me on the back. I am a joke, Sean, a household joke who can find love for everyone but herself."

Sean's arm tightened around her waist. "Stop saying that. You aren't a joke, Ellie. As for love, don't you know the Bible says 'do not stir or awaken love until the time is right'? Did you ever think that just maybe the time wasn't right?"

"No, I didn't."

"Well, maybe that's what it is. Maybe God knows you aren't ready for that. Or maybe you aren't the holdup at all. Maybe your future husband is the one who isn't ready."

She sighed. "I sure wish he'd hurry up. I'm tired of waiting."

He laughed. "What has you in such an all-fired hurry all of a sudden?"

"I don't know." She bit her lip. "Sometimes I think something must be wrong with me since I've never had anything close to a beau."

He stiffened. "There isn't a thing wrong with you."

She ignored his comment and narrowed her eyes. "You know what I think the problem is? All of the men in this town see me as a little sister."

"Stop acting like one and they'll stop treating you like one."

She pursed her lips to the side. Now, that was an interesting statement. She wasn't exactly sure how to do that but something had to change and it might need to be her behavior. She was plumb tired of being looked at merely as the town's source of amusement. She wanted to prove that she was more than that. She wanted to prove that she was worthy of being wanted.

Sean finished the dance with her before leading her to the table where their families sat. He pulled out the empty chair that had been left between Lawson and Kate for her, then went to sit beside Lorelei. As he did, Nathan cleared his throat. "Since we're all gathered here, I have an announcement to make. As you know, the horse ranch Kate and I started almost ten years ago has been doing very well lately. We've decided to expand."

This certainly wasn't news to Ellie, but she offered her congratulations, anyway. However, Nathan wasn't finished. "As part of that expansion, I decided to hire a new foreman. I'm pleased to announce that Lawson has agreed to take the position."

Happy gasps circled the table and Ellie's was among them. Her gaze flew to Lawson just as he gave a bashful shrug. "Surprise! I hope y'all don't mind that I'm going to stick around."

"Mind?" Sean's tone portrayed how completely ridiculous he found the question. "Why would we mind? This is great."

Ms. Lettie seemed to be glowing. "Does this mean no more traveling? You'll be settled in Peppin permanently?"

Lawson nodded. "The opportunity came at just the right time. I was ready to retire my badge."

Doc's approval shone in his eyes. "It will be good to have you home."

"It's perfect. Does this mean you'll live at the ranch again?" Ellie glanced at Kate for confirmation. "Perhaps in the cabin? Or will we build something new?"

Lawson shook his head. "The cabin will do just fine for me. I don't need anything fancy."

"We'll get that figured out soon," Nathan said just as Maddie and Jeff passed the table.

Jeff paused to speak to Ellie. "Thanks again, Ellie. If it wasn't for that list—"

"I know. You're welcome." She didn't mean to be abrupt, but really! Enough was enough.

The couple stepped away from the table. Lawson's voice drew her gaze as he regarded her. "What did Jeff say about a list?"

She leaned back in her chair as her family and closest friends launched into the story she was sick and tired of hearing. Sean caught her gaze and she returned his wry grin with a roll of her eyes. She took a sip of punch and managed to swallow her annoyance with a big gulp of the fruity concoction. Lawson sent her a measuring look once the story was through. "Looks like you've caused quite a stir."

She lifted her chin. "What else is new?"

Lawson chuckled. "Ellie, I'm just curious. Who did you match up with me?"

"I don't remember." Ellie's gaze swept toward Lettie and Kate before she settled on Lorelei's face. Lorelei looked as baffled as she. Suddenly, Ellie's confusion fled and she turned back to him. "You weren't living here, so you weren't on the list."

"That's too bad. It would have been nice to—"

"Oh." She gasped the word as she realized what

she'd just said. Her eyes widened. She stared into Lawson's hazel eyes for a drawn-out moment, vaguely aware his voice stumbled to a halt. She watched his gaze trail down to her lips—which had formed a perfect circle of incredulous indignation.

She dragged her gaze from his until she found Ms. Lettie's. The satisfaction on the woman's face told her everything she needed to know. A quick glance at her laughing sister confirmed it. Ellie shook her head at both of them even as she leaned back in her chair and pinned them with a look. "Ridiculous. You two are completely ridiculous."

Ellie heard Lorelei catch her breath but Ms. Lettie's knowing smile kept her from looking away. The woman lowered her chin and lifted one eyebrow as though to say "time will tell." Lawson's hand brushed her shoulder to gain her attention. She glanced up at him. He said something but all she could remember was earlier...the warmth of being in his arms and the sound of his voice in her ear. What had she felt the moment before she realized it was only Lawson? Attraction? Anticipation? She didn't want to label it.

Lawson—of all the silly ideas, to think that we might make a good couple. They were just friends—only friends. Besides, a man as attractive, interesting and worldly wise as he would never be interested in a simple girl like her, especially after all those years of courting Lorelei, the most sophisticated girl in town. Why would he want Ellie? No one else ever had. Except Donovan, who she really didn't want to count.

She realized Lawson was still talking and shook the cloud from her thoughts. "What did you say?"

"I said, let me in on the joke. I want to laugh, too."

Her breath pulled from her lungs as if she'd been cut.

Her gaze held his for a long moment then fell to her lap as she felt something within her snap. She slowly lifted her gaze to survey the faces of those around her. They were all waiting for her to say something. They wanted to laugh with her just like they'd done a thousand times before. But this time one thing was different.

She wasn't laughing.

She eyed her friends and family. "There is no joke, Lawson—not anymore."

Lawson eased his duffel bag from his shoulder to the floor of the cozy old cabin on the O'Brien property. This was the place where his life had truly begun nearly ten years ago when Kate and Nathan had taken him on as a farmhand and brought him into their family. In this cabin, he'd learned his first lesson about what it truly meant to belong somewhere. Only a few months after that, Doc and Lettie had become his legal guardians and his honorary parents.

It somehow felt right to begin again in this place— to once more forget the past that had been resurfacing in his thoughts so often. Glancing around the room, he took in a cleansing breath then quickly lost it when he spotted Ellie directly to his right. She stood on a stool she'd placed over a crate in an effort to reach a cobweb near the cabin's high ceiling. Every time she moved, the stool she perched on wobbled beneath her. Lawson strode over and plucked her from her perch.

"Hey," she protested as he set her on her feet. "I almost had it."

He nodded. "You certainly did…if *it* was a broken bone."

She wrinkled her nose at him then turned to gesture

to the rest of the cabin. "Well, how do you like your new, old place?"

He surveyed the table with two chairs that had been placed by the window with a planter filled with cheery yellow flowers. A bed with a simple quilt, a large trunk and a small wardrobe stood on the opposite side of the room. A comfortable-looking chair sat next to the fireplace. He smiled. "It looks nice, clean, homey. Did you do all of this?"

"Guilty." She removed the stool from the crate and set it near the door.

"You didn't have to."

"I know. I wanted to." She tucked a loose tendril behind her ear. "I missed you, you know."

"What was there to miss?" He knew he was fishing for compliments but he didn't care. Mostly, he just wanted her to prove that her statement was true.

She kicked a large dark blue-and-green rag rug to unroll it over the middle of the wooden floor. "Oh, I don't know. It just hasn't been the same since you left and Sean got married. The three of us used to be as thick as thieves—you, Sean and I. Nothing felt right without you here."

He believed her. He'd wanted to, anyway. It was a nice feeling—being missed by someone.

She surveyed the room then must have been satisfied because she allowed herself to collapse onto a kitchen chair. "I bet you didn't miss me."

"Of course I did." He sat across from her.

She shook her head. "You didn't but that's fine. You were busy bringing outlaws to justice. I wouldn't have missed me, either."

"It wasn't as exciting as you seem to think."

"What was it like, then?"

"It was like everything I've tried to forget."

That quieted her for a moment before she smiled sympathetically. "Well, you're home now. You can forget as much as you want."

Home. That one word sounded so sweet to his ear. He gave a solemn nod. "I was already planning on it."

"I've been wondering—" she fiddled with one of the flowers "—why do the Rangers call you Lawless?"

Lawson stared at Ellie, then frowned. "Now, where did you hear that?"

"Nathan sold a few horses to the Rangers. While he was in Austin, he asked about you. They told him you were one of the best Rangers on the force. They also told him you'd picked up the moniker *Lawless*. Why?"

He averted his gaze from her questioning eyes. "They assigned me the worst criminals, Ellie. Sometimes that meant I had to take risks, be ruthless and do things I wouldn't dream of in any other situation. I never broke protocol but I've certainly bent my fair share of rules."

She frowned. "They called you that because you bent a few rules?"

He gave a slow nod. She narrowed her eyes. It was clear she knew he wasn't letting her in on the whole truth. Well, that was too bad because he wasn't about to tell her that almost the entire Ranger force thought he'd make a better outlaw than a Ranger, and loved to tease him about it. He didn't find it particularly funny. Nor did he want his name to be associated with the term *outlaw,* especially if some of those foggy memories of his childhood were accurate. He figured it was time for a change of subject.

"Now it's my turn to ask a question. What was so important about me not being on that list of yours?"

He asked the question before he could second-guess the wisdom of pursuing something that had upset her so much earlier.

Ellie was quiet for a long moment as if debating whether or not to tell him before she surprised him again by glancing up with teasing eyes. "Now that really *is* a dangerous question. You'll probably wish you hadn't asked, but since you want to know so badly, I'll tell you."

He gave her a nod. "I'll take my chances."

She leaned forward. "The whole point of the list was to find out who my match might be, right?"

"Right."

"Well, after I'd gone through the list without finding anyone, Ms. Lettie took the paper and looked it over. She told me I'd left someone off but she wouldn't tell me who it was."

He found himself leaning forward, as well. "That was me, right? I was the one you left off because I wasn't in town."

"Exactly." She sat back as if that settled everything.

Lawson stared at her. "You'll have to explain this to me, Ellie, because I still don't get it."

"You were *the one*."

"*The one* what?"

Ellie laughed. "Lawson, really. Think about it. You were the only man left."

"So?"

"So—" her voice took on a bit of exasperation "—Ms. Lettie and Kate, they think that you and I...well, that we would be...what did Kate say? Oh, that we could be very good...*together*."

Lawson stared at her for a long moment as understanding slowly dawned. "What?"

She smirked. "That's what I said."

He tried to wrap his mind around that thought. Honestly, it wasn't as hard as it should have been. He swallowed. His thoughts raced back to his recent interactions with Ellie—from his impulsive act of catching her in his arms at first sight to his pretend proposal. If he was honest with himself, he'd have to admit that he hadn't been treating Ellie like a sister. At least, not since he'd gotten back. In fact, if it were some other woman, he might have seen his behavior as flirtatious.

He ducked his head to keep her from reading his thoughts. He was crazy. He had to be. There was no way he could be attracted to little Ellie. Of course, she wasn't so little anymore. How old was she now? Twenty-one? She was pretty much a woman by now, wasn't she? His voice came out a little strained. "Ma and Kate really said that about us being good together?"

She sent him a curious glance. "It's funny but you don't seem nearly as shocked as I was. I thought they were completely ridiculous."

A wry grin lifted his lips. "I remember."

Her eyes widened. "Oh, that isn't to cast any sort of disparagement on you. I didn't mean that at all."

"I didn't think so."

"Good. I mean I'm sure some gal would be lucky to have you. I just can't imagine—" Her face twisted into a strange expression, as though she was desperately trying to conjure up some image of the two of them together.

He tried not to let that bother him…but why *was* it so hard for her to imagine? He shook his head. They were friends—nearly family. So Ellie had grown up. That didn't mean anything had to change between them or even that it should. He met her gaze with a grin. "It is pretty hard to imagine, isn't it?"

Her green eyes started dancing. "Well, since you won't have me, either, I guess I'd better start waiting at the train station for some handsome stranger to disembark. That looks to be my best bet."

He laughed along with her though he had to admit it was a bit forced. The thought of some stranger sweeping into town and carrying Ellie off didn't sit well with him. It was just his protective nature at work, he assured himself. That's all it was and nothing more. He was here to work. He was here to start over.

Most important, he was here to forget.

Chapter Three

Ellie thanked Mr. Johansen then tucked the small brown-paper-wrapped package under her arm. "Lawson and I will be back with the wagon to pick up the list of goods Kate ordered."

Lawson had moved out to the ranch less than a week ago and ever since then, Ellie hadn't been able to turn around without finding him nearby. She knew it was mostly due to the fact that they now lived on the same ranch. Still, a part of her wondered if a little tiny bit of it was through Kate's machinations. After all, Kate usually liked coming into town but today had sent Ellie in her stead. Nathan sent Lawson and so they had gone to town together with express directions to eat lunch there.

Guilt sprang onto her conscience. Of course, Nathan was busy, which was why he'd hired Lawson in the first place, and Kate had her hands full tending three children too young to go to school. Perhaps she really was imagining it. Mr. Johansen's voice pulled her from her short reverie. "I'll have the boys waiting by the loading dock in about thirty minutes."

Ellie nodded and managed to make it all the way out the door and a few steps down the sidewalk before she tore open the brown package. The colorful cover of the dime novel looked even more intriguing than it had in the catalog. She opened the cover to reveal the first page and found herself in the midst of a stagecoach robbery. Her heart skipped a beat. She carefully read each word as she stepped onto Main Street's raised wooden sidewalk.

Suddenly, a hand caught her arm and firmly pulled her to a stop. Ellie glanced up from the page only to realize that if not for the restraining hand on her arm, her next step would have sent her tumbling off the sidewalk. Her eyes widened then traveled to the man who stood slightly beside her with his hand still protectively on her arm. Lawson shook his head. "You really need to be more aware of your surroundings."

She wrinkled her nose at him as he led her to the shiny display window of the mercantile. Pointing at it, he leaned toward her. "Look at the reflections in the window."

The angle of the bay window reflected a clear image of the things behind her—including a man standing next to a tall chestnut mare tied to the nearest hitching post. "Donovan."

"He appeared just as I left you to walk to the livery. He seemed content to stay on his horse until you exited the mercantile...alone."

"He always does that. I think it's the only way he can work up the nerve to talk to me." She laughed at his skeptical frown. "He's harmless."

"Well, someone else might not be."

Her gaze shot to his hazel eyes. "Am I your latest assignment, Lawson? And here I thought you'd left the Rangers."

"So did I." He tucked her hand in his arm and led

her across the street. They both jumped at the sound of Maddie's joyful greeting through the café's large front window. The woman waved at her as though she'd just seen her long-lost best friend. *I understand that she's grateful that my list motivated Jeff enough to talk to her, but isn't this a little too much?*

The rest of the folks in the café turned to look. She could feel their eyes tracking her as she followed Lawson inside. She glanced around the room. Everyone was smiling at them. An entire table composed of Judge Hendricks, Mr. Potters and Joshua Stone lifted their coffee cups in a congratulatory toast. Lawson seemed just as bewildered as she did by the positive response. "Ellie, why is everyone smiling?"

"I don't know."

Maddie couldn't stop grinning as she led them to their table. "This is so wonderful! I don't know why no one thought of it before. You two are just perfect for each other. Y'all had us fooled into thinking you were just friends but now we all know better, don't we?"

Ellie felt her cheeks warm. She darted a glance at Lawson before she met Maddie's gaze. "What are you talking about?"

"Oh, you don't have to be coy, dearie." She patted Ellie's shoulder. "The whole town knows about your secret engagement. Don't worry. We haven't said a word to your families."

"Our secret what?" Lawson's question came out rather loud.

Maddie picked up the menu from the table. "Mrs. Greene saw you propose, Lawson. It's been all over town for days."

Ellie's gaze flew to Lawson. She glared at him. "Mrs. Greene saw you propose." She couldn't imagine anyone worse to have seen Lawson's little prank. Mrs. Greene was, ironically, the biggest gossip in town and one of the strictest moralists. Not to mention that she'd always held a particular grudge against Ellie for all of her childhood pranks.

Lawson seemed to be at a loss for words but guilt was written all over his face. A quick glance around the room told her everyone was watching so she stood to her feet. "Everyone, please listen closely then spread the news like wildfire. Lawson and I are not, nor have we ever been, engaged."

Mrs. Cummins set down her coffee with a thud. "But Mrs. Greene saw him kneel down and ask you."

"I was joking."

Maddie frowned at Lawson. "What an awful thing to joke about."

Ellie sent him a look seconding that, then turned to the crowd again. "Mrs. Greene also should have noticed that I punched him in the arm afterward. That's obviously not how a woman says yes to a man."

Judge Hendricks cleared his throat. "Well, Ellie, you've always been sort of a tomboy."

"As a child, not as an adult…usually." She sank to her chair. Maddie studied the two of them. "So y'all aren't engaged?"

"No," they answered together, setting the whole café to rumbling.

"Well, don't that beat all," Mr. Potters muttered.

"A real shame, that's what it is," Mrs. Cummins announced.

"Well, folks, this just isn't right." Maddie put a hand on Ellie's and Lawson's shoulders. "These two would make a fine couple, wouldn't they?"

"The best!" someone yelled and others chimed in to agree.

Ellie rose to her feet again. "Now, hold on. I think I'd know if Lawson and I would make a fine couple, wouldn't I?"

People reluctantly agreed.

"Then you can trust me when I say we aren't a couple."

People adamantly *dis*agreed. Maddie held up a stilling hand to her patrons. "Ellie's right. We can trust her on this. You just tell us who you matched Lawson with on the list of yours and we'll let this all go."

"Oh." Ellie swallowed then glanced down at Lawson. His expression said they were done for, which was discouraging and slightly insulting at the same time. Her fingers clenched the side of her chair. "Well, he wasn't on the list so that can't be considered. Now—"

"That explains why you couldn't find the one meant for you." Maddie caught her hand. "He wasn't on the list, darlin', but he was *your* match."

"Don't I have something to say about that?" Lawson seemed more amused than he should have been in this situation, especially when a firm "no" echoed through the café. Ellie eyed him. Why wasn't he more upset?

"We can't abandon Ellie in her time of need." Maddie released them and turned toward her patrons. "Didn't Mrs. Greene say that Ellie deserves this after everything she's done for the town?"

"Mrs. Greene said that?" Ellie turned to Lawson. "Why would Mrs. Greene say that?"

"That *is* strange," he admitted with the beginnings of a grimace.

Maddie ignored them. "Well, that settles it."

Lawson jumped up. "Wait. That settles what? What's going on?"

Oh, now *Lawson decides to look nervous.*

"You just leave that to Peppin, folks." Mrs. Cummins said. "You just leave that to Peppin."

Just like that, it was over. Maddie promised to bring them each a special on the house. The other patrons went back to their food. Ellie and Lawson were left to stare about in shock.

Ellie spoke first. "I have chills and I'm not sure why."

Lawson understood her feelings exactly. He didn't have chills but he did feel a strange foreboding settle in his gut. He'd done his best to ignore what he'd convinced himself were just fleeting flashes of attraction to Ellie. Living in the old cabin on the Rutledge ranch for the past week or so hadn't made that easy. Especially since he tended to take his meals with the Rutledge family—and Ellie, train the horses with Nathan—and Ellie, complete barn chores with Nathan, Nathan's son Timothy—and Ellie. She seemed to be everywhere at once being helpful or kind or getting into mischief.

He'd almost wondered why Nathan hadn't just increased Ellie's responsibilities around the farm rather than hire him as foreman. After all, her talent for settling down high-strung horses was remarkable. Then he discovered that Nathan didn't only need the talented horse trainer he had in Ellie, but also the brawn her slim frame didn't carry and the business acumen she seemed to intentionally avoid.

Once he settled down into the new job and got used to being in Peppin again, his perception of her would go back to normal. It was obvious Ellie didn't see him as anything other than a friend, almost a brother. And that was the way it was supposed to be. He wasn't about to pin his heart on a girl who would no doubt reject him. The last thing he needed right now was for the town to bluster in and make things even more confusing. Unfortunately, it looked as if that was exactly what was about to happen.

He shook his head. "Well, Ellie, it looks like all of your matchmaking efforts are about to be repaid to you."

"Courtesy of Mrs. Greene. Why does that sound so threatening?" She shivered. "I think she incited this on purpose. Probably because she knows you'd never…"

He almost let that comment slide before deciding against it. "I'd never what?"

She lifted her chin to continue solemnly, "No matter how hard matchmakers might try, you're the one man who'd never fall in love with me. You're the only man in town unrelated to me who has a legitimate reason to treat me like a little sister."

"Ellie." Not knowing what else to say that wouldn't make them both feel more awkward, he covered her hand to comfort her.

She shook her head as her large green eyes filled with tears. "No, it's true. I tell you, it's true. She saw me punch you afterward. She knew what that meant. She did this on purpose to get back at me for who knows what."

"Then don't let her." He handed her his handkerchief in case one of the tears tried to escape. "Don't let her know it bothers you. Just go about your life as if it doesn't matter to you. We won't let it determine our behavior one way or the other."

She nodded. She pulled in a deep breath, seeming

to will back her tears. Maddie approached to serve their food and eyed their clasped hands. They immediately pulled apart. She smiled, as the town's plan was working already. Lawson's gaze flew to Ellie when she gasped. "What's wrong?"

She straightened abruptly. "There's Mrs. Greene. I should talk to her."

"I don't think that's a good idea." He stared after her as she strode out the door. It clanged shut with a plaintive cry of the bell. He suddenly realized everyone was watching him. He stared right back at them. Maddie gathered Ellie's plate. "I'll box it up for her and she can eat it on the way home."

"Thank you."

"Fine way to start a romance," she muttered as she walked away.

Chapter Four

Ellie frowned as she hurried across Main Street toward where her childhood nemesis stood outside of Sew Wonderful Tailoring. For years, she'd assumed her antagonistic relationship with Mrs. Greene wasn't something worth contemplation. Now she wasn't so sure.

Perhaps if she'd apologized for her mischievous youth years ago instead of just letting the pattern continue, she wouldn't be in this mess now. The funny thing was that Ellie didn't believe it was entirely her fault. She'd sensed Mrs. Greene's disapproval for as long as she could remember. Once she'd realized nothing she did changed the woman's opinion of her, she'd decided she might as well live up to those low expectations and have fun while doing it. It had been a silly, childish decision for sure, and one that had gotten her into scads of trouble.

"When I was a child I spoke as a child but when I became an adult I put childish things away."

Isn't that in the Bible somewhere? Her heart beat rapidly in her throat even as her steps hastened in resolve. "Mrs. Greene, may I speak to you for a moment in private?"

The woman slowly turned from surveying the window to look at Ellie with a measuring stare. Her response came slowly but with precision. "Certainly."

"The courtyard is always quiet," she suggested. At Mrs. Greene's nod, she led the woman toward the courthouse then stopped beside one of the courtyard's benches. This was going to be either the wisest or the stupidest things she'd ever done. She cleared her throat. "I'd like to apologize for the way I behaved when I was younger—"

Mrs. Greene laughed. She laughed! "You must want something from me pretty badly if this is the approach you're taking. What is it, then?"

Taken off guard, Ellie pulled in a steadying breath before replying. "M-Maddie at the café says you've been telling everyone that I'm engaged to Lawson."

"Yes?"

"But I'm not!"

Mrs. Greene sniffed disdainfully. "Well, of course you are. I saw him get down on his knee and propose. It's pure nonsense keeping the engagement hidden when you know both families will approve. Why should I keep your secret for you?"

"It isn't a secret! I mean, it isn't an engagement!" Ellie shook her head to clear her confusion. "Lawson was just teasing me—he proposed as a joke. As soon as he was done, I punched him on the shoulder and then we both had a good laugh about it. That was it! Or it should have been, except that you had to go and tell everyone. Now the whole town has gotten the wrong idea."

"Have they?" Mrs. Greene tilted her head. "Are you sure?"

"Yes, I'm sure! I thought it was obvious we were

joking and that you were just telling people it was real as a prank. You know, like the ones I used to pull." She probably shouldn't have reminded Mrs. Greene about the pranks. The woman's face turned a little red so Ellie rushed on. "I just thought that if we talked—if I apologized for the way I used to behave—maybe you could tell people that you were mistaken."

"Hmm." There was a long pause as Mrs. Greene pondered the matter. "No."

Ellie was so stunned that it took her a minute before she could speak. "No?"

"I don't believe I will." Mrs. Greene's laugh was tinged with pity. "Did you really think a half-sincere apology would fix everything? Oh, no. I think it's high time someone gave you a taste of your own medicine."

"What medicine? I don't spread false stories about other people."

"No. You prefer true ones," Mrs. Greene said before she paled slightly then hurried on. "Never mind, Ellie. I accept your apology but I doubt anything I say will stop this train now that it's on the tracks. Everyone will begin meddling in your life just as you've always meddled in theirs. We'll see how you like it."

Ellie surveyed the woman carefully then shook her head slowly. "That isn't what you meant about getting a taste of my own medicine. What true story do you think I spread?"

"I really must go."

Ellie stopped the woman with a quick hand on her arm. "No, Mrs. Greene. I think you'd better stay and tell me what this is all about. I've always sensed you didn't like me. I'd like to know why."

Mrs. Greene stared at her. "You really don't remember?"

She shook her head. "Should I?"

Ire momentarily rose in the woman's eyes. She gave a tight nod then sat down on the bench. "I daresay you should. I certainly do."

Ellie waited as Mrs. Greene gathered her thoughts. Finally, the woman met her gaze. "I used to be good friends with your mother. You remember that, at least."

"Vaguely." She took the seat at the far side of the bench. "I was only eight when they died."

"I know," Mrs. Greene said quietly. "Once I went to visit your mother. You were home from school because you weren't feeling well. You'd fallen asleep on the settee as your mother and I talked, so I felt it was all right if I shared a confidence. Your mother was so sweet. She even prayed that I would accept the fact that God's love had covered my sins. That was the end of it, or so I thought.

"The next day my daughter came home crying." Mrs. Greene surveyed her scathingly. "You hadn't been asleep after all. You'd heard every word and repeated it to your friends at school. The whole town knew in a matter of hours."

Ellie frowned in confusion. "Knew what?"

Mrs. Greene's words were quiet, steady, yet bore a trace of shame. "I bore my daughter out of wedlock."

Ellie gasped—not at Mrs. Greene's words but at what that meant about her. "You mean, I told everyone that?"

"You certainly did."

"Oh, no. I'm so sorry!"

The woman fiddled with her reticule. "Your parents came to me a few days later and apologized. They said you repeated the story without knowing what it meant. Unfortunately, the rest of the town did."

"My parents…" she murmured as she blinked away a vague semblance of a memory. It returned with vengeance. She remembered overhearing the conversation, telling the older girls and feeling so important when they gasped. She also recalled the disappointment on her parents' faces when she'd admitted it. The disappointment in their voices…

That vague feeling of guilt overcame her with startling intensity. Quickly, she pushed it away—blocked those memories from her thoughts. She didn't want to examine them. She didn't want to remember. She rose abruptly from the bench to look down at Mrs. Greene. "Don't tell me any more. I understand. I'm sorry. I—I don't want to talk about this ever again."

Odd, how Mrs. Greene didn't seem startled by her reaction. She just nodded slowly. As if she knew something Ellie didn't.

"Everyone has something to be ashamed of, Ellie," Mrs. Greene said quietly. "You exposed my secret and humiliated me and my family in front of the whole town. But you're not innocent, either. The things you've done have brought down terrible consequences on your family, too."

Ellie stared at the woman. What terrible consequences? What had she done that caused so much harm? Could it be possible that after all these years of suppressing it, that strange sense of guilt actually meant *something?* Was it something Mrs. Greene—and Mrs. Greene only—was somehow intimately aware of? It must have to do with her parents…with their disappointment in her. She swallowed. "I don't know what you're talking about."

"Perhaps not." The woman smiled ruefully. "Perhaps it's just as well you don't. We won't speak of this again. I have to go."

She watched Mrs. Greene walk away then sank onto the bench. She felt so guilty—almost dirty. She wasn't sure how long she sat there but she slowly became aware of the man standing before her. She shook the clouds from her head to meet the stranger's blue eyes. "I'm sorry. What did you say?"

"I said I'm new here. I just got off the train, in fact. I'm looking for the boardinghouse."

"The boardinghouse—" That's as far as she got before tears began to run down her cheeks.

A look of panic crossed the young man's face before he sat beside her and handed her a handkerchief. "There, now. If it's such a horrible place, I won't go anywhere near it."

She gave a watery laugh. "I'm sorry. The boardinghouse is a wonderful place. I just had an unsettling conversation, that's all. You mustn't mind me."

"Ellie, I've been looking all over for you."

She jumped up to greet Lawson. "I'm sorry for leaving you like that. I just had to speak to Mrs. Greene."

He eyed the handkerchief in her hand. "I'm guessing that didn't go well."

"She said some awful things. She also said that she thought the story was true when she shared it—but even now that she knows it isn't, she'll do nothing to stop it from spreading. I was right. She wants to get back at me for…everything."

"Well, let her have her fun." He caught her arms to give them a supportive squeeze. "We won't let it bother us."

A weak smile was all she could offer in return. After all, he wasn't the one with an ominous secret lurking somewhere in a memory. A throat cleared behind them. She followed Lawson's gaze when it traveled past her to the man standing patiently by the bench. "Oh, this man saw that I was upset and tried to cheer me up. I'd introduce y'all but I don't think I caught your name. I'm Ellie O'Brien and this is Lawson Williams."

The stranger's smile slipped into what almost seemed like alarm for an instant before he held out his hand to Lawson. "I'm glad to meet you both. I'm Ethan Larue. I'm sure y'all have a lot to discuss so I think I'd better get going."

Ellie managed to give him directions to the boardinghouse and he was soon on his way. "I'm sorry I was angry earlier."

He shrugged. "That's all right. I was angry, too— at the town, I mean. I hope they didn't offend you too badly."

"Offend me?" she asked with disbelief. "Why would I be offended? You're a wonderful person, Lawson. You're intelligent and funny and…"

His lips titled into that slow grin of his and he held up a hand to stop her. "I meant I hope they didn't offend you by suggesting you needed help finding a match— not that you may have been offended to be matched with me."

"Oh," she breathed, feeling her cheeks begin to warm. Why was it that she couldn't even have a simple conversation without making some silly mistake?

He eyed her. "It's kind of a crazy idea they have, isn't it?"

"Uh-huh," she muttered, in an effort to save face. "Plain crazy. That's what it is."

Lord, I just have the knack of getting myself into uncomfortable situations whether verbally or otherwise.

It's just one of my many faults, I know, but if there's any way You can help me fix that I'd be forever grateful. She bit her lip. As for the town's matchmaking—well, she'd much rather focus on that than her altercation with Mrs. Greene and its mysterious implications.

Lawson ignored the sweat mottling his brow as he pounded another wooden stake into the ground. Nathan followed slowly behind him, digging the holes the new fence posts would soon go in. "We've got company."

He glanced up as a rider approached. It took him a moment to realize the rider was Chris Johansen. The distance between them dissipated, allowing Lawson to see him more clearly. The man's hair was slicked back and it was also obvious that he had taken special care with his clothing. However, it was the bouquet of wildflowers that gave away the true nature of the man's mission.

"It looks like you have some competition," Nathan teased.

Nathan and Sean had gotten a kick out of the town's decision to hitch him to Ellie, and his supposed "court-ship" had been a running joke ever since. Sean laughed so hard that Ellie had been put out with him for the entire week. It was a little disheartening how against the whole thing she actually was. Not that he'd planned to do anything about the attraction that had started stirring in his chest during Founders' Day. He knew where stirrings like that eventually led—to a little white chapel and tiny booties.

Whether he'd really make a good husband and father was anybody's guess. He'd been willing to try with Lorelei but when she'd walked out on their wedding, he'd started to wonder if maybe God's will was involved in keeping him single. The past ten years of his life had been wonderful but he'd been branded by the first fourteen, and that scar wasn't going to go away. Even if he could somehow trust himself not to emulate his memories, he wasn't sure he would be enough to make a woman stay. His first mother had abandoned him. Lorelei had literally run from him. Despite Lettie's affection, he kept wondering when she'd reach her limit and decide she didn't want him. He'd spent a year away from home and she hadn't forgotten him. It was practically unfathomable.

Meanwhile, Lawson and Ellie had figured out the best way to avoid the town's tricks was to simply avoid the town itself. So far, so good, but now it seemed the town had come to them and not at all in the way they'd expected. Chris pulled his horse to a stop. Lawson drove the stake into the ground with one last swing then stood to greet the man since he was closest. "Hello, Chris."

Chris dismounted then turned to greet Lawson with a wary look. "Hello, Lawson. I'd like to see Nathan in private, if you don't mind."

Lawson nodded then turned to Nathan for direction. "Why don't you go get Ellie and tell her to meet us in the house?" Nathan suggested.

"Yes, sir."

"Thanks, Lawson."

Lawson waved off Nathan's thanks then made the long walk to the barn in search of Ellie. He found her near the back in the stall with a mare that was due to foal in the next few weeks. Her hands were carefully examining the mare's stomach. She looked up when he neared and he propped his boot on the stall's gate. "You have a visitor."

"I do?" She tilted her head curiously. "Who is it?"

"Christian Johansen," he said, carefully pronouncing each syllable.

"Why didn't he just come inside?" She gave the mare one last pat then climbed the few rungs of the gate until she was able to sit on top of it. She lifted her legs over the gate then pushed herself around to face him.

He tilted back his Stetson to look up at her. "It isn't that kind of a visit."

She braced her palms against the wooden railing beneath her. "What kind of visit is it, then?"

"Why don't you just open the gate and walk out?" he asked when she began to lean forward as if ready to jump down.

His question made her hesitate long enough to set her off balance. Her hands began to slip from the railing. He caught her around the waist and carefully lowered her down to keep her from tumbling the rest of the way. She found her footing then leaned back, accidentally trapping his hands between her waist and the stall gate behind her. Her green eyes sparkled as she looked up at him. "That wouldn't be nearly as exciting."

"Probably not," he admitted as he tried to ignore the way his heartbeat increased.

"What kind of visit wouldn't let Chris come to the barn?"

"A courting kind of visit." Grateful for the reminder, he shifted her weight forward just long enough to reclaim his hands, then took a large step back. Ellie looked positively perturbed.

"You're kidding me, right?"

"Nope. He's talking with Nathan and is going to meet you in the house. You should clean yourself up. You have a dirt smudge on your cheek." He gestured to the affected area. She lifted her shoulder and wiped her cheek on her shirt. That only left more residue. He grinned. "There's your problem."

He lifted her chin to the side then carefully wiped the smudges from her cheek with his handkerchief. He stuffed the handkerchief back in his pocket, released her chin and stepped back. "That's better. Now you'd better get in there."

Her green eyes sought his for a long moment before she smiled. "Yes, sir."

Ellie and Kate disappeared into the parlor to whisper together. Lawson figured he might as well stick around and get a drink of water before he headed back into the heat. He had just poured himself a cup when Nathan and Kate's oldest child, Timothy, burst through the back door. "I was digging up potatoes. That makes a man awfully thirsty."

"It sure does, partner." Lawson handed him the cup and poured himself another. "Slug that down. I bet it will help."

"Thanks." The dark-haired boy showed his gap-toothed grin and did just that.

The front door opened and Lawson heard Nathan and Chris enter. Chris went immediately into the parlor while Nathan joined them in the kitchen. "Looks like the men are taking over the kitchen. Kate's going to stay in the room with them."

"Chris, if you came about that silly list, you should know that I'm not going to talk about it anymore."

Lawson's eyebrows rose at the faint but clear sound of Ellie's voice, then he stared into the hall that separated the kitchen from the parlor. He looked at Nathan. The man shrugged. "There are thin walls in the old part of the house."

Lawson grinned. "No kidding."

Timothy frowned. "Who was that man you were walking with?"

"I didn't come here for the list, Ellie. I came here for you."

"That was Chris."

Ellie's voice sounded in response but Lawson couldn't hear what she said because Timothy started talking. "That didn't look like Chris. That looked like some kind of fancy man all gussied up."

Lawson laughed. Nathan shook his head. "Chris got all gussied up because he came to court Ellie."

Timothy turned to Lawson. "I thought you were courting her. At least, that's what the other kids say at school."

"Those were just rumors," Lawson said. "Don't believe them. You'd know for sure if I was courting your aunt."

"How?"

"You'd see me doing it, kiddo."

"I can't hear—" Nathan complained before he could catch himself. He turned to Timothy. "How about a piece of your ma's cake? You can have some if you're very quiet."

Lawson shook his head. "Shameless."

"Ellie, I've wanted to court you for a year now."

"Why didn't you?"

"I knew you thought we were only friends. I don't want to be only friends anymore. I know you're courting with Lawson and I respect that, but I couldn't go any longer without letting you know how I feel about you. I wanted you to know that before you did something you couldn't take back."

"For the last time, I am not engaged to Lawson."

There was a pause, then her voice became gentler. "You've been such a good friend to me—"

"But it could change into something better if you gave us a chance."

"No, I honestly can't imagine us being anything more than just friends. I see you like a brother. Nothing more."

Nathan gave a nod of approval.

"You said the same thing about Lawson."

"I know, and I'm not going to marry Lawson, either."

"Does he know that?"

"Yep." Lawson nodded just as Ellie said, "Goodness, yes."

"Then why not—"

"Chris, let's forget all of this and go on as we always have."

"Poor man," Lawson said while Ellie said goodbye to Chris. "That has to hurt."

Nathan nodded. "That's about what I expected but I did warn him. I guess that means you and Ellie are still on the road to matrimony."

Lawson shook his head at Nathan's teasing. "For the record, when I asked she said 'no' so there is no possible way we're engaged or courting."

Ellie breezed into the kitchen to grab Kate's mending basket. "It would have served you right if I had said yes. What would you have done then?"

He shrugged nonchalantly as he returned her challenge with his own. "Picked out a ring."

"Oh, sure." She breathed in disbelief but that uncertain look in her eye told him she'd picked up on that slight vein of truth in his voice. "We would have one-upped each other right to the altar."

"Probably."

"Well, if you gentlemen are done eavesdropping, you should probably get back to work." She sent them a knowing look over her shoulder before she breezed out of the room.

Yep, she had them figured out, all right. He turned to share a chagrinned grimace with Nathan only to find the man scrutinizing him thoughtfully. Lawson cleared his throat then decided he'd better follow Ellie's advice before Nathan asked him to explain that comment about the ring. He wasn't sure he wanted to explain it to himself.

Chapter Five

Ellie carefully slid her hand down Delilah's leg until she reached the mare's foot. She gave it a little squeeze and Delilah immediately kicked up her leg so Ellie could clean out her hoof. The horse leaned into Ellie's side then began nipping at the ribbon she'd used to tie back her hair. Ellie pushed the horse away with her shoulder. "Stop it, silly. You're going to topple both of us over."

She heard Nathan's confident steps pound toward her on the barn floor. "Ellie, you have another visitor."

She glanced up in surprise. It had been two days since her last visitor. Frankly, she'd been stunned by Chris's attempt to woo her. She hoped she hadn't hurt him with her reply. She knew how saddening it could be to discover that someone you were interested in saw you only as a sibling. After all, that was the story of her life in this town. She let out a world-weary sigh then released Delilah's hoof and straightened up. "Who is it this time?"

Nathan grinned wryly and opened the gate to the stall, knowing better than to give her the option to climb over it. "I guess you'll find out when you see him."

She glanced back at him for some clue but he was already striding past her out of the barn. She followed him into the sunlight. It took a moment for her to realize the whole Rutledge family and Lawson had gathered to watch the proceedings. The man wasn't waiting for her inside like Chris had. Instead, he sat on the top of his wagon with a piece of hay stuck in his mouth. Ellie barely contained the urge to groan. "Hello, Mr. Turner."

"Call me Donovan." He jumped down from the wagon to grab her hand. He shook it up and down repeatedly as his eyes wandered across her face as though memorizing her every feature.

She carefully pulled her hand from his sweaty palm and attempted to smile sweetly. "I don't suppose you're here to buy a horse?"

"No, ma'am. I heard you got yourself engaged to this fellow, but I won't believe it until I see it." Donovan threw a frown at Lawson then grasped her left hand in both of his. He stared at it for a long moment before bursting into a grin. "There's nothing there."

Ellie sighed. "I know."

She jumped when he let out a whoop of joy then rolled her eyes, which caused her nieces and nephew to giggle. Suddenly he was herding her toward his wagon. Literally. He just turned toward her and started walking so she began backing up until he stopped at the front of the wagon. She glanced past him to meet Nathan's gaze. He stepped closer to the wagon to keep an eye on them.

Donovan reclaimed her attention by placing a hand on her arm. "Darlin', I've got something here that will make you wonder what you ever saw in that fellow."

"Really, Donovan?" She glanced past him to Lawson. He didn't look particularly concerned, with that poorly concealed half smile on his face. Then again, why should he be? He was just there to watch the show like everyone else.

"This is for you."

He reached under the wagon seat and pulled out a small, white piglet with black spots.

She stared at it for a long moment then lifted her gaze to Donovan's pale gray eyes. "You brought me a pig?"

"Yes, ma'am. I sure did." Her nieces squealed in delight but Donovan sent a glare over his shoulder at the sound of Lawson's disbelieving laugh. "It's the best of the litter. I thought you could use it on the farm."

She bit her lip to keep from laughing then couldn't stop the incredulous smile that followed. "That's very thoughtful, but I can't accept a gift like that."

"Sure you can."

She shook her head. "I'm afraid I can't because I'm not going to let you court me. You're a very nice man but I just don't feel that way about you."

He dropped his head and pulled the piglet closer. "Shucks, ma'am. I know that you feel that way now. I just had to take a chance and let you know how I felt so's I can try to change your mind." Each time he spoke, the sleeping pig's ears jerked toward the sound. The man lifted his head to stare at her. "I've watched you at church, Ms. O'Brien, and your faith is inspiring."

"That's nice of you to say." She glanced over his shoulder to meet Nathan's suspicious gaze.

"I watch you every time you come to town. Sometimes I even follow you a little. It always brightens my day to see you."

"That's…" She paused. *Very strange.* "Something

you probably shouldn't do. Follow me around, I mean. You should stop."

"Yes, ma'am, I understand." He glanced down at the pig then thrust it under her nose. "You should still take the pig."

"I don't think—" She stopped trying to reason when he lifted one of her arms and slid the pig into it. "Oh, well, if you're sure."

"I'm positive. It's yours. No strings attached. Just because you're you." He smiled hopefully. "If you like, I can stop by to check on it—"

She cut him off with a shake of her hand. "If you leave it, that's it."

"I reckon that's all right." He patted the pig on its head. "Cute little fella, isn't he?"

She glanced down at the animal in her arms and smiled. "He is cute and very little. Thank you."

When she glanced up she found Donovan was still watching her. "Yes, sir. The man who takes you for a wife is going to be a mighty lucky man."

Nathan must have seen that as his cue because he stepped forward. "Donovan, I think you and I should have a talk about what's appropriate when it comes to young ladies."

Ellie slipped away just as Kate and her children stepped forward to look at the pig. Kate's wary eyes darted to Donovan as her children crooned to the animal. "He's a strange man. You'd do well to stay away from him. He may be harmless, but it pays to be careful."

"I've been doing my best."

"Well, Nathan will be on high alert, too, as I'm sure Lawson will."

"I appreciate that." She left the piglet in an empty

stall under the watchful eyes of the children then went to finish Delilah's hooves. She found Lawson had beaten her to it. "You don't have to do that. I can finish what I started."

"It's fine," he said, but didn't glance up from his work. "Maybe you could start on Samson."

"Delilah was the last one." She propped her boot on the gate of the stall and watched him work, noticing the controlled power that surged through each motion.

"This will only take a minute." He released Delilah's hoof then straightened to meet her gaze. "It looks like our supposed engagement lit a fire under some of your suitors."

She crossed her arms along the stall's gate and leaned against it. "It's awfully silly."

"Silly?" He eyed her carefully, then turned away to run his hand down Delilah's back leg to get the horse to lift her foot. "You know I think I've got you figured out, Ms. O'Brien. The ruse is up."

She frowned at him in confusion. "What are you talking about?"

"You don't really want to get married."

"Of course I do. That's the most ridiculous statement I've ever heard."

"So you say." He finished cleaning Delilah's hoof and turned to face her. "Yet, over the past few days, you've managed to discourage two completely different types of men."

She shrugged nonchalantly. "So what if I did? I didn't like them, that's all."

Lawson rubbed his chin in thoughtful speculation. Delilah nudged him in the back, forcing him to take two steps toward her. "What about Chris?"

She narrowed her eyes. "What about him?"

"He said his feelings for you changed a long time ago." He braced his hands on either side of her arms and tilted his head. "Are you saying you really didn't notice?"

"I had no idea," she said honestly.

"I think that leads us to the crux of the matter."

She raised her brows expectantly. "Which would be?"

He gave a slow smile, and shook his head. "You, Ellie O'Brien, are afraid to take off the blinders you've fashioned."

"What blinders?"

"The ones that keep you from seeing yourself as everyone else sees you—as a kind, beautiful, spontaneous woman."

She stared at him in awe. He thought she was beautiful? Hadn't he always thought of her as one of the boys? Hadn't he always seen her as a surrogate little sister? Apparently, somehow that had changed. He now saw her as beautiful—a woman. She swallowed. Why did that send her heart galloping in her chest?

He carefully guided her chin up until she was forced to meet the knowing smile in his eyes. "You're the kind of woman who wouldn't have any trouble finding herself a husband, if she didn't try so hard to cross every suitable man off her list or give him away to her friends."

She didn't have anything to say because she'd suddenly realized why those relatively suitable men had seemed so unsuitable. She realized it because she was staring the reason right in the face. She, Ellie O'Brien, had a crush on Lawson Williams.

She barely withheld a groan. She had no idea how long this had been going on but she needed it to stop.

Talk about embarrassing! He obviously didn't feel the same way. He thought proposing to her was so ridiculous that he'd turned it into a joke! Just because he said she was a beautiful woman didn't mean he considered her a woman he'd want to pursue. Goodness, he'd only been trying to encourage her. It didn't mean anything. As though to confirm her assessment, he stepped back and shook his head. "You need to give one of those men on your list a chance, Ellie."

She gathered her wits enough to lift an impervious eyebrow at his statement. "No, I don't."

He grinned. "Then I stand by my other statement. You aren't really searching for a husband. So what are you searching for?"

"Love," she said softly. "The kind of love that Nathan has for Kate and Sean has for Lorelei. I *do* want that, Lawson. I just haven't found a man who can love me like that or at least a man that I want to be loved by. I think if I had that, why, I might be a different person altogether."

He frowned at her. "What's wrong with the person you are now?"

"Do I really need to list my faults for you? I'd rather not." Especially since some of them she couldn't even admit to herself. Nevertheless, she'd been achingly aware of them lately…ever since Mrs. Greene mentioned consequences from the mistakes Ellie had made in the past—whatever they were.

"No, you don't have to do that," he said, then shook his head. "I still think you're selling yourself short in many respects."

She backed away from the stall's gate so he could walk through it. "Well, I think I just have a very clear view of my weaknesses."

A very *clear view,* she thought with a sideways look at Lawson as they walked to the corral. She planned to overcome one of them as quickly as possible to save both of them from embarrassment.

"Lawson, are you decent? Your parents came early to help set up for the party and want to see your cabin."

He froze at the sound of Ellie's voice as he glanced around in a panic at his messy cabin. Why hadn't he folded his clothes instead of dumping them in the chair near the cold fireplace? He probably should have swept out the dirt he'd tracked in. "Stall them for a minute, will you? This place is a mess."

An awkward silence seeped through the closed front door. He sighed and grabbed his shirt. "They're standing right next to you, aren't they?"

"Yep." Her muffled voice continued cheerily, "Lawson has been such a big help setting up for Maddie and Jeff's engagement party. I kept finding one more little thing for him to do so I'm afraid I've made him late getting ready."

He heard his parents respond but didn't bother to try to decipher what they were saying. Instead, he stuffed his clothes into the trunk at the end of his bed, straightened his bedding, pushed the chair under the table and hoped they wouldn't notice the dirt on the floor. He opened the door as he tucked his shirt into his pants. "Welcome to my humble home."

Lettie stepped inside wearing a pert little blue bonnet over her dark brown hair and carrying a basket that filled the cabin with the smell of freshly baked apple pie. "What a cute little cabin."

Doc chuckled as he clasped Lawson on the shoulder. "Lettie, that isn't exactly what a man wants to hear about his first home as a bachelor."

Ellie leaned against the doorway to peer inside. "Well, it should be cute. I picked out all the decorations."

"Did you?" Lettie asked with new interest.

"She did. I'm afraid all I added was the mud."

Doc nodded proudly. "That's the best part."

Ellie frowned, then stepped past him to sit at the table and pick up the planter filled with brown flowers. "You didn't water them."

"Was I supposed to?" He was quickly distracted when Lettie opened his cabinets to fill them with all sorts of colorful concoctions in glass jars. His stomach gave a low rumble of appreciation. "Preserves?"

"Of course." She set the pie on the counter next.

Doc sat in the chair now free of Lawson's laundry. "It's been a couple of weeks now. Are you're still happy you resigned from the Rangers?"

"Yes, sir."

Lettie looked relieved then straightened her shoulders in pride. "I think my boy is ready to settle down."

The significant wink she tossed Ellie's way wasn't lost on Lawson. He coughed to cover his laugh then shot a glance at Ellie to see her reaction. She rolled her eyes at them both. "Don't smirk at me, Lawson Williams. Talk to your mother."

He turned to Lettie and found her looking absurdly innocent. "Now, Ma, just because I came home doesn't mean I'll marry the first girl who asks me."

Ellie gasped and straightened in her chair. "Who's asking?"

"I haven't even thought about looking for a wife yet."

Ms. Lettie frowned. "Why ever not? Every man

needs roots. Doc and I have done our best to provide some for you these past years but you deserve more than that. You deserve a family of your own."

Lawson met his ma's gaze directly. "Not every man is supposed to have a family of his own. I'd even go so far as to say that some men shouldn't."

Lettie shook her head at Lawson's statement. "Well, you are the type of man who *should* have a family. You'd make a wonderful husband and father. Isn't that right, Ellie?"

"I think I'd better go change before the other guests start showing up." She rose from the table to stand in front of him. Her dancing green eyes captured his. "Be on your guard, my friend. The whole town is coming to this shindig. This is just the beginning."

She handed him a clean sock she'd somehow managed to pick up, then waved at his parents before she sashayed out the door. Lettie delicately cleared her throat, making him aware that he was still watching that vacant door. He felt a dull heat creep across his jaw. He pulled another sock from his trunk then grabbed his boots to sit down at the table. As he put them on, Lettie served the pie. "She's getting to you, isn't she?"

He glanced up to discover that she was enjoying a lot more about this situation than the pie she was eating. He glanced at Doc for help. The man was watching him over the top of his spectacles as he would a patient in an examination room. Lawson stomped his foot into the boot a little harder than necessary. "Come on, Pa. Y'all can't gang up on me here."

Doc walked over to stand behind his wife and gave her shoulder a little squeeze. "It's obvious you and Ellie have a special connection. Don't tell me it's just because y'all are friends. There's more to it than that. The whole town can see it, even if y'all can't admit it."

He leaned onto the table with his elbows and rubbed his jaw. "Fine. I admit that I'm attracted to her but I wasn't planning on doing anything about it. Why do I get the feeling that y'all think I should?"

"Eat your pie, dear." Lettie pushed the plate closer to him as she'd done many times in the past. Since there was never a problem that a slice of one of her pies couldn't help solve, he did as he was told. She set her plate aside and leaned closer. "I know that Ellie thinks she has the corner on matchmaking in this town but what some people, Ellie included, may not realize is that she learned everything she knows from me. Therefore, the true question here is not 'What do we think *you* should do?' but rather 'What can *we* do for *you?*'"

His fork lowered to his plate. His eyes widened then flew from Lettie to Doc then back again. "Are y'all suggesting that I— That we—"

He didn't want to finish his question because the answer was on their faces as plain as day. They wanted his permission to matchmake. No, they wanted more than that. They wanted his full cooperation. An echo of Lettie's words whispered through his heart. *You are the type of man who should have a family. You'd make a wonderful husband and father...*

He wasn't sure if he could believe that completely but if he ever wanted those words to describe him, he'd have to start somewhere. Maybe this was that place. Maybe this was the start of the "someday" he'd always longed for where he'd have his own family—a real family with someone. They weren't talking about a vague "someone," though. They were talking about Ellie. This was the same girl he'd pushed off the top of the waterfall more than once. The girl who'd helped him study for school. The woman who could suddenly make his heart race with a mere touch.

"She doesn't feel that way about me." He wasn't even aware that he'd stated that out loud until Doc responded.

"How will you know for sure if you don't take a chance?"

"I don't want to ruin our friendship."

"Son, you've always made me proud with the way you haven't let fear hold you back from doing the right thing," Doc said gently. "Don't give in to fear now. Any relationship worth having is worth taking a risk."

Quiet descended as everyone waited for him to make his decision. He swallowed then gave a shallow nod. "All right. I'm going to do it. I'll pull back the moment I sense she's the least bit uncomfortable but I want to see where this goes. Does that make me crazy?"

Lettie shook her head. "That makes you brave."

The rich timbre of Chris Johansen's fiddle filled the air with a lively melody that nearly drowned out the low crackle of the fire. One last drop of juice from Ellie's piece of sausage sizzled in the flames before she pulled out her skewer. She skirted the fire to sit next to Lorelei on a wooden bench and fanned her food to help it cool. An odd look crossed Lorelei's face. "You do know where that's from, don't you?"

"The kitchen."

"I mean—originally."

Her gaze trailed down to the kebab. Suddenly, she realized she was probably eating one of her piglet's cousins. She set the skewer onto a discarded plate. "I think I'm full."

Lorelei giggled. "I'm sorry. I shouldn't have done that."

"Don't worry. I've had too much food already." Ellie pulled in a deep breath as she surveyed the happy scene in the field around her. Folks stood or sat in groups while Maddie and Jeff shared a kebab near the outskirts of the firelight. Lorelei leaned toward her. "I heard Chris came calling. How did that go?"

She pulled the list from her pocket. "I crossed him off the list."

"So...not well."

"It wasn't that bad. It just wasn't right." She bit her lip and glanced around the field. "When I cross someone off I try to match them with someone else, but I haven't figured out Chris's match yet."

"It will come to you." Lorelei leaned over to steal a peek at the list. "It looks like the field is narrowing."

"Rapidly. Most of the men left are the ones I don't know as well."

"Who is that man who came with Amy?"

Ellie glanced around until she found the man talking with Lawson a bit closer to the house. "That's Ethan Larue. He's staying at the boardinghouse—that must be how Amy knows him. I met him in town the other day. He seems nice but I don't think he's planning to stick around long so I didn't put him on the list."

"Is Lawson on it now?"

She shook her head then changed her mind and shrugged. "I guess it's only fair to add him. He deserves to find a good match as much as anyone else— maybe even a little more."

Lorelei set her elbow on the back of the bench and rested her cheek in her palm as she leaned in. "Who would you match him with? Sophia?"

Ellie's gaze darted to Chris's sister. "I had Sophia in mind for someone else."

"Helen?"

Ellie shook her head. The schoolteacher would be a good match for someone with children. *Of course!* She smiled then put the woman's initials by a name on her list. "No."

"You?"

She stilled. Her eyes shot to Lawson. The firelight painted him in shades of gold simultaneously softening and contouring his handsome features. He caught her watching. Their eyes held for a moment before he flashed a grin and winked. Her heart lurched down a few rib bones before fluttering back into place. "I don't remember him being quite so…"

"Attractive?" Lorelei laughed softly. "So you don't mind if your family and friends do a little matchmaking?"

"For my part, I'll admit that I wouldn't mind. But what makes you think he'd want to be with me? Everyone in town's all but thrown me into his arms and he hasn't shown any interest yet."

"Hmm. Do you think we're taking the wrong approach?"

Ellie started to argue that that wasn't what she'd meant, but then she stopped to think about it. "Well, that may be part of it. Blatant suggestions like we've been getting tend to make couples more resistant—at least when they're together. Now, if they're apart, then it helps to encourage the idea of a romance. Mainly, y'all just need to be less obvious about pretty much everything."

"Got it." Lorelei gave her a parting smile then hurried away as if she couldn't wait to start coordinating everything.

Ellie chuckled. *Well, Lord, I asked for a little help in finding a match for myself and You sent me an entire town. I sure do appreciate it. Now if only I could convince myself it will do any good.*

Chapter Six

Lawson drowned his bemused smile with another gulp of lemonade as he glanced at the man beside him. He had no idea what Ethan Larue was talking about. He'd stopped paying attention the moment Ellie looked up and smiled at him from across the fire. Her golden hair was swept up and away from her neck, leaving her shoulders bare save for the pale green cap sleeves of her dress. He wasn't used to seeing her all fancied up like this. Normally she wore a simple blouse and split skirt around the ranch and left any fancier fare for Sunday services. He'd called her beautiful when they were in the barn, but now she was truly stunning. And very distracting.

Guilt pulled his focus back to the conversation just in time to realize that Ethan was staring at him expectantly. Lawson grasped for some clue of what the man had been saying. He came up empty. He cleared his throat. "Well, now. I couldn't say."

Ethan nodded thoughtfully. "It would probably be hard to tell without an official census. There are plenty of interesting people here, though, and they've all been so kind and welcoming. It makes a man think about settling down and starting a new life."

"Are you planning to settle here, then?"

"No. I'm not exactly the settling type." He glanced out at the field and frowned as if looking right into his past. "My mother died when I was eight. I lost my father when I was thirteen. I was put in an orphanage a few years before I was able to leave. I learned a long time ago that it's pointless to put down roots."

"I understand. I'm—"

"You understand?" Ethan gave a bitter laugh. "I appreciate your sympathy but—"

"No." Lawson met his gaze unflinchingly. "I said I understood and I meant it."

"Really?" A slightly victorious smile pulled at the man's lips for an instant before he tempered it. "Tell me about it."

Lawson stilled. Why did he just feel as though he'd just walked into a trap? Had Ethan been waiting to hear Lawson's story? But why would he? Lawson scanned the man's features, looking for anything familiar in them. As a Ranger, he'd made his share of enemies. Enemies who'd do a good deal to learn his background and find out where he was vulnerable. But Lawson couldn't find anything there to legitimize his suspicions. He'd give Ethan, if that was his real name, what he wanted for now.

He began with a grim smile. "I don't remember a time when my parents weren't drinking or fighting. When I say fighting, I don't just mean yelling or screaming words no child should hear. I mean…" He swallowed against the emotion that rose in his throat. "Let's just say there was a lot of abuse involved. Most of that time is just a blurry memory. I try to keep it that way."

Ethan gave a curt nod but didn't try to interrupt.

"I must have been about nine or ten—maybe eleven—" he hated that he could never be completely sure "—before they left me."

"What do you mean, 'they left me'?"

Lawson was startled awake by a banging on the door. He sat up and watched the shadow of his mother's petite frame race across the white sheet that separated his little corner from the rest of the cabin. His father's shadow staggered into the room. His familiar walk seemed a little off—almost listing. His mother gasped and guided his father into a chair. "What happened? You're bleeding something fierce."

He groaned. "You aren't drunk, are you, woman?"

"I had a couple but I'm not drunk yet."

"Good. I need you to bandage me up then we've got to get out of here."

"The job went bad?"

"Course it did. Why do you think I'm bleeding like a stuck pig?"

"I guess that means you won't get paid. The rent's due in the morning. Maybe you should have thought about that before you messed up whatever you were supposed to do."

"The rent! I could have the sheriff on my tail and you want to talk to me about the rent!"

Lawson sighed and snuggled back under the threadbare cover with no other choice than to listen to another argument. "You get that look out of your eye. Don't even think of hitting me tonight or I'll push you out the house and let you die on the street where you belong! Do you really think the sheriff is after you?"

"Probably so. They couldn't pin anything on me, though. I wasn't sloppy enough to leave evidence."

"Don't be a fool. That hole in your side is all the evidence they need."

"That's why I say we've got to leave here and tonight. I'm in the clear if no one sees this."

"What makes you think I'm coming with you?"

"Do you want to be put in jail as an accessory?"

"Accessory to what? No, don't answer that. I'm coming. Let me get the kid."

"No. The kid stays."

Lawson's eyes flew open. He saw his ma pause before she set the suitcase on the table. "Are you crazy? We can't just leave him here."

"He'd slow us down. Have you looked at the boy lately? He's skinnier than a ragweed and twice as puny. We can't even provide for ourselves in the best of times. How are we going to provide for him on the run? Send him to your family. They'll take him in, won't they?"

"I suppose they'll have to. I know, I'll write a letter and pin it on him. That will explain everything. Have you got any money I can leave with him?"

"I've got a dollar."

Lawson pretended to be asleep when his mother stepped through the sheet. It only took a second for her to pin something on his raggedy shirt. She paused then whispered, "I know you're awake. You have to trust me. This is for the best. You know how mean your pa gets when he drinks and you know how silly I get. Neither of us is getting better. Look at me, Lawson."

He slowly did as she commanded. Her bright blue eyes stared as though she was memorizing his every feature. "I'm no good but I love you. That's why I'd rather see you gone than bleeding to death from a beat-

ing one day. Promise me you won't be like your father or me. Promise."

"Yes, Ma," he whispered.

He watched her sweep from the room. Her shadowy form grabbed the suitcase then disappeared. He jumped from the bed and slipped around the white sheet in time to see his father turn to close the front door. The man caught sight of him and hesitated for just a moment. Their eyes held. "You stay inside tonight. You hear me?"

Lawson leaned against the wall then gave a single nod in response. The door closed. He stared at it for a while. His gaze swept the disheveled but empty cabin. Then, turning on his heel, he slipped back into his cot, pulled the covers over his head and waited for daylight.

"I don't think I ever believed my mother's reasons for leaving me behind." He shrugged. "Whatever they used to justify it in their own minds, they abandoned me."

"That's awful."

"That's just the beginning. The landlord was a big man and I was scared of him so I ran before he could come for the rent. I couldn't read the note they left. I was afraid if I showed it to someone else they'd send me to an orphanage like the one my father said he'd take me to if I was bad. I wandered from town to town doing whatever jobs I could manage and stealing food when I couldn't get work. Let me tell you, Ethan, you lived a charmed life in that orphanage. People don't treat children well in bawdy Western towns. I've got the scars to prove it. Some of them are still visible."

He stared at the man who would no longer meet his gaze. "Is that enough or do you want to know more?"

"That's enough."

"Good." Lawson was quiet for a moment then decided to take a risk. "Now, who are you going to give that information to next?"

Ethan tensed, his startled eyes flying back up to meet Lawson's.

Lawson smirked in satisfaction. Man, he was good. He leaned forward to press his advantage. "You're pretty good but you aren't professional. Your face gives too much away. You should work on that."

"I don't know what you're talking about."

Lawson laughed. "Oh, come on, Ethan. I know you're digging around for someone. Tell me who it is."

Ethan just stared at him. "I'm not digging for anyone. I shouldn't have asked. I didn't know it would be so painful for you. Don't let it ruin your evening. I'm not going to let my past cheat me out of a dance with one of those lovely ladies over there. Excuse me."

Lawson didn't believe him for a moment, but Ethan ignored his silence and walked toward Amy and her sisters. Meanwhile, Lawson valiantly pushed away the heaviness that settled around his soul. He never went through a visit to his past unscathed.

Sean appeared at his side with Lorelei in tow. "I convinced Chris to play a few more dances before putting away his fiddle. The rest is up to you, my friend."

It took Lawson a moment to figure out what Sean was talking about. "My parents told you about our conversation in the cabin, didn't they?"

Sean grinned. "Why do you think they brought it up?"

"Of all the—" He shot a frown at his parents then slid his wary gaze to Ellie. "That was supposed to be private."

Sean slipped an arm around his wife as she swayed

in time with the lively music. "You agreed to let us help so they had to tell us."

"Don't worry. Ellie won't know a thing about it." Lorelei winked at him as she tugged her husband toward the circle of dancers. "Now, go get her before someone else does."

"What have I gotten myself into?" he mumbled as he searched for Ellie in the crowd. He found her already dancing with Clayton Sheppard, a young farmer who was a good friend of Jeff's. However, when Clay caught sight of him, the man led Ellie closer to Lawson. Clay sent him a questioning look, which Lawson returned with a nod. Clay gave Ellie one last twirl, which placed her right in front of Lawson.

They both stilled along with pretty much everyone else on the field. Ellie's gaze held his before it slid away to take in the fact that everyone was waiting for something to happen. "What? Are they expecting me to kiss you or something?"

He swallowed a chuckle. "Well?"

Her eyes widened until she realized he was waiting for her to place her hand in his. "Is that an offer to dance?"

"It is."

She frowned. "We're giving people all sorts of wrong ideas. You know that, don't you?"

"Can't give people something everybody already has so I reckon we might as well have a little fun."

She considered this for a moment then made a show of resting a hand on his shoulder and placing the other in his. His free arm went around the small of her back. They waited for the right moment in the music before he led her into a quick two-step to Chris's robust rendition of "Cotton-Eyed Joe." A cheer echoed across the field but it was Ellie's warm smile that chased away the heavy memory of his past.

Ellie pulled in a refreshing breath of dawn air as she urged Starlight into canter through the woods toward the farm. It still smelled like rain from the heavy deluge that had lulled her to sleep last night. She had awakened before dawn and finished her chores in the barn early so she would have time to ride Starlight before getting ready for church.

She burst from the woods near the old cabin where Lawson was staying. She didn't see any movement inside of it so she assumed he must already be doing his chores. She guided Starlight across the cleared land toward the barn. Suddenly a small white object dashed from the barn toward the pasture. She leaned over the saddle horn to stare. Was that her pig? It was. Her breath caught in her throat. It must have escaped. She urged Starlight faster. Her shout pierced the still morning air. "Lawson! Lawson!"

She pulled Starlight to a stop outside the pasture fence then vaulted over it. The pig streaked toward her, running in a zigzag pattern. She heard Lawson call her name and glanced up in time to see him running out of the barn. Good. She needed help catching it. She refocused her attention on the pig. The little thing slowed to a trot and stared up at her with a wary eye. She took a calm step toward it. It took off again. She whirled and chased after it.

It ran straight toward the tree line. Her eyes widened. If it went into the woods she would never find it. Suddenly the pig turned and ran straight up the middle of the field away from the woods and the few horses Lawson must have already let out to pasture. Relief filled her. Mud began to cling to the bottom of her skirt, making it harder to walk. She stopped for a moment to catch her breath. The pig stopped almost immediately. She narrowed her eyes. The pig stood frozen. She stepped toward it. The pig began walking away. She stopped. The pig stopped. She let out a huff of frustration. "Great."

"Ellie, stop!"

She glanced behind her to see Lawson closing in on her. Three horses followed on his heels. "Good," she yelled back. She motioned him to her left. "You go that way."

"No."

She frowned at him over her shoulder then started running. The pig started running. It veered sideways so she tried to cut it off. She was getting closer. "Now, Lawson! Go that way quickly."

A hand caught her arm and she screamed. She'd been so focused on the pig she hadn't realized Lawson was behind her. He pulled her to a stop. She fought to free herself from his grasp. Finally, she pinned him with a glare. She said between gasps, "You were… supposed to…go that way!"

He shook his head. "I'm trying to tell you. Don't chase it."

"Of course I'm going to chase it." She pulled in a deep breath. "It's my pig. I don't want it to escape." She swallowed. "Now stop talking and help me."

"But Ellie, I'm trying to tell you that the silly pig—"

"The pig." She gasped. She turned from him to scan the field for the pig. It had stopped running to wallow in a mud puddle about ten feet away.

"Ellie—"

"Hush!"

"Fine. Do it your way."

"I will," she breathed as she carefully approached the pig. It was apparently too busy wallowing in the mud puddle to notice. Mud began to creep up the sides of her boots. It dragged at the hem of her skirts. She hiked it up several inches. Each time she pulled her boot from the mud it made a loud sucking sound.

She froze as the pig's ears jumped. She took another large step as it gave one last good wallow, then turned onto its stomach to stare at her. It was so close. She diverted her eyes so she wouldn't threaten it. Then she knelt. The pig stood to its feet and took a step toward her. Her eyes widened. This was too easy. She reached out to it very slowly. The pig took another step toward her.

Suddenly it tried to bolt past her. She lunged in a twisting motion toward it. She managed to get one hand on it before it slipped through her fingers. She landed facedown in the mud. She lay there for a stunned second before she managed to push herself onto her forearms. She glanced up in time to see its curly-tailed behind racing back toward the barn.

She closed her eyes. She heard the squish-pop of Lawson walking toward her through the mud. Finally, he stopped in front of her. She eyed his muck-covered boots for a moment. Pushing her stomach away from the mud, she didn't even bother to stand up. Instead, she plopped onto her bottom and braced her arms behind her to look up at Lawson.

She lifted her eyebrows, daring him to comment. He did an admirable job of keeping his laughter in check, though he couldn't stop the way his golden eyes danced. He knelt beside her as a smile barely tilted the corner of his lips. "I let your pig out every morning. He runs around the pasture for ten minutes then comes back to the barn on his own. He likes the exercise."

"Oh, no." A smile rose unbidden to her lips. A giggle slipped out without her permission. Lawson started chuckling and that just made everything funnier. Her sides began to ache as the tension of the past week seeped out of her. She finally gathered herself enough to send Lawson an expectant look. "Well, don't just sit there. Help me up."

He rose to his feet then extended a hand down to her. He gave a powerful tug that pulled her from the puddle. Mud oozed between their palms, causing her hand to slip from his. She gasped as she nearly tumbled back into the mud, but at the last moment his other arm stole around her waist. He hauled her to his chest and set her feet on the ground.

"That was entirely too much trouble," she muttered against his shirt.

"What?"

She pushed away slightly to look up at him just as he lowered his head to hear her more clearly. They both stilled. Lawson's eyes flashed to hers. Her eyes widened. His arms tightened around her. Her gaze fell to his lips before resting on the top button of his shirt. The still morning air filled with the sound of slightly winded breaths. "I just… I said—trouble."

"Oh," he said as if her statement made a lick of sense. "You lost your shoes."

It wasn't the best line to give the girl he'd almost kissed but it was the only thing Lawson could think of at the moment. It was a wonder he'd been able to come up with anything at all with her hand pressed against his chest, her lips inches away. Despite the cold mud seeping into his shirt, she felt warm in his arms. He released her and retrieved her boots as slowly as possible to give himself time to think.

Telling his parents—and apparently the whole town with them—that he didn't mind their matchmaking didn't mean he should haul off and kiss the woman two days later. He had to let the matchmakers do their job and warm Ellie up to the concept, first. The idea of pursuing something with Ellie still sent a bolt of fear straight to his chest. His relationship with Lorelei had been easy. They'd both been so disengaged. He'd only experienced a few surface feelings.

That would not be so with Ellie. She was so open with her thoughts and feelings, so full of emotion. She would expect the same warmth and openness from him, which would mean he'd have to let down his guard completely. His past had taught him being that invested in someone wasn't wise. He knew better than to hand out even a piece of his heart without thoughtful consideration. If he did decide to approach Ellie with his heart in his hands, it would be after prayerful deliberation. For now, he'd just handed her the boots.

The question in her eyes made him wonder if she'd felt the same powerful tension between them or just wondered why he was acting so strange. He needed to pull himself together. "I guess we'd both better get cleaned up."

A confused frown flashed across her lips before she took her boots and began to walk away. She turned to smile at him as she walked backward. "Thank you for trying to stop me."

"That's what—" *friends are for.* He couldn't quite get himself to complete that statement so he just finished with, "You're welcome."

She gave him a jaunty wave and picked her way across the field toward the house. He grabbed his Stetson from the mud where it had fallen a few feet away, hit it against his leg to clean it off then turned to watch her go. He'd learned a long time ago that he could trust God with his heart, but could he trust Ellie? More important, could he trust himself to be the man she deserved—the kind of man she wouldn't walk away from?

Chapter Seven

Kate hadn't even asked why Ellie showed up at the kitchen door covered in mud. She'd just ordered Ellie to wash in the creek and return in her Sunday best in time for church. She'd washed away the mud with little difficulty but she couldn't rid herself of the memory of being in Lawson's arms. She'd been there many times in the past for a hug, so why did that one feel so different? Why did it feel so real? She even imagined for a moment that he might erase the distance between them with a kiss.

Wishful thinking—nothing more, nothing less. That was the same kind of thinking that had led their families to sandwich him next to her in this pew through some rather crafty maneuvering.

Lawson leaned over to whisper beneath the closing hymn of the church service. "Did you say something?"

Had she said that out loud? She just smiled and shook her head. A small hand tugged her skirt. She glanced down at her four-year-old niece, who whispered, "I want to see Aunt Lori play."

Ellie obediently lifted her niece onto her hip so she could see around the grown-ups to where Lorelei played the piano at the front of the church. Grace rested her curly red head on Ellie's shoulder as Pastor Brightly gave his closing prayer. "Lord, give us the strength to meet life's challenges. Give us discernment as we seek Your will, and courage to perform it. Help us to be a demonstration of love to those around us and to remember that the greatest love of all is found in You. Amen."

Ellie looked up and frowned at Pastor Brightly, then quickly bowed her head when he opened his eyes to smile at the congregation. "Go in peace."

She put her niece down but kept hold of her hand as they followed Lawson and their families toward the sanctuary door. Donovan stood as she passed the aisle where he sat. He held her gaze for a moment then smiled when he looked at Grace. "Do you like children?"

"Yes."

"That's good."

Why can't you be a little less strange? She frowned at him before hurrying on. Mrs. Brightly, the pastor's wife, pulled her into a warm hug when they reached the door of the church. "I hope you're going to help us with the box social next week. You were indispensable at the Founders' Day celebration."

She released Grace to go play with the other children. "I was already planning to come early."

"Perfect!" The woman stepped aside to continue her conversation with Ellie. "Lorelei mentioned you might be willing to help with the children's Sunday school we're trying to start."

"Yes, I told her I was interested in serving as an alternate."

"You'll be wonderful with the children. I'm afraid

we still need one more person. Do you think Lawson might want to help?"

"Lawson?" She looked at Mrs. Brightly a little more closely and realized… *She knows. I wonder who else is aware that I've sanctioned the matchmaking. Probably the whole town.* She felt a telling heat begin to warm her cheeks. "I'll ask him."

Mrs. Brightly gave her arm a squeeze then moved on to the next parishioner. Ellie found Lawson and was surprised when he immediately agreed to help with the Sunday school. Before she had time to question him about it, Rhett appeared in front of them. "Ellie, is Lawson in the Bachelor Club?"

"In the—" She shook her head and blinked at him. "What?"

He passed his hat back and forth between his hands. "I don't know. I made it up because I wanted to know if it's all right to talk about the Bachelor List in front of Lawson."

"Yes!" Lawson's response was entirely too quick and enthusiastic. "I would like to be admitted into the club."

"There is no club."

"As the club's founding member, I welcome you," Rhett replied, ignoring her.

"Please don't make a club." Her protests were in vain because the two men shook hands heartily.

"Thank you. I'm honored." Lawson tipped his head toward Ellie. "We'll need a president."

Rhett grinned. "I nominate Ellie O'Brien."

"No!"

"I second the motion."

"Carried."

Her mouth opened and closed without any sound before she finally managed, "You can't—"

"Madame President," Rhett drawled then gave a slight bow, "I'd like to discuss the match you gave me."

"Who did you get?"

"Amy."

Lawson tilted his head for a moment then nodded. "I could see that happening."

"Well, it isn't. That's the problem. Amy doesn't even know I'm alive."

Ellie glanced at Lawson expectantly.

"Oh, no. I'll leave the advice giving to you, Madame President."

She sighed. "Have you tried talking to her?"

"No." He grimaced at his shoes as though it was all their fault. "I *can't* talk to her. When she's around, my mind freezes up and my words come out all wrong. Do you know what I mean?"

"Yes," she said with certainty as her mind replayed the difficulty she'd had that very morning. Lawson shifted slightly and she suddenly remembered that he was *right there*—listening to her every word. Her eyebrows rose, she bit her lip and dared to slide her gaze to his. He had a bemused expression on his face. She swallowed. "I mean everyone experiences that at some point. After all, it's just a nervous reaction. It doesn't only happen with romantic relationships and…"

When a hint of a half smile played at Lawson's lips, she decided it was best to stop talking altogether.

"How did you overcome it?"

Apparently, I haven't. "I suppose you just have to push through it. Practice. Talk to her about something small and keep it short. Then each time after that, try to increase the length of conversation and the depth of the topic. You'll grow more comfortable over time."

"I can do that."

Ellie smiled. "Yes, you can."

"Thank you, Ellie." He reached down and gave her a hug then shook Lawson's hand before heading across the church lawn. She watched as he hesitated a moment then gathered his courage enough to speak briefly with Amy and Isabelle. She hadn't even realized that she and Lawson had moved closer together, smiling like proud parents as Rhett made his move, until she heard the disapproving sniff behind her.

Ellie knew that sniff—she'd had its disapproval aimed at her through most of her childhood. She pulled in a steeling breath then turned to face Mrs. Greene with a smile. "Good morning."

The woman's eyes darted back and forth between Ellie and Lawson. "Well, isn't this a cozy scene? Are y'all sure y'all aren't hiding an engagement? You can tell me. I'm good at keeping secrets. Isn't that right, Ellie?"

A sick feeling filled Ellie's stomach but she stood taller and lifted her chin. "No, ma'am. It's plain wrong, but thanks for the offer. Have a good day."

She escaped Mrs. Greene's intimidating frown with Lawson in tow. He caught her arm to slow her flight and leaned toward her to ask, "What was that about?"

She shook her head and began walking toward the church without even making a conscious choice to do so. Lawson followed her. "Why is she always rude to you? She seems to get along well enough with the rest of your family these days."

"She hates me." She skirted the church door to walk around the side to the peaceful grounds behind it. "She's hated me for a very long time."

"Is there a reason for this hatred?"

She glanced at him. "There is but please don't ask me what it is."

They both stilled when they realized where they'd ended up after their brisk walk. Shafts of warm sunlight poured through the canopy of tall oak trees that shaded the quiet cemetery. She didn't have to walk far down the cobblestone path before coming to her parents' headstones. Their deaths were one of the young town's earlier tragedies. She closed her eyes and the storm that had taken their lives raged once more in her memories.

His voice was as hushed as their surroundings seemed to demand. "Ellie, what is going on? What was Mrs. Greene talking about?"

"I don't know. I think it ties back to something bad I did—something about my parents."

"She could be making it up just to make you uncomfortable."

"It's real." Her breath rushed from her lungs with a sigh, leaving her with nothing but a whisper. "I know it's real but I can't remember. I don't want to remember."

"Then don't." His hand gently caught her arm and he turned her away from the grave to face him. "We forget things because we have to in order to move on. It's more than a necessity. It's a gift."

"It doesn't feel like a gift."

His eyes deepened to a troubled olive-brown. "I've tried to forget so many things in my past, Ellie, but the memory of it is like a bruise that never fully healed. Don't wish that on yourself. Let Mrs. Greene live with her memories and her hate while you leave them buried."

A soft smile gradually rose to her lips while his

hand fell away. "This reminds me of Pastor Brightly's sermon."

"It does? All I remember is him mentioning something about the sins of the fathers not being visited on the sons."

"Right, but there was something after that. Oh, what did he say?" She pursed her lips as she tried to remember. "It was something like, 'God's grace is experienced…fully experienced…when we have the courage…to believe that the past no longer defines us.'"

He began to lead her to the front of the church. "I've never been that courageous."

"Neither have I." She glanced over her shoulder once more before the cemetery was hidden from her view. "Do you think our lives would be very different if we were?"

"I know mine would be."

She let that answer rest for a moment but her curiosity got the better of her. "How?"

He stilled as a slow revelation seemed to overtake him. For some reason, it twisted the side of his mouth into a frown. Her eyes widened with intrigue. He just looked at her, gave a funny little smile and left her wondering.

Lawson hefted the thick wooden board then held it in the right position for Nathan to pound it into place with his hammer. Thankfully the field had dried enough that they were able to keep working on the new corral fence. Lawson was glad to have a task that didn't take much thought, since his mind was full of Ellie. He'd learned something valuable after that mud bath yesterday. Ellie was attracted to him. Her response to Rhett's question hadn't clued him in to that as much as her reaction to having said it. She'd looked guiltier than a cat swimming in a bucket of milk and just as uncomfortable. That made things infinitely more complicated because if the attraction was mutual, he might have to stop thinking about being brave and actually take a real step in that direction.

Nathan's mind seemed to be on a similar track because he asked, "So what happened in the field yesterday between you and Ellie?"

Lawson tossed him a sideways glance. "What makes you think something happened?"

"You were up to your knees in mud and Ellie was covered in it." Nathan paused his hammering to glance up in amusement. "There has to be a story in there somewhere."

Lawson told Nathan about the pig's morning run and how Ellie reacted to it.

Nathan laughed and shook his head. "That girl. She's something else."

"She sure is." Lawson grinned.

"So did you kiss her?"

The question was asked so casually that it took a moment for it to process. When it did, Lawson nearly dropped the board he was holding then glanced at Nathan with a frown. "What kind of question is that?"

"A perfectly normal one." Nathan wiggled his eyebrows. "Did you?"

"No." He paused then murmured, "Almost."

"How do you *almost* kiss someone?"

Lawson knew right then and there that letting that slip had been a bad idea. "You realize what you're about to do in time to be sensible."

"Well, then." Nathan pushed against the fence to

test its stability. "I guess I'd better ask—what are your intentions toward my little sister-in-law?"

"Nothing I'm ready to declare."

That didn't mean he hadn't thought about developing some. He had. He'd thought about it when he'd gotten home and proposed. He'd thought about it in that café when she'd bemoaned being paired with the one man who would never love her. He'd thought about it yesterday when she'd asked how his life would be different if he believed his past didn't matter.

"Why don't you have any intentions toward my little sister-in-law?"

Lawson froze and stared at Nathan in shock. "Did you really just say that?"

Nathan grinned then crossed his arms. "Look, I don't want to pressure you, but if you have feelings for Ellie I hope you'll pursue them."

"You *are* serious," he said with a bemused smile. "Why?"

"Your personalities fit together like puzzle pieces. Where she's weak, you're strong and vice versa. What I notice most is that she lightens you up and you keep her grounded. She's a dreamer so she needs that. Your past weighs on you at times so you need her, too." Nathan shrugged. "Maybe I'm just being selfish, but I like the idea having you in our family."

Lawson lifted his brows. "You really mean that?"

"Sure I do. I couldn't think of a better man for her." He pushed against the fence post to test its sturdiness. "You have my blessing if you ever want it."

Of course he wanted it, but that fact raised so many questions. *What if this just ends up like other important relationships have in the past? What if I'm not enough*

*to make her stay? If it doesn't work out, what would
happen to my relationship with the O'Briens?*

His shoulders straightened in determination. Hadn't
he told himself over and over that he was nothing like
his birth parents? He was supposed to believe it by now.
And like Doc had said, any relationship worth having
was worth taking a risk. Ellie was worth it.

A burst of joyful laughter pulled Ellie's attention
from the strawberry bush to her six-month-old nephew.
He waved a dandelion then laughed as the seeds van-
ished into the air. Ellie caught his gaze and grinned.
"I don't think I've ever seen anyone have so much fun
with a dandelion before."

Kate watched her son lunge toward Ellie. "Pretty
soon he'll be crawling and getting into everything.
That's when the real fun will start."

Ellie dropped another berry into the large pail then
picked up her nephew and deposited him in her lap. He
squirmed until his back rested against her stomach then
smiled up at her. "You're like a ray of sunshine, aren't
you, little Matthew?"

She glanced up to find Kate watching her curiously.
"You've been pretty quiet until now, Ellie. Is everything all right?"

"I was just thinking about how Ma used to take us
berry picking." She reached a bit deeper into the bush
for more berries.

"That was fun, wasn't it? I'm a little surprised you
remember it. You were so young."

"Not too young to cause trouble," she said, then
wished she hadn't when it immediately made her think
of Mrs. Greene.

Kate laughed. "No. You were never too young for that."

Ellie bit her lip. She hated that Mrs. Greene seemed to know something about her that she didn't know about herself. Or rather—something she'd tried to keep from knowing. Surely, those mysterious "consequences" of her actions couldn't have been that bad. Then again, telling the whole world Mrs. Greene's secret had been bad enough. What could top that?

She steeled herself before quietly asking, "Kate, did you ever get the feeling that our parents might have been disappointed in me for some reason?"

"What? No. Why do you ask?"

She shrugged. "Oh, I don't know. It's just a feeling I get sometimes. Or maybe it's a memory."

Kate frowned and surveyed her searchingly. "Our parents were just as proud of you as they were of Sean and me."

I don't think she knows. She'd finished school by that point so she wasn't there when I spread the rumor. Sean might remember it happening but I don't think he knows I started it, either. My parents and Mrs. Greene were the only ones who knew where it originated. But what were the consequences for my family?

"There you go looking pensive again. What are you thinking about now?"

She groped about for some other subject and went with the first thing that came to mind. "Just that I need to start planning what I want to achieve as a maiden aunt for the rest of my life, since my Bachelor List scheme didn't work."

Kate rested her berry-stained hand on her knee in exasperation. "You don't need to give up on a husband. You just need to be patient and stop worrying about it."

"I'm not worrying. I'm planning for the next practical step." She grinned teasingly. "I figure I'll need to find a house in town and take in a few cats to keep me company."

"Stop it, Ellie. This is serious." Kate's fiery blue gaze met hers. "We are long overdue for a talk. I have a few things I need to set straight with you."

Matthew dropped his dandelion. "Uh-oh."

Ellie picked it up for him then eyed her sister as she whispered, "Brace yourself, Matthew. Your ma's on the warpath."

Kate ignored her but narrowed her eyes. "You are twenty-one years old. That is entirely too young to start planning a life alone. Can you look me in the eye and tell me you know without a shadow of a doubt that God called you to be single?"

"No."

"Then you need to start praying that God will lead you to the right man or make it clear that you aren't supposed to have one." Kate leaned forward to catch her hand. "Ellie, dear, I want you to be honest with me about something."

Ellie decided it was best to stick to one-word responses. "Anything."

"I know what Ms. Lettie thinks and I know what the town thinks, but what are your feelings toward Lawson? Tell me the truth. There is no right or wrong answer."

Ellie sighed. Of course Kate would ask that. She was getting plumb tired of it being mentioned and having to think about it so much. Yet, as she stared back into her sister's eyes she didn't see laughter or teasing, she saw only concern. She tightened her grip slightly on Kate's hand then shrugged lightly. "We've always been friends."

"I know," Kate replied softly as Matthew used both of his hands to pat theirs.

"It's only since he returned that..." Ellie searched Kate's face for a moment, wondering if she should let her sister in on the emotions she'd barely acknowledged to herself. "That I've started to like him as more than a friend."

Kate's eyes widened and a slow smile spilled across her face. Her voice was low as though they were sharing secrets. "You aren't pulling my leg, are you?"

"No!" She covered her mouth then laughed at her vehemence. "I'm not saying I'm in love with the man."

"But there's potential." Kate glanced past her at the sound of girlish giggles. "Grace and Hope, y'all are not too far away for me to see you throwing berries at each other. Pick up each one of them and put them in the pail where they belong."

"Yes, ma'am," the sisters chorused.

Ellie shrugged. "I'm afraid I'm just being silly."

"You aren't."

"Oh, but I am! You don't seriously think he'd be interested in me, do you? I certainly don't. I thought for a moment he was going to kiss me the other day but now I think I was just imagining it."

"If he might have almost kissed you, why don't you think he'd be interested in you?"

"I have no delusions about myself. I know what I am and what I'm not. I'm not nearly as beautiful as Lorelei. I don't have it all together like you. I'm not nearly as nice as Ms. Lettie." She brushed an errant tear away and frowned. "I have no idea why I'm crying."

"You're crying because you're being too hard on

yourself. Stop comparing yourself to other people. You are a wonderful person, Ellie O'Brien. I can't believe you don't know that."

"You have to say that because you're my sister."

"I have to say it because it's true. I ought to know *because* I am your sister. I raised you, for goodness' sake. I know you. I know you mean well even if what you do only seems like mischief to others. I know you have a wholesome beauty that you haven't stopped long enough in front of a mirror to notice. I know you haven't had a beau because you've been too busy trying to plan everyone else's love life to care about your own."

Ellie gave a watery laugh. "Why do you always say exactly what I need to hear?"

Kate smiled gently. "It's not my words you needed to hear, silly. It's God's. You need to figure out what He says about you in His words because I know it doesn't match up with any of the things you just said. His opinion is what's really important—not mine or some man's, right?"

"I guess," she said with a frown. She should believe that. It just didn't seem true. At least, it didn't feel true.

"As for moving into town with a bunch of cats, I think we both know that's just silly. This farm is Ma and Pa's legacy. They left it to you and Sean as much as they left it to me. That means you have every right to stay here for as long as you want. Nathan and I are happy to have you here. I never meant to make you feel unwelcome."

"You didn't—I was just being silly."

Grace bolted past them. "Papa!"

Ellie glanced up in surprise to see Nathan heading toward them on his mount with Lawson beside him on his own. Grace stopped abruptly as though suddenly realizing how she was supposed to approach the horses. Hope joined her as Nathan dismounted a few feet away. Kate stood to greet her husband. "You have perfect timing. We've filled all our pails and could use some help carrying them to the house."

"We'd be happy to help." Nathan's gaze flashed to Lawson then slid to where Ellie still sat with Matthew. "Wouldn't we, Lawson?"

Ellie narrowed her eyes suspiciously at Nathan when Lawson quickly agreed. What was going on with those two? Lawson approached her with his hat in his hands. "How can I help?"

"Hold him for a minute."

He looked a little panicked but took Matthew from her hands while she stood to her feet. She settled her nephew on her hip. Lawson picked up the huge pail before grabbing the reins of his horse. Kate and Nathan strolled ahead of them. The girls shared the saddle while Kate led the horses and Nathan carried the two large pails.

Nathan said something to Kate, who glanced back to look at them in surprise. A smile flashed across her face before she turned back around. Kate responded to Nathan. He actually winked at them. Ellie nearly winced, then risked a sideways glance at Lawson. He caught her looking. She wrinkled her nose. "Subtlety doesn't exactly run in the family."

He chuckled. A beat of silence hovered between them before Lawson cleared his throat. "There's going to be a barn raising at the Sheppards' place next weekend."

"Yes, I heard Clay mention it."

"I was wondering if you'd do me the honor...of going with me."

It took a moment for the meaning of his words to process. By that time, they'd both stopped walking and she found herself in danger of getting lost in hazel eyes that shone with cautious hope. "Are you— Do you..."

"Maybe the town and our families aren't entirely crazy. Maybe they are." His chest rose and fell with a deep breath that rushed out in one sentence. "I think we should find out."

"What does that mean?" Her heart was beating at a full gallop but her mind couldn't seem to catch up.

"I'm not sure. We could just see what happens. If you don't think that's right then we can forget the whole thing—"

"No." She bit her lip when the word escaped a bit too quickly and she forced herself to slow down. "I think that's fine."

"You do?"

She nodded.

"All right. Then we'll just see what happens, I guess."

"I guess so."

Their eyes held for another moment before they started walking again. She wasn't exactly sure how to classify the agreement she and Lawson had just come to. They weren't exactly courting—or were they? Either way, it looked like the matchmaking might be starting to work, so she kept her mouth shut and played with the baby. Perhaps Kate was right and she didn't need to give up on finding that transformative love she longed for after all.

Chapter Eight

Ellie stood outside the door of the church's storage room while she waited for the arrival of the first entries into the box social. She saw Mrs. Greene arrive and hoped beyond anything the woman wouldn't approach her. Of course, she had to be the first to follow Marissa Brightly's instructions to check the picnic baskets in with her. Ellie greeted her pleasantly and tried to act as if nothing had happened that day by the courthouse. Mrs. Greene managed to do the same except for that knowing glint in her eye.

Ellie felt that look right to the pit of her stomach. She'd allowed her courtship with Lawson to become a welcome distraction from her fears but they were still there—taunting her when she tried to go to sleep. She couldn't stand it anymore. She'd figure this out as soon as she could. Otherwise, Ellie would have to live not only with that feeling of guilt, but with Mrs. Greene lording over her with whatever special knowledge the woman had.

Amy Bradley and her younger sister, Isabelle, were the next to arrive. Ellie forced a cheerful greeting to her lips and ushered them inside the room so she could write down their names and a description of their lunch baskets for Pastor Brightly. Isabelle watched the proceedings with a curious smile. "Why are we being so secretive this year?"

"We're just trying to liven things up. We're also trying to spark some competition to raise a bit more money," Ellie explained. "That schoolhouse roof needs a lot of work."

"I think it's a wonderful idea," Amy said as she set her basket down on the table.

Isabelle rolled her eyes. "You're just happy Rhett won't know to bid on yours."

Ellie's gaze shot to Amy. "What have you got against Rhett, anyway?"

"Nothing in particular," she said with a vague wave of her hand.

"It's just something in general," Isabelle informed Ellie wryly. "Amy here has sworn off men since that Silas Smithson character left town without a word. I gave that resolve about two weeks but it's lasted for a year now."

"Amy, why didn't you tell me?" Ellie must be slipping. How did she not already know this?

Amy shrugged and sent her sister an unappreciative look. "Well, I haven't exactly been shouting it from the rooftops. Thank you, Isabelle. You don't think it's silly, do you, Ellie?"

"It isn't my place to judge."

"Isabelle, please take note of that statement and apply it the next time you want to give advice." Amy squeezed Ellie's hand gratefully then left the room.

Isabelle sighed. "I wish you would have said something in Rhett's favor. She hasn't been any fun lately.

She wouldn't have even entered a basket if Mother hadn't insisted."

"What's wrong with her?"

"I wish I knew. She's been in love with someone for the past few years and now it's as though she feels nothing."

"Who has she been in love with?"

"Who hasn't she been in love with? My sister has fallen in love more times than I can count."

Ellie chuckled. "Well, then, it's good that she's taking some time out from love. Perhaps it will help her figure out who she really loves."

"Maybe so, but I'm rooting for Rhett."

A few other women entered the room as Isabelle left, so it was a few minutes before Ellie stepped outside the door. She was surprised to find Chris waiting for her. He held up a basket. "This is Sophia's."

She frowned. "Why didn't she bring it herself?"

"I wanted to talk to you."

She almost asked why, then remembered what he'd said the last time he'd tried to talk to her. She glanced around for any sign of Lawson but he'd said he wouldn't be able to come early. "I'm not sure that's a good idea."

"We've always been good friends, haven't we? I thought that meant I could at least have a conversation with you."

Her shoulders relaxed and she smiled. "You're right, Chris. I'm sorry for being prickly. Let me check in that basket while you tell me what's on your mind."

"Are you really courting Lawson?"

She glanced up from her list to meet his gaze. "As far as I can tell."

He frowned. "What does that mean?"

It meant she wasn't sure. They were more than

friends but less than a couple. As far as she could tell, that meant he liked her but didn't want to be her beau yet. She couldn't fault him for that exactly. No one else had shown even half as much interest in her... until now, apparently, when men kept coming out of the woodwork.

She eyed Chris thoughtfully. "Why do you want to know?"

"I was hoping that since you just want to be friends with me, you might be willing to tell me who my match is."

She let the tablet fall to her side as she tilted her head. "Aren't you moving on a little too fast for someone who's supposed to be in love with me?"

His jaw tightened. "Don't tease me, Ellie. It's cruel."

"I'm sorry, Chris. I didn't mean to be." She sighed then leaned back against the door frame and crossed her arms with the tablet in front of her. "I haven't figured out everyone's match yet."

"You mean I don't have one."

"Yet."

He lowered his head in disappointment. "Did you give Amy one?"

"Did I give...?" she echoed, then met his gaze when he looked up. "Amy," she breathed in realization. "Didn't you two go to the harvest dance together last year?"

He crossed his arms and lifted his chin to stare down at her. "She threw me over for that fancy out-of-town fellow who broke her heart."

"I remember." She frowned. "Wouldn't that have been right around the time you said you started developing feelings for me?"

Either her eyes were playing tricks on her or her friend was blushing. "Maybe."

Her mouth fell open for a moment. She clamped it shut then placed her hand on her hip. "Tell me the truth, Chris Johansen. You were settling for me, weren't you? I was your last choice."

He just stood there, not giving an inch, then his arms slowly relaxed to his side. "I don't suppose you could talk to her for me?"

"No!"

"I didn't think so." He handed her the basket then walked away.

She glared at his back for a moment then placed the basket inside the room, muttering to the Lord, "Of all the nerve, expecting me to fall at his feet when he doesn't even care a whit about me and is in love with someone else entirely."

"Who's in love with someone else?" Lawson's deep voice asked from the door. "I hope you don't mean me."

She gave a startled jump then whirled to face him. He lifted his eyebrows to prod an answer from her and she realized she hadn't given him one. "I don't."

"Good, because it wouldn't have been true." He surveyed the room filled with baskets. "Are you going to tell me which one of these is yours?"

She shook her head. "It's against the rules. Why don't you help me move all of these to the sanctuary? It's almost time to start."

After Ellie handed Mrs. Brightly the list of entries, she wandered back over to the seat Lawson had saved for her on the same pew where Nathan and Kate sat with Ms. Lettie and Doc. When the third basket came up for sale, Lawson leaned over to her conspiratorially. "I recognize that basket. It's my ma's."

With that, he lifted his hand to place the first bid. Doc immediately leaned over to challenge. "Are you trying to steal my woman, Son?"

Lawson grinned, but before he could answer, Chris yelled, "I bid a dollar."

She turned to stare at him in confusion. He just met her gaze with a grim nod. Suddenly. another man yelled, "One dollar and ten cents."

She whirled around to face the front of the church to find Donovan standing with his hands obstinately on his hips. "They think it's mine."

Doc finally had a chance to bid. Donovan hesitated a moment then sat down. No one else spoke up after Doc so he won the basket. Lawson sent her a sideways glance then rubbed his hands together. "This is going to be fun."

Lawson randomly started bidding on many of the baskets after that. Chris and Donovan followed suit, which drove the prices up until Lawson dropped out. After that, Chris and Donovan would stop, which allowed the person who really wanted the basket to step in and purchase it. Finally, Isabelle's basket came up. Lawson continued to bid on it more intensely than he had the others.

People began to whisper their speculations on whether or not it was Ellie's basket or someone else's. Chris dropped out of the running so it was just between Lawson and Donovan. Lawson stopped bidding, leaving Donovan with the prize. Isabelle stepped forward and did not look pleased. For that matter, neither did Donovan.

Pastor Brightly held up the lunch Ellie had prepared next. It was packed in a medium-size picnic basket that had been whitewashed and covered in bright yellow fabric. "I'm told this cheerful basket is filled with fried chicken, hashed potatoes, fruit and chocolate cake. Let's start the bidding at fifty cents."

Ellie waited for Lawson to start the bidding. He didn't. This was obviously going to be one of the baskets he didn't bid on. Unfortunately, no one else did, either. Embarrassing silence permeated the air. "Who will make the opening bid?"

She bit her lip.

Pastor Brightly cleared his throat. "Why don't we start at thirty, then?"

Her fingers clenched. Clayton Sheppard raised his hand. She had a bid. One bid. That was better than nothing. She unclenched her fingers and felt her shoulders relax. Lawson's arm pressed against hers. She glanced up to find him watching her carefully. He smiled slowly. "I thought so."

He raised his hand. "Sixty."

Just like that a bidding war erupted. Chris jumped in the game. Nathan put up a bid, then Sean tried to make things interesting. Finally, Chris and Lawson began duking it out for the highest bid. Obviously, Lawson was serious about this one. Pastor James was desperately trying to keep up. A third bid from Donovan threw him for a moment before he paused. "Donovan, I told you three times now. You can't bid anymore once you've won a basket. Why don't you and Isabelle find a spot to eat? Now, where were we?"

Lawson stretched his arm so it landed on the pew behind Ellie. "You were just about to sell me that basket."

"A dollar fifty," Chris yelled from the pew behind her.

"This is ridiculous," Ellie murmured. She turned to look for Amy and found the girl seated with the rest of her sisters. Amy was only paying cursory attention to the drama unfolding on the auction block. She seemed more interested in exchanging furtive glances with Rhett. Ellie hissed to Chris, "Would you stop it? I promise you're not doing yourself any favors with this."

He followed her gaze to Amy then hesitated. "I withdraw my last bid."

"Then the last bid was from Lawson for one dollar and thirty cents. Going. Going—"

"Two dollars!"

A mixture of gasps and groans filled the church at the sound of the new voice from the back of the church. Ellie turned in her seat with the rest of the congregation to find Ethan Larue leaning nonchalantly against the back wall.

Lawson turned to find Ethan's gaze settled on him in open challenge. Who was this man and why did he keep inserting himself into Lawson's affairs? Granted, Lawson had willingly bared his past to the near-stranger but that didn't mean he trusted him. Far from it. He still believed Ethan was up to something underhanded. Rhett hurried across the aisle to ask lowly, "Is he in the club?"

"Not a chance."

Rhett nodded like a Ranger receiving his first assignment. "Put your hand up and leave it there. We'll do the rest."

Ellie leaned over as he did just that. "What are y'all whispering about?"

"Why is he bidding on your basket?"

"I don't know why anyone does anything these days," she moaned.

Lorelei's father, Mr. Wilkins, leaned across the aisle to slip something into his hand. Lawson glanced down and realized he now held three rolled-up dollar bills. Ellie nudged him. She opened her hand to reveal more than a dollar's worth of coins. "Mrs. Cummins passed us this. It's from her row."

Lawson shook his head in amazement. The town was giving Lawson the money to up his bid. Once Ethan realized what was happening, he bowed out with a grin that said he'd never intended to win in the first place. The man was starting to get under his skin. One of these days, when there wasn't a crowd of people watching, Lawson intended to find out why. For now, though, he had four dollars and fifty cents worth of a lunch basket to eat. He stole a glance at Ellie's flushed cheeks and knew it was worth every penny.

Tap. Bam. Tap. Bam. Lawson reached for another nail but it rolled off the end of the roof of the unfinished barn and fell two stories to hide in a bush. He picked another nail, tapped it into place and drove it through. He'd gotten so used to building things in the weeks he'd been home that he could probably save himself time by driving the nail through the board in one blow. He just didn't trust himself to get it right the first time.

"Lawson, why are you still here?" Rhett's yell sounded loudly over the noise of construction and the distant sound of singing. "Your shift is over. Go find that pretty girl of yours and give someone else a turn up there!"

Laughter and hoots echoed through the new walls of the building. Lawson smiled in case anyone was watching, although he wanted to groan. Bringing Ellie to the barn raising seemed to have given the town the last piece of evidence they needed to convince themselves that he and Ellie were meant to be. Pretty soon they'd convince themselves he'd proposed again. By next month, the town would have them married and living in his cabin. The way everyone was rushing things made him nervous. Didn't they realize he needed to take this slow, make sure everything was going to work out before he put his heart on the line completely?

"I hear you, Rhett. I guess I got a little distracted, but I'm leaving now." His feet hadn't been on the ground floor for long before Ethan Larue approached him. Lawson took a deep drink of water then gave the man a suspicious look. "Is there something I can help you with?"

"I need to talk to you. It's important."

"What is it?"

Ethan's gaze swept the rafters of the barn and the crowded area outside before he shook his head. "We'd better find someplace quieter."

He reluctantly followed Ethan away from the ruckus of the barn raising toward a quiet spot near the Sheppards' house. Lawson took stock of his opponent. The man wasn't armed as far as he could tell. "I think you'd better sit down," Ethan said.

Lawson frowned but complied by wrangling a wooden crate. "I think you'd better tell me what this is all about, Ethan."

"You were right at the party. I did come here to find out about you. I wasn't given permission to reveal why until yesterday." Ethan sat on the crate across from him and watched him intensely. "I lied about my last name. It isn't Larue. It's Lawson."

Lawson placed his elbows on his knees as he leaned forward. "Your last name is my first name?"

"Actually, your first name is your mother's maiden name."

"How would you know that?" He shook his head in confusion. "I don't even know that."

"Your mother, Gloria, was my aunt."

"My…" Lawson stared at him. "That means you're my cousin."

"That's right."

He had a cousin. He stared at Ethan blankly for a moment as he went over the facts he'd just heard. "You said *was*. Is she dead?"

"I don't know. She'd run off by the time my father died and your father took me out of the orphanage."

"My father is Doc Williams." Lawson's firm tone brokered no question. His thoughts stumbled about as he tried to figure out what to call the man Ethan knew. "This other man—he took you out of the orphanage and you lived with him?"

"Yes."

"I'm sorry."

"Don't be. He treated me well." Ethan ignored Lawson's disbelieving scoff. "You don't have to call him *this other man*. You remember his name, don't you?"

He shook his head.

"Well, surely you remember your own last name."

"It's Williams."

Ethan frowned but his tone was patient. "No."

Lawson ran a hand through his hair and suddenly realized it trembled. His words came out harshly. "I don't remember."

"It's Hardy."

"Hardy," he whispered before another blow landed across his small jaw. He reeled but the stranger's rough hands held him upright.

"Speak up, boy. I want my friends to hear you.

*What's your last name?" The drunk slurred then shook
him until his brain rattled.*

"I said it's Hardy!"

*The man's bloodshot eyes held his. "Your father's
name is Clive."*

*"Yes, sir." He whimpered when the man let him fall
to the ground, then carefully rubbed his jaw.*

*"I told you, friends, I told you. That's the kid. His
father will pay big to get him back." The man whirled
toward him. "Don't move. We're taking you back to
Papa...right after I finish this drink."*

*Lawson pulled his knees to his chest and crossed
his arms around them. His pa didn't want him. What
were these men going to do when they found that out?*

*One of the painted ladies came down the stairs and
frowned at the blood on his face. She shot a look toward
the men who were too deep in their cups to notice when
she offered him her hand. He hesitantly took it and allowed her to lead him into the kitchen. She cleaned his
face before handing him a sack. "I know those men.
They don't mean well by you. Take this and run."*

*He stared at her in shock. She didn't want him, ei-
ther. "You promised I could stay on and wash dishes."*

*"I know I did but if you stay, they'll hurt you worse.
I can't stop them. You run away and don't ever come
back to this town. Too many people here know you're
Clive's son. With that reward on his head, there will
be plenty more like those men wanting to use you to
get to him. Promise me you'll run."*

"Yes, ma'am."

*"Oh, and Lawson, you've got to protect yourself in
the next town. You can't tell anyone who you are. From
now on you don't have a last name. If anyone asks,
you're just Lawson. You hear me?"*

"Lawson!"

He snapped back to reality to find Ethan watching him in concern. "What?"

"I said he wants to see you."

"Who does?"

"Your father."

"No."

"At least think about it."

"I don't have to think about it. The answer is no." He shot to his feet, nearly overturning the crate in his haste. He searched the crowd for Nathan and found him sitting next to Sean. "Nathan, I need you to take Ellie home. I'm not feeling well."

"You look pale. Maybe I should drive you," Sean offered.

"No." The word came out louder than he intended. He thanked them then turned away. He realized it would be rude to leave Ellie without saying anything but it couldn't be helped. He needed to be alone. He needed to think. So this was it. For the past ten years, he'd been waiting for the other shoe to drop. It finally had.

The world seemed to slow down yet rush with color and sound—memories that he had to fight back. He had a cousin. His mother was probably dead. His father wanted to see him. He was filled with disbelief. There had to be a way to salvage this. He'd just ignore it. Ethan would go away. Lawson would go back to the life he'd created. He'd go back to hope, to Ellie's pure smile, to moments when he'd thought maybe his past could be erased.

Somehow he knew it wouldn't be that easy.

Chapter Nine

The incessant hammering from the barn raising rooted Ellie on as she held her breath and gulped down a full glass of water. She placed a hand on her stomach as she waited to see if her hiccups had been sufficiently drowned by the deluge. Her next hiccup was followed by a frustrated groan. She'd spent the past five minutes trying everything she could think of to get rid of the annoying condition she was in.

"Miss Ellie, you sure look pretty today!" She jumped and turned to find Donovan Turner standing a bit too close for comfort. He leaned even closer in concern. The piece of hay in his mouth bobbled as he asked, "What's wrong?"

"Nothing." She waited for a moment then smiled. "You scared the hiccups right out of me, though."

He grinned. She scanned the crowd for Nathan and found him talking to Sean and Lawson. Donovan fiddled with the Stetson in his hands. "How is Hamlet?"

She shifted out of the way of a passing woman, which conveniently placed her farther away from Donovan. "Who?"

"The pig I gave you."

"Oh, I didn't know it already had a name."

He nodded. "It's Shakespeare—one of his trage-dies."

"Yes, I know."

"You know Shakespeare?"

"Not personally." He didn't seem to think that was funny so she bit her lip to hide her smile. "I read a few of his plays in school."

"Did I ever tell you that I was an actor in a troupe?" He shifted closer as though her surprise gave him permission to do so. "We toured the panhandle and made a lot of money."

"How did you end up running a pig farm?" She nearly winced when she realized she'd gotten him started on his favorite subject. He'd trapped her good this time. She cast a pleading look over his shoulder to where her oblivious brothers stood before he blustered on. Where had Lawson gone? He'd asked her to come with him. Didn't he care that she'd been cornered?

Something in her question must have hinted at dis-approval because Donovan shifted into more of a com-bative stance. "What's wrong with my pig farm? You've never been there so how could you have formed an opinion?"

She suddenly remembered Kate's warning not to encourage the man or be alone with him. She glanced around the bustling activity of the barn raising. Well, she wasn't alone with him. However, it was probably best if she moved along. "I'm sure your pig farm is just fine."

"I'm glad to hear you say that." He ducked his head then decided to peer at her instead. "The truth is I like you a lot, Miss Ellie, more than that dandy you're spooning with now. Anyone can see he's just going along because the town's making him. And, where is he now?"

Donovan's words hit a little too close for comfort. She shifted farther away from him. "I don't know, but I'm afraid I don't return your feelings, Mr. Turner."

His eyes narrowed. "It's because of my pig farm, isn't it?"

Why couldn't he understand that she just didn't like him? She'd already said it once. Did she need to tell him that he made her uncomfortable or that she didn't trust him? Her pause must have lasted too long. She jumped when he abruptly slammed his Stetson on his knee, somehow managing to make a loud popping sound in the process.

"Doggone. It is the pig farm. If I'd known, I never would have bought— Oh, here comes your brother. I'll see you later." He hurried away like a cat with its tail on fire.

Nathan placed a protective hand on her shoulder as he stared after Donovan with a frown. "Was he bothering you?"

She squeezed his hand appreciatively. "I find him slightly annoying, but other than that, not really. He scared my hiccups away at any rate."

Nathan crossed his arms. "Well, I told him to leave you alone and he ignored me. That doesn't bode well. The next time he tries that, be curt with him. He has to get it through his head that you're off-limits."

"He always seemed so harmless before."

"A rattlesnake seems harmless until it starts to shake."

She shivered at the analogy. "Aren't you descriptive?"

"I'm supposed to tell you Lawson left because he

wasn't feeling well. You'll ride home with me and Kate."

Ellie looked at him in concern. "Do you think we should send word to Doc?"

"Doc's delivering a baby."

"Even so, someone should check on Lawson."

"I know. We won't stay here much longer. You can check on him yourself."

Nathan kept his promise and less than an hour later, Ellie knocked lightly on the door of Lawson's cabin. He didn't respond. She shifted the large basket Kate had filled with anything and everything Lawson might need to cure whatever ailed him, and knocked again. Finally, his voice called from deep inside the cabin. "Who is it?"

"Ellie."

A moment later he opened the door with what seemed to be reluctance. Her eyes widened at his disheveled appearance. His short brown wavy hair looked as though he'd combed it with his fingers in myriad directions. He wore the same cream-colored shirt from earlier but it was half-unbuttoned and haphazardly tucked into the waistband of his brown pants. He didn't bother to meet her gaze. Instead, he stared down at his bare feet. "Sorry for leaving early."

"That's all right," she said, looking everywhere but the expanse of his exposed chest. "I understand why."

His gaze jerked to hers. "Ethan told you?"

"No, Nathan told me you were sick. I didn't see Ethan." His eyes lowered but not until she saw a hint of relief there. "I'm sorry if I awakened you. Are you feeling any better?"

He shrugged then leaned against the door frame. "I suppose."

"It must have come on suddenly."

He hardly seemed to hear her. He stared unseeingly at some distant object. "I'll be fine."

She wasn't so sure about that. He certainly seemed dazed. She remembered Nathan acting the same way when he'd had a high fever. "You don't have a fever, do you?"

He shook his head but she lifted her hand to his forehead, anyway. Suddenly, his hazel eyes focused on her. For the first time since he opened the door, he seemed exactly like himself, only somehow more intense. Her hand drifted back to her side. "Kate sent this basket. I don't even know what's in it."

He reached out and caught her arm to pull her closer.

"She threatened to send Nathan with the shotgun if I didn't come back in ten minutes."

His gaze captured hers. His other hand cradled her jaw while his thumb brushed her cheek.

"I told her that wasn't funny but she…" She stopped trying to talk the moment his forehead touched hers. How she'd managed to speak at all as breathless as she felt was beyond her. They stood there for a moment, neither of them speaking or moving. Finally, he lifted her chin and kissed her. She immediately began to pull away from the new sensation then hesitated. His hand pressed gently against her back and she allowed him to guide her into another kiss.

It seemed to take him a moment to gather his thoughts. His gaze finally found hers. "You didn't slap me."

She let out a breathless laugh. "Did you think that I would?"

"I wasn't sure."

She pushed away from his chest slightly to look up

at him and dared to ask, "Lawson, what is happening here? I can tell you aren't sick but obviously something is wrong. Won't you tell me what it is? Maybe I can help."

"You can't help, but thank you." He leaned down to kiss her once more then set her away from him. "You'd better go. Tell Kate I'll be fine in the morning."

He quickly took the basket then shut the door behind him, leaving her with no choice but to walk away. Nathan was still unhitching the horses from the wagon so she wandered into the barn and found him in the tack room. "How is he?"

She watched him put away the last harness. "I don't think we need to send for Doc."

"That's good." He closed the tack room door and grinned. "You and Lawson seem to be getting pretty close these days. I'm really happy for y'all, Ellie. I told him courting you would be the right thing to do."

"Thank you. I…" Suddenly, her heart gave a little hiccup of disappointment. "Wait. You *told* him that he should do it?"

"I sure did. I also said he would be perfect for you and that we'd love to have him in our family if things progress."

"Oh." She tilted her head to watch him closely. "Was that before or after he asked your permission?"

"Well, he didn't ask for my permission exactly."

"I see."

"Did I say something wrong?"

She squeezed her brother-in-law's shoulder to try to chase the furrow from his brow. "No, you were very sweet. Lawson hasn't officially said that we're courting, which is fine. I just wanted to make sure I was reading the signs right."

"I'm sure you are. Be patient. Lawson tends to hold his feelings close to his vest." He led her out of the barn and closed the door behind them. "How about a game of checkers before dinner?"

"Thanks, but I think I'll take a walk."

A few moments later, the few horses out in the pasture ran up to greet her when she reached their fence. Starlight was the only one who stayed when they realized she hadn't brought them any treats. She rubbed the horse's strong neck. "I wish I could be as sure as Nathan is, Starlight."

Instead, Donovan's words sifted through her mind to reveal the doubts she'd been afraid to face. What if she was mistaken and he was right? What if Lawson was only expressing an interest in her to please the town and their families? If so, then it was her fault because she'd encouraged everyone to matchmake on her behalf. Essentially, that meant that poor Lawson had the whole town pressuring him to be in a romantic relationship with her. Even the people who he normally went to for advice, like his parents and Nathan, had gotten caught up in the matchmaking fever.

What if I made the wrong choice in encouraging the matchmakers? Did I even stop to consider how Lawson might feel about that? No, because I wanted to feel important. I wanted to feel wanted. Isn't that exactly how I made an enemy out of Mrs. Greene? What if the same thing ends up ruining my relationship with Lawson?

She shook her head to rein in those thoughts. It was too much to take in. Maybe it wasn't true. Maybe the town wasn't the driving force behind his decision to court her.

She pulled back to look into her horse's large brown

eyes. "He kissed me, Starlight. That has to mean something, right?"

Starlight gave a low nicker of agreement. A flash of color in the woods that led to the creek drew Ellie's attention for a moment until Starlight nuzzled her shoulder. When she looked again there was nothing there, so she patted her horse's shoulder. "I know you love me, darling. That wasn't in question."

Her gaze slid to the cabin and she bit her lip. *At least now I know to keep my eyes open. I'll find out the truth and if I've made a mistake—if I've made him feel obligated to court me—then I'll fix it. Even if it hurts me to do so.*

Lawson sank onto the chair realizing he'd nearly frightened Ellie away during that little interlude at the door. He glanced down at his shirt and grimaced at the sight of the collar hanging open. He'd been changing when he'd heard her knock. He'd become so afraid that Ethan might have followed him that he'd forgotten what he was doing. Then he'd gone off and kissed her.

That kiss had been building inside of him since their muddy foray in the field, but he wasn't sure if he'd done right to give in to it. Lawson didn't kiss women often but when he did, it meant something. Usually that something was that they were eventually going to hightail it out of his life.

He pulled in a calming breath as he continued unbuttoning his shirt. A metal button broke from its place and tumbled to the ground. He placed his boot over it to keep it from rolling away then froze.

His raggedy boot covered the gleaming metal coin that rolled his way. He tried to look nonchalant as the gentleman stopped to look around. The man muttered about hearing something fall before he continued on his way. Lawson picked up the coin with a satisfied grin.

A moment later, he ducked under the swinging doors of the nearest saloon. No one seemed to notice him stop and stare to get his bearings. None of these rowdy places had exactly the same layout. He spotted an empty stool at the bar so he climbed it and placed his elbows on the shiny wood. The bartender did a double take then ignored him. Lawson frowned at him.

"Hey, I'm thirsty. I found five cents and I want a drink."

The man next to him glanced down and pushed away from the bar. "Starting them a little young, aren't you, Cal?"

The burly bartender turned to greet him as though unsure whether to laugh or snarl. "You're chasing away my customers."

He held up the shiny nickel. "How about it, Cal?"

"You've got a smart mouth." Cal didn't seem to think it was a bad thing because he grinned. "How old are you, anyway?"

"I don't know."

A man sidled up to the bar and winked as he slid a few coins toward the bartender. "Give the boy a drink on me."

"Sure, Lem." Cal quirked a brow. "What'll it be, son? Whiskey, Scotch or gin?"

Lawson shrugged. "No one ever asked me that before. They usually just give me water or sarsaparilla."

"Whiskey," Lem said.

Lawson's eyes widened as everyone began throwing money on the counter in front of him to place bets on whether he'd drink it or not. The tension mounted as he took the cup into his hand. He wrinkled his nose dubiously at the smell of the liquid, then lifted the glass to take a sip. Suddenly, a man on his left snatched the glass from his hand and threw its contents in Lem's face. "You no good—"

The man didn't get to finish before he reeled from Lem's punch. Lawson suddenly found himself in the middle of a brawl. Noticing everyone was distracted, he gathered all the money and crawled out on his hands and knees.

He stuffed the money in his pockets and grinned. He was rich! He could buy himself a sandwich, some new clothes and maybe even some new boots. Not in this town, though—the next one. It wouldn't do to get caught. He glanced back at the saloon to make sure he was in the clear, then started making tracks...

Lawson clenched the button tightly in his closed fist. He leaned back against the chair and closed his eyes. His memories would have their fun for a while. There was no avoiding that. He'd grit his teeth and bear it because they wouldn't last forever—not when he'd finally found someone in the present he might be able to hold on to. The choke hold of his past couldn't be as strong as it seemed...or could it?

Chapter Ten

Nathan had told him that someone was interested in buying a few of their horses and that he wanted Lawson to help with the deal. But when the next morning rolled around, Lawson could hardly keep his mind on his job. To say that he'd had a rough night was a bit of an understatement. He hadn't been able to shake those memories or the feelings they inevitably brought with them of anger, abandonment and fear. Between that and the preparations for the important buyer coming today, he hadn't had time to speak with Ellie. He wanted to make sure that he hadn't hurt her feelings by refusing to tell her what was bothering him.

In the meantime, he needed to get his head together enough to show the buyer the horses' full potential so he wouldn't make Nathan lose the sale. He finished the last exercise near where the buyer—who'd insisted they call him Alex—stood talking to Nathan. Alex nodded in appreciation. "Nathan, you have some of the finest horses I've seen in a long time. I'd like to buy the three you showed me today."

Nathan shook the man's hand. "Let's go inside and talk specifics."

Lawson finally found himself alone with Ellie. He circled the arena on Sheba a few times to cool the mare down then stopped the horse in front of where Ellie stood. "I'm sorry about yesterday."

"What are you sorry for?" She stepped onto the bottom rung on the fence and peered up at him with what seemed to be trepidation. "Kissing me?"

"What do you think?" He leaned across the saddle horn to kiss her pert nose. Her cheeks turned rosy and a hesitant smile tugged her lips but she stepped down from the gate leaving a big gap between their heights. Lawson dismounted. "I just wanted to make sure I didn't mess anything up with my strange behavior."

"Your strange, *unexplained* behavior." She lifted a prodding brow.

"Right. So we're fine?"

She held his gaze long enough to tell him that she was aware of his not-so-artful avoidance, then gave a single nod. "I am if you are."

He covered the hand she'd placed on the fence between them. "Good."

"When did all of this start between us, Lawson?" She placed her other hand on top of his. "Was it at the café when the town suggested it? Or maybe at the engagement party?"

"I don't know. I kind of think it started that first day I got back."

"You do?"

He smiled at the strange tone of hope in her voice. "Sure. Of course, it took me a while to figure it out, and I probably wouldn't have done anything if our families hadn't encouraged it."

Her gaze dropped from his and she pulled her hands away. "They were pretty convincing, weren't they?"

Before he could respond, they spotted Alex ambling toward them from the house. Ellie smiled at him. "Did you want another look at them, sir?"

"No need. The contract is signed." The man propped his boot on the fence and trained his gaze on Lawson. "I'd like to speak to this young man alone for a minute."

Ellie sent him a curious and questioning glance. At his shrug, she left him alone with the man. Lawson absently tied the horse's reins to the fence as he watched her go. Alex shifted slightly. "You haven't been able to keep your eyes off that gal since I got here. I looked at your ma the same way before she ran off and left me."

Lawson's entire being stilled. He slowly turned from the closed door of the farmhouse to pierce the shadowed gaze of the man before him. Alex removed his Stetson and met Lawson's eyes straight on. "I guess I should introduce myself properly. I'm Clive Alexander Hardy."

"Clive Hardy." The words came out in a disbelieving echo.

Clive nodded as a slight smile briefly appeared on his lips. "I'm your father."

Lawson stared at the man in shock. He had the strangest sense that those words should make him feel something, but he couldn't seem to feel anything at all. Finally, he spoke as though from rote memorization. "No, you aren't."

"I can prove it."

A slow leak of anger began to drip from his soul to his tongue. "I don't care if you can prove it."

Lawson suddenly realized that the man didn't have to. If someone looked, really looked, it was obvious. They were practically the same height and build, though Lawson was a bit taller and Clive was stockier. The man had remnants of the same brown hair in his silver hair and beard. The shape of their eyes was different but the hazel coloring was the same. His jaw tightened. "You should go."

Clive shook his head. "I didn't come all this way just to purchase a few horses. I want to talk to you."

The frayed thread he'd been holding on to for years suddenly snapped. "How dare you? How dare you possibly think you can just waltz into my life like this? I told Ethan I didn't want to see you but you ignored that completely."

"I was already on my way." Clive held his gaze urgently. "I wanted to see you."

"Why? How did you expect me to react? Did you think this would make me happy?"

"I guess not," Clive drawled. "I thought I'd at least try to start a relationship—"

Lawson shook his head in disgust. "I don't want anything from you and you're too late to give it. I think you'd better leave."

Clive stared at him for a long moment, then smiled wryly as he put his Stetson back on. "I guess I have no one to blame but myself for the way you turned out—just like me."

His eyes narrowed. "What does that mean?"

Clive shrugged lightly. "You've got the same anger, same stubborn mindset, apparently the same weakness for pretty women, and from what I hear, you'd make a pretty good outlaw."

"I'm nothing like you." The crack in his voice belied the firmness he was searching for.

"Sure you are. Don't fool yourself into thinking otherwise. You're a Hardy, from your hazel eyes to that smile you flashed when you met me. I think it's about time you figured that out."

"I asked you to leave."

Clive tipped his hat. "Sure, for now. But this isn't over, kid."

Lawson hardly waited for the man to head toward the house before he mounted Sheba and pointed her toward the woods. It was only when he dismounted at the creek that he was able to reel in his racing thoughts and breathe. It wasn't fair. After all this time and all the ways he'd struggled to distance himself from his past, he'd wanted to believe that he was finally free of it. He wasn't. It kept reaching out to pull him back—forcing him to remember who he was, where he'd come from, what kind of person he could expect to be. He'd never truly forgotten, but having his father come and point it out seemed like the stamp in the wax that sealed his fate.

He'd even thought that he might be able to create a new life with Ellie. Oh, he hadn't let himself truly plan that far ahead, but the intention had been there all along. He'd been working up his courage bit by bit in preparation for that final plunge. Too bad it was all for nothing. His father's sudden appearance served as a stark reminder of what usually happened when he let people too close—they left.

He picked up a rock and tossed it into the lazy creek. It was his parents' fault. When they left him, they'd left some sort of invisible mark that warned others off or so it seemed. Maybe it was the Hardy family curse— abandoning or being abandoned by the ones who were supposed to love you the most. Whatever caused it, the result was the same. He was still lacking, still missing that special ingredient that would make him worthy of the family he'd always wanted.

"Who am I fooling?" he muttered above the low grumble of the waterfall. He wasn't enough. It was time he realized that.

Ellie placed a stilling hand over her nieces' to end their exuberant hand game when Alex stepped back into the parlor with his hat in his hands. "It's been nice to meet all of you but I think it's time I head back to town. Nathan, would you mind if we left now?"

"Certainly not." Nathan set Matthew in Kate's arms and picked up his Stetson.

They followed him outside and Ellie's gaze immediately went to the corral. "Where's Lawson?"

Alex put his Stetson on and tugged its brim low as he walked toward the buggy. "I don't know. He took off on one of my new horses."

Ellie shot a concerned look at Nathan before hurrying to keep pace with the man. "What? Why? What did you say to him?"

The man stopped to frown down at her. "That's a private matter."

She surveyed him in confusion. What private matter could a stranger have to discuss with Lawson? The man looked pale in the sunlight and the twitch in his jaw showed that he was upset about something. "What happened?"

"Ellie," Nathan cautioned.

"Well, something must have."

Alex looked at her with new interest. "Why do you care? Who is my— Who is he to you?"

"He's…" She glanced away to search for the right word. Her what? Could she say he was her beau? She wasn't sure. Her friend? Somehow that didn't seem appropriate or meaningful enough. She met Alex's gaze again. The color of his eyes seemed to change from green to gold. She suddenly realized they were hazel, just like... She caught her breath as she took in his height, his build, his age. She stepped back. "Perhaps I should ask who he is to you."

His gaze faltered. She didn't wait for further confirmation before bolting for her mount. It took her nearly thirty minutes to find Lawson skipping rocks at the creek. The wildflowers from weeks ago had withered away and a new batch hadn't yet come in to replace them, so the only contrast to the greens and blues of the creek and surrounding forest was Lawson's dark shirt. He turned at the sound of Starlight's hooves. Their eyes met for a moment before he sent another rock skittering across the surface of the slow-moving creek. "Did he tell you?"

"I guessed." She dismounted and pushed away the tendrils of her hair that had managed to come loose during her ride. "What are you going to do?"

He shrugged as his gaze transferred back to the creek. "I told him to leave. What else is there to do?" Panic filled his voice. "He is leaving, isn't he?"

She stepped slightly closer to place a comforting hand on his arm. "He was the last time I checked."

He nodded then sent another rock hopping with a bit too much force. "I'm so angry, Ellie. I told Ethan I didn't want to meet him, and Clive completely ignored that. He just came, anyway. I should have known. He never respected anyone's choices but his own."

Confusion lowered her brows. "What does Ethan have to do with this?"

His gaze leapt to hers. "His real name is Ethan Lawson. He's my cousin."

She stared at him in awe. "You have a cousin."

"Apparently, I have a lot more than that."

Her hand slipped from his arm. She picked up a smooth, round rock and studied it as she turned it over in her hand. "How long have you known about this?"

"Since the barn raising."

Well, that explained his mysterious behavior. She sent the rock skipping across the water. "What did your father want?"

"I think he wanted to build some sort of relationship with me."

"And you didn't want that?"

He threw the last rock into the creek then turned to face her defiantly. "Why should I?"

"Maybe you should at least consider it." She lifted one shoulder in a slight shrug. "You know my parents died when I was eight. I hardly remember them. Sometimes I wonder what it would be like if I could just sit down with them at least once to find out who they were, what they wanted out of life…" Anxiety filled her but she continued, "What they think of me."

"My parents were nothing like yours. I wish I could forget everything about them and I've certainly tried." He frowned. "I remember all too vividly who that man is and what he's like."

"Maybe he's changed."

"Maybe he hasn't." He set his jaw stubbornly. "Either way, I don't intend to find out. For so long, I've been trying to prove I'm not like him. I became a Ranger to show I'd uphold the law and not break it like he did, but even that didn't work. They called me Lawless and said I'd make a better outlaw than a Ranger."

She wasn't sure what to do about that or what to say to comfort him. He made the decision for her by turning away and stuffing his hands in his pockets as he stared at the creek. "Why are you here, anyway?"

"I thought… I thought you might want me to be with you."

"I don't. Not anymore. Not the way it has been." He turned to face her, his intense gaze arresting her. "I want us to go back to being friends and nothing more."

"But an hour ago you said—"

"I said what I thought you wanted to hear. That doesn't make it true."

This shouldn't surprise her. It was just what she'd suspected. Still, she had to hear it from his own lips to believe him. "It's because our families and the whole town pressured you into it, isn't it?"

Confusion flashed across his face an instant before realization took hold. Some of his intensity left him but determination tightened his jaw. "They did—I can't deny it."

"I suspected as much. I'm sorry. I shouldn't have encouraged them." She let out a short laugh. "You must have thought me so desperate. I needed a whole town to make you consider courting me and even that—" She cut herself off with a shake of her head. "Well, that's one thing you don't have to worry about anymore, at least. I'm willing to stay with you as a friend, if you like. However, you probably want to be alone."

He gave a short jerk of a nod then turned away. "You should leave."

She stared at his strong back for a moment, wanting to protest, but she wasn't going to force her presence on him if he didn't want it. She mounted Starlight and turned to look at him once more before she was swallowed by the woods. His head was bowed, his shoulders low—he looked defeated. He wasn't the only one.

She forced her gaze forward. *I knew this was a possibility. I should have prepared myself.*

Tears flooded her vision and fell in large drops on her skirt. "Lord, why am I always making these stupid mistakes and messing everything up? Please, don't let my willfulness ruin our friendship. I have no idea what he is going through right now but I ask that You work things out for Lawson. He needs to know You have good plans for his life.

"As for me…" She sighed. "I think it's time I stop trying so hard to figure out everything happening around me and just figure myself out."

That meant gathering enough courage to get to the bottom of the guilt she'd always struggled with. She'd at least gotten off to a good start by asking Kate about her parents a while ago. Of course, she hadn't gained anything from her inquiry—no information, no peace. Just the fearsome realization that the answers she needed must lie within her own mind. She just prayed she'd have the courage to find them.

Chapter Eleven

Lawson rested his forehead on the warm hide of Rosie, one of the milking cows, as he stole a glance across the aisle where Ellie patiently waited for her pesky piglet to mosey out of its stall for its morning jaunt. She turned toward him so he trained his gaze back on the bucket. She walked toward him, anyway. "Good morning, Lawson."

"Good morning."

"You missed breakfast." She placed her hands on the stall railing and leaned back as she surveyed him. "Aren't you hungry?"

He finally lifted his head to meet her gaze. "No, I ate something at my cabin."

"Oh." She stilled as though contemplating the fact that he'd never done that before. No doubt she was trying to figure out if he was avoiding her or just people in general. The answer was both.

She'd given him a convenient excuse for ending things between them yesterday. He'd wanted to keep himself from feeling the pain that might one day accompany her leaving but he hadn't planned on hurting her to do it. He hadn't truly realized how much using that excuse would hurt her until she'd laughed at how desperate and unwanted she must have seemed to him. He'd been both of those things before and Ellie was neither. He hated that he'd made her feel that way, but there was nothing he could do now. The deed was done. He had to make sure it accomplished what he needed it to because in the end he was probably saving them both from heartache.

She leaned against the stall gate. "Aren't you going to talk to me, Lawson?"

"There's nothing to say."

Her voice was quiet and sincere. "Please don't push me away. I know I made a mistake by trying to change our friendship into something it wasn't. I'm sorry for that but I don't want to let it ruin our friendship."

"You're right." He wouldn't have to lose her completely if they could just stay friends. "I'm sorry. I'm not sure how to deal with all of this."

"Neither am I."

She looked so miserable that he halfway rose to take her into his arms, then sat down with a thud. *Friends,* he reminded himself, *nothing more and nothing less.* He swallowed against the sudden lump in his throat. "Give me time, Ellie. I'll be back to my old self soon enough."

She gave him a compassionate smile then nodded once before walking away. A moment later, he glanced up to find Nathan standing in her place. His boss crossed his arms. "Do you want to tell me what's going on between you and Ellie?"

"There's nothing going on." His gaze dropped down to the pail between his boots. "We called it off."

A moment of silence stretched between them. "That's a shame. You're going through a rough time,

Lawson. This may not be the best time to make major decisions."

"The decision has been made."

"Fine, but I don't think we need that much milk. Give Rosie a rest, will you?"

He suddenly realized the pail had quite a bit more milk than they usually used. He grimaced, then stepped away from the cow with an apologetic pat. "Sorry, girl."

"Timothy," Nathan called as his son stepped into the barn. "Come take the milk to your ma. I need to talk to Lawson."

"Yes, sir." The boy skipped over and took the pail from Lawson.

Lawson smiled dubiously. "It isn't too heavy for you, is it?"

"No, I'm strong. See?" The boy grinned over his shoulder as he left.

"We need to talk about the Hardy contract." Nathan held up an official-looking document. "It was signed with a stipulation."

Lawson took the contract from him. "What kind of stipulation?"

"The full payment will be collected when the horses are delivered, which has to be within two weeks."

Lawson nodded, realizing he hadn't even considered the fact that Clive would need to come back for his horses.

"He also paid for one week of training with the horses and his men." Nathan sat down behind a modest desk and looked up at Lawson. "I'd like you to do this, Lawson. It's part of your job. Besides, one of the main reasons I hired you was so I wouldn't have to leave my family to make deliveries like this. However, I understand that the circumstances surrounding this particular contract are unusual. If you don't want to go, I won't make you. I hope you will consider it, though. Not for the job, but for yourself."

He shifted uncomfortably. "What do you mean?"

"I mean that the past has a funny way of creeping up on us." Nathan shook his head and Lawson knew he was speaking from experience. "Trust me. Sometimes you can't truly move on until you deal with the problems you left there."

Lawson tried to ignore the chills that raced down his arms at that statement. "My first instinct is to say no but I'll consider it."

"Good." Nathan eased the moment with a smile. "You should know that I'm giving you a few days off. Let's see. Today is Thursday. Once you finish today, you don't have to report in until Monday."

Lawson frowned. "What? Why? I didn't ask for time off. I want to work."

"Then work hard today. I think you could use a few days with Doc and Ms. Lettie. Besides, this would be a good opportunity for you to decide about that contract and get a bit more perspective on your relationship with Ellie."

Lawson stared at his longtime friend-turned-boss and frowned, realizing the only answer Nathan would accept was yes. He shrugged and gave in. "All right, Nathan, if that's what you want I guess I need to make the most of my day here. I think I'll go find something to throw."

Nathan's dark eyes began to twinkle. "The stalls could use some new hay."

He rubbed his hands together. "That sounds perfect."

He climbed up to the loft and began tossing the heavy bales into disorganized submission on the barn floor. That allowed some of the pent-up aggression to ease out of him. At least, it did until he was interrupted.

"You look like you're spoiling for a fight."

Lawson stilled then turned to find his cousin peering over the loft floor with a knowing smile on his face. He watched Ethan scale the last few rungs of the ladder to stand a few feet away with his Stetson in his hands. "Who let you in here?"

"Ellie."

"Figures." Lawson grunted, then turned to push another hay bale over the edge. "You have a lot to answer for, Ethan. I thought I told you I didn't want to see that man."

"*That man* doesn't often take no for an answer."

Lawson paused to glance at him. "What do you want?"

"I thought you'd like to know Uncle Clive went back to the ranch this morning. He was pretty broken up. Not that it would matter to you." Ethan took a seat on one of the bales.

"Is that all?"

Ethan was quiet for a moment. "You should have taken a swing at him and gotten it out of your system."

Lawson turned to stare at him. "Whose side are you on?"

He gave a careless shrug. "Uncle Clive was the only family I had until I found you. We're cousins and in my book that means something. Besides, if you got some of that anger out of your system, maybe it would leave some room to let your family in."

Lawson frowned at him skeptically.

"We could go a round or two if you want." Ethan sized him up. "I think I can take you."

Lawson narrowed his eyes. "You couldn't, but it doesn't matter. I'm not going to fight you."

"We probably would have more than a few times if we'd grown up together."

Who is this man? Lawson couldn't figure him out. He knew nothing about his cousin except that they were related by blood and that didn't bode well. The unnerving thing was that Ethan seemed to know more about him than he knew about himself. He cleared his throat and decided to start digging for clues about both of them. "You're younger than me, aren't you?"

"By a few years." Ethan frowned. "Please tell me you know how old you are?"

Lawson shook his head. "Do you know?"

"I'm twenty and you're twenty-three."

"Are you sure?" At Ethan's nod, he tilted his head. "I'm younger than I thought."

Ethan laughed. "How old did you think you were?"

"Somewhere around twenty-five." He hesitantly took a seat near Ethan but not close enough to be friendly. "I guess I've had a lot of life experience."

"You were nine when they left you. From what I've gathered, that would have made you about thirteen when you came to this town. They took good care of you here, didn't they?"

He nodded. "Better than I deserved."

"We could compare stories, if you like."

"I'd rather not."

Ethan grabbed his Stetson and stood. "I'm staying at the boardinghouse in town. If you change your mind about swapping stories or have any other questions, just stop by and see me. I've given my notice at the livery so I'll be here for another two weeks."

Lawson nodded. He returned Ethan's wave before

the man disappeared down the ladder. He moseyed over to the window in time to see Ethan pause to talk with Ellie, then ride off. One of these days he might take Ethan up on that offer. Until then, he had work to do.

Ellie shaded her eyes from the sun and seemed to look directly at him. Even from this distance, he could feel the concern telegraphing from her. He swallowed. Nathan was right. A little time away from the farm would be good for him.

Ellie probably should have told her family that she and Lawson had called it quits. Oh, wait. She had. It just didn't seem to change her family's perception of them as a couple or the seating arrangements at dinner. She realized that as soon as her fingers slid their usual path across Lawson's warm palm to settle in his grasp for grace that evening. When Timothy's lengthy monologue came to an end, she tried to divert her thoughts from the man beside her but failed miserably.

She passed him the sweet potatoes while gleaning a sideways glance. He caught her watching him and captured her gaze before she could look away. His hazel eyes deepened to a dark shade of olive. The corners of his mouth softened into an almost smile before an unreadable mask slipped into place and he glanced away. He'd made it clear that he'd lied about wanting to be more than friends. Odd, it hadn't felt like a lie. It had felt natural and right.

She pushed those thoughts from her mind. She wouldn't do this to herself. It would be foolish to pine for a man who didn't want her—had never wanted her. She might make a lot of mistakes but never the same one twice.

Supper passed in a flurry of chatter, though neither

she nor Lawson added much to the conversation. Afterward, the men moved to the sitting room with the children, which gave Ellie the opportunity to talk freely with her sister. Kate must have realized it, too, because she glanced up from the bowl she was washing. "It's strange to see how things have changed between you and Lawson."

"Yes," Ellie admitted as she swept a dry towel across the wet plate in her hands. "It's for the best."

"Is that really how you feel?"

She absently accepted the bowl Kate handed her. "All I know is that I should have accepted that he wasn't interested in me from the start and left it alone. Instead, I messed up our friendship. The silliest part is that now I can't imagine myself with anybody else."

A moment of quiet descended around them, interrupted only by the sound of the game taking place in the sitting room. Kate's voice softly filled the void. "Are you in love with him, Ellie?"

She finished drying the bowl before setting it aside and leaning back against the counter with a sigh. "Am I? I can recognize it in everyone else but when it comes to my own feelings and Lawson's, I seem to be lost. I'm beginning to think I wouldn't know love if it came up and bit me. If this is it, then I guess I was expecting more."

"More what?"

"Oh, I don't know. More of a difference in me and the way I feel about life in general."

"Ellie, loving someone doesn't make your problems go away." Kate shook her head wryly. "If anything, it just adds the other person's problems to the mix. The benefit is that you are able to solve them together."

"I see." So did that mean she should try to help Lawson with his problems? She could support him and encourage him even if it was only as a friend.

Kate smiled at her discouraged tone. "Have you ever heard the saying 'Love is friendship set on fire'?"

"No."

"Well, I think it's true. I had to learn to appreciate Nathan as a friend before I was able to consider him as anything more."

"But Lawson and I have been friends for years."

"Yes, and I've never seen a more romantic friendship in all my life. That's why I say going back to that might help you both. Give it time. He's dealing with a lot right now and it looks like you have a lot to figure out, too. Don't give up yet."

Ellie wasn't entirely sure that was wise. She just kept hearing that familiar refrain explaining why he'd really sought her out. The whole town had been fooled into thinking their "romantic" friendship should turn into more. The whole town—including her. How could she move past her feelings if she let herself slip right back into the old routines? "What if Lawson can't love me?"

"Then you'd have to let it go, but I think it's worth finding out. Don't you?" Kate handed her the last dish then wiped her hands on a dry towel. "Didn't you say something about giving Nathan and me a child-free evening for once? The children finished their homework and there is a bit of time left before bed. Why don't you and Lawson play with them?"

Ellie rolled her eyes then laughed. "What? Are you charging for advice now? I wish you'd told me before I asked."

"You don't have to—"

"I want to. It will be fun," she said as she carefully put away the dishes. "Besides, I can take a hint."

"What hint?" Kate asked innocently.

"I know I didn't offer, though I should have." She lifted a coy eyebrow at her sister. "You must really want to be alone with Nathan."

Kate sent her a mischievous look. "Like I said, don't forget to invite Lawson. He might want to go along and he could definitely use a bit of fun."

It took Ellie a moment to catch on. "Oh, you're still matchmaking, aren't you?"

Kate shook her head piteously. "You're right. You really are lost when it comes to love."

Ellie popped her with the damp towel, then skedaddled out the kitchen before Kate could retaliate. Everyone looked up when she abruptly danced into the sitting room. She glanced behind her once more to make sure she hadn't been followed, then smiled. "Who's up for a game of tag?"

Lawson gave an approving nod sending Timothy sneaking through the trees toward Ellie. She gasped and whirled in the opposite direction, which happened to be directly into Lawson's path. He sidestepped her tumbling strides but caught her arm and somehow managed to keep them both upright. A small hand slapped Ellie's back, then his. "Freeze, both of you!"

They automatically froze in their somewhat awkward positions. Suddenly, Lawson's gaze snapped to Ellie's nephew. "Wait. What just happened? I thought we were partners."

Timothy stepped away from them to scan the landscape. "No more teams. It's every man for himself."

Ellie shifted to frown at the boy in protest. "You can't play freeze tag without teams. Who is going to unfreeze us?"

Timothy's eyes lit up as he spotted his prey. "Hope. You have to stay frozen until she tags you."

That is not going to happen, he thought with a glance at the woman practically in his arms. Once Timothy ran off, Lawson stepped away before he could change his mind and do something foolish. He'd almost refused to help Ellie mind her nieces and nephew. However, he'd decided to leave for town first thing in the morning to stay with his parents as Nathan had ordered, and if he hit the hay too soon he'd just spend hours sorting through stacks of old memories.

He'd told himself a game of tag would be far easier than that. After all, the children would provide a buffer. He stared at the three small retreating forms and shook his head. *Some buffer they are.*

"Great. Now they're just hitting each other." Ellie stepped up beside him.

"I'd say it's more of a spirited tap."

She laughed. "I guess I'll let them run around a bit more then call them in."

"I think I'll go to my cabin. I have some packing to do before the morning."

"You're leaving?"

"Yes…" He watched a strong breeze suddenly toss her hair into disarray, hindered only by the single ribbon that kept her golden locks from her face. He glanced away and struggled to regain the vein of conversation. "Nathan practically insisted I take the weekend off. I'm going to spend some time with my folks."

"That will be nice." She finally corralled her hair enough for her to catch his gaze. "That means I won't see you again until church on Sunday."

He cleared his throat softly. "I guess not."

Disappointment seemed to settle in her eyes and a

strange warmth filled his chest at the sight of it. He stepped away to grab his Stetson from where he'd tossed it on the grass earlier. He managed to ease the tenuous moment with a nod and half smile. "See you later."

He walked away and that should have been the end of it but it wasn't. He still had the sense that they were connected—tethered together almost. The rope wouldn't break no matter how far across the field he traveled. It just seemed to stretch along with him.

As he stopped to say goodbye to the children, he managed a quick look back at her. She must have felt his gaze for she lifted her hand in a wave. He returned the gesture before his long strides ate up the rest of the distance to his cabin. He wasn't sure what was worse—watching her walk away later or having to do it himself every day.

Chapter Twelve

Lawson leaned back on the cushioned wicker bench on his parents' porch with a discontented sigh at his cousin's stubbornness. "So you really won't try to convince your uncle to cancel that clause of the contract?"

Ethan shrugged from his perch on the matching wicker chair. "I told you, the main reason he bought those horses was to make sure you'd come to the ranch. He isn't going to cancel any clause."

"Surely, if you reason with him—"

"Not a chance, cousin."

Lawson's lips edged upward in amusement. Ethan had a habit of reiterating their relationship to each other. He'd managed to sneak that word in multiple times over dinner. Lawson wanted to find it annoying but he actually almost liked the sense of belonging it gave him. "Fine. There are some things a man has to do for himself and this might be one of them."

Ethan's eyebrows shot up in surprise. "Are you coming to the ranch, then?"

He pressed his lips together to keep from speaking an answer he didn't want to give one way or another. He had no problem traveling to a ranch for business

446 A Texas-Made Match

purposes. He could even stomach going to a ranch his father owned. The problem was that once there, another reckoning with his father seemed inevitable. He'd won the first round but he wasn't sure he'd come out on top in the next one.

"I don't want to," he said as the door opened and Doc joined them with a tray of after-dinner coffee, obviously prepared by Lettie. Lawson felt relief unwind his tense shoulders. "You're joining us, aren't you?"

The distinguished-looking gentleman smiled as he put the tray on the table next to the chair. "I was hoping for an invitation, hence the coffee, but I don't want to intrude."

"You're no intrusion, Pa." Lawson used the term purposefully with a quick glance at Ethan to see how his cousin processed that. His parents had been as stunned as she was at the news of Clive's visit, but their support and encouragement had left no doubt in Lawson's mind about who truly deserved the titles "Ma" and "Pa."

Ethan shifted uneasily but didn't protest when the older man settled onto the other end of the bench. "Lawson was just saying he didn't want to go to Uncle Clive's ranch."

Doc nodded. "It isn't a decision to be made lightly."

"I'd be more willing to go if I knew that Clive wouldn't try to—"

Ethan's blue eyes snapped. "Get to know his only son?"

Just like that, anger began to simmer in his chest. "He had a chance to do that and he lost it. That was his choice. I don't feel the need to make things easier on him by walking into his lair."

"He isn't a villain."

"To you."

"Villain or not," Doc said, calmly easing the tension, "ignoring his existence, his wishes or the past won't make any of this go away. Maybe you need this, Lawson."

"I don't want to go," he repeated, then shook his head. "I just have this awful feeling that seeing him again is inevitable, and you're right. I have to face this."

"Have you prayed about this?"

"Besides praying I wouldn't have to go?" Lawson shook his head. "No."

"I'll call your mother out and we'll do it as a family."

Lawson began to agree but paused when Ethan stood to his feet. "In that case, I think I should leave. Please tell Ms. Lettie I said thank-you for a delicious meal. It was nice to meet you, Doc. I'll be around."

Lawson stood. "Where do you think you're going?"

Ethan froze. "The boardinghouse."

"Are you a praying man?"

Ethan nodded, then shrugged. "On occasion."

Lawson glanced at Doc. "Think that will do?"

"I'm sure the Lord will be happy to hear from him."

"Pa said *family,* Ethan." He crossed his arms. "I'm pretty sure that somehow means you, unless you need to call me 'cousin' a few more times to make sure."

Ethan didn't seem to know how to respond at first. He cleared the emotion from his throat a few times before he nodded. "I reckon I can manage an *Amen* as well as anybody. I practiced in church last Sunday so I'm not that rusty."

"I heard there's going to be a prayer meeting," Lettie said as she preceded her husband onto the porch. "We should have started the evening this way but I think it's a good way to end it, too. 'Pa,' will you lead off?"

"I'd be glad to." Doc waited for Lettie to settle on the bench next to Lawson before he sat in the chair beside Ethan and bowed his head. "Heavenly Father, first and foremost, Lettie and I want to thank You for entrusting us with Your son Lawson."

Lawson swallowed as his ma's hand found his and squeezed in agreement.

"When Nathan asked if we'd give a young man a chance at a better future, I had a feeling we were giving ourselves the best possible future as well, and I was right. Now, we ask that You give Lawson the strength, wisdom and courage he needs to face his past. Give him peace."

After a moment of silence, Lettie took her turn. "God, I pray for Clive right now."

Lawson couldn't help but tense at her words.

"I can certainly understand him wanting to get to know Lawson. I pray that if it's Your will, it will happen in Your time and in Your way. Whether he knows You or not, let this situation draw Clive closer to You."

It was Lawson's turn. He knew it, so he cleared his throat of the emotion clogging it. "I just want to do the right thing, Lord." For some reason, that made him think of Ellie. He was doing the right thing by letting her go, wasn't he? "Help me to be strong. Help me to make the right choices. Help me to know what those are."

Ethan was quiet for so long that Lawson wondered if it might be best to let him off the hook. When Ethan finally spoke, his deep voice was quiet but entreating. "All I ask is that You teach us—all of us—how to be a family."

Family. Was it made of blood? He stole a glance at his cousin. Or law? He rubbed his mother's cool hand.

He closed his eyes and saw Ellie standing in the field with the wind blowing in her hair. Or love? Was any of it enough to truly bind people together? Ten years ago, that downtrodden boy without a last name would have said no, but tonight—tonight, he wanted to say yes more than anything. Would this feeling of belonging disappear if he surrendered to it? Maybe. Maybe not. It was too precious for him to take that chance, so he settled for the next best thing. He pushed that desire into the corner of his heart where only God could see it, then allowed his whisper to blend with the voices that echoes around him in a final "Amen."

Ellie snuggled deeper into the cushions of Ms. Lettie's comfortable settee with her eyes closed against the morning sunlight in an effort to doze. The corners of her mouth tipped upward slightly when the settee sank to the right a few moments later. Lawson's deep voice drawled in amusement, "You look like you either need a nap or a cup of coffee."

"Probably both." She kept her eyes closed to concentrate on the rich tone of his voice.

"Why are you so sleepy?"

"I stayed up most of the night reading. I didn't even look at the clock until it was too late—literally and figuratively." She lifted her lashes to meet his gaze with a wry smirk. "Of course, I also woke up an hour earlier than normal to teach Sunday school to imaginary students."

"'What Sunday school?'" he asked, quoting Pastor Brightly's exact words.

She shook her head. The man had wandered into the church to find them waiting for their pupils to arrive. After twenty minutes without anyone coming, they'd been ready to give up, anyway. Pastor Brightly had informed them that Sunday school had been canceled due to a lack of attendance last week. Apparently, children didn't like the idea of going to school an additional day of the week.

"I can't believe no one told me." She shifted more to the left for a better view of Lawson, who sat at the opposite end of the settee with his ankle propped on his knee.

He placed his arm on the back of the settee. "I guess I should warn you that the town isn't taking the news that we broke things off very well. They're actually pretty up in arms about it."

"I assumed they would be." She fiddled with the fringe on the pillow resting between them. "They were the ones who convinced you to pursue me in the first place so they're bound to be disappointed that their efforts weren't enough."

Lawson shifted slightly away. "Where are my parents? We should leave soon."

Ms. Lettie made a timely entrance into the parlor with Doc right behind her. "We're ready when you are."

"Thanks for letting me rest here until the service." Ellie corralled her slightly mussed hair back into place as she stood. "I don't know what else I would have done with myself."

Doc smiled fondly at her. "You're always welcome here. Shall we go?"

Doc offered his arm to his wife and the two set off, leaving Lawson and Ellie to follow. They walked the rest of the way to the church in silence where they confused the gathering parishioners by arriving together, then immediately separating. Ellie managed to avoid anything more than a few concerned and curious glances as she wound her way to her sister-in-law. They barely had time to exchange a hug before Lorelei sent her a warning look. "Don't look now, but the Peppin Inquisition is on its way."

She barely had time to turn around before Maddie, Sophia, Amy and Isabelle appeared at her side. Maddie immediately pulled Ellie into an embrace. "Oh, my dear, dear friend. We are so sorry to hear about you and Lawson. You must feel awful."

"Thanks, girls," she said when she could breathe again. "I'm fine. We weren't even officially courting so you don't need to worry about me."

Amy searched her face with a frown. "Don't tell me you're the one who broke his heart and not the other way around?"

"Hardly." She glanced at Lawson who was across the churchyard no doubt getting the same treatment from Sean, Jeff, Rhett and Chris. "It seems that all the matchmaking from the town and our families made him think he needed to pretend emotions he wasn't feeling. I shouldn't have encouraged y'all. It was all a big mistake, nothing more."

Silence followed her statement as the girls exchanged significant looks with each other. Maddie finally broke the silence. "Ellie, did he say that was the reason he broke things off?"

"Yes." She couldn't interpret the strange looks on her friends' faces. "What?"

Lorelei stepped closer and whispered as if Lawson might overhear, despite their distance away from him. "It just can't be true, that's all. He encouraged us to matchmake the same as you. Oh, he didn't give us pointers like you did at Maddie and Jeff's engagement party, but he told his parents that he was willing to cooperate. I promised him myself that you wouldn't find out he was in on it."

Sophia smiled. "You see, Ellie? You didn't make a mistake."

She felt a weight lift off her soul as those words settled into her mind. Her words came out more as an exclamation than a question. "Why would he lie to me?"

Amy shushed her, throwing a quick glance over her shoulder at the men. "He was probably trying to hide the real reason. That's the way men are. He's probably upset about something else entirely."

Sophia nodded. "Whatever the reason, we know for sure that it isn't what he told you."

"I don't know. He isn't usually one to lie. And come to think of it, he didn't actually say that was his reason. I brought it up, and he just agreed. Maybe he doesn't want to tell me the real reason because it's something worse. Either way, I'm not sure the reason matters if the bottom line is that he doesn't want to be more than friends with me."

"Of course it matters," Lorelei protested.

Ellie glanced around the circle of her friends who nodded adamantly. "But, even when we tried being more than friends, he didn't seem that serious about me."

"Serious?" Maddie asked. "The only other girl he ever expressed interest in he was willing to marry."

Lorelei laughed. "He wasn't half as interested in me as he has been in you, which proves to me that he knows he has a shot at creating something incredible with you. For some reason he doesn't want to admit, he's willing to walk away from that. All I can say is don't make it that easy for him."

The church bell rang to announce the service would

start in a few minutes, so the girls dispersed, save Lorelei, who lingered for a moment. "Did you ever finish that list you were making?"

"Actually, I forgot about it. I guess I've been distracted."

"Perhaps you should finish it." Lorelei gave her a little wink then left. Ellie spotted Kate, Nathan and their children arriving, so she excused herself to meet up with them. Someone started matching her steps. *Donovan Turner.*

"Hello, Miss Ellie. You'll be pleased to know that I sold my farm."

She stopped abruptly to face him. "You did what? Why?"

"It was keeping us apart." He removed his hat.

She stared at him in shock. "Please tell me you didn't sell your farm because of me."

He puffed out his chest proudly. "Sure I did. Now that you're no longer with Lawson there is nothing to stand in our way."

"My goodness!" She glanced around and though no one seemed to have noticed their interlude, she kept her voice quiet but urgent so as not to embarrass him. "You've got to get your farm back. No, don't shake your head. Please stop smiling at me and listen. I am not interested in you, Mr. Turner. It has nothing to do with whether or not you're a pig farmer. You won't seem to heed my brother-in-law but you need to listen to me. You have to stop this. You're making me uncomfortable. I don't want you to seek me out anymore. Do you understand me?"

As she spoke, the smile on his face slowly faded to confusion then disappointment. "But, there's no other girl for me. We have to be together."

"There is another girl somewhere who's right for you but I'm afraid it isn't and never will be me."

His eyes seemed to harden.

She softened, realizing her words must have wounded him mightily. "I'm sorry if I hurt your feelings. I'm not trying to. Honest, I'm not. Just please find someone else. Oh, and talk to Judge Hendricks. Maybe he can help you get your farm back."

She hurried away holding her breath until she was sure he wasn't following her. When she reached Kate and Nathan she told them what happened. They both assured her she'd done the right thing. Even so, the look in Donovan's eyes after she told him they'd never be together was not one she'd soon forget.

The end of Lawson's match burst into flame a moment before he led his mount through the barn door. He turned to light the lantern that normally hung inside the door, but realized it was missing just as he spotted its golden glow reflecting off the window near the south side of the barn. It illuminated a rather familiar feminine form that slept cuddled uncomfortably on a wooden chair. His lips pulled into a slight smile before he trained them into a curious frown.

A few moments later, his horse properly settled for the night, he surveyed Ellie's slumbering features. She looked pure, innocent in the pool of light that spilled across her features into her golden hair and down her yellow dress. The open dime novel in her hand had slowly slipped from her lax fingers to dangle perilously toward the ground. As he watched, it broke free from her grasp. He instinctively tried to catch it before it could fall and awaken her but it didn't do any good for she startled awake.

He stepped back and closed the book. "I didn't mean to frighten you."

"That's all right." Her hand sleepily rubbed across her cheek then slipped into her hair. "I wasn't supposed to be sleeping, anyway."

"What are you doing in here this time of night?" He handed her the book.

"Abigail is foaling. It's her first and Nathan wants to make sure there aren't any complications. I'm supposed to keep watch until eleven o'clock, then he's taking over."

He eyed the mare that appeared to be sleeping. "Did you tell Nathan that you didn't sleep much last night?"

"No. It's my own fault for staying up late. I'm not going to shirk my duties because of that."

"I see." He wandered down the aisle until he found a stool, then carried it back to where Ellie sat. "I'll keep watch until Nathan gets here. You go on to bed."

Her eyes widened but she shook her head. "You don't have to do that. Besides, I'm awake now. Perhaps you could stay a while to keep me awake."

He stared at her, thoroughly confused. She'd been sending him mixed signals since the day after they'd broken things off. He should have rejected her invitation. He should have gotten up and walked away or insisted she leave. He knew that so why did he nod? Why did he straddle the stool and allow a companionable silence to fall between them? It was probably because he was a little bit crazy and very foolish. Or, maybe he was just curious about how she managed to read her book upside down without knowing it. He glanced at Abigail. "Are you sure that horse is foaling?"

He'd managed to startle her again. Had she fallen back to sleep? She set her book aside. "She was before

I went to sleep. You don't suppose she already had it and I slept through it?"

"I don't think so."

She went back to reading her book upside down. He wondered how long she could keep it up then she lifted her green eyes to his. "Have you decided about the trip?"

He nodded but glanced away. "I'm going."

She let that answer stand for a moment before she softly asked, "Why?"

He rolled his shoulders in a shrug. "I've always had that one fear lurking in the back of my head that I was like my father or would somehow end up like him—them, really…my parents. No matter what I do I can't seem to make it go away. Until now, I've never had the opportunity to know—really know how we're similar or different. Now I do."

He glanced up to meet her gaze with intensity. "The only thing I want less than to see my father again is to live with that thought haunting me for the rest of my life. Either way, I've got to know."

"I know what you mean about having a fear hanging over you." She rubbed her arms and frowned. "Only I'm not sure I'm brave enough to face up to mine."

"What is it?"

"I don't know. Isn't that the strangest thing?" Her voice quieted as she stared into the distance. "Mrs. Greene knows part of it. Maybe she knows all of it but I don't want to ask her. It has something to do with my parents."

"I remember you mentioning this at the graveyard."

"Yes, and you told me to forget about it but I can't. You see, I don't remember much about my parents but I do remember that they were full of life and laughter.

Then one day they were gone. They just died. They were too young to die." She bit her lip. "Ever since then, in the back of my head, I've always had this fear—this nagging sense that I did something to make them go away."

He frowned. "That's hard to imagine from what I've heard of your parents. They didn't choose to die like my parents chose to leave."

Her eyes refocused on his, and a wan smile touched her lips. "My head says you're right but my heart isn't convinced."

"I understand." He would have continued the conversation but Abigail decided to remember that she was going to have a foal. Lawson watched her carefully as she began to pace. Everything seemed to be progressing normally. As Lawson kept an eye on the nervous mare, Ellie subtly turned her book right side up and began to read. It wasn't long before the book was drooping in her hands again. He shook his head. "Aren't you ready to give up yet?"

She didn't respond so he whispered a promise to Abigail that he'd be back, then managed to lift Ellie from the chair into his arms. She stirred but he was fairly certain that she was too sleepy to realize he was taking her to the farmhouse. He mounted the steps to the porch, then called her name to awaken her. "Do you think you can stand?"

"Mmm-hmm."

He glanced down to meet her mischievous eyes with a frown. "You little faker. You were awake the whole time."

She didn't go far when he set her down. In fact, she left her arms around his neck and leveled her deep green eyes at him in the evening shadows. "All right,

I'm a little faker. I admit it. I think you'd better admit something, too."

"What?" He thought about removing his hands from her waist but got distracted when she poked him in the chest.

"You are a faker, too."

He released her. "What are you talking about?"

One of her hands slipped to her hip as she lifted her chin. "You agreed with me when I said that you only courted me because everyone was pressuring you, but that's not the truth. You didn't feel pressured by the town's matchmaking. You *encouraged* it. You wanted to be more than friends just like I did."

He should deny it but the hurt in her eyes after he'd ended their fledgling courtship kept him from doing that. He rubbed his stubbly jaw and turned his gaze to the star-covered sky so he wouldn't have to look her in the eye. "Who told you?"

"It doesn't matter. The whole town knew." She tugged him slightly closer, arresting his attention once more. "Why did you let me believe something that wasn't true?"

"I didn't know it would hurt you as badly as it did. I just… I thought it would be simpler than telling the truth."

"What is the truth?"

He lifted his hand to cradle her chin and swept his thumb against her smooth cheek as he faced it for the first time himself. He cared for Ellie as a friend but his feelings went far deeper than that—so deep that they were dangerously close to love. It wouldn't be a weak sort of love, either. At least, not according to the feelings she'd inspired so far.

His past told him that if he let her that close—closer

than he'd let anyone before—she was bound to leave. Maybe not tomorrow or in a year, but one day. Somehow he had to make her understand.

"The truth is that I'm not the man for you, Ellie. You deserve so much more than what I have to offer. One day you're going to realize that I'm not enough and you're going to walk away. I don't want my broken heart trailing behind you."

She barely let him finish before she shook her head. "The only one walking away from this is you, Lawson. Not me. Maybe that's saving your heart but it's breaking mine and I won't stand by and watch it happen."

He tensed at her declaration. The last thing he needed was for her to make this more difficult than it already was. His hands found their way to her arms. "We agreed to go back to being friends."

She leaned into his touch and tilted her head back to meet his gaze in a challenge of temptation. A hint of a smile touched her lips. "Is that what this is? Then by all means, Lawson, let's be friends."

"Ellie," he groaned. "You're not being fair."

She swayed onto her tiptoes to give him a soft but lingering kiss. "Good night, Lawson."

He'd never heard anyone say his name like that before. Her voice caressed those two simple syllables as if they were something precious—as if he was something important and dear. It took him a moment to realize that he was the one holding on to her. He released her. "Good night, Ellie."

Chapter Thirteen

Ellie went into the house, hurried up the stairs to her room and peered out her window to see Lawson standing just where she'd left him. No doubt the shocked look on his face hadn't changed, either. A smile tilted her lips when he slowly walked toward the barn. She lit her lamp, then grabbed her nightgown and spun in a joyous circle. "I didn't make a mistake. I didn't! I actually did the right thing for once. Thank You, Lord!"

She changed into her nightgown, marveling at how close she'd been to letting him go without a fight. That *really* would have been a mistake. She still had a chance. She'd seen it in his eyes and heard it in his voice even as he'd told her he wasn't the man for her.

She pulled the Bachelor List from beneath her mattress, then settled onto the stool in front of her vanity to look at it. She'd given a match to nearly everyone on her list except Lawson. From the way he talked, he probably wouldn't give himself a match at all. He seemed to think love would expose something inside of him that would frighten her away. Didn't he know that wasn't the way romantic love worked?

What about God's love? she asked herself, then wondered where that thought had come from. She knew she had God's love. She knew that Lawson had it, too. Didn't he realize that it covered a multitude of sins? God would never leave him…and if Lawson gave her a chance, then neither would she.

She found a pencil, then proceeded to circle Lawson's name before placing her initials beside it with a deliberate flare. *I won't let him cheat himself and some fortunate woman out of a beautiful future—especially if that woman might be me.*

She blew out the lamp and slipped under the covers. Sleep beckoned her, lowering her defenses. A wisp of a memory fluttered through her mind. She could almost hear her mother's voice. *"You did a bad thing, Ellie. A very bad thing."*

Her sleep-laden lashes flew open as she instinctively pushed the thought away. She swallowed. Gathering her courage, she closed her eyes and allowed the memory to wash over her.

She looked up at her mother through tear-blurred eyes. Her father knelt beside her. "Do you know what you did wrong?"

"I told a secret."

"We have to fix this," her mother said.

Her father nodded, but looked doubtful. "There's a storm coming in."

"I know, but she's ruined Amelia!"

Her parents scolded her once more and she sulked off to the settee to watch the flurry of activity as her parents got ready to leave. She refused to say goodbye to them because she was smarting from their rebuke. They left and they never came back.

Ellie gasped as realization filled her then left her breathless. The guilt that she'd always felt in the back of her mind settled in the pit of her stomach and tripped up to her lips. "It's my fault. They left that day because of me…my stupid mistake… I wanted to feel important by telling others about Mrs. Greene. It's my fault they died."

These were the consequences Mrs. Greene had mentioned. And yes, they were just as awful as she'd promised. How could she face her siblings now knowing the truth? She couldn't tell them. Not after all these years. She didn't want to see them try to disguise their feelings to make her feel better. They'd tell her it wasn't her fault. They'd be lying.

I think I knew the truth all along. I was always afraid it was true—afraid I was right.

She could no longer hide from the memory or the disappointment she remembered hearing in their voices. They had been so disappointed in her—had died while still upset over what she had done. And if they had lived, she would have upset them so many more times with her endless stream of mistakes—except for Lawson. Despite her earlier fears, she hadn't made a mistake with him. It wasn't enough to rectify her earlier mistakes, but it was a start.

Pushing away her covers, she settled on her knees beside her bed in a position she only assumed when she desperately needed help. "Lord, I prayed that You would reveal what happened to me and You did. I don't know that I'm particularly grateful for that but I finally know. What am I supposed to do now? I'm so tired of feeling guilty and dirty. I thought knowing might relieve me of that but I just feel worse. Will You help me, please? Show me what to do."

She paused, realizing that was the first time in a very long time that she'd actually prayed for direction instead of just handing out an order. She grimaced. All right, so maybe she had a little to learn about walking with God instead of running ahead of Him. At this point, her sense of direction was so confused that she had no idea where she was, let alone where she was supposed to be going. Perhaps she'd try to let Him lead for a while just to see how it felt. Anything would be better than this.

Lawson ran a nervous hand through his hair. He hesitated for a moment then stepped into the Rutledges' kitchen for breakfast. A quick sweep of the room revealed that it was empty of everyone except Kate. She glanced up from the pancakes she was frying and placed her hand on her hip. "It's about time you showed your face in my kitchen, Lawson Williams. I was starting to get offended."

He grinned. "You know I can't stay away from your cooking for long."

"The laces fell out again, Ma." Timothy clomped into the room in his untied boots and stopped in his tracks at the sight of Lawson. "How come you don't eat breakfast anymore? Don't you get hungry?"

"I'm hungry today." He gestured the boy closer. "How about some help with those boots?"

As he helped Timothy straighten out the tangled laces, Nathan arrived in the kitchen with baby Matthew in his arms and chuckled when he spotted Lawson. "I wondered how long it would take you to get sick of your own cooking."

Timothy stopped him when he began tying the shoes. "Thank you, but I like to tie them."

Lawson settled into his chair just as Ellie entered with her nieces in tow. Surprise painted her features just as it had the rest of her family's. All right, so he couldn't blame them for being surprised. He'd been taking meals with them less often lately. Today he settled into his normal place at the table because for the first time in a long time he hadn't battled against his memories to win a few hours of sleep. No, last night he'd stayed awake thinking about Ellie.

He'd thought about the silly way she'd read her book upside down. He thought about the concern in her voice when they'd talked about his upcoming trip. He'd thought of the way she'd belittled her own courage. He'd thought about the words they'd shared at the door and the kiss she'd given him.

Ellie's familiar hand slipped into his. He stilled for a moment before he realized Nathan was praying a blessing over the meal and over the day. She promptly removed her hand from his once the prayer was over. As breakfast progressed he couldn't help but notice that Ellie seemed much more subdued than normal. He stole a glance at her to discover that her cheeks lacked their usual bloom and her eyes their usual sparkle. Had his rejection done this to her? She hadn't seemed discouraged last night. She'd seemed eager—even excited—to face the challenge of winning him over.

When nearly everyone was finished, Nathan cleared his throat. "Well, before everyone rushes off, you might all be interested in meeting the new addition to our ranch."

The whole table stilled except Grace and baby Matthew. Ellie leaned forward with the eagerness previously missing from her person. "Abigail had her foal."

"She had a healthy colt."

Kate grinned. "Now we get to name it."

After breakfast the entire family walked out to the

barn to welcome the new addition. As soon as Ellie's pig caught sight of them, it gave an attention-grabbing screech. Lawson veered his path to open the pig's pen. "Demanding little thing, aren't you?"

Ellie paused to watch the pig hightail it toward the field at a brisk trot. "He isn't very little anymore. He's growing fast."

"That only means he's becoming even bigger trouble."

She wrinkled her nose at him. "You never did like Hamlet."

"I don't mind the play or the pig. It's the man who gave it to you that I have a problem with."

"Donovan Turner?"

"Nathan informed me of his latest maneuver."

She rolled her eyes. "Nathan worries too much."

He quirked a dubious brow. "The man sold his farm."

"I know." She couldn't deny a grimace. "So he's a little crazy and a little strange. That doesn't mean he's dangerous like Nathan seems to think."

"No, it doesn't. But there's no harm in being cautious. Don't let your guard down around him, and don't go places alone." Having delivered his words of advice, he would have rejoined her family, but she caught his arm to keep him from leaving.

"I have something for you." She held up a folded piece of paper that she'd pulled from her pocket. "Let's call it a declaration of intent."

He caught her wrist to still her waving hand and took the paper from her. He opened it, trying his best to ignore the way she leaned against his arm to get a look at it, too. "What is this?"

"You'll figure it out."

He did. It didn't take him long once he realized it

was a list people who all had one thing in common—
they were bachelors. Most of the names were lightly
crossed out and were accompanied by a set of initials.
His name was last on the list. It wasn't crossed out. Instead, a bold circle set it apart from the others. He swallowed. "Those are your initials, aren't they?"

"Yep." She took the list, then folded it before placing it safely back in her pocket. "I thought you might
like to know that I'm serious about this."

"I guess it doesn't matter that I still don't think it's
a good idea."

She patted his arm as she led him toward the barn.
"Of course it matters. It just doesn't change what I'm
going to do."

"It won't work."

"I think you're just afraid that it will. One thing is
certain… I'm going to have a whole lot of fun trying."

He should be angry at her for ignoring his wishes.
He should make her give up this game right here and
now. He didn't for one very simple reason. He was
a man with a history of being abandoned, and being
sought out might be a welcome change—even if he
knew it wouldn't last. He would be leaving for Clive's
ranch in a couple of days, anyway. He just had to stay
strong until then.

A sharp whistle and a hiss of steam from the black
iron giant announced the arrival of the ten-fifteen train
into the station. As it lumbered to a stop, Ellie saw Lawson's face turn a couple of shades paler before he set
his jaw and stood a little straighter. For a moment she
wished Nathan hadn't trumped up a reason for her to
accompany Lawson to the station instead of him. While
she appreciated the few minutes she'd have alone with

Lawson, Nathan might have had a better idea of what to say to make this trip easier on Lawson.

She hadn't even realized she'd reached out to hold his hand or that he was holding it right back until she saw him staring down at it. He released her under the guise of collecting the lead ropes for the three horses he was taking with him. "Ethan better get here soon. I'm not doing this alone."

"I could always go with you."

The skeptical look she received told her just how likely that was to happen. "The town would love that. We wouldn't step more than a foot off the train when we returned before they'd make us get married."

She lifted a brow. "Maybe I should come then."

"That isn't funny."

"It wasn't a joke."

She realized it probably wasn't attractive to smirk, and glanced away from Lawson just as Jeff Bridger stopped to greet them. The metal deputy's badge on his chest barely outshone his smile. "Don't tell me you two are eloping?"

Her laughter clashed with Lawson's exasperated tone. "We aren't eloping."

Jeff's eyes twinkled. "A man can hope, can't he? Well, it's good to see you two together again."

"We aren't together," Lawson corrected. His gaze brushed her before he continued quietly. "At least, not the way you mean."

"Why are you two unchaperoned folks heading off by yourselves, then?"

"Lawson is taking those horses to a buyer. I'm just seeing them off." Her fingers tightened on Starlight's reins as she lifted her chin to indicate the horses under Lawson's control. It was always hard to say goodbye to them after she'd spent so much time helping raise and train them. Starlight seemed to sense her mood and shuffled closer until Ellie was able to lean against her.

Jeff eyed the other horses and whistled. "They sure are beautiful. I wouldn't want to handle all three of those horses alone, Lawson. Maybe you should take Ellie with you."

"No. Ethan Law—Larue is going with me." Lawson's brow lowered into a weary expression. "His uncle is the one who bought them. There's Ethan now. We'd better get these horses loaded."

They said goodbye to Jeff and met Ethan near the stock car. Lawson stepped forward to speak with the man in charge of loading the horses, so she turned to meet Ethan's blue eyes with a smile. "I have a surprise for you."

"For me?"

"Yes." She opened her reticule and pulled out his freshly laundered handkerchief. "I bet you thought I'd stolen it for good."

He chuckled. "To tell the truth, I'd forgotten all about it. Thanks for returning it. I'm glad to be leaving you much happier than I found you."

Lawson returned and tied the horses to a nearby hitching post. "Ellie, Wesley says Ethan and I should take our seats. Seems he's particular about loading the horses himself. Will you watch to make sure they get on all right?"

"Sure."

"Thanks. Time to go, Ethan."

"Bye, Ellie. I'll leave you two to say goodbye."

"Goodbye, Ethan." She returned his parting smile then turned to Lawson. "Well, I guess this is it."

"Yep. Remember to have Sean see you home." His

gaze met hers for an instant before it darted away. "See you in a week."

She blinked and he was already hurrying to catch up with Ethan. There was no way he was in that much of a hurry to start this trip, which could only mean that he was trying to avoid her. She should have expected that since he'd had plenty of practice at it over the past three days.

She narrowed her eyes, tied Starlight's reins to a post and rushed after him. "Lawson Williams, stop right there."

He frowned at her and didn't stop but slowed his pace. "Ellie, I have to catch the train."

"You know I care about you even if you refuse to admit that you return my feelings. You're leaving for a week. Can't you muster up something better than that pathetic excuse for a goodbye you just gave me?"

"You mean like a kiss?"

She froze in surprise. "Yes, if you're offering it."

"Well, since I'll be gone a whole week, I reckon one kiss wouldn't hurt." He slipped one arm around her waist and the other behind her back to dip her back slightly. He placed a gentle kiss on her forehead before setting her upright. "Goodbye, Ellie."

"You aren't half as funny as you think you are." She wrinkled her nose at his wink, then placed her hands on her hips and watched him walk away laughing. "We'll see who gets the last laugh when I buy my ticket and get on that train."

He sent her one last warning look before he mounted the steps and disappeared into the railcar. She rubbed her forehead. "I guess something is better than nothing."

The conductor gave another call as she wandered

back to where she'd left her horse. Starlight was gone. She glanced around the bustling train station. An ominous bang announced the closing of the last stock car. She turned to face the train with a dreadful sense of foreboding. She rushed to the attendant that had been helping Lawson. "Wesley, where is my horse?"

"How should I know?"

"You've seen my horse. She's white with a gray mane. I left her tied right there."

He washed his hand over his face. "Lawson told me to put all the horses tied there on the train."

Her frantic gaze flew to the stock car. "You have to get her off that train."

"That's impossible. The train will be leaving any minute. There's no time."

"But the train can't leave with my horse on it!" She glanced around for help and caught sight of Jeff standing nearby. "Deputy, please make this man take Starlight off that train."

"I told her I can't do that." The attendant shook his head. "Lawson said he was coming back. I'm sure he'll bring your horse."

She turned to Jeff entreatingly. She couldn't be sure but she thought she caught the tail end of a wink. "I saw the whole thing. You loaded that horse into a different stock car. Lawson will never know Starlight is there."

Wesley scratched his head. "Come to think of it, you might be right."

"You saw the whole thing? Why didn't you stop him?"

Jeff shrugged. "Maybe you're supposed to go on this trip after all. The Lord works in mysterious ways."

"Oh! You can't blame this on Him." She panicked as the train began to move. "What do I do?"

Jeff caught her arm and rushed her toward the passenger car. "You're going to get on that train. You can get off at the next stop and collect your horse, then ride back to town. Maybe you and Lawson will part better farther down the road."

"I don't want to see him. I just want my horse." The plan sounded crazy, but she didn't have time to think of an alternative. She hopped onto the moving train with his help. Bracing herself, she turned toward Jeff and yelled, "I don't have a ticket!"

He just waved and smiled. She wanted to throw something at him. This was ridiculous. She should jump off. She stared at the ground passing by in front of her. Too late to go back now. She gritted her teeth. "I've been bamboozled!"

Chapter Fourteen

There was nothing she could do but climb the stairs and open the door to the train car. She scanned it for Lawson and Ethan and found them seated at the very front of the car. They hadn't seen her. Her first instinct was to rush over to them and demand they do something to help her. Then she remembered her foolish jest to Lawson about joining him on the train. She quickly slid onto the nearest open seat. *He's going to think I'm trying to trap him into marrying me.*

The man across from her grinned. "You almost didn't make it."

She smiled weakly. "Did the conductor pass through here yet?"

"No, miss," he said before he disappeared behind his newspaper.

"Oh." She swallowed. "Good."

She probably only had a few minutes before she would be kicked off the train in high style. She closed her eyes. Well, that would be fine with her. She just wanted to get her horse and leave. She bit her lip nervously. Would the conductor be more or less lenient if she was traveling under the protection of two men?

She shifted in her seat to peek at them, then abruptly sank down in her seat when the conductor entered the car. Five minutes later, he made it down the aisle to stand in front of her. "Ticket."

"I don't have one," she said quietly as though a lack of volume might lessen the seriousness of her offense.

His lips turned down into what seemed to be a familiar expression to his face. "What did you say?"

She winced at the censure of his question and the weight of her traveling companions' glances. "I'm sorry. It really isn't my fault. You see, the man loading the livestock car accidentally put my horse on the train and he wouldn't let me get it off."

"So you thought that entitled you to a free ride?"

"No. I was still trying to figure out what to do when my friend took action and practically forced me on the train."

His eyes narrowed suspiciously.

She held up her right hand as though swearing on a Bible. "I'm telling the truth. I promise. You can let me off right now if you want. Please, just let me get my horse. Her name is Starlight. I've had her since she was born. The poor girl is probably scared crazy."

The man across from her lowered the newspaper and eyed first her, then the conductor. "If you stop this train, I'm getting off, too. It's already running late. I have places to be even if the rest of these folks don't."

The conductor frowned harder. "The next stop isn't for another fifty miles. I can't keep her on the train that long without a ticket."

"I can pay my fare—"

"I don't take money. I just take tickets."

The woman next to her shifted forward to enter the fray. "I hope you aren't seriously considering putting this young woman off the train. Look out the window. There's nothing out there but open land, rattlesnakes and probably a few outlaws. Anything could happen to her."

"Let her stay," the newspaper man said, as though that settled it.

The conductor crossed his arms. "All right, missy, you can stay until we get to the next stop. At that time I will personally see to it that you take your horse and yourself off this train. Do you understand?"

"Yes, sir."

"I will also report you to the company so they'll know what to do if you take any unplanned trips in the future."

Ellie let out a sigh of relief when he turned to the other side of the aisle. She waited until he left the car to thank her traveling companions. The man across from her sent her a conspiratorial wink before returning to his newspaper while the woman sitting next to her patted her hand comfortingly, and started a conversation that lasted for nearly the entire fifty miles.

The train finally stopped at the next station, and the disembarking passengers began to file past her. She started to rise but the man across from her shook his head. "Wait for the warden. He wanted to see you off personally, remember?"

"Oh, right." She perched on the seat again while her gaze combed the aisle for a sign of the conductor. She was greeted instead with the sight of Lawson and Ethan rising from their seats. This was their stop, too. She grimaced. If they didn't see her, she could return home without Lawson ever knowing she was here.

The man across from her began to fold his paper

and set it aside. She impulsively reached toward it. "I'm sorry. Do you mind if I borrow this?"

"Go right ahead," he said. "Though I'm pretty sure the conductor will recognize you, anyway."

"That's fine, but tell me when those two cowboys pass."

The woman next to her leaned in. "This is Texas, honey. You'll have to be more specific."

She glanced at the woman. "There are two young, particularly attractive ones."

"I see them." The woman smiled. "If I was you, I sure wouldn't hide from them."

Ellie bit her lip to keep from laughing and drawing attention to herself. A few moments passed before the woman told her she was safe. She let out a relieved sigh. She carefully folded the newspaper and handed it to the man just in time for the conductor to appear at her side. "This is your stop, miss."

She grabbed her reticule and stood. The conductor gestured with the Stetson in his hand for her to precede him. She hid a smile of confusion at his hat then started walking toward the exit. She stopped abruptly, realizing she should at least say goodbye to her new friends. The conductor grumbled at her to keep walking so she did—backward…just for a moment as she said goodbye. That was all it took to slam into someone.

The air rushed out of Lawson's lungs in a whoosh, stirring the curls of the blond woman who'd backed into him. He found it strange that the conductor reached out to steady him, not her. "Are you all right, sir?"

"Yes," he managed. The woman stiffened, murmured something unintelligible that could hardly pass for an apology, then kept her back turned as she moved past him. He returned his focus to the conductor. "I left my—"

His voice stopped abruptly as he reached out to catch the arm of the woman trying to sneak down the aisle. He tugged her around to face him. The woman bit the corner of her pink lips while her cheeks flushed, enhancing their rosy hue, and her large green eyes trailed up to meet his. *Ellie.*

His brain stopped working for a moment as he tried to reconcile that the woman was standing in front of him after he'd left her at the train station fifty miles back. He suddenly remembered her threat to follow him, so they'd be forced to marry. *No, she wouldn't do that.*

But why else would she be here? Why was she being escorted by the conductor? What was going on? He should ask her any or all of those questions but they fled when her mouth teased into a smile and she innocently quipped, "Hello."

"Hello." She was here but she shouldn't be and that pretty much summed up the past several days of his life. He'd avoided her, purposefully annoyed her, tried to discourage her, but she kept turning up just when he needed her—like right now when he was about to face his past head-on once and for all. He wasn't supposed to need her. He shouldn't be the least bit glad to see her and yet he couldn't deny that a little part of him was. *Just because she's here now, doesn't mean she's going to stay in my life forever. It's only been three days.*

He knew that, so why didn't he let her go? His thumb stroked her arm even as his heart seemed to dislodge just enough to connect with hers. Was it his imagination or did she lean into his touch? The conductor cleared his throat. "You said you left something?"

"My hat." His gaze flew to the conductor's before settling back on Ellie's.

"Here it is. I was going to take it to the lost and found."

A nearby passenger snickered. "It looks like he found something better."

"Wish I'd found it first," another drawled.

Lawson suddenly became aware of the gaping railcar of travelers. He took his Stetson and guided Ellie off the train. Ethan was waiting just where he'd left him. She explained how she'd ended up on the train as they collected the horses and recovered Starlight. He shook his head. "Why didn't you just wire ahead and tell me?"

She stilled. "I didn't even think of that. It all happened so quickly."

Ethan slid a sly glance his way before turning to Ellie. "You should stay. It will only take a week—"

"That isn't a good idea." Lawson frowned.

"You know just as much about these horses as Lawson, if not more."

He crossed his arms. "You mean I could have sent her instead?"

"It would be fun." Ethan tipped his head toward Lawson. "This fellow could use another ally, anyway, if you know what I mean."

Ellie's gaze stumbled back and forth between them. "Oh, I couldn't do that."

Lawson nodded firmly. "No, she couldn't. Come on. We have to wire Peppin to let your family know you're safe, then get a ticket for you to go back home."

"You'd let her travel unaccompanied?" Ethan asked, his disapproval apparent.

"Why not? She rode all the way here without—" He almost said "without incident" then caught himself when he realized it wasn't true.

"Just a minute," Ellie objected as she crossed her arms suspiciously. "Why couldn't I stay if I wanted to? Ethan is right. I'll get into all sorts of trouble if I go back alone—just see if I don't. Besides, there is a chaperone at Clive's ranch, isn't there?"

Ethan nodded staunchly. "Ruth, the housekeeper and cook, will keep everyone in line."

"You could use an ally. I'd be a great one, I promise." Her green eyes turned slightly desperate and very hopeful. "Besides, I wouldn't mind getting away from the ranch for a little while. A change would be good for me."

She was right. He could use another ally. Still, he wasn't sure it was an idea Nathan would approve of— Ellie by herself with only a housekeeper to protect her from any wayward ranch hands…and Clive. He shook his head. "I said no."

Ethan grinned as if that sealed the deal for Ellie to stay, and Lawson fought the urge to groan. Telling Ellie no, flat-out, was the best way to bring out her obstinacy. Lawson watched as her chin lifted and knew that she wouldn't back down now. "Haven't I mentioned to you once or twice that I make my own choices? I'll just wire home to make sure it's all right. What do you say to that?"

Lawson hid his smile at the ridiculous statement. "Your stubbornness is showing."

"Where's the telegraph office?"

Ethan offered her his arm. "Right over here."

She took his arm, then lifted her eyebrows at Lawson as if to say, *So there.* Lawson frowned. "Hold on, Ethan. I want to talk to you. Ellie, go on and send your telegram."

"What is it?" Ethan asked once Ellie left them.

"I am not comfortable bringing Ellie along to meet Clive. He never thought twice about hitting my mother. I'll not subject her to that."

Ethan's face paled slightly. "Uncle Clive isn't like that anymore. I've never seen him raise a hand to anyone, not even an animal. Ruth has never borne a scratch and she's lived with us for eight years. He's a different man than you remember."

"I hope so for your sake but I'm not willing to trust him that far."

"Then trust me," Ethan said quietly. "She'll be safe. I give you my word on that."

Lawson eyed his cousin. "If Clive so much as looks at Ellie wrong—"

"I'll personally buy her ticket home and see that she gets on the right train with Ruth to accompany her."

"Fine," he agreed. They joined Ellie inside the telegraph office and less than thirty minutes later, she received permission to stay from Sean. Her triumphant smile was quickly followed by a sigh of relief, leaving him to wonder if more than just a desire to be with him motivated her not to return home.

He put his hat on as they exited the office, and let out a deep breath. If he was being honest, he'd admit he was grateful for the distraction of Ellie's presence. His stomach had slowly but surely begun to climb toward his throat those last few miles into town. He felt like Daniel being led toward the lion's den. He swallowed. *Maybe it won't be that bad. Yeah, and maybe I can get away with "accidentally" leaving my Stetson somewhere again.*

It was too bad stalling didn't actually change the destination.

Lawson was relatively certain he'd seen this little meadow before. Just to make sure, he leaned forward to rest his wrists against the saddle horn and catch Ethan's attention. "How long would it take to get to Clive's ranch from here if we stopped going in circles?"

Ethan glanced up sharply then gave him a slow, guilty smile. "About twenty minutes."

"We've been going in circles? Why?" Ellie asked in exasperation.

"To make me think they're farther from town then they actually are. That way I'm less likely to leave abruptly. Isn't that right, Ethan?"

"Yep."

He shook his head. "I thought you were on my side."

"I thought you weren't in a hurry to get where we're going, anyway. It seemed to fit everyone's purposes."

Lawson pulled off his hat to let the breeze cool his face. "We might as well stop for a few minutes and stretch."

"Amen," Ellie muttered as she dismounted and they did the same.

Ethan frowned at her. "I thought you rode horses all the time."

"I do, but not for two hours straight after riding to town and then traveling by train."

Lawson took a swig from his canteen then slowly lowered it. His gaze scanned the woods for movement. His ears strained to listen. He put the canteen away while his right hand strayed to his holster. "Ethan, do you have neighbors close by?"

"No. Why?"

"We have company." He pulled his Colt from his holster. "Come here, Ellie."

Suddenly, four horsemen burst from the woods to surround them. Ethan's horse reared in protest as Ellie let out a startled scream. One of the men dismounted and edged toward her. "Saints above, aren't you a pretty sight? Do you belong to one of these never-do-wells?"

Lawson's protective instincts kicked in. He stepped closer to her saying a firm "yes" just as she squeaked out a "no." Her gaze collided with his in hope. "Yes?"

He eyed the men and Ethan for a moment. Realizing that everyone else looked particularly unconcerned about the situation, he slipped his gun back into its resting place. Another man dismounted. "Well, which is it?"

"Actually, I think that about sums it up." Ethan smirked. "What do y'all mean by rushing in here like that? You could have gotten yourselves shot. As it was, you scared the lady pretty good."

The first man pulled off his hat. "Sorry, miss. I guess we got a little overexcited."

Lawson snorted. "You think?"

Ethan smiled and gestured to the men. "Lawson, meet your father's ranch hands. Boys, this is Ellie. You aren't to bother her."

They grumbled for a minute, then offered to escort them the rest of the way. Lawson stepped forward to give Ellie a boost before anyone else could offer. As he passed her he mumbled, "Knowing my father, they're probably all a bunch of outlaws, anyway."

Her eyes lit with excitement. "Do you think so?"

"No." He ignored her laughter but it drew the attention of the other men. He frowned at them all. This was not good.

The churning of his stomach increased substantially when the ranch house came into sight. It was a large two-story, whitewashed with dark blue shutters that reminded him of bruises. The bright red barn and weathered gray outbuildings stood out on the green countryside. The property looked well maintained—almost picturesque, and a far cry from the bleak shantytown shack he remembered from his early childhood.

Clive was nowhere in sight as their caravan of sorts approached the house. Would Clive not come out to greet them? Perhaps he was busy in another area of the ranch. Lawson brought his horse to a stop near the steps of the house's porch. He unclenched his white-knuckled grip on the reins and warily surveyed his surroundings once more before dismounting.

That delay nearly cost him the prerogative of helping Ellie off her horse. She was obviously a skilled rider who needed no assistance, but the other men didn't seem to take that into account as they stepped toward her, then stopped in disappointment. Ellie gave him her thanks along with a curious look. He heard the door open behind him. Ellie stilled as her gaze trailed from that sound back to him.

Steeling himself, Lawson turned to face Clive. Tension filled the air as the man walked slowly along the porch. His footsteps sounded loudly on the hollow porch steps before being muffled by the grass at their base. Lawson found himself widening his stance, pulling back his shoulders and meeting the man's gaze straight on. Clive eyed him carefully.

Lawson narrowed his eyes. It almost felt as if he'd

been called out and Clive was waiting for him to make the first move so he could shoot him down fair and square. Lawson was wearing his gun belt, as was Clive, he noted. He didn't know how to gauge this man— this almost stranger with a violent past. Surely, this wouldn't turn into a fight.

Lawson's hand moved backward slightly—closer to his gun. Instead of the cold metal of his Colt, Ellie's warm fingers slid into his. She'd thought he'd been reaching for her. Maybe he had been. His hand tightened around hers. He let out a pent-up breath and managed a respectful nod. "Hello, Clive."

"I wasn't sure you'd come."

"Neither was I." He saw Clive notice their linked hands so he gestured to Ellie but didn't release her hand. He wasn't sure he could have if he'd wanted to, and he *didn't* want to. "You remember Ellie O'Brien."

Clive nodded. "Certainly. It's a pleasure to see you again."

"Thank you, sir."

Ethan stepped forward. "Ellie is here to help Lawson with the horses. I told her Ruth would look after her."

"Ruth will be glad of some female company. I know she's tired of mine." He turned to his men, ordering, "See that the horses are stabled. Ethan, let Ruth know of Miss O'Brien's arrival while I show our guests to their rooms."

Everyone hurried to do as they'd been told. Lawson pulled in a deep breath. He was here. He'd walk into the house and he'd stay for the required length of time but that didn't mean he'd be as submissive as everyone else in Clive's life seemed to be. Clive may not know it yet but they were going to do things Lawson's way, in Lawson's time. He'd start by getting at least half of

Nathan's money up front so Clive wouldn't be able to play any games with it.

Lawson was distracted from his thoughts when Ethan gave him a supportive clasp on the shoulder as he passed. Clive stood by the door waiting for them to enter. Let him wait. Lawson glanced down at Ellie to see if she was ready. She smiled encouragingly. He nodded. *All right, then. Let's do this.*

Chapter Fifteen

Ellie couldn't believe she was on a real, live cattle ranch just like she'd read about in her dime novels. No one was looking so she stretched her arms wide and pulled in a deep breath. They were a little too close to the barn for that to be entirely pleasant. She smiled, anyway. This trip was exactly what she'd needed. At home, she couldn't seem to get out from under the cloud of guilt she'd been feeling since the night she'd remembered the truth about her parents' deaths. Even if the busyness of the day momentarily pushed it away, the ranch still carried so many reminders of her parents that it wasn't long before it returned.

A change of scenery might be just what she needed. Unfortunately, this wasn't likely to be a joyful trip for Lawson. He walked ahead of her with his father and Ethan. The distance between Lawson and Clive and the tension that filled it was nearly palpable.

Lawson's face had turned inscrutable when his father stepped out of the house. Yet, even in that difficult moment, he'd had enough strength and courage to turn around to greet the man respectfully. She'd taken a risk in slipping her hand into his when he'd reached for the comfort of his Colt. She knew he wasn't going to draw, but doing so allowed her to show she was standing with him. His hand had tightened to hold hers right back. He hadn't released it, either—not until they had to go their separate ways in the house. That meant something, didn't it?

Ethan noticed she'd fallen behind the group and dropped back to walk with her. "What do you think of the ranch?"

"It's wonderful. How many head of cattle are there?"

"About a thousand."

"Is that a lot? It sounds like a lot."

"It's more than a little."

They shared a smile at his silly response before Ellie lifted her chin toward the men in front of them. "How is it going with them?"

"No fisticuffs yet," he said blithely.

She sent him a censoring frown. "I don't think that's something to joke about."

"I wasn't joking."

"You don't really think it might come to that, do you?" she asked, walking sideways so she could see his face.

"I hope not. They still have some serious issues to work through but I'm not sure either of them is prepared to do that yet." He shrugged. "I guess it's something to pray about."

She threw him a curious glance. "I don't think I've ever heard you mention prayer before."

He ducked his head. "I've been doing it more lately—mainly because Lawson seems to put such stock in it."

"He's a good man." She sent him a smile. "So are you."

"Thanks. I might not have known Lawson long, but

it's obvious that my cousin doesn't make it easy for anyone to get close to him." Ethan met her gaze seriously. "If you want him, you'll need to fight for him. Lawson told me the story of Uncle Clive and Aunt Gloria abandoning him. He remembers that feeling well, though he was only nine when it happened. He isn't going to pin his hope on anyone who can't convince him that it'll last."

She bit her lip. She didn't want to make anything worse between her and Lawson, but what else could she do to make it better? She watched Lawson stop at a nearby paddock as his father gestured to the large dark horse inside. His arms were crossed and his expression closed off. "I'm trying. I don't know how well it's working."

"He has feelings for you. Of that you can be sure. The rest is up to you."

She tilted her head as though that might help her discern the emotions to which Ethan seemed privy. Lawson caught her watching him and sent her a quizzical smile that quickly disappeared when he turned back to Clive. "Thanks, Ethan."

"You're welcome. Let's rejoin them. Lawson is starting to look nervous."

"What a beautiful horse," Ellie exclaimed at the sight of the large black stallion. The horse seemed agitated to be the subject of their examination.

Clive acknowledged her compliment with a nod but didn't bother to look her way. "This is Diablo. He's as mean as they come. There's never been a man that could stay seated on him."

Lawson eyed the horse skeptically. "This is the horse you want me to train? And you want me to do it in a week? That seems unrealistic."

"Diablo has the potential to be a great horse. He just needs to be gentled."

"I'll do my best but once the week is up I trust you'll stay true to your word and the contract by giving me the other half of the payment regardless of my results with Diablo."

"It's a deal." Clive put out his hand. After a moment of hesitation, Lawson shook it firmly. Clive cleared his throat. "We'll leave you two to decide how you'll go about this. Come along, Ethan."

Ethan obeyed but not before giving Ellie a significant look. She chuckled softly. It seemed she couldn't get away from matchmakers no matter where she went. Her laughter drew Lawson's attention so she wrinkled her nose. "Diablo is an awful name for a horse. Of course he'd act mean if everyone called him that. First things first, he needs a new name."

An amused smile tipped his lips slightly. "Like what?"

"Let's see." She crossed her arms on the paddock fence and surveyed the horse thoughtfully. "He looks like a Midnight to me."

He copied her posture, leaning onto the paddock fence, as well. "I guess so since you named your horse Starlight."

"They are kind of similar."

He sighed. "This is a ruse, you know."

"What is?"

"This whole thing." He turned to face her. "That stipulation for the horses to be delivered, this horse that has never been ridden—he's been using it all to get me here and keep me here."

"I figured." She paused then quietly continued, "But, you did choose to come."

"I know."

She touched his arm in concern. "How are you holding up so far?"

"Fine… I think. I know what's coming, though. I knew it when I came. I'll have to listen to him try to explain away leaving me behind. That's all right, though, because I have a few questions I'd like some answers to and I aim to get them."

She wondered if he caught the glimmer of admiration in her eyes before he turned his attention back to the horse. She certainly felt it. He was so brave not only to acknowledge his past but to travel all these miles to face it, as well. He didn't seem afraid—just determined. It was too bad she lacked the courage she saw in him. Not that there was anything left for her to face. Her parents were gone and there was nothing she could do to rectify that mistake.

Her situation with Lawson was different. She'd made her mistakes with him but perhaps that didn't have to be the end of the story. She didn't want it to be. *Lord, I know I said I'd try to follow Your lead. For the first time in a long time, I think maybe I will. I think I still have a chance. If I do…well, Lord, I intend to take it.*

The next few days passed without the altercation Lawson expected. He dedicated himself to Diablo—or Midnight, as Ellie renamed him. His interactions with Clive remained polite and distant, if slightly cold. That sufficed since Lawson rarely saw the man except for at mealtimes or when Clive would wander over to Midnight's stall to check on their progress—like now. Lawson tried not to let the man's presence distract him from his task. "Do you have the saddle blanket ready, Ellie?"

Her affirmative reply came softly so as not to

frighten the horse that flinched but otherwise didn't protest when Lawson stroked his mane. Ellie stood a few feet away outside the fence but close enough to be at his side at a moment's notice. That pretty much summed up her behavior during their visit so far.

He was grateful—incredibly grateful for her presence during all of this. She'd been supportive of him while managing to charm everyone from the ranch hands to the housekeeper to Midnight. Even Clive seemed to enjoy talking to her, though Ellie adhered to Lawson's plea that she keep her distance. Midnight stepped toward her to examine the blanket as she calmly approached the stallion. "He's doing well, isn't he, Lawson?"

"Better than I'd hoped," he admitted as his hands traveled across Midnight's back. "It helps that he's fallen in love with you along with everyone else at this ranch."

"Well, I wouldn't say *everyone*." The look in her green eyes betrayed a subtle hope that he might contradict her statement.

He wasn't sure how to respond to that and a quick glance over his shoulder at Clive told him this was not the time to try to figure it out. He forced his focus back on the horse. His fingers brushed over something hard. Frowning, he stepped closer to examine the horse and found a patchwork of scars across its back. He instinctively flashed accusatory eyes at Clive. "This horse has been abused."

Hurt swept across Clive's face before he managed to mask it. "Not by me. The previous owner thought beating the fight out of Diablo would tame him. That's why I convinced the man to sell the horse to me."

Ellie's fingers examined the black scars that were

nearly indiscernible from the horse's black coat. "The scars are old, Lawson."

He knew that but it hadn't changed his first thought. He glanced back at Clive wondering if he should apologize. He didn't. He wouldn't have meant it. Clive seemed to sense that.

"I understand why you might assume…" the man began then cleared his throat. "I'm not that person anymore."

Ellie mumbled something about getting sugar cubes for the horse, then left them alone. He watched her go, feeling his jaw tighten. So this was it—the moment he'd been planning for and dreading in equal measure. He released Midnight from the long lead rope. The horse wandered away as Lawson turned to face the man who was supposed to be his father. "Your name's Clive Hardy, isn't it?"

"You know it is."

"Then you're still the man who abandoned me."

Clive gave an accepting nod. "I guess to you I always will be."

He began coiling the rope in his hand with a bit more force than necessary. "Tell me. What kind of thoughts go through a man's head when he abandons his only son with nothing more than a dollar bill and a note no one else is literate enough to read?"

"Are you sure you want me to tell that story?"

"No, but it belongs to me as much as it belongs to you so I reckon I've a right to know."

Clive braced his boot on the last rung on the fence. "It will be no surprise to you to know I'd had a few drinks. Not enough that I couldn't function but just enough to make my judgment shady. I thought I needed the courage for the job I had to do."

"Which was?"

"Robbery." He pulled a pipe from his pocket and tapped it on the wooden fence. "It wasn't my first but it was my last. The whole thing was a disaster from start to finish. I got shot. I knew worse would happen if the sheriff or my boss caught up to me."

The story matched what Lawson remembered. "So you ran out on me. You thought I'd slow you down and you couldn't take the risk."

Clive didn't deny that. Instead, he continued, "It was the worst decision I ever made. Your mother never forgave me for putting her in that situation."

Lawson glanced past Clive toward the open land and shook his head. "She had a choice, same as you. Whatever happened, you were both equally guilty—equally wrong."

"After a couple of weeks, we came back to look for you." He tried to strike a match to light his pipe but gave up and tucked it away. "There was no trace of you."

He nodded. "I was young but I wasn't dumb. I knew you intended to leave me for good. The rent was due in the morning so I wasn't going to stick around just to get kicked out. I'm sure I was long gone by the time you two moseyed back."

"Well, your ma sort of snapped when we couldn't find you. She threw all the whiskey out of the house and told me if I ever came home drunk I'd sleep outside. A few rainy nights sobered me up enough to realize what a miserable cur I was. I thought that would make things better between me and your ma, but I'd done too much damage. One day she up and left. No note. No anything."

Lawson crossed his arms. If Clive was looking for

sympathy on that point, he wouldn't get any. He didn't seem to notice because he was staring off into the distance as if seeing the whole thing play out before him. "I think now she might have been in the family way and didn't trust me to be a better father than I'd been before."

"So I might have a sibling out there somewhere suffering from the same ill fortune of birth that I am."

Clive winced. "I don't know. Maybe. Once your ma left I went searching for both of y'all. I didn't find either of you. Instead, I found the only other male child in that area of Texas answering to the name of Lawson."

"Ethan."

Clive nodded. "I took him in and did for him what I should have done for you. One day I heard about a Ranger named Lawson Williams. I thought maybe it might be you at last. I had to find you. So I did."

"So you did and here I am.... I guess I'm supposed to feel better about all of this because you looked for me." Lawson eyed the man before him and shook his head. "I'm not sure how this makes up for what you did but if it feels good to see me here, to talk to me, to tell me your story—then I guess for you it was worth it." He ran his fingers through his hair. "To me, it isn't worth much. It doesn't change what I went through. It doesn't change who I am, or what you put me through. It wasn't just a matter of you abandoning me. As long as I carried your name, I got followed by your trouble. People who otherwise might have helped me didn't want anything to do with me when they learned I was your son."

He paused and let that sink in for a moment. "For better or worse, I'm still the one who gets left behind. The one that can't get the folks who matter—really matter—to stay, or to let *me* stay." He should shut his mouth but he couldn't seem to stop. "The O'Briens and the Williamses—they're the only ones who seemed to care enough to want to keep me. I wonder what they see that others don't. Or maybe it's just that they're blind to the thing that drives everyone else away." He glanced up at his father. "The thing that drove you away…from a nine-year-old boy who didn't even have sense enough to ask to go along. You wouldn't have let me, if I had. Would you?"

He didn't need to wait for an answer. He slipped through the corral fence and let the rope he held fall to the ground. He wasn't sure where to go. He just kept walking until he found a solitary place where he could sit under a shade tree. He was a grown man. This shouldn't bother him, but it did. It always had. He'd seen that abandonment repeated in his life time and time again—maybe even when it wasn't there… like with Ellie. He'd just come to expect it to happen eventually in each relationship. Even with God, he'd been afraid to get too close.

He shook his head. He couldn't remember the last time he'd thought about God. He couldn't remember the last time he'd prayed without prompting from others. He tilted his head back against the rough bark of the tree to stare at the patches of sky that peeked through the auburn canopy. "Are You still there or did You walk away, too?"

He could almost hear Nathan's words from that long-ago night when he'd first met the Lord. *You're part of God's family now. He'll never leave you or forsake you.* He swallowed. "That's a big promise. I hope You're living up to it."

A strange feeling filled his chest. It wasn't peace

exactly, just a powerful feeling that he wasn't alone in this. God might not be able to reach out and hold his hand like Ellie but He hadn't left. How else would Lawson have survived in those rough Western towns or found the O'Briens or settled with the Williamses?

If that was so—if God had been with him his entire life—then why had he been brought to this moment? What was the purpose? It hurt worse than many of the others. It was if all the pain he'd stuffed inside for so long finally popped like a loose button on one of those old raggedy shirts he used to wear.

A faint prickling sensation danced around his eyes. He fought it back. He hadn't cried when his parents left him and he wouldn't start now. He was stronger than that. He'd make it through. He always did. He'd leave this place soon, anyway. Maybe he'd never see Clive again. Maybe this was the last time he'd have to relive any of this. Maybe he'd finally be able to put his family shadows behind him once and for all. As soon as he left this ranch, he'd start looking toward the future. Whatever it was, it had to be better than his past. It just had to be.

Chapter Sixteen

Ellie was in the kitchen when Clive breezed through on the way to his study. He paused as if to say something, then shook his head and continued on. She followed him. "What happened?"

"Let's talk in my study."

She ignored the frown Ethan sent her from the sitting room when she shut the door part of the way behind her. Clive had never taken her into his confidence before and she didn't want to be interrupted. It was obvious that Clive and Lawson had finally gotten around to the talk that had been hanging over everyone's heads since the beginning of the trip. "How is he?"

"I don't know." He sank into a nearby chair with a sigh. "You can go after him if you wish but he might need some time to himself."

Ellie thought about this for a moment, then settled into the chair across from him. "I'll give him a few minutes."

"What was he like, Ellie, when you first met him?"

"He was a lot like Mid—Diablo. He was sort of wary about accepting any kindness. He had a lot of fight in him but was never violent. I got the impression he knew too much for his age—although I don't think we could ever figure out what age he was for sure."

Clive stood to riffle through some papers at his desk. "And now?"

"I think that tattered little boy is still a part of him but he's grown up since then. He has a dry sense of humor that is just sly enough to catch you off guard. He's very protective of women in general but especially the ones in my family and his adoptive mother. He's intelligent, hardworking, caring, gentle, yet he's always been a bit of a mystery to everyone. Even himself."

Clive finally took a piece of paper out of his desk, then settled back in the chair. "Does he know you love him?"

Her breath stilled in her throat. What was he talking about? *She* didn't even know she loved him.

All right, that wasn't entirely true. She was falling in love with him. She knew that. But how did a girl know when she was *completely* in love? Was there a sort of jarring sensation or did she just decide that she was? She glanced at Lawson's father. Or did someone have to tell her? She cleared her throat. "Honestly, Mr. Hardy, I'm not sure it would matter to him."

He seemed to understand what she meant for he nodded. "That's my fault as well as Gloria's. You're right. He is like Midnight. Isn't that what you call him? He's strong but with scars that run deep. I may not have inflicted them on the horse but I wielded that whip on my own son. That's a thousand times worse."

The man before her seemed to deflate. "You don't know how a mistake like that can eat at a man. Day in and day out to know that you were responsible for bringing harm to someone that close to you."

"Yes, I do," she said before she could stop herself.

She reached out to touch his hand. "I know that feeling exactly. I did something that had horrible implications for people I loved. It was a mistake but that didn't change the outcome."

He patted her hand. "My dear, if there's one thing I've learned it's that you can't change what happened. You have to accept that you made the mistake, examine it closely to learn from it, then move on. Don't let it define your life as I have let my mistakes define mine. Seek to make peace if you can. If you can't, let it go. I hope you'll let me know how it's resolved."

"*If* it's resolved." She didn't hold out much hope and she wasn't sure what good it would do to go poking around in the matter.

He handed her the paper in his hand. "I want you to have this. I'd give it to Lawson but I'm not sure he'd take anything from me. It's his birth certificate."

She glanced at the document. "His middle name is Clive. I don't think he knows that."

"I don't think he'd want to know."

"His birthday is this month—next week, in fact. Perhaps we can throw him a party at home. He'd like that."

Clive nodded, then looked past her to the window. "I think I see Lawson under that far tree. You should go to him."

"I will." She folded the worn birth certificate into her pocket as she muttered a quick goodbye and breezed past a concerned-looking Ethan to walk down the porch steps.

Lawson stood from his spot at the base of the tree when she neared. She stopped a few feet away and they just looked at each other. She wasn't sure what to say or do. He was obviously torn up inside over the conversation with his father. If she'd ask how he was he'd probably give her the same answer she'd gotten all week. "Fine... I think." That didn't say much. "You talked to Clive."

His eyes seemed slightly reddened. That broke her heart since she'd never seen him anywhere close to tears before. He glanced away, shoving his hands in his pockets. "It went about as I expected. The facts didn't change. I guess I'm just angry."

"At Clive?" She eased closer.

He nodded staunchly as if the words he said didn't really affect him. She knew better. "And Gloria, and the hand I've been dealt, and pretty much everything else."

"That's understandable."

Something in her voice must have caught his attention because he looked at her and caught her blinking away tears. He frowned. "Are you crying—for me?"

The incredulous tone in his voice made a tear slip free. "So what if I am?"

"That is not necessary." He pulled her toward him.

"Yes, it is." She resisted slightly so that she could look up at him. "Don't you dare comfort me at a time like this, Lawson Williams."

A smile played at the corner of his lips. "What's wrong with a time like this?"

"Nothing, except that *I* should be comforting *you!*"

He actually chuckled as he pulled her into his arms. She rested her cheek on his chest. He didn't bother to respond, which was just fine with her. She closed her eyes and prayed he wouldn't let go...ever.

His low voice rumbled against her ear. "You know something, Ellie?"

"What?" she whispered.

"You're getting to be like a bad penny," he murmured. Her eyes flew open. She pushed against his chest but he didn't let her go. "Now, hold on. I didn't mean that the way you took it."

"Oh?" she asked, tilting her head to stare at him in hurt disbelief. "How exactly did you mean it?"

"I meant it as a thank-you."

Her eyes dropped to the top button of his shirt. "You did?"

"Yes."

"Then you're welcome," she said, trying to ignore the fact that it hadn't sounded like much of a thanks. Surely he didn't think she was only throwing herself at him again. She wasn't. She was just concerned about him and a little bit in love with him. That was all.

"Hey," he protested as he lifted her chin to make her look at him. "That's what I really meant. I promise. To be honest, I don't mind you staying close. It's kind of nice."

Her eyebrows lifted incredulously. "Really?"

He nodded. "It's been the best part of this trip. That's for sure."

"Well, now," she drawled, allowing a slow smile to blossom on her lips. "That isn't really saying much, is it?"

"I guess not." She watched his gaze trail down her lips before he stepped away. "I don't know about you but I'm ready to go home."

What was she going to do when she got home? Would the guilt be as strong as it had been before? Her relationship with Lawson had taken a turn for the better. That should ease the burden, shouldn't it? She nodded. "So am I."

Maybe it won't be that bad. I can't stay away from home forever. I wouldn't want to, anyway. I can be

brave like Lawson. Lord willing, I can go home and
face this, then try to move past it.

The rhythm of the train wheels flying over the track
slowed considerably when it reached the outskirts of
town. Ellie tapped Ruth to awaken the woman who
had succumbed to the lulling beat nearly an hour ago.
The housekeeper was kind enough to accompany them
all the way to Peppin, though the two-hour train ride
hardly required it. Lawson was too busy peering out
the window for his first sight of town to notice their
chaperone's critical eye. Apparently, they passed inspection because the woman smiled and settled in for
the last few minutes of their journey.

Their goodbyes at the ranch had been short and to
the point. Lawson didn't have much to say to Clive but
he made sure that Ethan knew what to do to keep Midnight progressing. The greetings at the Peppin train station promised to be something else entirely. A small
crowd of their friends and family milled about. Lawson led the way as they filed out of the train with the
other passengers. He paused and pointed to a droopy
banner visible through the last window of the rail car.
"Why does that say *congratulations?*"

"Maybe it's for someone else." That was all she managed to say because as soon as he helped her down from
the train, their families rushed to greet them. Once
she finished hugging everyone, Nathan pulled her forward so that she stood before the droopy-banner group.
"Ellie, these folks won't believe me. Will you tell them
once and for all that you did not elope with Lawson?"

Before she could answer, Maddie stepped forward.
"It's been all over town since you left. Of course, we
knew you wouldn't have told your families."

She knew that with her answer, she could easily trap Lawson into an engagement and maybe even into a wedding, but she didn't want him that way. "We didn't elope. We aren't engaged. We don't need to be because we had a chaperone the entire trip. Her name is Ruth Gordon and she's standing right there by Lawson. Did that cover everything?"

"Goodness," Sophia Johansen exclaimed. "I don't understand. Don't you like Lawson?"

"Of course I do."

Rhett frowned at her but kept sneaking looks at Amy, who didn't appear to notice. "Doesn't he like you?"

Ellie would have glanced over her shoulder for Lawson's response but her attention snagged on a rather familiar figure leaning against the wall near the ticket booth. Donovan Turner observed the unfolding scene intently. When he saw her watching, he didn't smile. He just kept chewing at the piece of hay in his mouth. Suddenly uncomfortable, she pulled her gaze back to Maddie, who took over the line of questioning again. "Then why are y'all fighting this matchmaking so hard? Don't you know this town is just trying to help?"

"I appreciate that, but some things a man and a woman just have to figure out on their own." She held up a hand to stall their comments. "I know that's ironic coming from me after all the matchmaking I've tried to do over the years, but it's true."

Jeff slipped an arm around Maddie. "Well, I think if Lawson had a lick of sense he'd propose to Ellie right here and now."

Ellie exchanged an exasperated look with her family. "I give up."

"Now, hold on folks," Lawson said in an authoritative voice as he stepped up beside her. "I'm not sure you're taking Ellie seriously here. She's right. While we appreciate and originally encouraged the thought behind the matchmaking, we've had enough. Jeff, you went so far on the matchmaking scheme that you put Ellie on that train out of town. That was uncalled for. Something bad could have happened to her. The rest of you have been spreading rumors and listening to gossip. That isn't right, either. I'm saying it's got to stop. I proposed to Ellie once in jest and she turned me down flat. If I ever proposed to her again, it wouldn't be at the town's command. Now, I think it would be best if we all minded our own business."

The crowd dispersed rather reluctantly. Some of them looked offended. Others looked smugly satisfied. After all, Lawson hadn't said that he would never propose again—just that if he did it would be on his terms not the town's. It left room for hope.

Ellie smiled. Yes, it certainly did.

Crisp autumn wind swept across Lawson's skin as the buggy meandered down a country road toward town. It was good to be back in Peppin. It had been just over a week since their return from his father's ranch and with each day, he gained more distance from the dark past and painful memories he'd visited there. They were still a part of him. He suspected they always would be. But at least now the pain he'd felt so deeply had lessened to the old familiar throb.

Somehow he'd expected to feel some sort of peace or relief at finally facing his memories and his father. It never came. That just didn't seem fair. The experience had been unpleasant at best but now—thankfully—it was over, so where was he supposed to go from here? Forward, maybe? Where would that lead?

His gaze slid to the woman sitting next to him. Ellie had been edging deeper and deeper into his heart since he'd left the Rangers and moved back to Peppin. After the trip to his father's ranch, his attempts to stop her had become dangerously close to halfhearted. She'd stayed by his side despite his at times prickly behavior. She'd always been faithful in her friendship even when he rejected her, and it was obvious that she was open to something more.

It was foolish of him to even consider a relationship with her. Somehow that didn't stop him from thinking about it. The O'Briens, along with his adoptive parents, had always been the family of his heart. He knew for certain they loved him even if no one else did. That meant that Ellie, as one of them, might be the one woman who could possibly see past his faults to truly love him for a lifetime.

She was reading, so she didn't seem to notice that he slowed down to extend their trip into town. He glanced at the book, wondering what was interesting enough about it to keep her from talking to him. It took him a minute to realize it was upside down and probably had been the entire time. A slow grin spread across his face. "Ellie O'Brien, what are you up to?"

"What makes you think I'm up to something?" she asked innocently, not looking up from her book.

"What was the last sentence you read?"

She stilled. The book snapped shut and she tucked it away. "It's a beautiful day, isn't it?"

He shook his head in amusement but agreed. "It certainly is."

She played with the strings of her reticule for a moment. She was nervous, he realized, nervous to be alone with him on the short trip to town. He dared to shift slightly closer. "You look especially nice today."

"Do I?"

He nodded. Her hair had been swept into a loose chignon instead of simply being pulled back with a ribbon like usual. She was wearing a light green dress instead of the usual blouse and riding skirt, which made her eyes look even greener while the cool wind painted her cheeks with a bright hue of pink. "Is today a special occasion or something?"

Her eyes widened in what seemed to be alarm before he realized it was just confusion. "Why? Do I only look nice on special occasions? It's hard to work with the horses in a dress."

"No." He laughed. "I guess I was wondering if you might have done it on my account."

She watched him blankly for a moment, then turned toward him with interest. "You mean you're wondering if I stand by my declaration of intent."

He nodded as they reached the outskirts of town. "Pretty much."

"I stand by it."

"You're not going to give up?" He turned onto his parents' street.

"No! And if you think you can wait me out you have another think coming."

He hopped from the buggy to help her down. "How long are you planning to visit my mother?"

"All afternoon if I can," she said as they walked toward the door. "Doc will take me home. Don't forget that we're having dinner with Sean and Lorelei."

"I won't."

Ellie didn't bother to knock. She just opened the

door and hallooed the house. Lettie told her to come in. He would have gone in as well but Ellie turned to face him, effectively blocking his entry. "I want to talk to your mother privately."

"Why?"

"It's just woman talk. You wouldn't be interested."

"Something tells me I would be." He shifted to the right to try to get around her, but she wouldn't let him pass.

"I think you'd be more interested in hearing what I have to say to you." She waited for him to look her in the eye before she continued. "Lawson, I'm not going to force my attentions on you if you don't want them. If you can look me in the eye and tell me *honestly* that there isn't even the tiniest sliver of hope for us then I won't keep bothering you. Otherwise, I'm going to keep right on doing what I've been doing."

"Good."

A slow smile blossomed on Ellie's lips. "You mean it?"

"I mean it."

Love was the last thing his mother had spoken of before she'd abandoned him. Love didn't still a bottle of whiskey on trek to an eager mouth. It didn't still a hand before a painful slap. To him, that word hadn't meant much for a number of years. Yet, he was beginning to realize that to Ellie, that word meant something else entirely. She came from a family where love meant everything. Taking that into consideration, perhaps Ellie's love was something that truly would last—and that was more than worth capturing. He just needed to figure out some way to do it.

Chapter Seventeen

Ellie waited patiently for Lettie to turn away and check the icing recipe before she stole another taste of the chocolate fluff. It was delicious but she managed to school her ecstasy into an innocent expression before the woman turned around. When Lettie looked at her she was dutifully stirring the cake batter. "Are you sure Lawson doesn't suspect anything?"

Ellie shrugged. "Even if he realizes something is going on, he can't possibly know it's his birthday."

By this point he was probably the only person in town who didn't know. She'd invited half the town to his party tonight. She'd urged them all to be especially nice to him if they saw him in town but not to let the secret slip, no matter what. She prayed everyone would hold their tongue until then.

"He still thinks the two of you are the only ones invited to dinner at Sean and Lorelei's, then?"

"Yes, ma'am."

"Perfect." Lettie deftly handed her a napkin. "Everything is going according to plan."

Ellie lifted the napkin questioningly. "What is this for?"

Lettie tapped her own lips to indicate the chocolate

clinging to Ellie's. She ignored Ellie's guilty grimace to continue. "Maddie insisted on bringing enough fried chicken for everyone. Lorelei and her mother are working on side dishes. We have the desserts and Kate is at home trying not to look suspicious."

"She cooked his favorite foods for breakfast and lunch. He noticed but she pretended it was just a coincidence." Ellie carefully poured the batter into the baking pans. "Do you think the cake, pies and cookies will be enough?"

"Amelia said she'd bring apple turnovers so we'll have plenty. I don't think Peppin has ever seen a party like the one we're throwing. I hope he likes it."

"I'm sure he will." She slid the cake into the oven then froze. "*Amelia* is bringing turnovers? You don't mean Amelia Greene, do you?"

"Certainly."

Ellie closed the oven and turned to face Lettie. "I did *not* invite her."

"We invited the whole town," Lettie said absently as she measured out more cocoa.

"*Not* Mrs. Greene."

She glanced up to frown. "But she already said she was coming."

The last thing Ellie wanted was to spend what was supposed to be an enjoyable evening dodging disapproving looks from Mrs. Greene. Hardness entered into her voice as she insisted, "I don't want her there."

"Why, Ellie," Lettie said after a startled pause. "I don't think I've ever heard that tone from you before. Has something happened between you and Amelia? Other than the usual annoyances, I mean."

Ellie didn't want to lie but she didn't want to tell the truth, either, so she just remained silent.

Lettie narrowed her eyes. "The only time you are ever that quiet is when something is really bothering you. Why don't you tell me what it is?"

"I can't." Emotion nearly choked her voice.

"Sure you can. Keeping it a secret won't make it any easier to deal with."

The tears she'd been holding in for weeks suddenly tumbled down her cheeks. Lettie embraced her but allowed her to cry it out before handing her the napkin to dry her tears. She finally gathered her courage enough to reveal what was bothering her. "Mrs. Greene told me the truth about what I did—and how it led to my parents' deaths. Oh, she didn't tell me it was my fault in so many words but she told me about the rumor I spread, and that triggered the memory of my parents leaving that day because of me, because they had to go apologize to Mrs. Greene. It's my fault they braved the storm that took their lives."

Lettie's eyes began to flash. "Amelia had no business telling you that."

"Why not? It's true. I know it is."

"It's *not* true that you're in any way responsible for your parents' deaths. They did come to town to apologize to Amelia but they didn't have the accident on the way into town. They had it when they left."

"What difference does it make?"

Lettie sighed and brushed the hair away from Ellie's brow. "I was the last one to see them alive. Did you know that?"

"No." Ellie frowned. "I thought it must have been Mrs. Greene."

She shook her head. "Your parents stopped by my house on the way out of town. They told me how they'd apologized to Mrs. Greene for what happened and how she refused to accept the apology. They spoke to me of you, Ellie."

Ellie pulled in a deep breath. "They were disappointed in me, weren't they?"

"No! They knew you'd made a mistake but that in no way changed their opinion of you or their love for you. No one is perfect all the time, Ellie. They never expected that from you."

She allowed that knowledge to settle within her for a moment before the guilt returned with a vengeance. "But it's still my fault they died. They wouldn't have been out there in the first place if it wasn't for me."

"I've thought the same thing about myself over the years." She shook her head sadly. "If only I'd paid more attention to the storm, I might have noticed it was getting worse in time to warn them to stay in town. Then perhaps you wouldn't have lost your parents and I wouldn't have lost my best friend. 'If only' can't change what happened. Your parents made their own decisions and that is no reflection on you or me. Neither of us controls the weather, or has any say in God's plan. I'll never stop missing them, but it's not anyone's fault that they're gone."

"I don't know, Ms. Lettie. I've felt that shame and guilt for so long—even before I remembered what I'd done to make me feel that way. Hearing you say these things doesn't make it disappear." She hugged her arms about herself. "Why, I don't know what I'd do if Sean or Kate found out about this."

"Your siblings knew."

Ellie's eyes widened in a mixture of surprise, horror and confusion. "They did? But they never told me.

They never even acted as though they knew. I thought for sure they'd blame me even if they tried to hide it."

"Perhaps you should talk to them about it. However, I don't think they ever blamed you. That may be why they never made an issue of it."

Ellie shook her head in disbelief. "Mrs. Greene led me to believe she was the only one who knew about it. I've spent the last few weeks doing my best to keep this quiet."

"Amelia Greene needs to learn a few lessons about forgiveness. She's carried that anger in her heart until it turned her into a bitter woman. You just leave her to me."

"This is my battle."

"You are my best friend's daughter. If I can't fight for you against the likes of Amelia then who can? It's time she dealt with someone of her own age and standing. I mean to see that she does. Don't worry about her one more minute."

Ellie smiled at her. "Thank you for telling me all of this. I feel better—not exactly exonerated but better than before."

"I'm glad, dear." She paused thoughtfully before continuing, "I think in this situation, the only sin you might be guilty of is that you spread gossip when you were eight. I don't think you've indulged in that since then but you can ask God to forgive you of that and He will. However, if you really want to get rid of the guilt you feel, you need to forgive yourself."

"I know you're right." Ellie bit her lip.

"Yes, but knowing it and doing it are two separate things, aren't they? You have to make the decision for yourself. Think it over. I'll be praying for you."

"Thank you. I'm sure I'll need it."

* * *

Lawson followed Ellie up the porch steps of Sean and Lorelei's house, inspecting the hat in his hands thoughtfully. "Ellie, do you like this hat?"

"What?" she asked distractedly. "Yes."

"That's what I said when Mr. Johansen asked me at his mercantile. He said he wouldn't be able to sell that hat to anyone else and outright asked me to take it off his hands for practically nothing. Don't you think that's odd? This is a perfectly good hat and I feel kind of like I stole it."

Ellie stopped to survey him laughingly. "Maybe he meant it as a gift."

"Why would he give me a gift?" He reached out to stop her when she continued walking toward the door. "Come to think of it, that happened a lot today. Maddie wouldn't let me pay for the pie and coffee I had at her café."

"Uh-huh." She tugged him onward.

"Maybe the town is trying to make up for the match-making fiasco—"

"I don't think so." She knocked on the door.

"Well, it's downright peculiar."

Lorelei's voice called from inside, "Come in. The door is open."

"People have been really nice—almost overly so. There has to be an explanation." Ellie stared at him with an amused smile but she was listening intently, so he kept going. "Nathan took me aside to tell me what a good job I've been doing. At first I thought he was going to fire me or… Aren't you going to open the door?"

She stepped aside. "Be my guest."

He frowned but complied. She went in ahead of him

so he pulled the door closed behind them. He realized the house was full of people only an instant before they all yelled, "Surprise!"

He glanced around at the familiar faces in confusion before settling on Ellie's. The party must be for her. He echoed "surprise" to pretend that he'd known all along. Why hadn't anyone told him this was a surprise party for Ellie? He hadn't gotten her a present or anything. *Wait a minute. Ellie's birthday already passed.*

"What is going on?"

"It's your birthday," Ellie explained. "Everyone is here to celebrate you."

He pulled her closer as if that would give them some modicum of privacy. "Ellie, you know I don't celebrate my birthday because I don't know when it is."

"It's today. Your birth certificate says so." She handed him a folded piece of paper.

"My birth certificate?" He stared at the paper. *Lawson Clive Hardy.* His gaze stumbled over his middle name and he frowned before he moved on. *Born...* His head shot up. "It's my birthday!"

Cheers echoed through the room. Suddenly, he was receiving hugs from everyone, which was no small feat since it looked as though half the town had shown up. Everyone had a quick word or good wish for him. It was overwhelming. He was glad when his parents finally made it through the fray for their chance to hug him. "Y'all didn't have to do this."

Lettie smiled knowingly. "*We* didn't. Ellie was the main one who planned and carried this out."

Doc nodded. "A few others chipped in but it was her idea."

"Why would she go through the trouble of doing all

this?" He frowned as he spotted her talking with Amy, Sophia and Lorelei.

Doc placed a hand on his shoulder. "Son, I think it's pretty obvious to everyone how that girl feels about you. Don't you think it's about time you figured out what you're going to do about it?"

A wry smile touched his lips. "I'm working on it."

"Well, praise the Lord for that," Lettie said with such obvious relief that he laughed.

Lawson was surprised to discover that an entire meal had been planned in his honor. Sean and Lorelei's dining room was too small to accommodate a sit-down dinner inside, so pretty soon everyone headed outside to a small clearing behind the house. It seemed this was where the real party was to take place. Several long tables filled the clearing, including one that functioned as a buffet. Lanterns hung from the trees in preparation for nightfall. Guests wasted little time in filling their plates and settled in for a night filled with friends and laughter.

Lawson found himself seated at a table with his parents, the Rutledges and the O'Briens. They automatically saved the seat beside him for Ellie, who, after bustling about to make sure that all was well, finally made her way to the table. He waited until they were nearly finished eating to say, "I can't believe you did all of this for me."

She blushed in the fading light of sunset. "It was fun. Honestly, it sort of took on a life of its own once the town caught wind of it. I hadn't planned on this many people coming. Apparently, this town is very fond of you."

"I never would have imagined this many people really cared about me."

He didn't realize how pitiful that statement must have sounded until Ellie's eyes filled with compassion. "Of course they do. You grew up here. It's your hometown. You belong here."

"I didn't stumble into Peppin until I was fourteen," he corrected doubtfully.

She lifted her chin. "I don't see how that changes anything I just said."

He grinned slowly and shook his head. "That's because you're stubborn."

"This town is blessed to have you and we know it. You're blessed to have us, too, so it's equal all the way around." She hesitated a moment before shifting closer. "You know what I've realized since we came back from the ranch?"

He found himself leaning toward her. "What?"

"If your parents hadn't abandoned you, your life would be completely different and not necessarily for the better."

He stiffened slightly but decided to hear her out. "What are you getting at?"

"You would have stayed with them. Your father told me that coming to terms with leaving you behind was what made him turn his life around. If you were with them, your parents would have continued with the drinking, the fighting, the stealing. You would have been subjected to the lifestyle they led and the environment they lived in. You wouldn't have had the same opportunities. You probably never would have come to this town, which means you wouldn't have met Nathan. He's the one who led you to the Lord, so you may not even have become a Christian. Doc and Ms. Lettie wouldn't have adopted you. You would never have known what a normal family is supposed to be like.

You might have followed in your father's footsteps and become an outlaw. Should I go on?"

"No," he said quietly as he leaned back in his chair to take it all in. He'd known all along that he was blessed to live in a town like Peppin, to have met Ellie's family and have been adopted into one of his own. However, he hadn't been willing to connect his parents' abandonment to the life he led now. Was this what the Bible meant about God taking the bad and working it out for something good? Was that what grace was—being able to live in the "good" that wasn't a sensible outcome of life's events?

He remembered Pastor Brightly's sermon on the subject not so long ago. He'd focused on the Scripture about the sins of the fathers not being visited on the sons, but if he remembered correctly, there was another key component to living in grace—forgiveness. Suddenly, he thought about his father. He swallowed hard. Surely he didn't have to forgive his parents for what they'd done to him. It wasn't fair of God to ask such a thing of him.

What would I get in return for that, Lord? Would the pain go away? How about whatever stigma I might have that keeps people from loving me? Something inside of him seemed to check that thought and make him take stock of all the people who had gathered to celebrate him. It was then he realized the truth. People *did* care about him. They *did* love him. He was the one who kept holding back out of fear they would abandon him.

Would it take forgiving his parents to break free of that fear? His jaw clenched. He hoped not because he wasn't even sure if doing that was possible.

"Lawson, did I say something wrong?"

He glanced up to meet her concern and covered her

hand with his. "No. You said something right. I am a very blessed man. I appreciate the life God has given me. The problem is that the past is just always…there."

"I know it is but so is God." She glanced at their hands and turned hers to allow her fingers to thread through his. She met his gaze. "And so am I."

He stared at the incredible woman before him in awe. Physically she was so beautiful that she could make his heart forget to beat with just a look. But more important, she was everything he'd never allowed himself to hope for on the inside. She was warm, genuine, *committed*—and to him, no less. She saw past his protective barriers to the man he truly was. Yet, her time, her attention, even the look in her eyes, telegraphed that he mattered—not only to her but to the world in general.

He knew right then and there that she was the only woman he'd be willing to risk his heart for. He also knew that to do so would take courage on his part. Not just when he asked her to marry him, which he surely would, but every day for the rest of his life. It would take courage to believe that he was enough to make her stay. He couldn't—not yet…but one day. One day soon.

A throat cleared a few feet away. He suddenly realized how close he was to Ellie and how they must appear to everyone with their heads together and hands clasped. He released her hand to direct his attention to Lettie, who stood at his side. Her smile barely hid her excitement at the scene before her. "I hate to interrupt but I can't find the candles and it's nearly time to cut the cake."

"I think I left them in the kitchen." Ellie pushed back from the table. "I'll get them."

Both Ellie and Lettie walked away, leaving Lawson to take a swig of his forgotten glass of cider. He'd also forgotten that Ellie's brother had been sitting on the other side of her until Sean took the opportunity of her absence to turn toward him. "So when are you going to propose to my little sister?"

After a momentary pause in which he decided against playing dumb, Lawson set his cup aside and shrugged. "I'm not sure. I didn't even know I was going to marry her until about a minute ago."

Sean nodded. "Yep, I saw that poleaxed look from all the way over here."

"When the time comes will I be asking your permission or Nathan's or both?"

"Why don't the three of us talk about it on my day off next week?"

Lawson nodded soberly. No doubt they would have a few deep questions to ask, most likely spiritual in nature. Lawson would be ready for them. At least, he hoped he would be.

Chapter Eighteen

Ellie breathed a prayer of thanks for Lettie's timely interruption. She'd never seen Lawson's gaze quite as intense as it had been a few minutes ago and had certainly never been the subject of it. It had done funny things to her…chiefly, it had stopped her ability to think and hampered her ability to breathe. The connection between them had been so real—nearly tangible. What did it mean?

She brushed her cool hand across her warm cheek and tucked a wisp of hair behind her ear as she forced herself to focus on the task at hand. She entered the house to find a few stragglers remained. Her eyes narrowed at the sight of Mrs. Greene conversing with Donovan Turner in the sitting room. *I definitely did* not *invite him, either.*

"I guess some people think they can just show up anywhere whether invited or not," she muttered to herself as she snatched the candles from the counter, then searched for matches. She let a drawer close with a bit too much force. The bang was enough to draw the attention of the two people she was glaring at. Caught, she quickly turned her grimace into a detached smile, though she felt more like sticking out her tongue.

Mrs. Greene glanced away almost guiltily. No doubt she'd been gossiping about Ellie and Lawson. Donovan didn't have the sense to look away. He even offered Ellie a smile, which she pretended not to see before she breezed out the door. She *wouldn't* let either of them ruin her evening. She'd promised to leave Mrs. Greene to Lettie. She'd also promised Nathan and Lawson to avoid Donovan. She planned to do both of those things starting now.

She pulled in a deep breath of cool autumn air as she followed the lighted path back to the clearing. The combination of perfect weather and clear skies prepared the way for the dusky descent of twilight. It would be easy to enjoy the rest of the evening. If her resolve to do so was ever in danger, she knew she'd only have to take one look at Lawson's joyful if slightly stunned face to remember the true purpose of the evening.

She finally reached the clearing. As she glanced around for Lettie, a shadow separated from the trail behind her to step into the light. She swallowed her alarm. Donovan. He had probably been only a few feet behind her the entire time and she'd never even noticed. She tried to calm her nerves. There was no reason to be frightened. Perhaps he just happened to be walking the same direction at the same time.

Right, she thought sarcastically. Still, there was no real cause for her to be jumpy. It was just Nathan's overprotective warnings that had her on edge. He stepped toward her as if her frown was an invitation to speak. "I got my pig farm back."

Oh, thank goodness. He had some reason for seeking her out after all. "Did the judge help you?"

"No." His chest expanded with pride. "The man I sold it to gave me my deed back."

She tilted her head in confusion. "He *gave* it to you—just like that?"

His smile seemed to take on an almost sinister gleam in the dim light. "Well, I might have used a little persuasion."

She blinked and his smiled seemed normal again. She backed up a step. "I should probably go."

"What's the rush?"

"Ellie, there you are," Ms. Lettie said, unintentionally coming to her rescue. She didn't seem to notice that Ellie was speaking with someone else. Perhaps because Donovan remained in the shadows. "Let's put the candles on the cake. I think people are getting restless."

Grateful for the interruption, she gave a little wave to Donovan, then helped Lettie place the candles on the cake. After a few minutes, she was able to put the unsettling episode out of mind—or at least save it to examine later. They were about to light the candles when Lawson stopped them. "Before we cut the cake, I'd like to say a few words."

It took a moment for everyone to gather around. Ellie stepped closer to Lettie when Mrs. Greene appeared at her husband's side. Lettie whispered, "I haven't talked to her yet but I will."

Ellie nodded, then focused on Lawson. He cleared his throat, looking endearingly unused to being the center of attention. "I just want to thank everyone for coming. It means the world to me to have you all here. I can tell you right now that it's the best birthday I've ever had."

Laughter filled the air. Lawson grinned, seeming more at ease. "I've never had an opportunity like this where practically the whole town is listening to my every word. It probably won't happen again so I figure I'd better make the most of it by saying a few words to some very special people. Doc and Lettie, you raised me to be the man I am today. I don't think I tell you enough what that meant to me or how much *you* mean to me."

Doc stepped up to put his arm around his wife. "It's been an honor."

"It surely has," Lettie echoed.

Lawson nodded, took a moment to wrangle his emotions to a more manageable state and continued. "I'm also grateful to Nathan and Kate Rutledge. If you hadn't taken me in all those years ago, I don't want to imagine where I'd be or who I would be now."

Nathan grinned. "That was definitely one of our better decisions. Wouldn't you agree, Mrs. Rutledge?"

"It was." Kate nodded then teased, "He didn't stay with us for more than a few months back then but we have him now, don't we?"

Lawson laughed as did everyone else. "Aside from thanking you for hosting this shindig, Sean and Lorelei, what can I say? Y'all are just about the best friends a man could ask for."

Sean nodded his appreciation and Lorelei smiled but they refrained from commenting. Then Lawson looked at Ellie. Was it her imagination or did anticipation float through on a breeze? Suddenly, everyone was at attention. Her friends even leaned forward slightly. She barely refrained from rolling her eyes. What did they think was going to happen? A proposal? Not likely.

She tilted her head thoughtfully. *What is he going to say, though? I wonder if he'll try to be romantic or if he'll just focus on our friendship. No doubt every-*

one will pick whatever statement he makes apart in an effort to discern his feelings for me... He is taking an awfully long time to come up with something.

"Ellie," he began, "I think what I said to you earlier today made it pretty clear how much I've come to—" he cast about for an appropriate word before settling on "—*appreciate* your…ah…friendship."

It took her a moment to realize he was referring to their conversation in the buggy. "Oh. Yes, of course."

I will not *blush. That would give away too much to all of the folks staring at me right now.* For once her cheeks obeyed. A smile tilted her lips and she nodded at him in deference. *Very clever. You told me something yet managed not to tell them anything at all. Won't that leave everyone just itching to know what you said earlier today?*

He seemed to understand what she was thinking for he grinned. "I hear you are also the one to thank for coordinating this celebration. You did a great job. Now…how about that cake?"

"Yeah, Ellie, how about that cake?" Sean asked, obviously not referring to the cake and with no other purpose than to tease her.

He wasn't the only one wondering, because the conversations that should have continued now that Lawson was done with his announcement, didn't. She just smiled secretively as she lit the candles. "Wouldn't you like to know? It's too bad I'm not telling."

Sean winked at her as if he already knew. She wrinkled her nose at him then stepped aside so Lawson could make his wish and blow out the candles. It only took one breath from him to make those tiny fires go out but the one in her heart blazed all the brighter. She would just focus on that, not on the ache that filled her chest from her conversation with Lettie earlier today. Her gaze met Lawson's and somehow that made it easier to smile.

A nod from Nathan was enough to make Lawson push back from the table after their midday meal a few days later. Sean did the same. Lorelei looked at them in confusion. "Where are you men going in such a hurry?"

"We're just going to have a talk," Nathan answered. "Make sure we aren't disturbed, will you, Kate?"

"Since when do men talk?"

"Very funny." Nathan pressed a kiss on Kate's forehead before leaving the room.

"We promised the children we'd play with them," Lorelei reminded Sean.

He kissed her cheek. "We will when I come back."

Lawson looked at Ellie. She watched Sean leave the room then met his gaze with a cheeky smile. "I think I'm supposed to protest."

"And I'm supposed to kiss you." He glanced at the other women. "Or is that only for married folks?"

Kate shook her head and swept a hand in Ellie's direction. "Go right ahead."

Lorelei nodded. "Just keep it respectable."

He leaned over, lifted Ellie's chin and placed a kiss on the tip of her nose. "How was that?"

"Well done," Kate said.

As soon as he left the room he heard Lorelei ask, "What *did* he say to you on his birthday?"

He met the other men outside. Nathan told them to follow him, then led them into the barn and up the ladder to the hayloft. Lawson let out a low whistle once he saw a huge fort made out of hay. "That's impressive."

Nathan nodded. "The children started it. I told

them to take it down but as we moved things around, it turned into this instead."

Sean shook his head in awe. "Lawson, why didn't we think of doing this when we were children?"

"I don't know." He frowned. "Are we really going to have this discussion in a hay fort? What's wrong with the parlor?"

"The sound carries."

"I always forget that."

"Everyone does unless they're in the kitchen…except for me. Sometimes that's the only way I know what's going on in my own house." Nathan clasped him on the shoulder. "Now, stop being nervous and enjoy the moment. Let's go inside."

Lawson's first impression of the fort was right. It was impressive. It had four outer walls of hay. Each wall had a window and the front one had a door they had to crawl to get through. The inside was partitioned into three rooms. They found their hay chairs in the last one. Nathan was the first to start things off. "Sean tells me there is a question you want to ask me."

"I'd like to marry Ellie."

"I figured that." Nathan nodded, then leaned forward, bracing his elbows on his knees. "You know you're like a brother to Sean and me, so this discussion isn't so much about whether you're suitable or not. I told you a long time ago that I couldn't imagine a better man for our Ellie. However, we're still going to ask you some questions to make sure you know you're doing the right thing for the both of you."

"Fair enough."

"Why do you want to marry Ellie?"

"I love her."

"What does God say about it?"

The question threw him for a moment. He cleared his throat. "I can't say that I've heard a direct command from Him to marry her. It's just more of a knowing inside me."

That seemed to satisfy Nathan. Lawson turned to Sean expecting him to speak up now. He wasn't disappointed. "How has your father's sudden reappearance affected your relationship with Ellie?"

"I think it's made my feelings for her stronger. She stood by me during my trip to his ranch. That meant a lot to me."

Sean played with a loose piece of hay as he considered that. "Have you forgiven your father, Lawson?"

"I thought we were talking about Ellie," he said tensely.

"We'll get back to her." Sean tossed the hay on the floor. "This is important, too."

Lawson looked to Nathan, hoping the man might be able to get their discussion back on track. He was disappointed when his boss shrugged. "I'm concerned about that, too. For your sake, I hope you have, but I can tell you probably haven't. There is a lot of anger stored up inside of you, Lawson. You hide it well but it's been there as long as I've known you."

"Anger isn't always a bad thing," he countered.

"You're right. The Bible says there is such a thing as righteous anger. But I have a feeling that holding on to that anger has let a lot of other things slip in, as well."

"Like what, exactly?"

"Fear…self-doubt…maybe a little bitterness. Am I hitting anywhere close to home?" At Lawson's hesitant nod, he gave a grim nod. "I thought so."

"It isn't worth it, Lawson," Sean advised. "It isn't worth holding on to that anger if you have to forfeit so much to keep it. You're a good man but I don't think you realize that. You seem to still see yourself as that child who was abandoned. That hasn't been you for a very long time."

"I know." He sighed. "I've been thinking the same thing myself lately. I'm not sure how to forgive Clive, though."

Nathan shrugged and leaned back onto the hay wall. "I think you just have to let it go. Make the decision to forgive him even if you don't feel it, then let God work out the rest."

Sean nodded. "It may not happen immediately but it will in time."

"What about the anger?"

Nathan smiled wryly. "I've found that if I'm angry at someone it helps to pray for them. It's probably the last thing I want to do at the moment but it's effective eventually."

"I'll try that."

Sean nodded. "I asked you about your father because I see how your inability to forgive him—as wrong as he was—could transfer to others you care about, including Ellie. I love my sister but she isn't perfect, which means she's going to mess up. So what happens if she disappoints you in some way? Are you going to turn away from her? Or will you love her anyway and seek her out to show her that? That's the kind of love I want for both of you."

Lawson stared at the hay-laden floor thoughtfully. Had he ever loved in that way before? No, he hadn't. But that was the kind of love he'd always wanted for himself. If he hadn't given it then why did he expect to receive it?

He gritted his teeth. *I really have let my anger and*

*unforgiveness bind me to my past. Nathan and Sean
are right. I have to let it go. It's the only way to have
the life that I want.*

"All right, Lord," he prayed, hardly realizing he
spoke aloud until Sean and Nathan bowed their heads.
"I'm letting go of my anger and I choose to forgive my
father." He paused, realizing that was the first time he'd
ever called Clive that. Just like that, anger welled up
inside of him. He shook his head. "You know I don't
feel it but I guess I'll have to trust You to fix that. Help
me to love Ellie the way You love her. In Jesus' name,
Amen."

He eyed the men he'd hoped to call his brothers-in-
law. "I guess this means I don't have your permission
to marry Ellie."

Nathan and Sean exchanged a look before Sean said,
"Are you crazy? Of course you can marry Ellie."

"You mean it?" he asked, even as relief settled over
him in a thick wave.

Nathan nodded. "Everybody is working on something in their faith. If they aren't, then they should be.
That isn't enough to disqualify you. Just be mindful
of what we said. That prayer was proof you're already
working on it."

"How soon are you going to propose?"

"I don't know. I'd like to be a bit surer of her feelings for me before I ask."

Sean grinned. "The only way to know for sure is
to ask."

"I guess you're right." To be honest, the thought of
doing so slightly terrified him. If she said no, he'd just
keep loving her and hope eventually that love would

turn back into just plain friendship. Wasn't that the right answer? He hoped so because it was the only one he had.

Chapter Nineteen

Ellie placed her chin on her fist as she stared thought-fully out of the sitting room window toward the barn. "What do you think they're doing out there?"

Lorelei spilled a handful of jacks on the low table as she tried to beat her niece's record score. "They're probably playing Cowboys and Indians in that fort Timothy was telling us about."

Everyone giggled at that. Ellie sat back in her chair. "Oh, I haven't played that game in such a long time. I wish they would have invited me."

Lorelei glanced up with a grin. "I keep forgetting you were a tomboy growing up."

"I'll never forget." Kate groaned. "I thought I'd never see the end of those knee-patched bloomers you always wore."

"They were comfortable. I'll tell you that much." She glanced out the window. "Here they come. Oh, no!"

"Did someone get shot with an arrow?" Kate asked.

Dread filled her stomach as the men greeted their new visitor. "Worse. Mrs. Greene is here. What on earth could she want?"

A thousand awful scenarios played out in her mind

as they all came inside. When Mrs. Greene announced her desire to speak to Ellie alone, curious looks were exchanged but everyone left them alone in the parlor. Ellie closed the door firmly behind them. She smoothed her skirt, then turned around to face her foe. "How can I help you, Mrs. Greene?"

Mrs. Greene took a seat on the settee, though Ellie hadn't offered her one. "Please sit down. I'd like to say what I came here to say without you hovering."

Ellie took her sweet time in taking the chair next to the settee. "Go right ahead."

The woman pulled in a deep breath. "I did wrong by you and I'm sorry for it. You came to me that day hoping for reconciliation. Instead, I offered you your worst nightmare served on a silver platter."

"Ms. Lettie talked to you."

"She did. My conscience had been bothering me, anyway."

Ellie surveyed her for a moment. "I hope you know how hard it is for me to believe you're sincere right now."

"I don't know how I'd be able to prove it to you." She grimaced and took her handkerchief out of her reticule to twist it nervously. "I realized how upset your parents would be if they knew I'd let you take the full blame for their deaths. We didn't part on good terms, and as disappointed as they were in you for spreading the secret, I think they were equally disappointed in me for refusing to forgive a child's mistake. They told me if I so much as mentioned that episode in your presence I'd have them to deal with and not you. I guess all of that anger in me built and built until even your apology wasn't enough. I wanted to hurt you and I suppose I did. I don't expect you to forgive me, but I am sorry."

"I understand why you felt the need to tell me." Ellie sighed. "For some reason, forgiving you isn't that hard. It's me I can't forgive." She shook away her thoughts and stood. "Thank you for coming, Mrs. Greene. I hope this means we can call a truce. We've done enough damage to each other already, haven't we?"

"I reckon we have." Mrs. Greene reached out to squeeze her hand. "I truly am sorry. Goodbye, dear."

Having Mrs. Greene call her "dear" somehow took the last of Ellie's strength out of her. She managed to wait until the woman left before collapsing onto the chair. She covered her face with her hands and tried to ignore the tears that stole down her cheek. It made no sense to cry now. Mrs. Greene had apologized. That was one load off her shoulders.

Perhaps it was just the reminder of her hand in her parents' deaths that did it. She'd been so good at avoiding that fact since she'd gotten back from the ranch. She'd stopped thinking about it every hour and now only thought about it every day or so. She tried to put Clive's words into action. *Don't let one mistake define your life.* That had only worked to an extent. Maybe it was time to try Lettie's advice about forgiving herself.

Suddenly she was aware that she was not alone. She glanced up to find her entire family and Lawson filing into the room. A small cry of dismay filtered through her lips as she realized they had probably all gone to the kitchen, which meant they'd heard every word of her exchange with Mrs. Greene. She wiped the tears from her cheeks and grimaced. "All of you heard. Well, it's true. All of it's true. It's my fault our parents died. I didn't want to tell you, but Ms. Lettie said you already knew."

Kate nodded slowly. "I knew why they went into

town that day but I had no idea you thought it was your fault. Oh, my dear little sister."

Suddenly she was enveloped in her sister's arms. Tears fell freely down Ellie's face. "You don't have to pretend that you don't blame me. Please, don't. I couldn't stand it."

"No one has to pretend, Ellie. We don't blame you," Sean said fiercely as he wrapped his arms around them both. "You were a child. You couldn't have known what you said, let alone that Ma and Pa would rush out into a threatening storm the moment they found out."

Kate stepped back to look at her face. "Tell me you believe us."

Ellie searched their faces. She wasn't sure yet if she agreed with them, but she could see that they meant what they'd said. She nodded. Sean handed her a freshly pressed handkerchief from his pocket. As she wiped away her tears he said, "As for you not forgiving yourself…"

"Yes?"

His tone gentled. "I don't see the point of it. You aren't going to bring Ma and Pa back by doing that. You're only going to make us sad and yourself miserable."

"He's right, Ellie."

"I suppose." She sounded about as unconvinced as she felt. It seemed after that everyone else wanted a chance to hug her—even her nieces and nephew. Lawson hugged her last. Once she stepped from his embrace she turned to everyone else and offered a trembling smile. "So what's this I hear about a fort?"

The first fire of the season blazed in the farmhouse's fireplace the next evening. The snap of cooler weather seemed to make everyone huddle a little closer to each other for the Rutledge family's Bible reading. At least that was the excuse Lawson gave himself for his close proximity to Ellie. She sat beside him on the settee with her feet tucked under her and a shawl draped around her shoulders. Kate sat in the rocker with Grace on her lap. Hope and Timothy sat at their father's feet as he read. Baby Matthew was already asleep.

Everything around Lawson seemed peaceful, homey and warm. He was beginning to think this sort of life might be possible for him.... His gaze slid to Ellie. For them. He was going to ask her soon. He just needed to figure out what to do about getting a ring.

Nathan seemed to give special emphasis to the last few passages, which conveniently focused on forgiveness, before closing the Bible. Kate and Nathan ushered their children off to bed, leaving him alone with Ellie. Kate paused at the door on her way out. "Lawson, I finished mending that sweater of yours. Be sure to get it from me before you leave."

He agreed to find her as Ellie yawned and stretched like a drowsy cat. He smiled at her. "Don't tell me you were sleeping. I'm pretty sure Nathan read that selection specifically for us."

"I wasn't sleeping." She groaned as she pushed the wisps of hair away from her face. She'd taken to wearing it up more often but by the end of the day it always seemed to anticipate its escape from the orderly style. "I barely slept last night. I just lay awake thinking."

"About your parents?" At her nod, he frowned. "I had no idea you were going through that. I wish I could have helped you in some way since you've been so supportive of me."

"I was ashamed. I didn't want anyone to know. I thought it would be easier that way."

"Was it?"

"No." Her smile signaled she was ready to change the subject. "I know Nathan read those passages to try to help me forgive myself. Why do you think he was directing them at you?"

He smiled wryly. "I decided to forgive my father."

"Really?" She leaned forward with interest. "How is that working for you?"

"Better than I thought it would, actually." He rose to bank the fire. "It seems like you just have to decide that's what you're going to do and stick with it."

Her silence made him glance over his shoulder at her. She watched him thoughtfully for a moment then joined him in front of the fireplace. "I don't think I'm quite as brave as you are."

"I'm not brave. I just got tired of feeling so many negative emotions all the time." He shoveled ashes over the fire logs then paused, realizing this was as good a time as any to try to get one last reading on her feelings for him. Setting the shovel aside, he captured her gaze. "I thought maybe I'd try a few more positive ones for a change."

Her fingers stilled for an instant before they continued on their route to tuck an escaping piece of golden hair behind her ear. Curiosity tinged her green eyes with gold, or perhaps that was just from the remnants of the fire. "Like what, for instance?"

He hid a grin, thankful that somehow she'd asked exactly the right question. He stood to his feet. Should he tell her he loved her right here and now? He couldn't seem to form the words. Despite her talk of his bravery, he didn't have the courage to declare his independence from his personal history. Surely that's what those three little words would mean—that he believed the abandonment of the past would stop here and now because he loved her and she loved him. Or did she?

He might not be able to ask that question with words but he needed to know how she felt. She must have recognized his intent, for her eyes widened as he erased the distance between them. She didn't step away. He lowered his head. Her lashes drifted down to rest on her cheek, so she didn't see the hopeful smile that passed across his lips in the moment before he kissed her.

She leaned into him. One hand came to rest on his chest and the other behind his neck. His arms encircled her waist before he broke away to press a kiss against her temple.

Well, that settles it, he thought as he held her close. *There is no way she'd kiss me like that if she didn't love me.*

Footsteps sounded in the hall. He released her just before Nathan walked in. His friend took one look at them and raised his eyebrows. "Don't mind me. I just needed one of these lamps."

Ellie blushed then said good-night to both of them before slipping out of the room. Lawson ignored the knowing look on Nathan's face to ask, "Is Kate around?"

"In the kitchen, I think."

Lawson found Kate folding his sweater. "Thanks for doing this."

"You're welcome. Before you go… Nathan can't keep a secret from me to save his life so I wanted to give you this." She opened a small leather pouch and pulled out a ring. "This has passed down through the women in my family for generations. My grandmother gave it to my father before he asked Ma to marry him. Now, I'm giving it to you."

"Didn't you want it?"

She smiled. "Nathan gave me a ring of his own. I didn't want to refuse it. Lorelei ended up using her family's ring since she was an only child. I hoped to catch you before you made any arrangements and that you'd want to give it to Ellie."

"Of course I do." He accepted the gold ring from her to examine it carefully. Two hands embraced a heart-shaped emerald that rested under a crown. "I've never seen anything like this."

"It's a traditional Irish token of undying love called a Claddagh ring."

"I think I'd better keep it in that pouch until it's time for me to use it." He carefully slid the ring inside then tucked it into his shirt pocket. "I was thinking tomorrow might be a good time."

"You move fast."

He nodded. "I've made up my mind so I see no use in stalling. Do you think you could prepare a picnic basket for us? She'd probably enjoy another visit to the creek before it gets too cold."

Kate's blue eyes began to dance. "I'd be honored."

He nodded his thanks. He was finally going to put his past behind him. He was ready and he was pretty sure Ellie was, too.

Ellie spread out the picnic blanket on the grassy bank of the creek, making sure to stay far enough from the water to keep from getting muddy. She set aside the picnic basket Kate had given her and lay in a warm patch of sunlight to read her book as she waited for Lawson to arrive. It was awfully sweet of him to invite her on this picnic. She smiled, thinking of last night's kiss. His attentions had certainly been marked as of late. Perhaps he would ask to court her again soon. Then maybe she would have rectified at least one mistake. Not that doing so was the only reason she hoped he'd ask. After all, she was pretty sure this was what love must feel like.

Had it only been a few months since she'd resolved to find a husband and petitioned God to help her? She'd had no idea what a mess she was going to get herself into. Thankfully, that mess seemed to straighten out after she'd asked God to lead her in her relationship with Lawson. She was thankful for that so why did she still feel as if she was holding back? Why could she only say she was "pretty sure" this was what love was like?

She lowered her book to frown at it thoughtfully. *I guess I'm still expecting my problems to vanish because Lawson cares for me. Kate told me that wouldn't happen. Why am I still longing for someone to ride in on a white horse and save me—rescue me from the stains of my past?*

Suddenly, the words of a hymn she'd learned as a child sprang to her lips. "What can wash away my sins? Nothing but the blood of Jesus."

She sat up abruptly. How on earth could she have forgotten something as basic as that? Romance didn't have the power to heal her hurts or make her feel clean. Only God could do that. Even He could only do that if she let Him. Lawson could and had been a tool God used to accomplish that but ultimately the hero she longed for was God. Could that be right?

It was. She could feel it all the way down to her soul. "Oh, what a fool I've been! Lord, I'm so sorry! Forgive me for seeking a man when I should have been seeking You. Wash me clean. I let go of my past and place it in Your hands."

Relief spread through her and blossomed into a burgeoning sense of peace. She'd loved her parents with all of her heart. She never would have done anything to hurt them intentionally. She'd made a mistake but that hadn't changed their love for her. It hadn't changed God's love for her. They would never have wanted her to live a life filled with guilt. God certainly didn't. So…though a tear slipped down her cheek, she finally let them go. She finally let their memory rest in peace.

She smiled and allowed herself to fall back onto the blanket. What a long journey it had taken to get to this point, but she was here and that's what mattered. She shook her head ruefully. *Poor Lawson. All this time I've been putting unreal expectations on his love. Given his past, I wonder how he could even care for me at all.*

It would be different now. She was different now, changed by love—God's love—the way she'd wanted to be. She was so lost in her thoughts that she didn't hear the sound of Lawson's approach until his boots landed in her peripheral vision. She sat up to greet him with a smile that stalled on her lips.

It wasn't Lawson.

Alarm filled her as she met the too intense gaze of the man before her. *Donovan.*

Ellie quickly stood to her feet, clenching her book in her hands nervously as she faced the man who watched her with what appeared to be a desperate hunger. "Donovan, what are you doing here?"

His hands slipped into his coat pockets as he seemed overcome with a sudden shyness. "I've wanted to talk to you for days but you were never alone."

She crossed her arms. "Have you been watching me all that time?"

"I wanted to talk to you," he repeated, avoiding her gaze.

She took that as a yes. Her gaze swept the woods around her as she suddenly became aware of their seclusion. No one would hear her if she screamed for help. Then again, she might not need help. She met Donovan's gaze once more. Maybe he really did just want to talk to her. *Alone...after he's been watching me for days... I don't think so.*

Suddenly, relief surged through her as she remembered. "Lawson will be here soon. You should leave. Come to the house later today and we'll talk then."

His entire demeanor changed from shy to contemptuous. "You're meeting Lawson? Why? That spoils everything.... No, that makes it better...much better."

"Yes, it does," she agreed. No doubt Lawson would be able to handle him in no time. "You two can figure things out and I'll just stay out of it."

"You don't understand." He caught her arm, which was crossed at her chest and thus brought him uncomfortably close to her. "I love you. I won't stand for you being with him anymore."

Right. She stepped away from his touch. "I don't see how you have any say in that matter."

"Oh, I'll have a say, all right. As a matter of fact, you're going to do *exactly* what I say. Do you understand?"

"Certainly not. I—" Her words stopped abruptly when she saw the gun he eased from his coat pocket. She realized that for now it was probably best to stop talking and listen to what he had to say. "What do you want me to do?"

He grinned and rocked back onto his heels. "That's more like it. First things first. You're going to sit down right where I found you and act like nothing has happened when he rides up. Then you're going to break things off with him. I want to hear you do it so no mumbling or whispering or trying to warn him because if you do—" he waggled the gun in her face "—that's it for him."

She stared at him trying to understand the strange words he was speaking. He couldn't be serious. But he was. He definitely was. Fear muddled her thoughts. He seemed to realize that for he stepped forward with the gun pointed at her chest. "I know I'm scaring you, Ellie. I'm sorry for that but you have to do what I say. I promise not to hurt you, but one little slip and I'll kill him."

He took her arm and led her back to the blanket. "That's it. Sit down right there. Read your book. I'm going to hide. I'll be close enough to hear and see you jilt him. Don't make a mistake. Remember that now."

She closed her eyes. *Don't make a mistake. Don't make a mistake. Don't...*

You did a bad thing, Ellie. A very bad thing.

She pushed away the memories but her mother's disappointed words lingered in her head. *Maybe Lawson won't come. Oh, Lord, please don't let him come.*

Her eyes jerked open at the sound of approaching hoofbeats. Dread filled her stomach. She scanned the woods for some sign of Donovan. Nothing—but he was there. She could feel him watching her. Could he hear her accelerated breathing? Probably. It seemed to fill the air around her.

Lawson appeared, riding on Starlight's sire, Samson. A hero on a white horse, but that wasn't right. She couldn't let him save her. Instead, she had to save *him*.

Chapter Twenty

She watched Lawson dismount and approach her with a grin so full of joy that it nearly broke her heart. She glanced down at the lines of black text to get her bearings. *Regulate your breathing. Unclench the book. Good. Now, hold it casually. Pretend to read.*

He knelt on the blanket beside her. "Aren't you going to say hello to me?"

She glanced up to see him eyeing the book in her hands. She set it aside and folded her hands nervously in her lap. "Hello."

"Hello," he responded, then proceeded to kiss her. She melted into his arms just like she had last night until she remembered who was watching them. She placed a hand on his chest and forced herself away from him.

"Lawson," she chided.

He searched her face. "I was just making sure. After that greeting—"

"I need to talk to you."

"I need to talk to you, too." His fingers threaded through hers. She almost removed them but realized that their position probably made it impossible for Donovan to see that connection from wherever he hid, so she didn't pull away.

She lifted her chin. "I'm—"

"No. Let me go first."

She bit her lip and scanned the forest. He was insisting so she had to let him if she didn't want him to suspect anything was wrong. Would Donovan understand that? She glanced down at their hands. "All right. If you insist…"

"I do." He smiled at his statement for some reason, then raked his free hand through his hair. "I didn't think I'd be this nervous. I guess I'd better just come out and say it. I love you, Ellie O'Brien."

Ellie's head shot up. She stared at Lawson. She must not have heard him correctly. This could not be happening. Not now. "What did you say?"

He grinned. "I love you! I love everything about you. I love the small things like the way your hair is always slipping out of place and the way your eyes dance when you laugh. I love the big things like the way you stand by me no matter what."

"Oh, Lawson." Her words came out half ecstasy and half despair but he didn't seem to notice.

Sincerity filled his every word as he continued. "You know how hard it is for me to believe that anyone, especially someone as wonderful as you, could care for me, but I have to take this chance to ask you. Do you love me?"

This was the question she'd been asking herself for weeks. She hadn't been sure of the answer before but right at that moment, looking into his eyes, she knew without a doubt what the answer was. Yes, she loved him. It wasn't even a question anymore. He didn't have to change her life to make her love him. She loved him just the way he was—strong yet scarred, caring and gentle yet protective and fierce. He was a true friend, but one glance from him could make her head spin.

Her heart begged to shout those three words loudly enough to shake the heavens, but the jubilant sound would only turn into a death knell. She held his hand tighter as her gaze raked the woods. She knew what she had to say.

"Ellie?"

Her gaze caught his and held on for dear life. *Oh, what a silly fool I've been. I couldn't tell if I really loved him. Now I know I do. Yet, I'm going to break his heart and that will break mine just as surely.* She allowed her heart to show in her eyes. He saw that and relaxed. She swallowed. "No."

He froze. *"No?"*

"No. I don't. I think you'd better leave." The words sounded hollow to her ears but she prayed he'd obey them. She wondered if he noticed that despite her rejection she hadn't released his hand. *Please, know that means something. Know that as soon as I can get away from Donovan I'll run straight to you.*

He couldn't know that. He couldn't read her mind. He didn't even seem to notice that they held hands as his hazel eyes filled with hurt and confusion. "You're lying. You love me. I'm sure of it—even if you never said it directly. I'm going to stay right here until you tell me the truth."

"No!" she cried in alarm before she could catch herself. She had to make something up—anything to make him go away before Donovan got impatient and shot him. "I'm not going to explain anything. I said I don't love you and that's that. It's over between us. Leave me alone."

He glanced down at their hands then back at her face. "You don't mean that."

She was glad he realized that but it didn't make him safe. Ellie grew desperate. She threw one more glance toward the woods then pushed him away. "Will you *get out of here* already? Go away! *Please.*"

Lawson stared at her as if he'd never seen her before. She watched his hurt turn to anger. Finally, he stood to his feet, rushed to his mount and rode back down the trail he'd come. Tension seeped from her body in relief. Donovan surfaced from behind a nearby bush. "You were brilliant. That performance would have made any actress proud."

"Why would you make me hurt him like that?"

"He was devastated, wasn't he? That, my love, was just an unexpected little treat. I had no intention of running into Lawson but I'm glad now that I did."

She glared at him. "You are insane. What is the point of all this?"

An angry muscle jerked in his jaw before he smiled. "I wish you wouldn't insult me like that. I've never insulted you, have I?"

She gritted her teeth and glanced toward the forest where no sign of Lawson remained before turning back to him. "What do you want?"

"You," he said calmly. "I want you. You're coming with me."

Lawson only made it a short distance before he had to get off his horse and lean against a tree to gather himself. Ellie had rejected him—outright rejected him without even providing a reason. He'd thought she was different. He'd thought if any woman in the world could love him, it was her. He shook his head. She didn't want him. She'd shooed him away like a pesky fly. So everything she'd said before and everything she'd done... did that mean nothing to her? Did *he* mean nothing to her? She said she didn't love him but he'd been so sure that she did. Her kiss had told him so last night. What could have changed between then and now?

"It's just so strange." He took the Claddagh ring out of his pocket and held it tightly. That was the right word for that episode—*strange.*

He'd ridden in and she hadn't seemed to care a whit that he was there. She just kept reading her book...upside down. He'd realized that, which was why he'd had the courage to kiss her. She'd responded almost desperately yet she'd pushed him away, and had seemed distracted. She kept looking off into the woods as if something out there was more important than his profession of love. Even when she'd rejected him, she'd done it while holding his hand the entire time.

He stared unseeingly into the woods. Something must have happened between last night and this morning. Perhaps it had something to do with her parents?

He took a step on the path back toward the creek then hesitated. She'd rejected him once already. Why should he risk that again? Maybe he just wasn't good enough. Maybe there really was something wrong with him—something that others could only sense when they got close to him. He shook his head. That didn't explain his relationship with his adoptive parents and the rest of Ellie's family.

He pulled in a deep breath. "Well, Lord, what is it? Do I let her go and just assume something really is wrong with me? Or do I go after her and prove... what, exactly?"

That even though I've been abandoned I can still

find the courage to seek out those I love. That my past doesn't determine my future. That Ellie loves me...and something must be wrong.

He stopped walking to peer down the path before him as the training he'd received as a Ranger kicked in along with his common sense. A woman alone in a secluded area, distracted enough not to notice her book is upside down, nervously watching the woods, behaving in completely uncharacteristic ways, clinging to his hand yet pleading with him to leave. Something really was wrong. Even if that wasn't the case, even if he was only seeing what he wanted to see, he wouldn't let Ellie go without a fight.

He rushed down the path back to the creek. The sound of the waterfall grew louder and he slowed his steps to a stealthy pace. He veered off the main path to shield himself in the trees. He spotted the blanket, the book and the picnic basket but Ellie was gone. Had she run off or had someone taken her? He studied the ground around the blanket and found her boot marks along with his...and another set—too large to be hers and slightly too small to be his.

He followed the prints away from the blanket into the woods, where they circled around to a large bush. A slight indention in the soft ground told him someone had recently been kneeling here. The prints then traveled back toward the blanket. They stopped about four feet away from it then veered off to the left. Ellie's soon joined them. Someone was with her. Lawson couldn't be far behind them if they were on foot. His relief came too soon for he discovered the distinctive marks left behind by horseshoes.

He could go back for help or he could continue on by himself and stand a chance of actually catching them.

He was used to working alone as a Ranger so he let out a low whistle and Samson cantered toward him. He mounted the horse, then urged him on as they followed the tracks that would guide him to Ellie.

The smooth canter of Donovan's horse ate up the ground as the familiar hills around her family's farm faded into dense, unfamiliar woods. Dense except for the well-worn path they traveled on. A shortcut between their horse ranch and his pig farm, Donovan explained. It chilled her to realize how often he must have used it. It was unfortunate that no one had noticed it, but then her family tended to stay close to the farmhouse and barn. Interminable minutes passed by or at least it seemed that way since they were riding double and Donovan's arm stayed around her waist the entire time. She smelled the pig farm before she saw it.

They burst into a small clearing where a barn nestled close to a cabin. The pigs hardly seemed to notice their arrival. Donovan dismounted first then carefully helped her down. "I'm afraid I'll have to hold the gun on you while you stable the horse. I don't want to take any chance that you'll run off."

"What are you going to do with me?"

"I'll tell you once we get inside," he promised.

Minutes later she entered the cabin, taking stock of it while he barred the door behind them. It consisted of one room much like Lawson's, and it had probably been built around the same time. The first thing she noticed was that it was clean. Almost too clean. The bed stood against the back wall. The stove was in the corner while a table sat in the middle of the room. A warm bear rug covered much of the floor. Dozens of thin soft-cover books were stacked neatly next to the bed. Plays, she realized.

"Make yourself comfortable."

She glanced at her captor, then took the only chair at the table. She rubbed her arms against the slight chill that filled the room. He took that as his cue to warm a pot of coffee on the stove. Once done with that, he sat down on the bed and just looked at her with a contented smile on his face. *He really* is *unstable.* "Well, what do you want with me?"

"I want to marry you."

She sighed and crossed her legs and arms. "I guess it doesn't matter to you what I think about that."

"Of course it does," he chided. "I want you to be happy. I just know that you'll be happiest with me."

She bit her cheek to keep from laughing at that ridiculous statement. He really seemed to care for her in that strange, demented way of his. Other than poking a gun at her and threatening to shoot Lawson, he'd been very careful with her. She lifted her chin, daring to ask, "Are you going to hurt me?"

He shook his head and actually appeared offended. "I would never hurt you."

"I'm glad to hear that."

His jaw tightened. "Unless you try to leave, of course, but it would be for your own good."

"Of course," she said with a mirthless smile. "So how exactly do you plan to marry me? I have to give my consent to that, you know. Even if I did, someone else would probably object, like my brothers."

No doubt Lawson would, too, despite the way she'd been forced to treat him. However, she didn't think it would be wise to mention that to Donovan at the moment. He didn't look fazed by the prospect of anyone objecting.

"It won't matter if you want to or not. You'll have to do it." He rose to pour her a cup of coffee. "I'm going to keep you here all night. Come morning, your reputation will be ruined and we'll have to get married."

"Morning?" she asked skeptically. "As soon as my brothers figure out I'm missing, they'll start looking for me. What makes you think you'll have until morning?"

"They won't know where to look." He set the coffee in front of her, then produced a stale-looking cookie she recognized as being from Lawson's party a week ago.

She narrowed her eyes as she stared at the man. She hated to admit it but his idea was actually sort of clever…and sneaky, deplorable, heavy-handed and implausible. Her brothers would never force her into a marriage with Donovan. As long as he kept his promise not to hurt her, she would be fine. She just had to wait until someone found her. It was probably best to play along with Donovan and let him think she was cooperating, just to keep him happy.

She cleared her throat. "That's quite a plan, but if we're going to have to wait a while, I wish you would have let me bring my book so I'd have something to do."

"We can read one of these plays together." He smiled as he poured himself a cup of coffee, then placed it on the table to sort through his stack. "*Romeo and Juliet.* I'll play Romeo. I know the lines by heart. You will be my Juliet."

She took a sip of the coffee to cover her incredulous smile. She shouldn't look at him as if he was crazy. It wouldn't help in the long run. Too many looks like that and he was bound to get insulted. That would make him angry, which wasn't good because he got even crazier when he was angry. "That's perfect."

He opened one of the thin booklets and flipped through the pages before handing it to her. He stood before her and placed a hand over his heart while he dramatically quoted the lines of the play in a strange sort of accent. She stared at him in confusion. All she caught was something about pilgrims, lips and a kiss. He stopped speaking and waited expectantly. She glanced down at the book. *Pilgrims...lips...kiss... Oh!*

"Good pilgrim, you do wrong your hand too much, which mannerly devotion shows in this..."

The rhythmic prose seemed to calm his nerves, which in turn made her less jittery. The satisfied look on Donovan's face told her that she was safe for now. *Please, Lord, send help and quickly.*

Chapter Twenty-One

Lawson could barely believe his ears as he listened to Ellie's lyrical Texas drawl launch into a Shakespearean verse in response to Donovan's cockeyed accent. He wanted to glance into the half-open window he crouched under, but resisted the action that would have given away his presence prematurely.

It sounded as if she was safe for the time being. That was a relief—as was the fact that her rejection hadn't been of her own hand but rather Donovan's. He could tell that much from the man's ridiculous plan to both ruin and save Ellie's reputation, thus binding her to him forever.

Yeah, that's not going to happen—not on my watch. He frowned when a giggle sounded through the window. What was going on in there? He didn't have to wait long to find out. Ellie's voice was filled with disbelief. "Did people really talk like this?"

Despite the danger of the situation, a smile curved Lawson's lips. She was outright adorable. That's all there was to it. Apparently, Donovan didn't agree because disapproval filled his voice. "I thought you knew Shakespeare and liked it."

"I knew *of* it." Her tone was more carefully modulated this time. Obviously, she remembered that it would not be wise to displease Donovan at a time like this. "I like it fine. I'm just not used to it."

"Keep going. Don't break character again."

"All right." She continued on with the play.

Lawson shook his head as he listened. This was a fine situation, wasn't it? He had to get Ellie out of that man's clutches. He just wasn't sure how. He could go in with both barrels blazing but Ellie could easily get caught in the cross fire of any violence in such a confined space. He needed to go for backup and he knew exactly where to find it.

He said a silent prayer for Ellie's safety, then crept away from his window to where he'd left reliable Samson. The stallion's ears perked up at Lawson's approach as if he was reporting for duty. Lawson mounted up and rode back along the path that had made it easy for him to track them down, until he reached the ranch. He rode into the barnyard just as Nathan exited the farmhouse with Kate. They must have been waiting for him to return with Ellie. His guess was right because when he dismounted, Nathan's first question was "Where's Ellie?"

"Did she say yes?" Kate asked.

"I didn't ask because she said she didn't love me, but I think Donovan forced her to."

Nathan narrowed his eyes. "Donovan?"

"He was hiding in the woods. I figured something was wrong after she rejected me so I went back to find out. He's taken her to his pig farm. He plans to keep her there until morning so she'll have to marry him to save her reputation."

"That isn't going to happen." Nathan's voice was laced with steel. "I reckon you already have a plan."

He nodded. "Donovan doesn't seem like he'll hurt Ellie unless she tries to run off or makes him angry. She's been smart and playing it safe by humoring him. I think that will give you enough time to ride into town and get Sean."

Nathan nodded. "That's probably the best thing to do since he's the sheriff."

"In the meantime, I'm going to ride back and keep an eye on things. There is a hedge of bushes near the smokehouse that will make a good lookout place. Y'all can meet me there."

"Sounds like a plan. Let's ride out."

How long have I been here? Ellie wondered. She wasn't sure but it was long enough for them to have lunch and make their way to the end of the play with her playing all the women's parts and Donovan playing the men's…by heart…using different voices. He'd skipped a few scenes here and there but seemed to relish being the Romeo to her Juliet. Thankfully, he'd been too caught up in hearing her speak the dialogue to try to act out stage directions. She didn't bother to read them out loud, either. No need to remind him that Juliet was supposed to kiss Romeo at certain points, like now. She just skipped to… "Thy lips are warm."

"Lead, boy: which way?" He perched on the edge of the bed in anticipation of the death scene.

She ignored the chills of foreboding that rose on her arms by lifting the fork from the ham she had barely touched. "Yea, noise? Then I'll be brief. O happy dagger!" She lifted the fork into the air. "This is thy sheath." She glanced down for her next line then plunged the fork toward her heart. "There rust and let me die."

The fork fell to the ground as she slumped against the chair and closed her eyes. She could feel him staring at her so rather than face that odd intensity, she kept them closed. Perhaps she could get away with this for the rest of the play. There didn't seem to be much left of it. What would they do after that? Perhaps they'd start another play. She wouldn't mind it as long as her own ending didn't turn out as tragic as Juliet's.

She started listening to Donovan again when his voice changed to reflect a different character. "The ground is bloody; search about the churchyard…"

Are You still there, Lord? You are, aren't You? I can feel You with me even though I'm scared. I'm trying hard not to be. You'll save me. Please, hurry. I'm waiting for You.

Suddenly she wondered if God might be waiting for her to act. After all, Lawson was safe. Donovan had tucked his gun into his holster, so it wasn't exactly an immediate threat anymore. Maybe she could hit him over the head with something.

She peeked one eye open to survey the clean room. Then she saw it. Right there on the stove was salvation in the form of a frying pan. It was cast iron and looked heavy enough to pack a wallop that would knock Donovan out long enough to ride for help on that mare she'd unsaddled for him. She just needed a distraction.

She had the entire rest of the play to think one up and as soon as they were finished, she reverently closed the play. "You read beautifully, Donovan. I'd love to hear you do another one."

He beamed. "Would you, really?"

"Oh, yes." She handed him the play. "I'll make us some more coffee while you find the next one."

"What shall I do?" He knelt beside the stack of plays as she walked to the stove and filled the coffeepot with water from the pitcher. *"Macbeth?"*

"No." She grasped the handle of the frying pan.

"Othello?" His back was to her.

"No." She took a deep breath. She had to do this right the first time because there wouldn't be a second chance. She needed to swing hard and swing true like she had when she'd played baseball with the boys at school. She trained her gaze on the back of his head.

"Taming of the Shrew?"

She swung and hit him right on the perfect spot to make him slump forward soundlessly. "That's the one."

She took his gun then put the pan on the table before unbolting the door. She stepped out into the sunlight and glanced around to get her bearings. The barn was in front of her. That was all she needed to know. She was only a few feet from the cabin when she heard a roar erupt from inside. Her eyes widened but she didn't look behind her. Her only hope was to get on his horse and gallop away. She took off running, begging the Lord for help.

Lawson tensed when the cabin door opened. Nathan and Sean hadn't arrived yet but if Donovan was planning to take Ellie somewhere else, Lawson would have to stop him here and now. He watched in amazement as Ellie walked out alone toward the barn with her arms swinging as if she didn't have a care in the world. Then he saw the gleam of black metal in her hand and realized she probably didn't.

He rose from his hiding place just as a roar sounded

from inside the house. Ellie dashed toward the barn. He ran toward the house. Drawing his gun, he slid his back along the side of the house until he could peer inside the front door. Donovan was stumbling around inside, no doubt gathering weapons. Lawson cocked his gun. "Get your hands up where I can see them. Now!"

The man froze. Donovan turned slowly, then lifted fury-filled eyes to Lawson before he lifted his hand and threw a steak knife right at Lawson's chest. He dodged the worst of it as the blade whizzed past his shooting arm. Donovan used that distraction to rush past him. Lawson momentarily holstered his gun to tackle the man before he could escape more than a few yards.

They landed on the ground with a rolling thud. A blow landed across Lawson's jaw so hard that he tasted blood. His gun was wrenched from his holster but Lawson slammed his elbow into the man's arm, pinning it against the ground and sending the gun sliding in the dirt. Donovan threw his body toward it.

Lawson channeled the movement while shoving a hand down on the man's shoulder, then added his own strength until Donovan landed flat on his stomach. He knelt onto the man's back. Forcing his left arm behind his back, Lawson waited for the fight to drain from Donovan. A string of curses came out instead. Lawson jerked his arm a bit harder. "Watch your mouth. There's a lady present... I think."

He knew the moment the pain set in because Donovan stiffened. A moment later, he went limp. Lawson took that opportunity to scan his surroundings. Ellie was indeed present along with her two brothers. All of them had guns pointed toward Donovan. "Easy, folks. I'm down here, too, remember?"

Sean was the last to put his gun away. "I thought you needed help."

"It looks like I just need some handcuffs." He took the metal bracelets from Sean and clamped them on Donovan. "He's all yours, Sheriff."

Donovan somehow managed to turn his head enough to stare up at her with those desperate, chilling eyes of his. She wanted to turn away from his gaze but it held her still. She shook her head sadly. "The love you want so badly from me I can't give. However, there is Someone who can love you the way you deserve if you'll accept it."

He grunted as Sean hauled him to his feet again. "Who are you talking about?"

She gave a small smile and lifted her shoulders in a shrug. "God. No, don't look disappointed. His love is real and powerful. It doesn't hurt or try to control, like you did today. It gives life, it heals and it fulfills. It did that for me and it can do the same for you if you let it."

Donovan stared at her with his eyebrows drawn together, confusion in his eyes, and his mouth slightly agape. Had she been blabbering nonsensically? She realized the rest of the men were staring at her, too. Sean nodded at her as if in a silent *Amen.* A hint of pride touched Nathan's smile. Lawson? Well, he just stared at her with that unnervingly intense look he'd perfected at his birthday party.

Nathan cleared his throat. "Well said, Ellie. Now, I think we'd better get going."

Once Donovan was ready to be hauled to the town jail, Sean turned to Ellie and opened his arms. "Come here."

She stepped into his embrace as he gave her a fierce

hug that nearly lifted her feet off the ground. He set her away from him to look her in the eye. "I love you."

"I love you, too."

"If you ever scare me like that again, I'll tan your hide."

She lifted her chin. "I'd like to see you try."

He gently cuffed her on the chin, then mounted his horse. Nathan was the next to hug her. "We'll travel with y'all as far as the farm, then Sean and I'll go on into town with Donovan. You'd better ride with Lawson."

It wasn't long before the faithful drum of the waterfall filled the air. Ellie caught sight of the abandoned picnic basket and stiffened in resolve. She slid closer to Lawson in the saddle. "Stop the horse!"

"What?" He glanced over his shoulder in alarm. "Why?"

"I want to get down."

He immediately reined in Samson, most likely realizing she was going to get off whether he stopped or not. She dismounted with his help then placed a hand on his knee to keep him from doing the same before waving her curious brothers on. She turned to stare up at Lawson. He stared right back. "Is something wrong, Ellie?"

She tucked a piece of hair behind her ear and lifted her chin. "We're doing it again."

"Doing what?"

"The whole thing," she whispered fiercely. "The whole thing from the very beginning. I'll go sit on the picnic blanket and you ride in from over there just like last time."

Realization filled his eyes along with a hint of wariness. He rubbed his jaw and glanced toward the woods as though avoiding the sight of her and the place of her rejection. She held her breath. Surely he knew that she was asking for a chance to undo the mess Donovan had caused. *Please, let me fix this.*

He glanced down at her then gave one almost indiscernible nod before he urged Samson into a canter toward the woods. She rushed to the blanket and smoothed out the wrinkles wrought by the wind before she settled onto it with her book. It seemed like an eternity until she heard the plod of Samson's powerful hooves. She waited until Lawson dismounted before she glanced up with a greeting on her lips. The intense look in his eyes stole her breath and her words. "You aren't going to say hello this time, either?"

She stood to greet him. "Hello, Lawson."

"Hello, Ellie." He lifted her chin to place a kiss on her nose. "Suppose we skip all the rest and just get right down to it?"

"All right." She tossed her book aside. "In that case… I love you, too, Lawson Williams."

A startled look crossed his face. "You—you do?"

She giggled. "Of course I do, silly. Do you really think anything other than having a gun at your back would keep me from saying that? I love you and I'll say those words a thousand times a day if that's what it will take to convince you."

"I don't know. Just hearing it once had a pretty strong effect seeing as I love you, too."

"I know," she said solemnly. "Which is why I think you ought to marry me."

He made a coughing sound somewhere between a choked laugh and a gasp. "Are you proposing to me?"

"I reckon."

"Ellie." He let out a frustrated groan.

"What?"

He shook his head. Catching her left hand, he gave it a quick kiss before stepping back and kneeling at her feet. He pulled a ring from his pocket and presented it to her. "Will you marry me?"

She stared down at him as confusion gave way to realization. "You had that ring the whole time."

He nodded.

"Then the picnic was…"

He smiled.

She gasped. Her free hand covered her cheek as she stared into the woods where her brothers had disappeared with Donovan. "You were trying to propose, weren't you?"

He tilted his head as his eyes took on a familiar teasing gleam. "Actually, I'm still trying to propose but I'm not getting an answer."

She laughed. "Yes! Oh, yes!"

He began to slip the ring on her finger, then hesitated. "You're serious, aren't you?"

"Of course!" Her heart jumped to her throat. "Aren't you?"

He searched her face for a long moment. Finally, he stood to his feet and slid the ring into place. "I'm serious. I've never been more serious about anything or anyone in my life."

"Lawson Williams." She stared at him in awe. "Are you crying?"

He grimaced and scrubbed a stray of wetness from his cheek. "I don't know. I haven't done much of it before. I've never felt this much love before—from you, God, the town, our families. Maybe it was there all the time but I didn't trust that it was enough. Now that I do, I feel like my heart is going to burst, it's so full. I can hardly believe this is happening." His hand brushed reverently across her cheek, then strayed to her hair. "That somehow God loved me enough to let me end up with you."

"In that case, He must love me an awful lot, too." She smiled and swayed forward to kiss his damp cheek, then leaned against him when his arms encircled her waist. Resting her cheek against his firm chest, she sighed. "I can't explain it, but somehow I know that it was always supposed to end exactly like this."

"I think there's one thing we forgot." His voice rumbled in her ear.

She pulled away slightly to look at him. "What's that?"

Her confusion was short-lived, for his lips captured hers as completely as he'd captured her heart, leaving her breathless when he pulled away. "How's that for a finish?"

"I don't know. I think it also makes a pretty fine beginning."

Epilogue

The whole town showed for the wedding—or at least it seemed that way from the glimpses of the sanctuary Lawson managed to glean through the crack in the foyer door. Ellie was tucked out of sight in the storage/ bride's room. He'd sent everyone else away in preparation for this moment. He swallowed and straightened his tie a moment before the door opened.

"Nathan said you wanted to see me."

Lawson braced himself before meeting Clive's gaze. The man seemed just as nervous as he felt. Lawson cleared his throat. "I guess you were surprised to receive my invitation to come here for the wedding."

Clive allowed a nod. "I was surprised and pleased. Ellie is a wonderful young woman. I'm sure you two will be very happy."

"Thank you. The real reason I asked you here was to tell you something important." He pulled in a deep breath. "I forgive you."

"You forgive me?"

"Yes." He ran his fingers through his hair. "I know it may seem presumptuous for me to say that since you haven't said you wanted it but it's there all the same."

"I do want your forgiveness. I just didn't dare ask for it." Clive wiped his eyes, which had become suspiciously red. "What made you decide to forgive me?"

"First of all, I knew God wanted me to do it. Then I realized that despite how it may feel sometimes, I'm not that little boy you left behind anymore. I am a grown man who has been blessed enough to know the love of family, friends and a good woman. The past can't be rewritten. It is what it is. Now it's time for me to plan my future."

Clive stopped trying to hide his tears and scrubbed his face with a handkerchief. "I know it is too soon for this but I hope that one day that future might include me."

Lawson stared at the broken man before him. For the first time, he looked deep enough to see the regret, vulnerability and pain staring back. Gathering his courage, he held out his hand. "It isn't too soon, Clive."

Clive froze in stunned disbelief. Finally, he reached out and grasped Lawson's hand in a hearty shake. His voice was solemn. "Thank you."

Kate stepped out of the bride room and quietly interrupted the scene. "Ellie is almost ready, Lawson. I think you can go to the altar now."

With his past behind him and the future promising nothing but happiness, Lawson smiled. "I'm ready, too. Will you tell her I'm waiting for her?"

"I will." Kate smiled, then slipped her arms around him in a quick hug. "You've always been a part of our family but I'm so glad it's going to be official."

"So am I." He turned to Clive and grinned. "It's time to watch your son get married."

The ceremony was short and sweet. As the rest of the town migrated toward the hotel where the reception would take place, Ellie and Lawson slipped out the back of the church. Ellie wrapped her arms around Lawson's waist and kissed his cheek. "I am so proud of you."

He chuckled. "Why?"

"Kate told me that you and your father seem to be on better terms. That must have taken a lot of courage."

He shrugged, then nodded toward the graveyard before them. "So does this."

She followed his gaze to her parents' tombstones. She sank to her knees in front of them, heedless of the stains the grass might cause on her ivory dress, but aware of Lawson's supportive presence behind her. Pulling two roses free from her bouquet, she laid one on her mother's grave, then one on her father's. Her hand rubbed the names inscribed in cold stone. "I wish you could be here today. Sean walked me down the aisle and Kate helped me get ready. Y'all would have been so proud of them.

"Y'all would have been proud of me, too." She smiled and glanced back at Lawson when he stepped forward to place a comforting hand on her shoulder. "Y'all would have loved Lawson. Perhaps not as much as I do but that's how it should be, seeing as I'm his wife and all. I love you both. I'll see y'all one day and when I do I want the longest, fiercest hug any of us have ever experienced. Until then, I'll just appreciate everything God has given me."

She stood to meet Lawson's gaze and smiled. "He sure has given me a whole lot."

"And me."

She placed a stilling hand on his when he lowered his head toward hers. "Don't forget that the whole town is waiting for us at the hotel."

"Let them wait."

She allowed him one more kiss, then grabbed his hand and hurried him down the sidewalk into the hotel ballroom. The moment they stepped inside, the town burst into applause and the hotel band struck up a waltz. Lawson sent her a sideways glance. She shrugged. "I didn't do any of this. It was all the town's idea."

"Well, this explains why my mother insisted I brush up on my dancing." He held out his hand to her. She stepped into his arms and allowed him to lead her around the dance floor. Pretty soon Kate and Nathan joined in, then Sean and Lorelei. Finally, the dance floor crowded with people. As they whirled around the floor, Ellie pulled back slightly to look up at him. "About that Bachelor List…"

"What about it?"

She held up a folded piece of paper. "It's finished. Should we burn it?"

He chuckled. "I don't know but I think I'm entitled to look at the finished product first."

She tugged him away from the dance floor to a secluded spot near the door to the garden. "Can you believe I did this?"

"Yes," he said heartily. She sent him an unappreciative look, which only caused him to laugh. She handed him the list, then watched his eyebrows raise as his gaze darted back and forth from the list to the crowd. Finally, he let out a low whistle. "It would be an awful shame to destroy that valuable information."

She searched his face. "Do you really think that I was right—that this works?"

"Well, it worked for Jeff and Maddie." He slipped his arm around her waist. "It worked for us."

She wrinkled her nose. "I suppose it did in a way."

"Maybe you were right about all of them."

"That is highly improbable."

He smiled. "So what are you going to do?"

She eyed the list, then surveyed the room full of swirling dancers. Her gaze stopped on one slightly morose figure standing sentry behind the punch bowl. Ellie took the list from Lawson and squeezed his arm. "I think I know."

She wound her way to the punch bowl and stopped in front of Amy. The girl rushed around the table to give her a hug and exclaim about Ellie's wedding dress. Ellie thanked her then stepped slightly closer to lower her voice. "I want to give you something. What you do with it is up to you but do try to keep it safe and private."

Amy's brow furrowed. "What is it?"

"The Bachelor List." Ellie slipped the folded paper into Amy's hand.

Amy froze. She stared down at the paper, then immediately slipped it into her pocket as though sensing its secrecy. "Why did you choose me?"

"I can't say, exactly. It just seemed right."

Amy nodded gravely. "I'll keep it safe."

Ellie gave the girl a parting hug then returned to her groom, who waited for her away from the hustle of the reception, on a secluded nook of the hotel's garden porch. "Did she take the list?"

"She did." She pretended to dust off her hands. "I believe my work here is done."

"Either that, or you started something else entirely."

"That's what I meant." She gave him a saucy wink.

He grinned. "What am I going to do with you?"

"You'll figure something out." She stood on her tiptoes to place a quick kiss on his lips.

His arms caught her around the waist before she could step away. "I think I just did."

"Hmm." She lifted an eyebrow and glanced down at her left hand then back at Lawson. "I bet this means you're going to kiss me all the time now."

He caught her hand and kissed it. "What do you think?"

Her lips curved into a smile, issuing a standing invitation. "I think you'd better."

And so he did.

* * * * *

**IF YOU ENJOYED THIS BOOK
WE THINK YOU WILL ALSO LOVE**

LOVE INSPIRED

INSPIRATIONAL ROMANCE

Uplifting stories of faith, forgiveness and hope.

Fall in love with stories where faith helps
guide you through life's challenges, and discover
the promise of a new beginning.

6 NEW BOOKS AVAILABLE EVERY MONTH!

SPECIAL EXCERPT FROM

LOVE INSPIRED
INSPIRATIONAL ROMANCE

*When a young Amish woman returns home
with a baby in tow, will sparks fly with her
handsome—and unusual—neighbor?*

Read on for a sneak preview of
The Baby Next Door
by Vannetta Chapman.

Grace found Nicole had pulled herself up to the front door
and was high-fiving none other than Adrian Schrock.
He'd squatted down to her level. Nicole was having a fine
old time.

Grace picked up her *doschder* and pushed open the
door, causing Adrian to jump up, then step back toward
the porch steps. It was, indeed, a fine spring day. The sun
shone brightly across the Indiana fields. Flowers colored
yellow, red, lavender and orange had begun popping
through the soil that surrounded the porch. Birds were
even chirping merrily.

Somehow, all those things did little to elevate Grace's
mood. Neither did the sight of her neighbor.

Adrian resettled his straw hat on his head and smiled.
"Gudemariye."

"Your llama has escaped again."

"Kendrick? *Ya.* I've come to fetch him. He seems to
like your place more than mine."

"I don't want that animal over here, Adrian. He spits.
And your peacock was here at daybreak, crying like a
child."

Adrian laughed. "When you moved back home, I guess you didn't expect to live next to a Plain & Simple Exotic Animal Farm."

Adrian wiggled his eyebrows at Nicole when he seemed to realize that Grace wasn't amused.

"I think of your place as Adrian's Zoo."

"Not a bad name, but it doesn't highlight our Amish heritage enough."

"The point is that I feel like we're living next door to a menagerie of animals."

"Up, Aden. Up."

Adrian scooped Nicole from Grace's hold, held her high above his head, then nuzzled her neck. Adrian was comfortable with everyone and everything.

"Do you think she'll ever learn to say my name right?"

"Possibly. Can you please catch Kendrick and take him back to your place?"

"Of course. That's why I came over. I guess I must have left the gate open again." He kissed Nicole's cheek, then popped her back into Grace's arms. "You should bring her over to see the turtles."

As he walked away, Grace wondered for the hundredth time why he wasn't married. It was true that he'd picked a strange profession. What other Amish man raised exotic animals? No, Adrian wouldn't be considered excellent marrying material by most young Amish women.

Don't miss
The Baby Next Door *by Vannetta Chapman,*
available April 2021 wherever
Love Inspired books and ebooks are sold.

LoveInspired.com

LIEXP0321

LOVE INSPIRED

INSPIRATIONAL ROMANCE

UPLIFTING STORIES OF FAITH, FORGIVENESS AND HOPE.

Join our social communities to connect with other readers who share your love!

Sign up for the Love Inspired newsletter at **LoveInspired.com** to be the first to find out about upcoming titles, special promotions and exclusive content.

CONNECT WITH US AT:

 Facebook.com/LoveInspiredBooks

Twitter.com/LoveInspiredBks

Facebook.com/groups/HarlequinConnection